Carol Marinell her job title. Thri she put writer. relaxation and sl third question asl to look obsessed she crossed the fingers on her hand and answered swimming but, given that the chlorine in the pool does terrible things to her highlights – I'm sure you can guess the real answer.

Joanna Neil had her future planned. She enjoyed her work as an infant teacher and didn't envisage any changes to her way of life. But then she discovered Mills & Boon. She was surprised to find how absorbing and interesting they were and read them on a regular basis. The more she read, the more she had the overwhelming desire to write one. Encouraged by her family, she persevered until her first book was accepted, and after several books were published, she decided to write full time.

With a background of working in medical laboratories and a love of the romance genre it's no surprise that **Sue MacKay** writes medical romance stories. She wrote her first story at age eight and hasn't stopped since. She lives in New Zealand's Marlborough Sounds where she indulges her passions for cycling, walking and kayaking. When she isn't writing she also loves cooking and entertaining guests with sumptuous meals that include locally caught fish.

A&E Docs

December 2020 **His Baby Surprise**	March 2021 **Emergency Medicine**
January 2021 **Taming the Brooding Doc**	April 2021 **The Maverick Doc**
February 2021 **Her Knight in Shining Armour**	May 2021 **His Emergency Secret**

A&E Docs: Taming the Brooding Doc

CAROL MARINELLI

JOANNA NEIL

SUE MACKAY

MILLS & BOON

First Published in Great Britain 2021
By Mills & Boon, an imprint of HarperCollins*Publishers*
1 London Bridge Street, London, SE1 9GF

www.harpercollins.co.uk

HarperCollins*Publishers*
1st Floor, Watermarque Building,
Ringsend Road, Dublin 4, Ireland

ISBN: 978-0-263-28190-3

MIX
Paper from responsible sources
FSC™ C007454

This book is produced from independently certified FSC™ paper to ensure responsible forest management.

For more information visit: www.harpercollins.co.uk/green

Printed and bound in Great Britain
by CPI Group (UK) Ltd, Croydon, CR0 4YY

DR DARK AND FAR TOO DELICIOUS

CAROL MARINELLI

CHAPTER ONE

JUST CONCENTRATE ON WORK.

Jed said it over and over as he ran along the damp beach.

He ran daily, or tried to, depending on work commitments, but as much as he could Jed factored running into his day—it served as both his exercise and his relaxation, helped him to focus and to clear his head.

Just concentrate on work, he repeated, because after the last two hellish years he really did need to do just that.

Jed looked along the bay. The morning was a hazy one and he couldn't make out the Melbourne skyline in the distance. Not for the first time he questioned whether he had been right to take the position at the Peninsula Hospital or if he should have gone for a more prestigious city one.

Jed loved nothing more than a big city hospital—he had worked and trained at a large teaching hospital in Sydney and had assumed, when he had applied for jobs in Melbourne, that the city was where he would end up, yet the interview at Peninsula Hospital that he had thought would be a more a cursory one had seen him change his mind.

It wasn't a teaching hospital but it was certainly a busy one—it served as a major trauma centre and had an NICU and ICU and Jed had liked the atmosphere at Peninsula, as well as the proximity to the beach. Perhaps the deciding factor, though, had been that he had also been told, confidentially, that one of the consultants was retiring and a position would be opening up in the not-too-distant future. His career had been building up to an emergency consultant position and, his disaster of a personal life aside, it was where he was ready to be. When Jed had handed in his notice six months ago an offer had been made and he'd been asked to reconsider leaving, but Jed had known then that he had to get away, that he had to start again.

But with new rules in place this time.

Jed missed not just Sydney and the hospital he had trained and worked at but his family and friends—it had been the first birthday of Luke, his newest nephew, yesterday, another thing he hadn't been able to get to, another family gathering he had missed, when before, even if he hadn't been able to get there on the day, he'd have dropped by over the weekend.

A phone call to a one-year-old wasn't exactly the same.

But the decision to move well away had surely been the right one.

Still he questioned it, still he wondered if he had overreacted and should have just stayed in Sydney and hoped it would work out, assumed it was all sorted.

What a mess.

Jed stopped for a moment and dragged in a few breaths.

Over and over he wondered if he could have handled

things differently, if there was something he could have said to have changed things, or something he had done that had been misconstrued—and yet still he could not come up with an answer.

It was incredibly warm for six a.m. but it wasn't a pleasant heat—it was muggy and close and needed a good storm to clear it but, according to the weather reports, the cool change wasn't coming through till tonight.

'Morning.' He looked up and nodded to an old guy walking his dog. They shared a brief conversation about the weather and then Jed took a long drink of water before turning around to head for home and get ready for work.

He should never have got involved with Samantha in the first place.

Still, he could hardly have seen that coming, couldn't have predicted the train wreck that had been about to take place, but then he corrected himself.

He should never have got involved with someone from work.

Jed picked up the pace again, his head finally clearing. He knew what he needed to focus on.

Just concentrate on work.

CHAPTER TWO

'JASMINE?' IT WASN'T the friendliest of greetings, and Jasmine jumped as the sound of Penny's voice stopped her in her tracks.

'What are you doing here?' her sister demanded.

'I'm here for an interview.' Jasmine stated what should be the obvious. 'I've just been for a security check.'

They were standing in the hospital admin corridor. Jasmine was holding a pile of forms and, despite her best efforts to appear smart and efficient for the interview, was looking just a little hot and bothered—and all the more so for seeing Penny.

Summer had decided to give Melbourne one last sticky, humid day before it gave way to autumn and Jasmine's long dark curls had, despite an awful lot of hair serum and an awful lot of effort, frizzed during the walk from the car park to the accident and emergency department. It had continued its curly journey through her initial interview with Lisa, the nurse unit manager.

Now, as Penny ran a brief but, oh, so critical eye over her, Jasmine was acutely aware that the grey suit she reserved for interviews was, despite hundreds of sit-ups and exercising to a DVD, just a touch too tight.

Penny, of course, looked immaculate.

Her naturally straight, naturally blonde hair was tied back in an elegant chignon—she was wearing smart dark trousers and heeled shoes that accentuated her lean body. Her white blouse, despite it being afternoon, despite the fact she was a registrar in a busy accident and emergency department, was still impossibly crisp and clean.

No one could have guessed that they were sisters.

'An interview for what, exactly?' Penny's eyes narrowed.

'A nursing position,' Jasmine answered carefully. 'A clinical nurse specialist. I've just been to fill out the forms for a security check.' Jasmine was well aware her answer was vague and that she was evading the issue but of course it didn't work—Penny was as direct as ever in her response.

'Where?' Penny asked. 'Where exactly have you applied to work?'

'Accident and Emergency,' Jasmine answered, doing her best to keep her voice even. 'Given that it's my speciality.'

'Oh, no.' Penny shook her head. 'No way.' Penny made no effort to keep her voice even, and she didn't mince her words either. 'I'm not having it, Jasmine, not for a single moment. You are *not* working in my department.'

'Where do you expect me to work, then, Penny?' She had known all along that this would be Penny's reaction—it was the very reason she had put off telling her sister about the application, the very reason she hadn't mentioned the interview when they had met up at Mum's last Sunday for a celebratory dinner to toast

Penny's *latest* career victory. 'I'm an emergency nurse, that's what I do.'

'Well, go and do it somewhere else. Go and work at the hospital you trained in, because there is no way on earth that I am working alongside my sister.'

'I can't commute to the city,' Jasmine said. 'Do you really expect me to drag Simon for an hour each way just so that I don't embarrass my big sister?' It was ridiculous to suggest and what was even more ridiculous was that Jasmine had actually considered it, well aware how prickly Penny could be.

Jasmine had looked into it, but with a one-year-old to consider, unless she moved nearer to the city, it would prove impossible and also, in truth, she was just too embarrassed to go back to her old workplace.

'You know people there,' Penny insisted.

'Exactly.'

'Jasmine, if the reason you're not going back there is because of Lloyd…'

'Leave it, Penny.' Jasmine closed her eyes for a second. She didn't want to go back to where everyone knew her past, where her life had been the centre stage show for rather too long. 'It has nothing to do with Lloyd. I just want to be closer to home.'

She did—with her marriage completely over and her soon-to-be ex-husband having nothing to do with either her or her son and her maternity leave well and truly up, Jasmine had made the decision to move back to the beachside suburb to be close to the family home and the smart townhouse where her sister lived and to start over again, but with family nearby.

She wanted to be closer to her mum, to her sister and,

yes, she wanted some support, but clearly she wasn't going to get any from Penny.

It was career first, last and always for Penny, but then again it was the same with their mum. A real estate agent, though now semi-retired, Louise Masters had made a name for herself in their bayside village for being tough and no-nonsense. It was the rather more dreamy Jasmine who did stupid things like take risks with her heart and actually switch off from work on her days off—not that she didn't love her work, it just wasn't all that she was.

'We'll talk about this later.' Penny's blue eyes flashed angrily—it was the only feature that they shared. 'And don't you dare go using my name to get the job.'

'As if I'd do that,' Jasmine said. 'Anyway, we don't even share the same surname, *Miss* Masters.'

Penny was now officially a Miss—the title given to females once they gained their fellowship. It caused some confusion at times, but Penny had worked extremely hard to be a Miss rather than a Doctor—and she wasn't about to have anyone drag on her coat-tails as she continued to ride high.

'I mean it,' Penny flared. 'You are not to even let on that you know me. I'm really not happy about this, Jasmine.'

'Hey, Penny.' Her sister turned, and so too did Jasmine, to the sound of a deep, low voice. Had Jasmine not been so numb right now, so immune and resistant to all things male, she might have more properly noticed just how good looking this man was. He was very tall and though his dark brown hair was cut fairly short it was just a bit rumpled, as was his suit.

Yes, a couple of years ago she might have taken note, but not now.

She just wanted him gone so that she could get back to the rather important conversation she had been having with Penny.

'It's getting busy down there apparently,' he said to Penny. 'They just called and asked me to come back from lunch.'

'I know,' came Penny's clipped response. 'I've just been paged. I was supposed to be speaking with Legal.'

Perhaps he picked up on the tension because he looked from Penny to Jasmine and she noticed then that his eyes were green and that his jaw needed shaving and, yes, despite being completely not interested, some long-dormant cells demanded that she at least deign to acknowledge just how attractive he was, especially when his deep voice spoke on. 'Sorry, am I disturbing something?'

'Not at all.' Penny's response was rapid. 'This nurse was just asking for directions to get back to Emergency—she's got an interview there.'

'You can hardly miss the place.' He gave a wry smile and nodded to a huge red arrow above them. 'Follow us.'

'Mrs Phillips?' Jasmine turned as she heard her name and saw it was the receptionist from Security, where she had just come from. 'You left your driving licence.'

'Thank you.' Jasmine opened her mouth to say that she was soon to be a Ms, but it seemed churlish to correct it as technically she was still a Mrs—it was there on her driving licence after all. Still, in a few weeks' time she'd be a Ms and she'd tell everyone the same.

Jasmine couldn't wait for the glorious day.

For now, though, she followed Penny and her colleague towards Emergency.

'I didn't mean to literally follow,' Jed said, and he waited a second for her to catch up. Jasmine fell into reluctant step alongside them. 'I'm Jed…Jed Devlin—I'm a registrar in the madhouse, as is Penny.'

'Jasmine.' She duly answered. 'Jasmine Phillips.'

'So?' he asked as Penny clipped noisily alongside them. She could hear the anger in her sister's footsteps, could feel the tension that was ever present whenever the two of them were together. 'When do you start?'

'I haven't got the job yet,' Jasmine said.

'Sounds promising, though, if you've been sent up to Security.'

'They have to do a security check on everyone,' Penny said abruptly.

They all walked on in silence for a few moments.

'Here we are,' Jed said. 'See that big red sign that says "Accident and Emergency"?'

'How could I miss it?' She gave a brief smile at his teasing as they headed through the swing doors and stepped into Emergency. 'Thanks.'

'No problem.'

'Good luck,' Jed said.

Of course Penny didn't offer her best wishes. Instead, she marched off on her high heels and for a second Jasmine stood there and blew out a breath, wondering if she was mad to be doing this.

It clearly wasn't going to work.

And then she realised that Jed was still standing there.

'Do I know you?' He frowned.

'I don't think so,' Jasmine said, while reluctantly admitting to herself that they had definitely never met—his was a face she certainly wouldn't forget.

'Have you worked in Sydney?'

Jasmine shook her head.

'Where did you work before?'

She started to go red. She hated talking about her time there—she'd loved it so much and it had all ended so terribly, but she could hardly tell him that. 'Melbourne Central. I trained there and worked in Emergency there till I had my son.'

'Nice hospital,' Jed said. 'I had an interview there when I first moved to the area, but no.' He shook his head. 'That's not it. You just look familiar…'

He surely hadn't picked up that she and Penny were sisters? No one ever had. She and Penny were complete opposites, not just in looks but also in personality. Penny was completely focussed and determined, whereas Jasmine was rather more impulsive, at least she had been once. She was also, as her mother had frequently pointed out throughout her childhood whenever Jasmine had burst into tears, too sensitive.

'There you are!' Jasmine turned as Lisa came over and Jed made his excuses and wandered off.

'Sorry,' Jasmine said to Lisa. 'They took ages to find all the forms I needed.'

'That's Admin for you,' Lisa said. 'Right, I'll walk you through the department and give you a feel for the place. It just got busy.'

It certainly had.

It had been almost empty when Jasmine had first arrived for her interview and the walk to Lisa's office had shown a calm, even quiet department, compared to the busy city one Jasmine was more used to. Now, though, the cubicles were all full and she could see staff rushing and hear the emergency bell trilling from Resus. Not for the first time, Jasmine wondered if she was up to the demands of going back to work in a busy emergency department.

The last two years had left her so raw and confused that all she really wanted to do was to curl up and sleep before she tackled the process of healing and resuming work, but her ex didn't want to see their son, let alone pay child support, and there was no point going through appropriate channels—she couldn't wait the time it would take to squeeze blood from a stone, but more than that Jasmine wanted to support her son herself, which meant that she needed a job.

However much it inconvenienced Penny and however daunted she was at the prospect.

'We do our best with the roster. I always try to accommodate specific requests, but as far as regular shifts go I can't make allowances for anyone,' Lisa explained—she knew about Simon and had told Jasmine that there were a couple of other single mums working there who, she was sure, would be a huge support. 'And I've rung the crèche and said that you'll be coming over to have a look around, but you know that they close at six and that on a late shift you don't generally get out till well after nine?'

Jasmine nodded. 'My mum's said that she'll help out for a little while.' Jasmine stated this far more generously than her mother had. 'At least until I sort out a babysitter.'

'What about night shifts?' Lisa checked. 'Everyone has to do them—it's only fair.'

'I know.'

'That way,' Lisa explained, 'with everyone taking turns, generally it only comes around once every three months or so.'

'That sounds fine,' Jasmine said confidently while inwardly gauging her mother's reaction.

It was a good interview, though. Really, Jasmine was confident that she'd got the job and, as she left, Lisa practically confirmed it. 'You'll be hearing from us soon.' She gave a wry smile as Jasmine shook her hand. 'Very soon. I wish you didn't have to do orientation before you start—I've just had two of my team ring in sick for the rest of the week.'

Walking towards the exit, Jasmine saw how busy yet efficient everyone looked and despite her confident words about her experience to Lisa, inside she was a squirming mess! Even though she'd worked right up to the end of her pregnancy she hadn't nursed in more than a year and, again, she considered going back to her old department. At least she'd maybe know a few people.

At least she'd know where things were kept. Yet there would still be the nudges and whispers that she'd been so relieved to leave behind and, yes, she should just walk in with her head held high and face the ugly rumours and gossip, except going back to work after all she had been through was already hard enough.

'Jasmine?' She turned as someone called her name and forced back on her smile when she saw that it was Jed. He was at the viewfinder looking at an X-ray. 'How did you get on?'

'Good,' Jasmine answered. 'Well, at least I think I did.'

'Well done.'

'I'm just going to check out the crèche.'

'Good luck again, then,' Jed said, 'because from what I've heard you'll need it to get a place there.'

'Oh, and, Jasmine,' he called as she walked off, 'I do know you.'

'You don't.' Jasmine laughed.

'But I know that I do,' he said. 'I never forget a face. I'll work it out.'

She rather hoped that he wouldn't.

CHAPTER THREE

'HOW DID YOU GO?' her mum asked as she let her in.

'Well,' Jasmine said. 'Sorry that it took so long.'

'That's okay. Simon's asleep.' Jasmine followed her mum through to the kitchen and Louise went to put the kettle on. 'So when do you start?'

'I don't even know if I've got the job.'

'Please,' her mum said over her shoulder. 'Everywhere's screaming for nurses, you hear it on the news all the time.'

It was a backhanded compliment—her mother was very good at them. Jasmine felt the sting of tears behind her eyes—Louise had never really approved of Jasmine going into nursing. Her mother had told her that if she worked a bit harder at school she could get the grades and study medicine, just like Penny. And though she never came right out and said it, it was clear that in both her mother's and sister's eyes Penny had a career whereas Jasmine had a job—and one that could be done by anyone—as if all that Jasmine had to do was put on her uniform and show up.

'It's a clinical nurse specialist role that I've applied for, Mum,' Jasmine said. 'There were quite a few applicants.' But her mum made no comment and not for the first time Jasmine questioned her decision to move close to home. Her mum just wasn't mumsy—she was successful in everything she did. She was funny, smart and career-minded, and she simply expected her daughters to be the same—after all, she'd juggled her career and had independently raised Jasmine and Penny when their father had walked out.

Jasmine wanted nothing more than to be independent and do the same; she just wanted a pause, a bit of a helping hand as she got through this bit—which in her own way her mother had given. After four weeks of living at home Louise had had a very nice little rental house come onto her books—it was right on the beach and the rent was incredibly low and Jasmine had jumped at it. It was in other areas that Jasmine was struggling, and nursing with all its shift work wasn't an easy career to juggle without support.

'I'm going to have to do nights.' Jasmine watched her mother's shoulders stiffen as she filled two mugs. 'A fortnight every three months.'

'I didn't raise two children just so that I could raise yours,' Louise warned. 'I'll help you as much as I can for a couple of months, but I take a lot of clients through houses in the evenings.' She was as direct as ever. 'And I've got my cruise booked for May.'

'I know,' Jasmine said. 'I'm going to start looking for a regular babysitter as soon as I get the offer.'

'And you need to give me your off duty at least a month in an advance.'

'I will.'

Jasmine took the tea from her mum. If she wanted a hug she wasn't going to get one; if she wanted a little pick me up she was in the wrong house.

'Have you thought about looking for a job that's a bit more child friendly?' Louise suggested. 'You mentioned there was one in Magnetic…' She gave an impatient shrug when she couldn't remember the terminology.

'No. I said there was a position in MRI and that even though the hours were fantastic it wasn't what I wanted to do. I like Emergency, Mum. You wouldn't suggest Penny going for a role she had no interest in.'

'Penny doesn't have a one-year-old to think of,' Louise said, and then they sat quietly for a moment.

'You need to get your hair done,' her mum said. 'You need to smarten up a bit if you're going back to work.' And that was her mum's grudging way of accepting that, yes, this was what Jasmime was going to do. 'And you need to lose some weight.'

And because it was either that or start crying, Jasmine chose to laugh.

'What's so funny?'

'You are,' Jasmine said. 'I thought tea came with sympathy.'

'Not in this house.' Her mum smiled. 'Why don't you go home?'

'Simon's asleep.'

'I'll have him for you tonight.'

And sometimes, and always when Jasmine was least expecting it, her mum could be terribly nice. 'My evening appointment cancelled. I'm sure you could use a night to yourself.'

'I'd love that.' Jasmine hadn't had a night to herself since Simon had been born. In the weeks when she'd first come home and had stayed with her mum, the only advantage she had taken had been a long walk on the beach each morning before Simon woke up. 'Thanks, Mum.'

'No problem. I guess I'd better get familiar with his routines.'

'Can I go in and see him?'

'And wake him up probably.'

She didn't wake him up. Simon was lying on his front with his bottom in the air and his thumb in his mouth, and just the sight of him made everything worth it. He was in her old cot in her old bedroom and was absolutely the love of her life. She just didn't understand how Lloyd could want nothing to do with him.

'Do you think he's missing out?' Jasmine asked her mum. 'Not having a dad?'

'Better no dad than a useless one,' Louise said, then gave a shrug. 'I don't know the answer to that, Jasmine. I used to feel the same about you.' She gave her daughter a smile. 'Our taste in men must be hereditary. No wonder Penny's sworn off them.'

'Did she ever tell you what happened?' Jasmine asked, because one minute Penny had been engaged, the next the whole thing had been called off and she didn't want to talk about it.

'She just said they'd been having a few problems and decided that it was better to get out now than later.'

Before there were children to complicate things, Jasmine thought, but didn't say anything. It was her mum who spoke.

'I know it's tough at the moment but I'm sure it will get easier.'

'And if it doesn't?'

'Then you'd better get used to tough.' Louise shrugged. 'Have you told Penny you're applying for a job at Peninsula?'

'I saw her at my interview.'

'And?' Louise grimaced. They both knew only too well how Penny would react to the news.

'She doesn't want me there—especially not in Accident and Emergency,' Jasmine admitted. 'She wasn't best pleased.'

'Well, it's her domain,' Louise said. 'You know how territorial she is. She used to put thread up on her bedroom door so she'd know if anyone had been in there while she was out. She'll come round.'

And even though she smiled at the memory, Jasmine was worried that Penny wouldn't be coming round to the idea of her little sister working in her hospital any time soon.

Jasmine was proven right a few hours later when, back at her own small house, adding another coat of paint in an attempt to transform the lounge from dull olive green to cool crisp white, there was a loud rap at the door.

'Can you knock more quietly?' Jasmine asked as she opened it. 'If Simon was here—'

'We need to talk,' Penny said, and she brushed in and straight through to the lounge.

If Louise hadn't exactly been brimming with understanding, then Penny was a desert.

Her blouse was still crisp and white, her hair still perfect and her eyes were just as angry as they had been when she had first laid them on Jasmine in the hospital corridor earlier on that day. 'You said nothing about this when I saw you last week,' Penny said accusingly. 'Not a single word!'

'I didn't exactly get a chance.'

'Meaning?'

She heard the confrontation in her sister's voice, could

almost see Pandora's box on the floor between them. She was tempted just to open it, to have this out once and for all, to say how annoyed she still felt that Penny hadn't been able to make it for Simon's first birthday a couple of months earlier. In fact, she hadn't even sent a card. Yet there had been no question that Jasmine herself would be there to join in celebrating her sister's success.

Or rather celebrating her sister's *latest* success.

But bitterness wasn't going to help things here.

'That dinner was to celebrate you getting your fellowship,' Jasmine said calmly. 'I knew you'd be upset if I told you that I had an interview coming up, and I didn't want to spoil your night.'

'You should have discussed it with me before you even applied!' Penny said. 'It's my department.'

'Hopefully it will be mine soon, too,' Jasmine attempted, but her words fell on deaf ears.

'Do you know how hard it is for me?' Penny said. 'All that nonsense about equal rights… I have to be twice as good as them, twice as tough as any of them—there's a consultancy position coming up and I have no intention of letting it slip by.'

'How could my working there possibly affect that?' Jasmine asked reasonably.

'Because I'm not supposed to have a personal life,' was Penny's swift retort. 'You just don't get it, Jasmine. I've worked hard to get where I am. The senior consultant, Mr Dean, he's old school—he made a joke the other week about how you train them up and the next thing you know they're pregnant and wanting part-time hours.' She looked at her sister. 'Yes, I could complain and make waves, but how is that going to help things? Jed is going after the same position. He's a great doctor but he's only been in the department six months and I am not going to lose it to him.' She shook her head in frustration.

'I'm not asking you to understand, you just have to believe that it is hard to get ahead sometimes, and the last thing I need right now is my personal life invading the department.'

'I'm your sister—'

'So are you going to be able to stay quiet when the nurses call me a hard witch?' Penny challenged. 'And when you are supposed to finish at four but can't get off, are you going to expect me to drop everything and run to the crèche and get Simon?'

'Of course not.'

'And when I hear the other nurses moaning that you hardly ever do a late shift and are complaining about having to do nights, am I supposed to leap to your defence and explain that you're a single mum?'

'I can keep my work and personal life separate.'

'Really!'

It was just one word, a single word, and the rise of Penny's perfect eyebrows had tears spring to Jasmine's eyes. 'That was below the belt.'

'The fact that you can't keep your work and personal life separate is the very reason you can't go back to Melbourne Central.'

'It's about the travel,' Jasmine insisted. 'And you're wrong, I can keep things separate.'

'Not if we're in the same department.'

'I can if they don't know that we're sisters,' Jasmine said, and she watched Penny's jaw tighten, realised then that this was where the conversation had been leading. Penny was always one step ahead in everything, and

Penny had made very sure that it was Jasmine who suggested it.

'It might be better.' Penny made it sound as if she was conceding.

'Fine.'

'Can you keep to it?'

'Sure,' Jasmine said.

'I mean it.'

'I know you do, Penny.'

'I've got to get back to work. I'm on call tonight.' And her sister, now that she had what she came for, stood up to leave. Jasmine held in tears that threatened, even managed a smile as her sister stalked out of the door.

But it hurt.

It really hurt.

CHAPTER FOUR

IT WAS HER favourite place in the world.

But even a long stretch of sand, the sun going down over the water and a storm rolling in from the distance wasn't enough to take the harsh sting out of Penny's words.

Jasmine hated arguments, loathed them and did her very best to avoid them.

She could still remember all too well hearing the raised voices of her parents seeping up the stairs and through the bedroom floor as she had lain on her bed with her hands over her ears.

But there had been no avoiding this one—Jasmine had known when she'd applied for the role that there would be a confrontation. Still, she couldn't just bow to Penny's wishes just because it made things awkward for her.

She needed a job and, no matter what her mother and sister thought of her chosen career, nursing was what she was good at—and Emergency was her speciality.

Jasmine wasn't going to hide just because it suited Penny.

It had been cruel of Penny to bring up her relationship with Lloyd, cruel to suggest that she wasn't going back to Melbourne Central just because of what had happened.

It was also, Jasmine conceded, true.

Finding out that she was pregnant had been a big enough shock—but she'd had no idea what was to come.

That the dashing paramedic who'd been so delighted with the news of her pregnancy, who'd insisted they marry and then whisked her off on a three-month honeymoon around Australia, was in fact being investigated for patient theft.

She'd been lied to from the start and deceived till the end and nothing, it seemed, could take away her shame. And, yes, the whispers and sideways looks she had received from her colleagues at Melbourne Central as she'd worked those last weeks of her pregnancy with her marriage falling apart had been awful. The last thing she needed was Penny rubbing it in.

'I knew I recognised you from somewhere.' She looked over to the sound of a vaguely familiar voice.

'Oh!' Jasmine was startled as she realised who it was. 'Hi, Jed.' He was out of breath from running and—she definitely noticed this time—was very, very good looking.

He was wearing grey shorts and a grey T-shirt and he was toned, a fact she couldn't fail to notice when he lifted his T-shirt to wipe his face, revealing a very flat, tanned stomach. Jasmine felt herself blush as for the first time in the longest time she was shockingly drawn to rugged maleness.

But, then, how could you not be? Jasmine reasoned. Any woman hauled out of a daydream would blink a few times when confronted with him. Any woman would be a bit miffed that they hadn't bothered sorting their hair and that they were wearing very old denim shorts and a T-shirt splashed with paint.

'You walk here?' Jed checked, because now he remembered her. Dark curls bobbing, she would walk—sometimes slowly, sometimes briskly and, he had noticed she never looked up, never acknowledged anyone—she always seemed completely lost in her own world. 'I see you some mornings,' Jed said, and then seemed to think about it. 'Though not for a while.'

'I live just over there.' Jasmine pointed to her small weatherboard house. 'I walk here every chance I get—though I haven't had too many chances of late.'

'We're almost neighbours.' Jed smiled. 'I'm in the one on the end.' He nodded towards the brand-new group of town houses a short distance away that had been built a couple of years ago. Her mother had been the agent in a couple of recent sales there and Jasmine wondered if one of them might have been to him.

And just to remind her that he hadn't specifically noticed her, he nodded to another jogger who went past, and as they walked along a little way, he said hi to an elderly couple walking their dog. He clearly knew the locals.

'Taking a break from painting?' He grinned.

'How did you guess?' Jasmine sighed. 'I don't know who's madder—whoever painted the wall green, or me for thinking a couple of layers of white would fix it. I'm on my third coat.' She looked over at him and then stated the obvious. 'So you run?'

'Too much,' Jed groaned. 'It's addictive.'

'Not for me,' Jasmine admitted. 'I tried, but I don't really know where to start.'

'You just walk,' Jed said, 'and then you break into a run and then walk again—you build up your endurance. It doesn't take long.' He smiled. 'See? I'm addicted.'

'No, I get it.' Jasmine grinned back. 'I just don't do it.'

'So, how did you go with the crèche?' He walked along beside her and Jasmine realised he was probably just catching his breath, probably pacing himself rather than actually stopping for her. Still, it was nice to have a chat.

'They were really accommodating, though I think Lisa might have had something to do with that.'

'How old is your child?'

'Fourteen months,' Jasmine said. 'His name's Simon.'

'And is this your first job since he was born?' He actually did seem to want to talk her. Jasmine had expected that he'd soon jog off, but instead he walked along beside her, his breathing gradually slowing down. It was nice to have adult company, nice to walk along the beach and talk.

'It is,' Jasmine said. 'And I'm pretty nervous.'

'You worked at Melbourne Central, though,' he pointed out. 'That's one hell of a busy place. It was certainly buzzing when I went for my interview there.'

'Didn't you like it?'

'I did,' Jed said, 'but I was surprised how much I liked Peninsula Hospital. I was sort of weighing up between the two and this…' he looked out to the bay, '…was a huge draw card. The beach is practically next to the hospital and you can even see it from the canteen.'

'I'm the same,' Jasmine said, because as much as she loved being in the city she was a beach girl through and through.

'You'll be fine,' Jed said. 'It will take you ten minutes to get back into the swing of things.'

'I think it might take rather more than that.' Jasmine laughed. 'Having a baby scrambles your brains a bit.

Still, it will be nice to be working again. I've just got to work out all the shifts and things.'

'What does your husband do?' Jed took a swig from his water bottle. 'Can he help?'

'We're separated,' Jasmine replied.

'Oh. I'm sorry to hear that.'

'It's fine,' Jasmine said. She was getting used to saying it and now, just as she was, it would be changing again because she'd be divorced.

It was suddenly awkward; the conversation that had flowed so easily seemed to have come to a screeching halt. 'Storm's getting close.' Jed nodded out to the distance.

Given they were now reduced to talking about the weather, Jasmine gave a tight smile. 'I'd better go in and watch my paint dry.'

'Sure,' Jed said, and gave her a smile before he jogged off.

And as she turned and headed up to her flat she wanted to turn, wanted to call out to his rapidly departing back, *'It's okay, you don't have to run—just because I don't have a partner doesn't mean that I'm looking for another one.'*

God, talk about put the wind up him.

Still, she didn't dwell on it.

After all there were plenty of other things on her mind without having to worry about Jed Devlin.

CHAPTER FIVE

THERE WAS, JASMINE decided, one huge advantage to being related to two fabulously strong, independent women.

It sort of forced you to be fabulously strong and independent yourself, even when you didn't particularly feel it.

The hospital squeezed her in for that month's orientation day and after eight hours of fire drills, uniform fittings, occupational health and safety lectures and having her picture taken for her lanyard, she was officially on the accident and emergency roster. Lisa had, as promised, rung the crèche and told them Simon was a priority, due to the shortage of regular staff in Emergency.

So, just over a week later at seven o'clock on a Wednesday morning, two kilograms lighter thanks to a new diet, and with her hair freshly cut, Jasmine dropped her son off for his first day of crèche.

'Are you sure he's yours?' Shona, the childcare worker grinned as Jasmine handed him over. It was a reaction she got whenever anyone saw her son, even the midwives had teased her in the maternity ward. Simon was so blond and long and skinny that Jasmine felt as if she'd borrowed someone else's baby at times.

Until he started to cry, until he held out his arms to Jasmine the moment that he realised he was being left.

Yep, Jasmine thought, giving him a final cuddle, he might look exactly like Penny but, unlike his aunt, he was as soft as butter—just like his mum.

'Just go,' Shona said when she saw that Simon's mum looked as if she was about to start crying too. 'You're five minutes away and we'll call if you're needed, but he really will be fine.'

And so at seven-twenty, a bit red-nosed and glassy-eyed, Jasmine stood by the board and waited for handover to start.

She never even got to hear it.

'I've decided to pair you with Vanessa,' Lisa told her. 'For the next month you'll do the same shifts, and, as far as we can manage, you'll work alongside her. I've put the two of you in Resus this morning so don't worry about handover. It's empty for now so I'll get Vanessa to show you around properly while it's quiet—it won't stay that way for long.'

'Sure,' Jasmine said, in many ways happy to be thrown straight in at the deep end, rather than spending time worrying about it. And Lisa didn't have much choice. There wasn't much time for handholding—experienced staff were thin on the ground this morning, and even though she hadn't nursed in a year, her qualifications and experience were impressive and Lisa needed her other experienced nurses out in the cubicles to guide the agency staff they had been sent to help with the patient ratio shortfalls this morning.

Vanessa was lovely.

She had been working at the hospital for three years, she told Jasmine, and while it was empty, she gave her a more thorough tour of the resuscitation area as they checked the oxygen and suction and that everything was stocked. She also gave her a little bit of gossip along the way.

'There's Mr Dean.' Vanessa pulled a little face. 'He likes things done his way and it takes a little while to work that out, but once you do he's fine,' she explained as they checked and double-checked the equipment. 'Rex and Helena are the other consultants.' Jasmine found she was holding her breath more than a little as Vanessa worked through the list of consultants and registrars and a few nurses and gave titbits of gossip here and there.

'Penny Masters, Senior Reg.' Vanessa rolled her eyes. 'Eats lemons for breakfast, so don't take anything personally. She snaps and snarls at everyone and jumps in uninvited,' Vanessa said, 'but you have to hand it to her, she does get the job done. And then there's Jed.' Jasmine realised that she was still holding her breath, waiting to hear about him.

'He's great to work with too, a bit brusque, keeps himself to himself.' Funny, Jasmine thought, he hadn't seemed anything other than friendly when she had met him, but, still, she didn't dwell on it. They soon had their first patients coming through and were alerted to expect a patient who had fallen from scaffolding. He had arm fractures but, given the height from which he had fallen, there was the potential for some serious internal injuries, despite the patient being fully conscious. Resus was prepared and Jasmine felt her shoulders tense as Penny walked in, their eyes meeting for just a brief second as Penny tied on a large plastic apron and put on protective glasses and gloves.

'This is Jasmine,' Vanessa happily introduced her. 'The new clinical nurse specialist.'

'What do we know about the patient?' was Penny's tart response.

Which set the tone.

The patient was whizzed in. He was young, in pain and called Cory, and Penny shouted orders as he was moved carefully over onto the trolley on the spinal board. He was covered in plaster dust. It was in his hair, on his clothes and in his eyes, and it blew everywhere as they tried to cut his clothes off. Despite Cory's arms being splinted, he started to thrash about on the trolley

'Just stay nice and still, Cory.' Jasmine reassured the patient as Penny thoroughly examined him—listening to his chest and palpating his abdomen, demanding his observations even before he was fully attached to the equipment and then ordering some strong analgesia for him.

'My eyes…' Cory begged, even when the pain medication started to hit, and Penny checked them again.

'Can you lavage his eyes?' Penny said, and Jasmine warmed a litre of saline to a tepid temperature and gently washed them out as Penny spoke to the young man.

'Right,' Penny said to her young patient. 'We're going to get some X-rays and CTs, but so far it would seem you've been very lucky.'

'Lucky?' Cory checked.

'She means compared to how it might have been,' Jasmine said as she continued to lavage his eyes. 'You fell from quite a height and, judging by the fact you've got two broken wrists, well, it looks like as if you managed to turn and put out your hands to save yourself,' Jasmine explained. 'Which probably doesn't feel very lucky right now.

'How does that eye feel?' She wiped his right eye with gauze and Cory blinked a few times.

'Better.'

'How's the pain now?'

'A bit better.'

'Need any help?' Jasmine looked up at the sound of Jed's voice. He smelt of morning, all fresh and brisk and ready to help, but Penny shook her head.

'I've got this.' She glanced over to another patient being wheeled in. 'He might need your help, though.'

She'd forgotten this about Emergency—you didn't get a ten-minute break to catch your breath and tidy up, and more often than not it was straight into the next one. As Vanessa, along with Penny, dealt with X-rays and getting Cory ready for CT, Jasmine found herself working alone with Jed on his patient, with Lisa popping in and out.

'It's her first day!' Lisa warned Jed as she opened some equipment while Jasmine connected the patient to the monitors as the paramedics gave the handover.

'No problem,' Jed said, introducing himself to the elderly man and listening to his chest as Jasmine attached him to monitors and ran off a twelve-lead ECG. The man was in acute LVF, meaning his heart was beating ineffectively, which meant that there was a build-up of fluid in his lungs that was literally drowning him. Jim's skin was dark blue and felt cold and clammy and he was blowing white frothy bubbles out through his lips with every laboured breath.

'You're going to feel much better soon, sir,' Jed said. The paramedics had already inserted an IV and as Jed ordered morphine and diuretics, Jasmine was already pulling up the drugs, but when she got a little lost on the trolley he pointed them out without the tutting and eye-rolls Penny had administered.

'Can you ring for a portable chest X-ray?' Jed asked. The radiographer would have just got back to her department as Jasmine went to summon her again.

'What's the number?' Jasmine asked, but then found it for herself on the phone pad.

Jed worked in a completely different manner from Penny. He was much calmer and far more polite with his requests and was patient when Jasmine couldn't find the catheter pack he asked for—he simply went and got one for himself. He apologised too when he asked the weary night radiographer to hold on for just a moment as he inserted a catheter. But, yes, Jasmine noticed, Vanessa was right—he was detached with the staff and nothing like the man she had mildly joked with at her interview or walked alongside on the beach.

But, like Penny, he got the job done.

Jasmine spoke reassuringly to Jim all the time and with oxygen on, a massive dose of diuretics and the calming effect of the morphine their patient's oxygen sats were slowly climbing and his skin was becoming pink. The terrified grip on Jasmine's hand loosened.

Lisa was as good as her word and popped in and out. Insisting she was done with her ovaries, she put on a lead gown and shooed them out for a moment and they stepped outside for the X-ray.

Strained was the silence and reluctantly almost, as if he was forcing himself to be polite, Jed turned his face towards her as they waited for the all-clear to go back inside. 'Enjoying your first day?'

'Actually, yes!' She was surprised at the enthusiasm in her answer as she'd been dreading starting work and leaving Simon, and worried that her scrambled brain wasn't up to a demanding job. Yet, less than an hour into her first shift, Jasmine was realising how much she'd missed it, how much she had actually loved her work.

'Told you it wouldn't take long.'

'Yes, well, I'm only two patients in.' She frowned as he looked up, not into her eyes but at her hair. 'The hairdresser cut too much off.'

'No, no.' He shook his head. 'It's white.'

'Oh.' She shook it and a little puff of plaster dust blew into the air. 'Plaster dust.' She shook it some more, moaning at how she always ended up messy, and he sort of changed his smile to a stern nod as the red light flashed and then the radiographer called that they could go back inside.

'You're looking better.' Jasmine smiled at her patient because now the emergency was over, she could make him a touch more comfortable. The morphine had kicked in and his catheter bag was full as the fluid that had been suffocating him was starting to move from his chest. 'How are you feeling?'

'Like I can breathe,' Jim said, and grabbed her hand, still worried. 'Can my wife come in? She must've been terrified.'

'I'm going to go and speak to her now,' Jed said, 'and then I'll ring the medics to come and take over your care. You're doing well.' He looked at Jasmine. 'Can you stay with him while I go and speak to his wife?'

'Sure.'

'I thought that was it,' Jim admitted as Jasmine placed some pillows behind him and put a blanket over the sheet that covered him. After checking his obs, she sat herself down on the hard flat resus bed beside him. 'Libby thought so too.'

'Your wife?' Jasmine checked, and he nodded.

'She couldn't remember the number for the ambulance.'

'It must have been very scary for her,' Jasmine said, because though it must be terrifying to not be able to breathe, to watch someone you love suffer must have been hell. 'She'll be so pleased to see that you're talking and looking so much better than when you came in.'

Libby was pleased, even though she promptly burst into tears when she saw him, and it was Jim who had to reassure her, rather than the other way around.

They were the most gorgeous couple—Libby chatted enough for both of them and told Jasmine that they were about to celebrate their golden wedding anniversary, which was certainly an achievement when she herself hadn't even managed to make it to one year.

'I was just telling Jasmine,' Libby said when Jed came in to check on Jim's progress, 'that it's our golden wedding anniversary in a fortnight.'

'Congratulations.' Jed smiled.

'The children are throwing us a surprise party,' Libby said. 'Well, they're hardly children…'

'And it's hardly a surprise.' Jed smiled again. 'Are you not supposed to know about it?'

'No,' Libby admitted. 'Do you think that Jim will be okay?'

'He should be,' Jed said. 'For now I'm going to ring the medics and have them take over his care, but if he continues improving I would expect him to be home by the end of the week—and ready to *gently* celebrate by the next.'

They were such a lovely couple and Jasmine adored seeing their closeness, but more than that she really was enjoying being back at work and having her world made bigger instead of fretting about her own problems. She just loved the whole buzz of the place, in fact.

It was a nice morning, a busy morning, but the staff were really friendly and helpful—well, most of them. Penny was Penny and especially caustic when Jasmine missed a vein when she tried to insert an IV.

'I'll do it!' She snapped, 'the patient doesn't have time for you to practise on him.'

'Why don't you two go to lunch?' Lisa suggested as Jasmine bit down on her lip.

'She has such a lovely nature!' Vanessa nudged Jasmine as they walked round to the staffroom. 'Honestly, pay no attention to Penny. She's got the patience of a two-year-old and, believe me, I speak from experience when I say that they have none. How old is your son?' She must have the seen that Jasmine was a bit taken aback by her question, as she hadn't had time to mention Simon to Vanessa yet. 'I saw you dropping him off at crèche this morning when I was bringing in Liam.'

'Your two-year-old?'

'My terrible two-year-old,' Vanessa corrected as they went to the fridge and took out their lunches and Vanessa told her all about the behavioural problems she was having with Liam.

'He's completely adorable,' Vanessa said as they walked through to the staffroom, 'but, God, he's hard work.'

Jed was in the staffroom and it annoyed Jasmine that she even noticed—after all, there were about ten people in there, but it was him that she noticed and he was also the reason she blushed as Vanessa's questions became a bit more personal.

'No.' Jasmine answered when Vanessa none-too-subtly asked about Simon's father—but that was nursing, especially in Emergency. Everyone knew everything about everyone's life and not for the first time Jasmine wondered how she was supposed to keep the fact she was Penny's sister a secret.

'We broke up before he was born.'

'You poor thing,' Vanessa said, but Jasmine shook her head.

'Best thing,' she corrected.

'And does he help?' Vanessa pushed, 'with the childcare? Now that you're working…'

She could feel Jed was listening and she felt embarrassed. Embarrassed at the disaster her life was, but she tried not to let it show in her voice, especially as Penny had now walked in and was sitting in a chair on the other side of the room.

'No, he lives on the other side of the city. I just moved back here a few weeks ago.'

'Your family is here?' Vanessa checked.

'Yes.' Jasmine gave a tight smile and concentrated on her cheese sandwich, deciding that in future she would have lunch in the canteen.

'Well, it's good that you've got them to support you,' Vanessa rattled on, and Jasmine didn't even need to look at Penny to see that she wasn't paying any attention. Her sister was busy catching up on notes during her break. Penny simply didn't stop working, wherever she was. Penny had always been driven, though there had been one brief period where she'd softened a touch. She'd dated for a couple of years and had been engaged, but that had ended abruptly and since then all it had been was work, work, work.

Which was why Penny had got as far as she had, Jasmine knew, but sometimes, more than sometimes, she wished her sister would just slow down.

Thankfully the conversation shifted back to Vanessa's son, Liam—and she told Jasmine that she was on her own, too. Jasmine would have quite enjoyed learning all about her colleagues under normal circumstances but for some reason she was finding it hard to relax today.

And she knew it was because of Jed.

God, she so did not want to notice him, didn't want to be aware of him in any way other than as a colleague. She had enough going on in her life right now, but when Jed stood and stretched and yawned, she knew what that stomach looked like beneath the less than well-ironed shirt, knew just how nice he could be, even if he was ignoring her now. He opened his eyes and caught her looking at him and he almost frowned at her. As he looked away Jasmine found that her cheeks were on fire, but thankfully Vanessa broke the uncomfortable moment.

'Did you get called in last night?' Vanessa asked him.

'Nope,' Jed answered. 'Didn't sleep.'

Jed headed back out to the department and carried on. As a doctor he was more than used to working while he was tired but it was still an effort and at three-thirty Jed made a cup of strong coffee and took it back to the department with him, wishing he could just go home and crash, annoyed with himself over his sleepless night.

He'd had a phone call at eleven-thirty the previous night and, assuming it was work, had answered it without thinking.

Only to be met by silence.

He'd hung up and checked the number and had seen that it was *private*.

And then the phone had rung again.

'Jed Devlin.' He had listened to the silence and then hung up again and stared at the phone for a full ten minutes, waiting for it to ring again.

It had.

'Jed!' He heard the sound of laughter and partying and then the voice of Rick, an ex-colleague he had trained with. 'Jed, is that you?'

'Speaking.'

'Sorry, I've been trying to get through.'

'Where are you?'

'Singapore… What time is it there?'

'Coming up for midnight.'

'Sorry about that. I just found out that you moved to Melbourne.'

He had laughed and chatted and caught up with an old friend and it was nice to chat and find out what was going on in his friend's life and to congratulate him on the birth of his son, but twenty minutes later his heart was still thumping.

Two hours later he still wasn't asleep.

By four a.m. Jed realised that even if the past was over with, he himself wasn't.

And most disconcerting for Jed was the new nurse that had started today.

He had found it easy to stick to his self-imposed rule. He really wasn't interested in anyone at work and just distanced himself from all the fun and conversations that were so much a part of working in an emergency department.

Except he *had* noticed Jasmine.

From the second he'd seen her standing talking to Penny, all flustered and red-cheeked, her dark curls bobbing, and her blue eyes had turned to him, he'd noticed her in a way he'd tried very hard not to. When he'd heard she was applying for a job in Emergency, his guard had shot up, but he had felt immediate relief when he'd heard someone call her Mrs Phillips.

It had sounded pretty safe to him.

There had been no harm in being friendly, no chance of anything being misconstrued, because if she was a Mrs then he definitely wasn't interested, which meant there was nothing to worry about.

But it would seem now that there was.

'Thanks, Jed.' He turned to the sound of Jasmine's voice as she walked past him with Vanessa.

'For?'

'Your help today, especially with Jim. I had no idea where the catheter packs were. It's good to get through that first shift back.'

'Well, you survived it.' He gave a very brief nod and turned back to his work.

'More importantly, the patients did!' Jasmine called as she carried on walking with Vanessa.

They were both heading to the crèche, he guessed. He fought the urge to watch her walk away, not looking up until he heard the doors open and then finally snap closed.

Not that Jasmine noticed—she was more than used to moody doctors who changed like the wind. For now she was delighted that her first shift had ended and as she and Vanessa headed to the crèche, Jasmine realised she had made a friend.

'He's gorgeous!' Vanessa said as Jasmine scooped up Simon. 'He's so blond!'

He was—blond and gorgeous, Simon had won the staff over on *his* first day with his happy smile and his efforts to talk.

'This is Liam!' Vanessa said. He was cute too, with a mop of dark curls and a good dose of ADD in the making. Jasmine stood smiling, watching as Vanessa took about ten minutes just to get two shoes on her lively toddler.

'Thank goodness for work,' Vanessa groaned. 'It gives me a rest!'

'Don't look now,' Vanessa said as they walked out of the crèche, 'they're getting something big in.' Jed and Lisa were standing outside where police on motorbikes had gathered in the forecourt. Screens were being put up and for a moment Jasmine wondered if her first day was actually over or if they were going to be asked to put the little ones back into crèche.

'Go.' Lisa grinned as Vanessa checked what was happening. 'The screens are for the press—we have ourselves a celebrity arriving.'

'Who?' Vanessa asked.

'Watch the news.' Lisa winked. 'Go on, shoo…'

'Oh,' Jasmine grumbled, because she really wanted to know. She glanced at Jed, who looked totally bored with the proceedings, and there was really no chance of a sophisticated effort because Simon was bouncing up and down with excitement at the sight of police cars and Liam was making loud siren noises. 'I guess I'll have to tune in at six to find out.'

And that was the stupid thing about Emergency, Jasmine remembered.

You couldn't wait for the shift to finish—even today, as much as she'd enjoyed her shift, as soon as lunchtime had ended, she had been counting the minutes, desperate to get to the crèche and pick up Simon.

Except that the second she had finished her shift, she wanted to go back.

'I've missed it,' she told Vanessa as they walked to the car park. 'I was looking at a job in MRI, but I really do like working in Emergency.'

'I'm the same,' Vanessa admitted. 'I couldn't work anywhere else.'

'The late shifts are going to be the killer, though,' Jasmine groaned, 'and I don't even want to think about nights.'

'You'll work it out.' Vanessa said. 'I've got a lovely babysitter: Ruby. She's studying childcare, she goes to my church and she's always looking for work. And if she can deal with Liam she can more than handle Simon. She's got really strict parents so she loves spending evenings and sometimes nights at my place.' She gave Jasmine a nudge. 'Though I do believe her boyfriend might pop over at times. Just to study, of course…'

They both laughed.

It was nice to laugh, nice to be back at work and making friends.

Nice to sit down for dinner on the sofa, with a for-once-exhausted Simon. 'Come on,' Jasmine coaxed, but he wasn't interested in the chicken and potatoes she was feeding him and in the end Jasmine gave in and warmed up his favourite ready meal in the microwave. 'I'm not buying any more,' Jasmine warned as he happily tucked in, but Simon just grinned.

And it was nice to turn on the news and to actually feel like you had a little finger on the pulse of the world.

She listened to the solemn voice of the newsreader telling the viewers about a celebrity who was '*resting*' at the Peninsula after being found unconscious. She got a glimpse of Jed walking by the stretcher as it was wheeled in, holding a sheet over the unfortunate patient's face. Then Jasmine watched as Mr Dean spoke, saying the patient was being transferred to ICU and there would be no further comment from the hospital.

It wasn't exactly riveting, so why did she rewind the feature?

Why did she freeze the screen?

Not in the hope of a glimpse at the celebrity.

And certainly not so she could listen again to Mr Dean.

It was Jed's face she paused on and then changed her mind.

She was finished with anything remotely male, Jasmine reminded herself, and then turned as Simon, having finished his meal and bored with the news, started bobbing up and down in front of the television.

'Except you, little man.'

CHAPTER SIX

JED DID CONCENTRATE on work.

Absolutely.

He did his best to ignore Jasmine, or at least to speak to her as little as possible at work, and he even just nodded to her when they occasionally crossed paths at the local shop, or he would simply run past her and Simon the odd evening they were on the beach.

He was a funny little lad. He loved to toddle on the beach and build sandcastles, but Jed noticed that despite her best efforts, Jasmine could not get him into the water.

Even if he tried not to notice, Jed saw a lot as he ran along the stretch of sand—Jasmine would hold the little boy on her hip and walk slowly into the water, but Simon would climb like a cat higher up her hip until Jasmine would give in to his sobs and take him back to the dry sand.

'You get too tense.' He gave in after a couple of weeks of seeing this ritual repeated. He could see what Jasmine was doing wrong and even if he ignored her at work, it seemed rude just to run past and not stop and talk now and then.

'Sorry?' She'd given up trying to take Simon into the water a few moments ago and now they were patting a sandcastle into shape. She looked up when Jed stood over her and Jasmine frowned at his comment, but in a curious way rather than a cross one.

He concentrated on her frown, not because she was resting back on her heels to look up at him, not because she was wearing shorts and a bikini top, he just focused on her frown. 'When you try to get him to go into the water. I've seen you.' He grinned. 'You get tense even before you pick him up to take him in there.'

'Thanks for the tip.' Jasmine looked not at Jed but at Simon. 'I really want him to love the water. I was hoping by the end of summer he'd at least be paddling, but he starts screaming as soon as I even get close.'

'He'll soon get used to it just as soon as you relax.' And then realising he was sounding like an authority when he didn't have kids of his own, he clarified things a little. 'I used to be a lifeguard, so I've watched a lot of parents trying to get reluctant toddlers into the water.'

'A lifeguard!' Jasmine grinned. 'You're making me blush.'

She was funny. She wasn't pushy or flirty, just funny.

'That was a long time ago,' Jed said.

'A volunteer?'

'Nope, professional. I was paid—it put me through medical school.'

'So how should I be doing it?'

'I'll show you.' He offered her his hand and pulled her up and they walked towards the water's edge. 'Just sit here.'

'He won't come.'

'I bet he does if you ignore him.'

So they sat and chatted for ten minutes or so. Simon

grew bored, playing with his sandcastle alone, while the grown-ups didn't care that they were sitting in the water in shorts, getting wet with each shallow wave that came in.

Jed told her about his job, the one he'd had before medical school. 'It was actually that which made me want to work in emergency medicine,' Jed explained. 'I know you shouldn't enjoy a drowning...'

She smiled because she knew what he meant. There was a high that came from emergencies, just knowing that you knew what to do in a fraught situation.

Of course not all the time; sometimes it was just miserable all around, but she could see how the thrill of a successful resuscitation could soon plant the seeds for a career in Emergency.

'So if I drown, will you rescue me?'

'Sure,' Jed said, and her blue eyes turned to his and they smiled for a very brief moment. Unthinking, absolutely not thinking, he said it. 'Why? Is that a fantasy of yours?'

And he could have kicked himself, should have kicked himself, except she was just smiling and so too was he. Thankfully, starved of attention, Simon toddled towards them and squealed with delight at the feeling of water rushing past his feet.

'Yay!' Jasmine was delighted, taking his hands and pulling him in for a hug. 'It worked.'

'Glad to have helped.' Jed stood, because *now* he was kicking himself, now he was starting to wonder what might have happened had Simon not chosen that moment to take to the water.

Actually, he wasn't wondering.

Jed knew.

'Better get on.' He gave her a thin smile, ruffled Simon's hair and off down the beach he went, leaving Jasmine sitting there.

Jed confused her.

Cold one minute and not warm but hot the next.

And, no, being rescued by a sexy lifeguard wasn't one of her fantasies, but a sexy Jed?

Well…

She blew out a breath. There was something happening between them, something like she had never known before. Except all he did was confuse her—because the next time she saw him at work he went back to ignoring her.

As well as confusing, Jed was also wrong about her getting right back into the swing of things at work. The department was busy and even a couple weeks later she still felt like the new girl at times. Even worse, her mum was less than pleased when Lisa asked, at short notice, if Jasmine could do two weeks of nights. She had staff sick and had already moved Vanessa onto the roster to do nights. Jasmine understood the need for her to cover, but she wasn't sure her mum would be quite so understanding.

'I'm really sorry about this,' Jasmine said to her mum as she dropped Simon off.

'It's fine.' Louise had that rather pained, martyred look that tripped all of Jasmine's guilt switches. 'I've juggled a few clients' appointments to early evening for this week so I'll need you to be back here at five.'

'Sure.'

'But, Jasmine,' Louise said, 'how are you going to keep on doing this? I'm going away soon and if they can change your roster at five minutes' notice and expect you to comply, how are you going to manage?'

'I've a meeting with a babysitter at the weekend,' Jasmine told her mum. 'She's coming over and I'll see how she gets on with Simon.'

'How much is a babysitter going to cost?' Louise asked, and Jasmine chose not to answer, but really something would have to give.

Paying the crèche was bad enough, but by the time she'd paid a babysitter to pick Simon up for her late shifts and stints on nights, well, it was more complicated than Jasmine had the time to allocate it right now.

'How are things with Penny at work?' Louise asked.

'It seems okay.' Jasmine shrugged. 'She's just been on nights herself so I haven't seen much of her, and when I do she's no more horrible to me than she is to everybody else.'

'And no one's worked out that you're sisters?'

'How could they?' Jasmine said. 'Penny hasn't said anything and no one is going to hear it from me.'

'Well, make sure that they don't,' Louise warned. 'Penny doesn't need any stress right now. She's worked up enough as it is with this promotion coming up. Maybe once that's over with she'll come around to the idea a bit more.'

'I'd better get going.' Jasmine gave Simon a cuddle and held him just an extra bit tight.

'Are you okay?' Louise checked.

'I'm fine,' Jasmine said, but as she got to the car she remembered why she was feeling more than a little out of sorts. And, no, she hadn't shared it with her mum and certainly she wouldn't be ringing up Penny for a chat to sort out her feelings.

There on the driver's seat was her newly opened post and even though she'd been waiting for it, even though she wanted it, it felt strange to find out in such a banal way that she was now officially divorced.

Yes, she'd been looking forward to the glorious day, only the reality of it gave her no reason to smile.

Her marriage had been the biggest mistake of her life.

The one good thing to come out of it was Simon.

The *only* good thing, Jasmine thought, stuffing the papers into her glove box, and, not for the first time she felt angry.

She'd been duped so badly.

Completely lied to from the start.

Yes, she loved Simon with all her heart, but this was never the way she'd intended to raise a child. With a catalogue of crèches and babysitters and scraping to make ends meet and a father who, despite so many promises, when the truth had been exposed, when his smooth veneer had been cracked and the real Lloyd had surfaced, rather than facing himself had resumed the lie his life was and had turned his back and simply didn't want to know his own son.

'Are you okay?' Vanessa checked later as they headed out of the locker rooms.

'I'm fine,' Jasmine said, but hearing the tension in her own voice and realising she'd been slamming about a bit in the locker room, she conceded, 'My divorce just came through.'

'Yay!' said Vanessa, and it was a new friend she turned to rather than her family. 'You should be out celebrating instead of working.'

'I will,' Jasmine said. 'Just not yet.'

'Are you upset?'

'Not upset,' Jasmine said. 'Just angry.'

'Excuse me.' They stepped aside as a rather grumpy Dr Devlin brushed passed.

'Someone got out of the wrong side of bed,' Vanessa said.

Jasmine didn't get Jed.

She did not understand why he had changed so rapidly.

But he had.

From the nice guy she had met he was very brusque. *Very* brusque.

Not just to her, but to everyone. Still, Jasmine could be brusque too when she had to be, and on a busy night in Emergency, sometimes that was exactly what you had to be.

'You've done this before!' Greg, the charge nurse, grinned as Jasmine shooed a group of inebriated teenagers down to the waiting room. They were worried about their friend who'd been stabbed but were starting to fight amongst themselves.

'I used to be a bouncer at a night club.' Jasmine winked at her patient, who was being examined by Jed.

Greg laughed and even the patient smiled.

Jed just carried right on ignoring her.

Which was understandable perhaps, given that they were incredibly busy.

But what wasn't understandable to Jasmine was that he refused a piece of the massive hazelnut chocolate bar she opened at about one a.m., when everyone else fell on it.

Who doesn't like chocolate? Jasmine thought as he drank water.

Maybe he was worried about his figure?

He stood outside the cubicle now, writing up the card. 'Check his pedal pulses every fifteen minutes.' He thrust her a card and she read his instructions.

'What about analgesia?' Jasmine checked.

'I've written him up for pethidine.'

'No.' Jasmine glanced down at the card. 'You haven't.'

Jed took the card from her and rubbed his hand over his unshaven chin, and Jasmine tried to tell herself that he had his razor set that way, that he cultivated the unshaven, up-all-night, just-got-out-of-bed look, that this man's looks were no accident.

Except he had been up all night.

Jed let out an irritated hiss as he read through the patient's treatment card, as if she were the one who had made the simple mistake, and then wrote up the prescription in his messy scrawl.

'Thank you!' Jasmine smiled sweetly—just to annoy him.

She didn't get a smile back.

Mind you, the place was too busy to worry about Jed's bad mood and brooding good looks, which seemed to get more brooding with every hour that passed.

At six a.m., just as things were starting to calm down, just as they were starting to catch up and tidy the place for the day staff, Jasmine found out just how hard this job could be at times.

Found, just as she was starting to maybe get into the swing of things, that perhaps this wasn't the place she really wanted to be after all.

They were alerted that a two-week-old paediatric arrest was on his way in but the ambulance had arrived before they had even put the emergency call out.

Jasmine took the hysterical parents into an interview room and tried to get any details as best she could as the overhead loudspeaker went off, urgently summoning the paediatric crash team to Emergency. It played loudly in the interview room also, each chime echoing the urgency, and there was the sound of footsteps running and doors slamming, adding to the parents' fear.

'The doctors are all with your baby,' Jasmine said. 'Let them do their work.' Cathy, the new mum, still looked pregnant. She kept saying she had only had him two weeks and that this couldn't be happening, that she'd taken him out of his crib and brought him back to bed, and when the alarm had gone off for her husband to go to work… And then the sobbing would start again.

She kept trying to push past Jasmine to get to her baby, but eventually she collapsed into a chair and sobbed with her husband that she just wanted to know what was going on.

'As soon as there's some news, someone will be in.' There was a knock at the door and she saw a policeman and -woman standing there. Jasmine excused herself, went outside and closed the door so she could speak to them.

'How are they?' the policewoman asked.

'Not great,' Jasmine said. 'A doctor hasn't spoken to them yet.'

'How are things looking for the baby?'

'Not great either,' Jasmine said. 'I really don't know much, though, I've just been in with the parents. I'm going to go and try to find out for them what's happening.' Though she was pretty sure she knew. One look at the tiny infant as he had arrived and her heart had sunk.

'Everything okay?' Lisa, early as always, was just coming on duty and she came straight over.

'We've got a two-week-old who's been brought in in full arrest,' Jasmine explained. 'I was just going to try and get an update for the parents.'

'Okay.' Lisa nodded. 'You do that and I'll stay with them.'

Jasmine wasn't sure what was worse, sitting in with the hysterical, terrified parents or walking into Resus and hearing the silence as they paused the resuscitation for a moment to see if there was any response.

There was none.

Jed put his two fingers back onto the baby's chest and started the massage again, but the paediatrician shook his head.

'I'm calling it.'

It was six twenty-five and the paediatrician's voice was assertive.

'We're not going to get him back.'

He was absolutely right—the parents had started the resuscitation and the paramedics had continued it for the last thirty-five futile minutes. Jasmine, who would normally have shed a tear at this point before bracing herself to face the family, just stood frozen.

Vanessa cried. Not loudly. She took some hand wipes from the dispenser and blew her nose and Jed took his fingers off the little infant and sort of held his nose between thumb and finger for a second.

It was a horrible place to be.

'Are you okay?' Greg looked over at Jasmine and she

gave a short nod. She dared not cry, even a little, because if she started she thought she might not stop.

It was the first paediatric death she had dealt with since she'd had Simon and she was shocked at her own reaction. She just couldn't stop looking at the tiny scrap of a thing and comparing him to her own child, and how the parents must be feeling. She jumped when she heard the sharp trill of a pager.

'Sorry.' The paediatrician looked down at his pager. 'I'm needed urgently on NICU.'

'Jed, can you…?'

Jed nodded as he accepted the grim task. 'I'll tell the parents.'

'Thanks, and tell them that I'll come back down and talk to them at length as soon as I can.'

'Who's been dealing with the parents?' Jed asked when the paediatrician had gone.

'Me,' Jasmine said. 'Lisa's in there with them now. The police are here as well.'

'I'll speak first to the parents,' Jed said. 'Probably just keep it with Lisa. She'll be dealing with them all day.'

Jasmine nodded. 'They wanted a chaplain.' She could hear the police walkie-talkies outside and her heart ached for the parents, not just for the terrible news but having to go over and over it, not only with family but with doctors and the police, and for all that was to come.

'I'll go and ring the chaplain,' Greg said. 'And I'd better write up the drugs now.' He looked at the chaos. There were vials and wrappers everywhere, all the drawers on the trolley were open. They really had tried everything, but all to no avail.

'I'll sort out the baby,' Vanessa said, and Jasmine,

who had never shied away from anything before, was relieved that she wouldn't have to deal with him.

'I'll restock,' Jasmine said.

Which was as essential as the other two things, Jasmine told herself as she started to tidy up, because you never knew what was coming through the door. The day staff were arriving and things needed to be left in order.

Except Jasmine *was* hiding and deep down she knew it, had been so relieved when Jed had suggested keeping things with Lisa. She screwed her eyes closed as screams carried through the department. Jed must have broken the news.

She just wanted to go home to her own baby, could not stand to think of their grief.

'Are you okay, Jasmine?' Vanessa asked as she stocked her trolley to take into Resus, preparing to wash and dress the baby so that his parents could hold him.

'I'll get there.' She just wanted the shift to be over, to ring her mum and check that Simon was okay, for the past hour not to have happened, because it wasn't fair, it simply was not fair. But of course patients kept coming in with headaches and chest pains and toothaches and there was still the crash trolley to restock and plenty of work to do.

And now here was Penny, all crisp and ready for work.

'Morning!' She smiled and no one really returned it. 'Bad night?' she asked Jed, who, having told the parents and spoken to the police, was admitting another patient.

'We just had a neonatal death,' Jed said. 'Two weeks old.'

'God.' Penny closed her eyes. 'How are the parents?'

'The paediatrician is in there with them now,' Jed

said. Jasmine was restocking the trolley, trying not to listen, just trying to tick everything off her list. 'But they're beside themselves, of course,' Jed said. 'Beautiful baby,' he added.

'Any ideas as to why?' Penny asked.

'It looks, at this stage, like an accidental overlay. Mum brought baby back to bed and fell asleep feeding him, Dad woke up to go to work and found him.'

She heard them discussing what had happened and heard Lisa come in and ask Vanessa if the baby was ready, because she wanted to take him into his parents. She didn't turn around, she didn't want to risk seeing him, so instead Jasmine just kept restocking the drugs they had used and the needles and wrappers and tiny little ET tubes and trying, and failing, to find a replacement flask of paediatric sodium bicarbonate that had been used in the resuscitation. Then she heard Penny's voice…

'The guidelines now say not to co-sleep.'

And it wasn't because it was Penny that the words riled Jasmine so much, or was it?

No.

It was just the wrong words at the wrong time.

'Guidelines?' Jasmine had heard enough, could not stand to hear Penny's cool analysis, and swung around. 'Where are the guidelines at three in the morning when you haven't slept all night and your new baby's screaming? Where are the guidelines when—?'

'You need to calm down, Nurse,' Penny warned.

That just infuriated Jasmine even more. 'It's been a long night. I don't feel particularly calm,' Jasmine retorted. 'Those parents have to live with this, have to live with not adhering to the *guidelines*, when they were simply doing what parents have done for centuries.'

Jasmine marched off to the IV room and swiped her ID card to get in, anger fizzing inside her, not just towards her sister but towards the world that was now minus that beautiful baby, and for all the pain and the grief the parents would face. Would she have said that if Penny hadn't been her sister?

The fact was, she *would* have said it, and probably a whole lot more.

Yes, Penny was right.

And the guidelines were right too.

But it was just so unfair.

She still couldn't find the paediatric sodium bicarbonate solution and rummaged through the racks because it had to be there, or maybe she should ring the children's ward and ask if they had some till pharmacy was delivered.

Then she heard the door swipe and Jed came in.

He was good like that, often setting up his drips and things himself. 'Are you okay?'

'Great!' she said through gritted teeth.

'I know that Penny comes across as unfeeling,' Jed said, 'but we all deal with this sort of thing in different ways.'

'I know we do.' Jasmine climbed up onto a stool, trying to find the IV flask. She so did not need the grief speech right now, did not need the debrief that was supposed to solve everything, that made things manageable, did not really want the world to be put into perspective just yet.

'She was just going through the thought process,' Jed continued.

'I get it.'

He could hear her angrily moving things, hear the upset in her voice, and maybe he should get Lisa to speak to her, except Lisa was busy with the parents right now and Greg was checking drugs and handing over to the day staff. Still, the staff looked out for each other in cases like this, and so that was what Jed did.

Or tried to.

'Jasmine, why don't you go and get a coffee and…?' He decided against suggesting that it might calm her down.

'I'm just finishing stocking up and then I'm going home.'

'Not yet. Look—' he was very patient and practical '—you're clearly upset.'

'Please.' Jasmine put up her hand. 'I really don't need to hear it.'

'I think you do,' Jed said.

'From whom?'

'Excuse me?' He clearly had no idea what she was alluding to, but there was a bubble of anger that was dangerously close to popping now, not just for this morning's terrible events but for the weeks of confusion, for the man who could be nice one minute and cool and distant the next, and she wanted to know which one she was dealing with.

'Am I being lectured to by Dr Devlin, or am I being spoken to by Jed?'

'I have no idea what you're talking about. You're distressed.' He knew exactly what she was talking about, knew exactly what she meant, yet of course he could not tell her that. Jed also knew he was handling this terribly, that fifteen minutes sitting in the staffroom being debriefed by him wasn't going to help either of them.

'I'm not distressed.'

'Perhaps not, but I think it would be very silly to leave like this. It would be extremely irresponsible to get into a car and drive home right now, so I'm suggesting that you go to the staffroom and sit down for fifteen minutes.' She stood there furious as she was being told what to do, not asked, she knew that.

'Fine.' She gave a terse smile. 'I will have a coffee and then I'll go home, but first I have to put this back on the crash trolley and order some more from pharmacy.'

'Do that, and then I'll be around shortly to talk to you.' Jed said, 'Look, I know it's hard, especially with one so young. It affects all of us in different ways. I know that I'm upset…'

She didn't say it, but the roll of her eyes as he spoke told him he couldn't possibly know, couldn't possibly understand how she felt.

'Oh, I get it,' Jed said. 'I can't be upset, I don't really get it, do I? Because I don't have a child, I couldn't possibly be as devastated as you.' His voice was rising, his own well-restrained anger at this morning's events starting to build. 'I'm just the machine that walks in and tells the parents that their baby's dead. What the hell would I know?'

'I didn't mean that.' She knew then that she was being selfish in her upset, but grief was a selfish place and one not easy to share.

'Oh, but I think you did,' Jed said. 'I think you meant exactly that.'

And he was right, she had, except that wasn't fair on either of them, because she had cried many times over a lost baby, it just felt different somehow when you had one at home. There was a mixture of guilt and pain tempered with shameful relief that it hadn't happened to her, because, yes, she'd taken Simon into bed with her, despite what the guidelines might say, and it wasn't fair on anyone.

It simply wasn't fair.

Jasmine had no idea how the next part happened. Later she would be tempted to ring Security and ask if she could review the security footage in treatment room two between seven twenty and seven twenty-five, because she'd finally located the sodium bicarbonate and stepped down from the stool and stood facing him, ready to row, both of them ready to argue their point, and the next moment she was being kissed to within an inch of her life.

Or was it the other way around?

She had no way of knowing who had initiated it, all she was certain of was that neither tried to stop it.

It was an angry, out-of-control kiss.

His chin was rough and dragged on her skin, and his tongue was fierce and probing. He tasted of a mixture of peppermint and coffee and she probably tasted of instant tomato soup or salty tears, but it was like no other kiss she had known.

It was violent.

She heard the clatter of a trolley that moved as they did.

It was a kiss that came with no warning and rapidly escalated.

It was a kiss that was completely out of bounds and out of hand.

She was pressed into the wall and Jed was pressing

into her; his hands were everywhere and so too were hers; she could feel his erection pressing into her. More than that she too was pushing herself up against him, her hands just as urgent as his, pulling his face into hers, and never had she lost control so quickly, never had she been more unaware of her surroundings because only the crackle of the intercom above reminded them of their location—only that, or shamefully she knew it could have gone further. Somehow they stopped themselves, somehow they halted it, except they were still holding each other's heads.

'And you thought driving would be careless and irresponsible,' Jasmine said.

He sort of blew out his breath. 'Jasmine…' He was right on the edge here, Jed realised, shocked at himself. 'I apologise.'

'No need to apologise,' Jasmine said. 'Or should I?'

'Of course not.' His mouth was there, right there, they were holding each other, restraining the other, and both still dangerously close to resuming what they mustn't. She could hear their breathing, fast and ragged and fighting to slow, and slowly too they let go of each other.

Her blouse was undone, just one button, and she didn't really know how, but he looked away as she did it up and moved away from him to pick up the flask she had dropped. She left him setting up his IV and went to head back out, but she could still taste him, was still not thinking straight. And then Lisa came in.

'Shouldn't you be heading home?'

'I couldn't find the paediatric sodium bicarb,' Jasmine said. 'There's only one left after this.'

'Thanks,' Lisa said. 'I'll get Joan to add it to the pharmacy order. Thanks for everything, Jasmine. I know that can't have been an easy shift.'

'How are the parents?'

'They're spending some time with him. The hospital chaplain is in with them and the police have been lovely.' Lisa looked at Jasmine. 'Maybe go and get a coffee before you go home.'

'I think I just want my bed,' Jasmine admitted. 'I just need to finish the crash trolley off and order some more of this.'

'I'll do that.' Lisa took the flask from her and they stepped aside as Jed walked past with his IV trolley. Very deliberately, neither met the other's eye.

'You go to bed and get a well-earned rest,' Lisa said.

Fat chance of that.

Jasmine did have a cup of coffee before she drove home.

Except she certainly wasn't hanging around to see Jed. Instead, she chose to head to the kiosk and get a takeaway.

And, of course, on the way to her car, she rang her mum.

'How was Simon last night?' Jasmine asked the second her mum answered.

'Fantastic. I haven't heard a peep out of him.'

'He's not up yet?'

'No, but he didn't go down to sleep till quite late.'

'You've checked him, though?' Jasmine could hear the anxiety in her voice

'I checked him before I went to bed. Jasmine, it's eight a.m. Surely it's good if he's having a little lie-in when he often has to be up at six for crèche?'

'Mum…'

She heard her mother's weary sigh as she walked through the house and then silence for a moment. She was being ridiculous, but even so, she needed the reassurance.

'He's asleep,' her mum said, 'and, yes, he's breathing.'

'Thank you.'

'Bad night?'

'Bad morning.'

'I'm sorry.' And then Louise started to laugh. 'He's just woken up—can you hear him?'

Jasmine smiled at the lovely morning sounds Simon made, calling out to anyone who was there, but she was dangerously close to tears a second later as she realised again just how lucky she was.

'Go and have a nice sleep and I'll see you here for dinner.'

'Thanks, Mum.'

Her mum could be so nice, Jasmine mused as she drove home. When she had Simon she was wonderful with him. Jasmine completely understood that her mother didn't want to be a permanent babysitter and she decided that when she woke up she *was* going to ring Ruby, Vanessa's babysitter, and maybe get together and see if they could work something out.

All the drive home she thought very practical thoughts, aware she was a little bit more than tired.

And upset.

And confused.

She parked in the carport and looked over at the beach, wondered if a walk might be soothing, but knowing her luck Jed would be running there soon and another encounter with him was the last thing either of them needed now.

So she showered and tried to block out the day with her blinds, set her alarm and did her level best not to think of those poor parents and what they were doing right now, but even trying not to think about them made her cry.

And it made her cry too, that she had been here twelve weeks now and Simon's father hadn't even rung once to see how he was, neither had he responded to the occasional photo of his son she sent him.

And then she got to the confusing part and she wasn't crying now as she went over the latter part of her shift.

Instead she was cringing as her mind wandered to a man who at every turn bemused her, and then to the kiss that they had shared.

She hadn't been kissed like that, ever.

Their response to each other's kiss had been so immediate, so consuming that, really, had the intercom not gone off, they'd have been unstoppable, and she burnt in embarrassment at the thought of what Lisa might have come in and found.

And she burnt, too, because in truth it was a side to him she had known was there—something she had felt the second he had jogged up to her on the beach. Jed was the first man to move her in a very long time, but she had never thought her feelings might be reciprocated, had never expected the ferocity of that kiss.

And she'd do very well to forget about it!

They had both been upset, Jasmine decided.

Angry.

Over-emotional.

It had been a one-off. She turned over and very deliberately closed her eyes. Yes, it would be a bit awkward facing him tonight but, hell, she'd faced worse.

She'd just pretend it had never happened.

And no doubt so would he.

She had her whole life to sort out without confusing things further.

And a man like Jed Devlin could only do that.

CHAPTER SEVEN

'MUM!' SIMON SAID it more clearly than he ever had before, and Jasmine scooped him up and cuddled him in tight the second she got to her mum's.

'You're early,' Louise commented. 'I said you didn't need to be here till five.'

'I didn't sleep very well,' Jasmine admitted. 'I'm going to go shopping at the weekend for some decent blinds.' Not that that was the entire reason! 'How has he been?'

'Okay. He's been asking after you a lot,' Louise said, when Jasmine rather wished that she wouldn't as she already felt guilty enough. 'Right, I'd better get ready.'

Louise appeared a little while later in a smart navy suit, with heels and make-up, looking every bit the professional real estate agent. 'How did you do it Mum?' Jasmine asked. 'I mean, you had evening appointments when we were little.'

'You were older than Simon when your dad left,' Louise pointed out. 'Penny's a good bit older than you and she was born sensible—I used to ask the neighbour to listen out for you. It was different times then,' she admitted.

Maybe, but nothing was going to fill the well of guilt

Jasmine felt leaving Simon so much and it was only going to get more complicated for him when she added a babysitter to the mix.

Still, she did her best not to worry about next week or next month, just concentrated on giving him his dinner, and when he spat it out she headed to her mum's freezer and, yes, there were chicken nuggets. He could eat them till he was eighteen, Jasmine thought, and let go of worrying about the small stuff for five minutes, just enjoyed giving him his bath and settling him, and then got herself ready for work.

There really wasn't time to stress about facing Jed, especially when her mum didn't get back till after eight, and by the time she raced into work the clock was already nudging nine but, of course, he was one of the first people she saw.

It was a bit awkward but actually not as bad as she'd feared.

As she headed to the lockers Jasmine met him in the corridor and screwed up her face as she blushed and mouthed the word, 'Sorry.'

'Me too,' Jed said, and possibly he too was blushing just a little bit.

'Upset, you know,' Jasmine said.

'I get it.'

'So it's forgotten?' Jasmine checked.

'Forgotten,' he agreed.

Except it wasn't quite so easy to forget a kiss like that, Jasmine knew, because through a restless sleep she had tried.

So too had Jed.

He was a master at self-recrimination, had been furious with himself all day, and that evening, getting ready for work, he'd braced himself to face her, to be cool and aloof, yet her blush and her grin and her 'sorry' had sideswiped him—had actually made him laugh just a little bit on the inside.

'I got you a present.' Vanessa smiled as, still blushing, Jasmine walked into the locker room and peered into the bag being handed to her. It was a bottle with ribbons tied to the neck. 'I think it should be real champagne, but sparkling wine will have to do. You can open it when you're ready to celebrate.'

'Thank you!' Jasmine was touched. 'I'll have a drink at the weekend.'

'I mean properly celebrate.' Vanessa winked. 'You can't pop that cork till…'

'It will be vintage by then.' Jasmine grinned.

It was a very different night from the one before.

It was quiet and the staff took advantage. Greg, the charge nurse, put some music on at the work station and when at four a.m. there were only a few patients waiting for beds or obs, instead of telling them to restock or reorder, he opened a book as Jasmine and Vanessa checked each other's blood sugars. They were low enough to merit another trip to the vending machine, they decided. Then they came back and checked each other's BP.

'It's so low!' Vanessa pulled a face as she unwrapped the cuff and Jasmine grinned, proud of herself for keeping her pulse and blood pressure down, with Jed sitting at the station.

He noticed how easily she laughed.

She noticed him, full stop.

Noticed that this time when she cracked open her chocolate he took a piece.

'Do you want your blood pressure checked, Jed?' Vanessa asked.

'No, thanks.'

Vanessa pulled a face at his grumpy tone. 'Do you work on it, Jed?' It was ten past four, well into the witching hour for night nurses, a quiet night, lights blazing, the humour becoming more wicked. 'Do you work on being all silent and moody?'

'No,' he said. 'I just work.'

'And that beard you're growing,' Vanessa pushed as Greg looked up and grinned, 'is it designer stubble?'

'No,' Jed said patiently. 'I went for a run when I got in from work and I was too tired to shave afterwards, and then I overslept.'

'You're sure about that?' Vanessa said. 'You're sure you're not a male model on the side?'

Jed had forgotten those times of late. He hadn't partaken in chit-chat and fun for a very long time, he'd been too busy concentrating only on work. Maybe he needed a coffee, maybe *his* blood sugar was down, because he was kind of remembering the harmless fun he had once had at work before it had all become a nightmare.

He sat there recalling the laughs that had been part of the job and he was almost smiling as Vanessa chatted on. There was such a difference between playing and flirting. Jed had always known that, he'd just forgotten how to mix the two of late, had lost one for fear of the other, but the atmosphere tonight was kind of bringing it back.

'When you go to the hairdresser's, do you ask them to leave that bit of fringe?' Vanessa teased. 'Just so it can fall over your eye?'

As he turned, Jasmine waited for a frown, for a sharp word, for a brusque put-down, but her smirking grin turned to a delighted one as he flopped his fringe forward, pouted his lips and looked over their shoulders in a haughty model pose.

And then as they screamed in laughter and even Greg did too, Jed got back to his notes.

Enough fun for one night, Jed told himself.

Except he'd set them off and now they were walking like models.

Greg was joining in too as he filled in the board, standing with one hand on his hip and talking in deliberately effeminate tones. Jed tried not to smile, not notice as he usually managed to—he had just blocked out this side of Emergency, had chosen to ignore the black humour and frivolity that sometimes descended.

And yet somehow it was coming back.

Somehow he was starting to remember that it wasn't all just about work.

And Jed knew why.

It was just that he didn't want to know why.

'I'm going for a sleep.' He stood. 'Call me if anything comes in or at six if it stays quiet.'

He could hear them laughing as he tried to rest.

And whatever they were doing it must be funny because he even heard the po-faced nursing supervisor, who must be doing her rounds, start to laugh.

Jed turned on the white noise machine but still he couldn't sleep.

He could do without this!

'Morning, sunshine!' Greg rapped on the door at six, but Jed was awake. He rolled out of bed and brushed his teeth, headed out, took a few bloods and discharged a couple of patients, and wished the place would pick up.

He got one query appendicitis and one very grumpy old man called Ken Jones. He had a chronically infected leg ulcer, which was being dressed by a visiting nurse twice a week, but he had decided at five-thirty a.m. that it was time to do something about it and had called an ambulance. He was very grubby and unkempt and had his radio with him, which was tuned in to a chat show.

'What's his blood sugar?'

'Eight,' Jasmine said.

'You're taking all your diabetic medication, Ken?' Jed checked.

'I just do what I'm told.'

'Okay.' Jed had already carefully examined the man and his leg and he chatted to him for a little while. 'I'm going to get the medics to come down and have a look at you,' Jed said, 'but it might take a while. We're really quiet down here but I know they're very busy up on the ward, so you might have to stay with us for a while. And we could look at the dressings nurse to come and have a good look at your wound and maybe try something new.'

'Up to you.'

'It could be a few hours,' Jed said.

'I don't make a fuss.'

Jed grinned as he walked out. 'He'll be ringing up the radio station to complain about how long he has to wait soon.'

'Does he really need to see the medics?'

'Probably not,' Jed said. 'Penny will probably clear him out by eight, but…' he gave a shrug, '…the old boy's lonely, isn't he? Anyway, he could do with a good looking over, his chest is a bit rattly and he's a bit dry. I'll run some bloods.'

'I'll order him breakfast,' Jasmine yawned.

She ordered a breakfast from the canteen and then checked on the query appendicitis. His drip was about through so she headed over to the IV room. When she swiped her card and saw that Jed was in there, sorting out his trolley to take the bloods, she nearly turned and ran.

But that would be making a big deal of things so instead she stepped in.

'We need to talk,' Jed said without looking up from his task.

'No we don't,' Jasmine said. 'Really, it's fine.'

'Sure about that?' Jed said, and then looked over.

And, no, she wasn't sure about that because the ghost of their kiss was there in the room. She could see the exact spot where he'd pressed her to the wall, feel again every feeling she had yesterday—except the anger, except the upset.

'What about we meet for coffee after work?' he suggested.

'People will see,' Jasmine said. 'You know what this place is like.' She certainly didn't want a hint of this getting back to Penny.

'I meant away from the hospital. Just to talk.'

She shook her head. She'd hardly slept yesterday and had to work tonight as well as stop by her mum's at five and give Simon his dinner.

'I just want to go to bed.' She opened her mouth to correct herself and thankfully they both actually laughed.

'I really,' Jasmine said slowly, 'and I mean *really* am in no position to start something. I know people say that, but I've got a whole lot of things to sort out before...' She shook her head. 'I'm not going there.'

'I get that,' Jed said. 'Believe me, I had no intention of getting involved with someone at work but yesterday, hell, these past weeks…' He wondered how something he had spent all yesterday regretting should be something he would happily do again right this minute.

'Is that why you've been so horrible?'

'I haven't,' he said, then conceded, 'Maybe a bit. We need to talk, maybe clear the air—because if we don't—'

'If we don't,' Jasmine interrupted, 'we're going to be caught making out in the IV cupboard.' She gave him a grin. 'And I have no intention of going there again.'

Except she was lying.

She was looking at his mouth as she said it.

And he was looking at hers.

Had Greg not come in, that was exactly what would have happened and they both knew it.

Yes, the air needed clearing.

CHAPTER EIGHT

'WHY IS HE waiting for the medics?'

Despite not having to start till eight, Penny was in at a quarter to seven, standing and staring at the admission board and determined to make the most of a rare opportunity to clear the board and start her working day with not a single patient.

'He's brewing something.' Jed shrugged.

'We're not a holding pen,' Penny said. 'I'll get the nurses to order him transport home.'

'Let him have his breakfast at least.'

'Of course he can have his breakfast—by the time transport gets here he'll probably have had lunch as well.' She glanced briefly at a weary Jed. 'You look awful.'

'It's easier when it's busy,' Jed yawned.

'Go home,' she said.

'I might just do that.' And then he looked at Penny, who was rather determinedly not turning round to face him, just staring fixedly at the board. 'Speaking of looking awful...' he waited till she reluctantly turned to face him and he saw her red swollen eye '...what happened?'

'I walked into a branch.'

'Ouch.' Jasmine walked over just as he was taking a look.

'Ooh.' She winced when she saw Penny's red eye. 'Penny, what happened?' And then she remembered she wasn't supposed to be her sister.

'My neighbour's tree overhangs,' she said darkly. 'Though it won't by the time I get home—I've left them a note, telling them what's happened and that they'd better cut it.'

Jasmine could just imagine she had, and what was in it. And she could picture the branch, too, and Penny's gorgeous old neighbours who would be so upset.

Trust Penny to handle things so sensitively!

Of course she said nothing.

'I'll have a look,' Jed said, and went to buzz Reception to get Penny an admission card.

'I don't need to be registered,' Penny snapped. 'It's just a scratch.'

'A nasty scratch on your cornea,' Jed confirmed a few minutes later. Penny was sitting at the nurses' station and Jed had put some fluorescein drops into her eye. It made her eye bright yellow but any scratches showed up green. 'You need antibiotic drops and to keep it covered. When was your last tetanus booster?'

'I can't remember,' Penny said. 'I'm sure I'm up to date.'

'Penny?' Jed checked, as Jasmine walked in.

'Ken Jones just spiked a temp—his temp's thirty-eight point nine.'

'I'll do cultures.' Jed grinned, and Penny rolled her tongue in her cheek because now the old boy would have to be admitted.

'I'll do them,' she sighed.

'Not yet,' Jed yawned. 'I'll just give you your tetanus shot.'

'I'll go to my GP.'

'Don't be ridiculous,' Jed said, already opening a trolley and pulling out a syringe.

It was then that Jasmine *had* to say something.

'I'll do that.' Jasmine smiled. 'You can do the cultures.'

'I'll do the cultures,' Penny said. 'You go home, Jed, and think about shaving.'

Jasmine said nothing, not a single word as they headed into a cubicle and Penny unbuttoned her blouse. She just handed her a wad of tissues as Penny started crying.

Penny was, as Jasmine knew only too well, petrified of needles.

Not a little bit scared, completely petrified of them, though she didn't blink when sticking them in others.

'If you breathe a word of this…'

She was shaking on the seat as Jasmine swabbed her arm.

'No, wait!' Penny said.

'For what?' Jasmine said, sticking the needle in. 'Done.' She smiled at her. 'You big baby.'

'I know, I know.' Penny shuddered. 'Just give me a minute, would you? Go and set up for those blood cultures.' She had snapped straight back to being Penny, except this time Jasmine was smiling.

Jed didn't think about shaving.

He had a shower and tried not to think about Jasmine.

And then he pulled on some running clothes and ran

the length of the beach and told himself to just concentrate on work.

Only this time it didn't work.

And he saw where she lived and her car pull up in her carport and he saw Jasmine minus an armful of Simon but holding a bottle of champagne, which confused him, and he tried to continue to run.

What on earth was he going to say to her if he knocked at her door?

At least nothing would happen, he consoled himself, as ten minutes later he found himself doing just that, because given he wasn't exactly fresh out of the shower, there would be no repeats of yesterday.

Except *she* was fresh out of the shower when she opened the door and he prided himself on the fact that he did not look down, that he somehow held her eyes, even though her dressing gown did little to hide her womanly shape.

'Bad timing?'

'A bit.'

'Well, I won't keep you from your champagne.' He didn't want to make her laugh, except he did so, only he wasn't here for that.

'It's in the fridge.'

'Good.'

'A present.'

'That's nice.'

'Well?' Jasmine demanded. 'Which Jed am I talking to this morning?' And she looked at him standing there, and she knew who it was—the beachside Jed, the man who made her smile, the Jed who had made his first appearance at work just a few hours ago.

'I like to keep my work and personal life separate,'

he offered as way of an explanation, only it didn't wash with Jasmine. Penny did too but she was a cow both in and out of work. Yet with Jed sometimes she felt as if she was dealing with two completely different people.

But she liked this one.

Really liked this one, and, no, maybe they weren't going anywhere, maybe it was just all a bit much for him, she was a mother to one year old after all, but that he was here, that at this hour of the morning he stood at her door, when sensible shift workers should be firmly asleep, proved the undeniable attraction.

'I just wanted to say that I am really sorry and that it won't happen again. There'll be no more inappropriateness.'

'And it won't happen again at this end,' Jasmine said. 'Nothing inappropriate…'

Jed nodded and turned to go, except she didn't want him to. She was tired of running from the past, tired of saving for the future—she just wanted a little bit of living for now.

'At least, not at work.'

And for two years Jed had kept things separate. Despite some temptations, he had kept fiercely to his rule.

But Jed's rules had never been tested at this level.

Had they not kissed yesterday he might have been able to walk away.

Had he not tasted lips that were exactly suited to his, he might have headed back to the beach and then home.

But more than that, her blush and eye roll and 'sorry' last night, her total lack of pursuit or demands meant more to Jed than Jasmine could possibly know.

Bottom line?

They wanted each other.

Not a little bit of want, it was a morning after a sleepless nights want. It was twenty-five hours since yesterday's kiss and for twenty-five hours it had been on both of their minds.

He walked into the hallway and his mouth met hers.

And his chin was even rougher than yesterday.

And yesterday, though their kiss had been fierce it had been tempered on both sides with bitter restraint.

But now they could have what they wanted.

Each other.

For now, at least, it could be as simple as that.

She didn't care that he was damp from running. He smelt fresh and male and she knew what was under that T-shirt, and as she pulled it up and over his head she didn't just get to glimpse, she got to feel, and, no, he wasn't annoyed at the intrusion this time.

He tugged at her dressing gown as his mouth was everywhere—on her lips, on her neck and on her breasts. Meanwhile, she pulled at his shorts, because he was pressed so hard into her, and they pulled apart just enough to get to the bedroom—they weren't in the treatment room now and they quickly celebrated the fact.

She wanted to see what she had felt and she manoeuvred his shorts and all things unnecessary and he kicked off his running shoes and stepped out of them and they were naked in seconds, and seconds from impact.

'Condoms.' She was on the floor, going through his shorts.

'I don't run with them.' Jed laughed.

She was at eye level with his crotch as she knelt up and pressed her lips to him, pleased with a brief taste. Too selfish to continue, she dashed to her tiny bathroom and pulled the cupboard under the sink apart for condoms that were somewhere in a box she hadn't sorted in ages.

She was uncaring as Jed watched her bottom sticking up as she searched in the cupboard and her breasts jiggling as she turned round and it was safer that he go back into the bedroom.

Oh, my.

It was all Jasmine could think as she walked back towards him, because he was better than anything she had fashioned in her mind. He was incredibly fit and toned. She should have been shy as she walked over, but shy was the furthest thing from her mind and anyway, he didn't wait for her to finish walking—both of them were happy to collide.

He was just so into her body, so wanting, and he didn't need to worry about speed or things moving too quickly for her because as his hands slid between her thighs and met her heat she was moaning and he was pushing her onto the bed, with Jasmine wondering where her inhibitions had gone.

She had hundreds of them, Jasmine reminded herself as he knelt over her and examined every inch of her, his eyes greedy with want.

A telephone book full of them.

Or she had, but they had just all disappeared today.

It was almost impossible to tear the packet for him.

And she found herself licking her lips as he slid it on.

She had never had sex like it.

She had never felt less mechanical in her life.

Thought had been replaced by pure sensation.

Him, she thought as he got back to kissing her.

Her, he thought as he reclaimed her mouth.

And then the power that remained sort of fused into one.

His fingers were there and she was wet and warm and wanted this just as much as he did.

'First time since…' She sort of braced herself and he held back and took a moment to not be selfish, even if she wanted him to be. Instead, he slid deeper into her with fingers that were skilled and frantic, and she left it to him, because he knew what he was doing. If they were quick it was mutual, if they were fast it was with begging consent.

Even with much preparation she was incredibly tense when the moment came and she willed him to ignore her. Slowly he pushed in, and she stretched and resisted and then stretched again, and he gave her a moment of stillness to get used to him inside.

Well, not really a moment because he knew he only had a few left in him but Jed left it for her to initiate movement, felt the squeeze and the pull on him as she tested herself as she moved herself up and down his long length.

Just when she thought she had adjusted, just when she pulled him in, he beat her to it and drove into her, and she met him and then he did it again and she tried to trip into his rhythm, except he was so hard and fast now it was bliss to not try, to simply let him, only it wasn't a passive response, it was more trusting.

Jed could hear Jasmine's moans and her urging, and he wished for a second she'd be quiet, because it made it impossible for Jed not to come, except she was starting to. He felt the lift of her hips and the arch of her into him, the feel of a slow uncurling from the inside, reluctant almost to give in to him, and then as he moaned his release she shattered.

She did, she just gave in in a way she never had, felt and delivered deeper than she ever had, and found out in that moment how much of herself she had always held back, the intensity fusing them for a moment in absolute bliss.

She lay there trying to get her breath back as he rested on top of her, and still they were one as reality slowly started to intrude.

She wasn't ready for a relationship.

He'd sworn to not get involved with someone from work.

Penny.

Promotion.

Simon.

Single mum.

Simultaneously the real world flooded its lights onto them and they both turned looked at each other for a long moment.

'Well,' Jasmine said. 'We must have both needed that.'

He laughed, actually laughed on the inside too as he had when she had mouthed 'sorry', and the doubts that had started hushed.

And they hushed some more as they lay in bed and drank Vanessa's sparkling wine that hadn't even had time to cool, and they congratulated each other on how fantastic that had been, rather than trying to work out where they were, and then she told him not what was on her mind but the truth.

'I have to go to sleep.'

'And me.'

'I hardly slept yesterday.'

'Me neither.'

'Jed, I don't know what happened. I don't really know what to say.' She was as honest as she could be. 'I'm nowhere near ready to get involved with someone, so I don't really know how we ended up here.'

'I do,' Jed admitted. 'Why the hell do you think I've been avoiding you since I found out you weren't married?'

'What?'

He just shrugged.

'Tell me.'

'You just...' He gave an embarrassed grin. 'Well, you know when you're attracted to someone? I suppose when I saw you talking to Penny and then she said you were here for an interview and then someone called you Mrs Phillips, well, I was relieved you were spoken for.'

Jasmine frowned.

'I don't like mixing work with things and thought I might have trouble keeping to that with you—it wasn't a logical thing, just...'

She did know what he meant.

Maybe it hadn't been quite an instant attraction, but that evening on the beach, when he'd lifted his T-shirt... Jasmine pulled back the sheet, looked at his lovely abdomen and bent over and ran her fingers lightly over the line there. He caught her hand as it moved down.

'I thought you wanted to sleep.'

'I do.'

'Then later.'

She set the alarm for that afternoon, before she remembered another potential problem. Penny.

'And no one at work is to know.'

'Suits me.'

'I mean it,' Jasmine said. 'What happened yesterday at work was wrong.'

'I'll carry on being horrible.'

'Good.'

'So much for clearing the air,' Jed said. 'Now it's all the more complicated.'

'Not really,' Jasmine yawned. 'Just sleep with me often and buy me lots of chocolate. My needs are simple.'

For that morning at least it really did seem as straightforward as that.

CHAPTER NINE

JED WAS NICE and grumpy at work and he deliberately didn't look up when she walked past, and Jasmine made sure there were no private jokes or smiles.

Gossip was rife in this place and the last thing she wanted was to be at the centre of it again.

No one could have guessed that their days were spent in bed. She just hoped he understood that it couldn't always be like this—that night shifts and her mother's help had made things far easier than they would be from now on. In fact, Jed got his first proper taste of dating a single mum that weekend.

Ruby was lovely.

'I'm hoping to work overseas as a nanny,' she explained to Jasmine, 'so I'm trying to get as much experience as I can and hopefully by the time I've got my qualification I'll have a couple of good references.'

She was very good with Simon, happy to sit with him as he tried to bang square pegs into round holes, and Jasmine could tell Ruby was very used to dealing with young children.

'My main problem is late shifts,' Jasmine explained.

'The crèche knows me,' Ruby said. 'I pick Liam up and I take him back to Vanessa's. I give him his dinner and bath and I try to get him asleep for Vanessa but Liam likes to wait up for her.'

Jasmine laughed. She and Vanessa had got the boys together a couple of times and Liam certainly had plenty of energy.

'Well, Vanessa and I aren't working the same shifts so much now,' Jasmine explained, 'so if we can try and work opposite late shifts…'

'It will all work out,' Ruby said. 'I can always look after them both some evenings.'

Jasmine was starting to think this could work.

So much so that for a try-out Ruby suggested she look after Simon that night, and for the first time in a very long time Jasmine found herself with a Saturday night free. To her delight, when Jed rang a little bit later she found that she had someone to share it with.

'It went well with Ruby, then?'

He asked about the babysitter as they were seated for dinner.

'She seems lovely,' Jasmine said. 'Simon didn't even get upset when I left.'

They were eating a couple of suburbs away from the Peninsula Hospital in a smart restaurant that overlooked the bay. Jasmine had taken a taxi because she hadn't been out in yonks and she wanted a glass or three of wine.

'I would have picked you up.'

'I know.' Jasmine smiled. 'But I've a feeling Ruby might gossip to Vanessa. I feel like I'm having an affair. It's too confusing to work out…' She looked up from the menu and went cross-eyed and Jed started to laugh.

'I can't do that.'

'It's easy,' Jasmine said. 'You just look at the tip of your nose and then hold it as you look up.'

'You've practised.'

'Of course.' She grinned.

And, cross-eyed or not, she looked stunning, Jed noted. Her hair was loose as it had been on the day he had met her on her walk on the beach, but it fell in thick glossy curls. Unlike at work, she was wearing make-up, not a lot but just enough to accentuate her very blue eyes and full mouth. 'What do you want to eat?'

'Anything,' Jasmine said. 'Well, anything apart from chicken nuggets.'

So instead of leftover nuggets there was wine and seafood, and conversation was easy, as long as it was just about food, about movies and the beach, but the second it strayed deeper there was a mutual pulling back.

'Will you go back to your maiden name?' Jed asked after a while.

'I don't know,' she admitted. 'I don't know if I should change Simon's…'

'So what is it?'

'Sorry?'

'Your maiden name?'

She didn't answer him, just peeled a prawn. She didn't even get a reprieve when he asked what had happened in her marriage, because for a marriage to break up when someone was pregnant it sounded as if something pretty serious had.

'I've got three hours, Jed.' She smiled, dipping a prawn in lime mayonnaise. 'In fact, two hours and fifteen minutes now. I want to enjoy them, not spend time talking about my ex.'

And later, when they were finishing up their heavenly dessert and he mentioned something about a restaurant in Sydney, she asked why he'd moved. His answer was equally vague and Jasmine frowned when he used her line.

'We've got thirty minutes till you need to be back for Ruby. Do we really want to waste them hearing my woes?'

'No.' She laughed.

But, yes, her heart said, except that wasn't what they were about—they had both decided.

They were going to keep things simple and take things slowly.

But it was difficult to find someone so easy to talk to and not open up, especially when the conversation strayed at one point a little too close to Penny. She'd mentioned something about how good it was to have Ruby, given her mum and sister were so busy with their jobs. As soon as she said it she could have cut out her tongue.

'Your mum's in real estate?' Jed checked, and she nodded. 'What does your sister do?'

It was a natural question but one she'd dreaded.

'She does extremely well at whatever she puts her mind to,' Jasmine evaded, reaching for her glass of wine.

'Ouch.' Jed grinned. 'Sore point?'

'Very.'

So he avoided it.

It was nice and going nowhere, they both knew that. It was an out-of-hours fling, except with each turn it became more complicated because outside work there were Simon and Penny and unbeknown fully to the other the two hearts that were meeting had both been incredibly hurt.

Two hearts that had firmly decided to go it alone for now.

They just hadn't factored in desire.

'It's like being a teenager again.' Jasmine grinned as he pulled the car over before they turned into her street and kissed her. 'My mum lives in this street.'

'We're not outside…?'

'No.'

'Good,' he said, and got back to kissing her.

They were under a huge gum tree that dropped gum nuts everywhere, but Jed risked the paintwork, grateful for the leafy shield, and they were ten minutes into a kiss that was way better than teenage ones she'd partaken in, right on this very spot, especially when Jed moved a lever and her seat went back a delicious fraction.

She could hardly breathe. He was over her and looking down at her, his hand was creeping up between her legs, and she could feel how hard he was. However, they could not take it even a fraction further here and she was desperate to pay Ruby and have her out of there, wanted so badly to have him in her bed.

And it would seem that Jed was thinking the same thing. 'I could wait till Ruby's gone.'

'No.' She hauled the word out, for if she regretted using it now, she knew she would regret it more in the morning if she didn't. 'I don't want that for Simon.' She looked up at those gorgeous eyes and that mouth still wet from her kisses and it killed her to be twenty-six and for it to feel wrong to ask him in. 'We're keeping things light,' Jasmine said. 'Agreed?' she prompted, and he nodded. 'Which is fine for me, but I won't treat his little heart lightly.'

'I know.'

'Next time we'll go to yours,' Jasmine suggested.

He looked down at her and the rules he'd embedded into his brain were starting to fade, because he had enjoyed being out, but now he wanted in.

'We'll see,' he said, because this was starting to be about a whole lot more than sex. He'd more than enjoyed tonight, had loved being in her company. The only bit that was proving difficult was leaving things here. 'Maybe we'll go out but eat more quickly?'

'Confusing, isn't it?' she said, and again she crossed her eyes and he laughed and then one more kiss and it ached to a halt.

Killed to turn on the engine and drive down the street and then turn into her own street and to park two doors down from her home.

To smile and walk out and to rearrange her dress as she let herself in.

To chat and pay Ruby and carry on a normal conversation, saying that, yes, she'd had a great night catching up with an old friend, and maybe she'd ask Ruby to babysit so that they could catch up again, perhaps as soon as next week.

But a week didn't seem so soon once Ruby was gone.

A night felt too long.

It killed her not to text him to come back.

CHAPTER TEN

'HI, JASMINE!'

She looked up at the familiar face of a paramedic who was wheeling a stretcher in.

'I haven't seen you in ages.'

'Hi, Mark.' Jasmine smiled, but there was a dull blush on her cheeks, and as Jed looked over to see how the new patient was, he couldn't help but notice it, couldn't help but see that Jasmine was more than a little flustered as she took the handover. 'What are you doing out here?'

'We're all over the place today,' Mark said. 'I had a transfer from Rosebud that got cancelled and then we were called out to Annie here.' Jasmine smiled at her new patient. 'Annie Clayfield, eighty-two years old, fell at home last night. We were alerted by her security when she didn't respond to their daily phone call. We found her on the floor,' Mark explained. 'Conscious, in pain with shortening and rotation to the left leg.'

He pulled back the blanket and Jasmine looked at the patient's feet and saw the familiar deformity that was an obvious sign of a hip fracture.

Annie was a lovely lady and tough too—she tried to hold back her yelp of pain as they moved her over as gently as they could onto the trolley.

Jed came over when he heard her cry and ordered some analgesic.

'We'll get on top of your pain,' Jed said, 'before we move you too much.' He had a listen to her chest and checked her pulse and was writing up an X-ray order when he saw one of the paramedics leave the stretcher he was sorting out and head over to Jasmine.

'So you're here now?'

'That's right.' Jed noted that her voice was falsely cheerful and he had no reason to listen, no reason not to carry on and see the next patient, except he found himself writing a lot more slowly, found himself wanting to know perhaps more than he should if they were planning to keep things light.

'I heard you and Lloyd split up?'

'We did.'

'What's he doing with himself these days?'

'I've no idea,' Jasmine said. 'We're divorced now. I think he's working in his family's business.'

As Jed went to clip the X-ray slip to Annie's door he saw the paramedic give Jasmine a brief cuddle.

'You had nothing to do with it, Jasmine, we all know that. You don't have to hide.'

'I'm not hiding.'

And there was no such thing as uncomplicated, Jed decided, looking at Annie's X-rays a good hour later and ringing down for the orthopaedic surgeons. They'd both agreed to keep it light, to take things slowly. Neither of them talked much, about families or friends or the past, and it should suit him, and yet the more he knew, or rather the less he got to know…

The more he wanted.

Despite all efforts to take things slowly, things were

gathering pace between them. They'd been seeing each other for a few weeks now—at least, whenever they got a chance.

They rang each other a lot, and went out whenever shifts and babysitters permitted, or more often than not they ended up back at his for a few stolen hours.

It just wasn't enough, though.

Concentrate on work, he told himself as he ran along the beach that night.

Except she was home, he knew it.

And Simon would be in bed.

And she wanted to keep that part of her life very separate.

So too did he, Jed reminded himself.

He caught sight of the city shimmering gold in the distance. Melbourne offered a gorgeous skyline but a different skyline from the one he knew so well.

He'd come here to get away, Jed reminded himself.

To finally focus on his career and get ahead.

Yet he looked at the tall gleaming buildings of Melbourne and as much as he loved Peninsula, there was something about the city, or rather a busy city emergency department.

And still Melbourne Central beckoned.

CHAPTER ELEVEN

JASMINE STARED AT the roster and gritted her teeth.

Jed was filling out blood forms and suitably ignoring her, and Penny was at her annoying best, suggesting that the nurses join her in Resus so that she could run through a new piece of equipment with them.

A new piece of equipment that had been there as long as Jasmine had and had been used often.

Honestly, the second the place was finally quiet Penny found a job or an activity for everyone.

No wonder she was so unpopular.

The roster had finally been revealed for the next eight-week period and as she tapped the shifts into her phone Jasmine could feel her blood pressure rising.

Yes, she was the new girl.

Yes, that meant that she got the rubbish shifts—but she had more late duties coming up than she could count, and lots of weekends too, which she would usually be glad of for the money, but of course the crèche wasn't open on weekends and, even though she'd been told it was only about once every three months, there was *another* stint of nights coming up in two weeks.

Her mum would be on her cruise by then.

'Problem?' Lisa checked.

'Just the nights,' Jasmine said. 'I thought it was every three months.'

'Well, we try and share it, but especially when someone's new I like to get them to do some early, so that was an extra for you.'

Was she supposed to say thanks?

She liked Lisa, Jasmine really did, and she was running a department after all, not Jasmine's childcare arrangements, but the pressure of shift work and single parenting, let alone trying to date, was starting to prove impossible.

Idly flicking through the patient bulletin, her eye fell on the perfect job for a single mum who actually wanted to have a little bit of a life too.

It was in the fracture clinic and was almost nine to five.

It was a level above what she was on now, but with her emergency experience she would stand a pretty good chance at getting it.

'Fracture Clinic!' Vanessa peered over her shoulder. 'You'd go out of your mind.'

'I'm going out of my mind looking at the roster,' Jasmine admitted.

'Don't think about it,' Vanessa said breezily. 'Something always turns up.'

Jasmine rolled her eyes as Vanessa walked out. 'I wish I had her optimism.'

'Jasmine.' She turned and smiled at the sound of Mark's voice. 'How are things?'

'Good.' Jed saw she was uncomfortable, saw she glanced over her shoulder to check whether or not he was there, and it was none of his business, he wanted it that way, yet he wanted to know what the problem was, why Mark thought she was hiding.

'Just giving you the heads up, no doubt you'll be alerted soon, but there's a nasty car versus bike on the beach road. Sounds grim.'

'Do we know how many?' Jed asked.

'That's all I've got but they're calling for backup.'

'Thanks.'

Jasmine let Lisa know and the orthopods were down anyway, looking at a fractured femur, and Lisa said to just wait till they heard more before they started paging anyone but that she'd let Penny and Mr Dean know.

Then Mark's radio started crackling and he listened, translating the coded talk of the operator. 'They're just about to let you know,' Mark said. 'One fatality, one trapped, one on the way—adult male.'

The alert phone went then and Lisa took it just as Penny appeared, looking brusquely efficient as usual.

'Car versus motorbike,' Lisa said. 'We've got the biker coming in, he's conscious, abdominal injuries, hypotensive.' She looked up at the clock. 'He's five minutes away and they've just freed the trapped driver, so he's on his way too.'

'I'll take the first,' Penny said. 'If that's okay with you, Jed?'

'Be my guest,' Jed answered, but Jasmine saw the clenching of his jaw and knew that Penny was seriously rattling him—she was always jumping in, always trying to take over anything that was remotely interesting.

'Have we paged the surgeons?' Penny asked.

'Done,' Jasmine said.

'Blood bank?'

'I've let them know.'

Penny gave no response, but with reason as the blast of a siren told them the ambulance was here. As the paramedics raced the patient in, Jasmine didn't blame Penny a bit for the curse she let out when she asked where the hell the surgeons were.

The patient, though conscious, was beyond pale. His pulse was thin and thready and Jasmine set to work, with Greg cutting his leathers off.

'Can you tell me your name?' Penny asked as she examined him.

'Reece.'

'And do you know where you are?'

He answered the questions when prompted but kept closing his eyes and drifting off. Jasmine could only just palpate his blood pressure manually and Penny wasted no time in drawing blood for an urgent cross-match and telling the porters to run it up.

'And I mean run!' he warned. 'Let's put the O-neg up.'

Penny was possibly up there with the most horrible doctors Jasmine had worked with. She was abrupt to the point of rudeness, gave no thanks, only barked demands, except…

She was brilliant.

'If they can't be bothered to get down here,' Penny shouted as Jasmine tried to locate the surgeons again, 'tell them that I'll meet them up in Theatre.'

The patient had had a spinal and chest X-ray, and despite the O-negative blood being squeezed in, his blood pressure was still barely discernible. It was clear he needed Theatre and Penny wanted him taken straight up.

Jed was dealing with the latest admission, and Jasmine quickly prepared Reece for theatre, loading his clothes into a bag and itemising his valuables—rings, wallet… But as she opened up the wallet Jasmine hesitated. There were loads of hundred-dollar notes—at best guess the wallet contained a few thousand dollars.

'Can someone check this with me?' Jasmine asked.

'I'll check it with you later,' Greg called. 'Just put it in the safe.'

'Can we just check it now?' Jasmine pushed, except Greg wasn't listening, so she popped her head around the curtain to where Vanessa and Lisa were assisting Jed. 'Can someone check this, please? He's got a large amount of cash.'

'Just pop it in the safe,' Lisa called. 'I'll count it when things have calmed down.'

'We're supposed to check it before we put it in the safe.' Jasmine's voice was shrill. 'We're not supposed to sign—'

'Here.' It was Penny who stepped in. 'Give it to me, Nurse. I'll put it in the safe.' She walked over and took the wallet, signed the piece of paper and threw the contents into the safe. Jasmine realised that she was sweating and she could feel Jed's eyes on her.

'Right,' Penny said. 'We need to get him up or he's going to bleed out.' She picked up the phone and told Theatre the same as Jasmine prepared the trolley for an emergency transfer, but her hands were shaking and her heart was thumping as she knew she'd made a bit of a scene.

'All okay, Jasmine?' Lisa checked as Jasmine walked past to get a space blanket to put over Reece on the way up to Theatre.

'We're just about to move him,' Jasmine said, and as Jed briefly looked up she felt the question in his brief gaze, knew she wasn't fooling anyone that everything was okay, least of all Jed.

'Reece.' Jasmine tried to explain things as best she could as she covered him with the space blanket. He was irritable now and struggling to remain conscious, and he wanted to wait till his wife got there before he went up. 'We're going to have to move you to Theatre now. Miss Masters will explain things.'

Which Penny did.

She was efficient, brusque but also terribly kind. 'I know you want to wait for your wife—I completely understand, but you're too sick,' she explained gently but firmly. 'I will talk to your wife myself as soon as she gets here. Is there anything you want me to say to her?' She glanced at Jasmine and Greg and at the anaesthetist who had just arrived. 'Could you all excuse us a moment?'

As Jasmine stepped outside to give Penny and Reece some privacy, there was a strange sting of tears in her eyes. It wasn't that she had seen a different side to her sister, rather she had seen a side to Penny that she had long forgotten.

Sitting on the stairs, hearing her parents argue, had terrified four-year-old Jasmine. It had been Penny who would take her back to bed, Penny who would sit beside her and tell her not to worry, that she would take care of things, that even if things did get bad, that even if Dad did what he was threatening and left, they would be fine.

'But what if we're not?' Jasmine would argue. 'What if we never see him?'

'Then we'll deal with it.'

And in their own ways and albeit not perfectly they had.

And as she ran up to Theatre with her sister, and

Penny told her to head back down, that she wanted to speak with surgeons, Jasmine knew that she hadn't just come back for the support of her family, neither had she taken the job here for the reasons she had so determinedly given.

She wanted to be close to Penny again.

CHAPTER TWELVE

'I'LL COME OVER after work.'

Jed was coming out of X-Ray as Jasmine walked back from Theatre and they found themselves walking together towards Emergency.

'It's fine.' Jasmine shook her head. 'I'll see you at the weekend. Ruby said that she could—'

'But you're upset tonight.'

'Don't worry, I'll be fine by Saturday.' She couldn't keep the brittle edge from her voice. Yes, she was happy keeping things light, but sometimes, on days like today, it was hard.

'I'm not expecting to be entertained,' Jed said. 'What happened back there?'

'Nothing.'

'Jasmine? Why did you get all upset over the safe? You know we can't just drop everything—the guy was bleeding out.'

'Just leave it.'

But Jed wouldn't.

It was a very long shift. Vanessa was on a half-day and Jasmine really wished that she herself was—she could feel Jed watching her, especially much later when Lisa came over and asked her to check the cash.

'Four thousand six hundred dollars. Agreed?' Lisa checked.

'Agreed,' Jasmine said, and because Penny had first signed for it, she had to be there too.

'I just rang ICU,' Penny said. 'He's doing much better. His wife told me that he was on his way to put down a deposit on a car—that's why he had so much cash on him.' She added her signature to the valuables book.

'Oh, the irony of it,' Lisa sighed, because in a car his injuries would have been so much less. 'Now, I know this is a lot of money and that it has to be checked,' Lisa continued, 'but it's not always possible to just drop everything. It's better to put it in the safe.'

'That's not what the protocol says,' Jasmine pointed out, and Lisa pursed her lips. 'It's been six hours now.'

'I didn't know you were such a stickler for protocol and guidelines, Nurse,' Penny smirked. 'The irony of it!'

'What was that about?' Lisa grinned when Penny waltzed off.

'I think that might have been Penny's attempt at humour,' Jed said, but she could feel his eyes on her, knew he was trying to talk to her, but as she had all day she did her best to avoid him.

Jasmine actually thought she had when she finally finished for the day and went to pick Simon up. But heading over to the crèche she found Jed at the vending machine outside.

'I'll come over later.'

'You know I don't want that. I don't want to confuse Simon.'

'We're not going to make out on the sofa,' Jed said. 'And I'm not going to stay the night till you think he's ready for that, but I do want to talk to you. You're nearly in tears and I don't get why. What happened at your old job?' He could see the blush on her cheeks but she said nothing, instead walked past him to pick up Simon.

Simon was happy and scruffy after a day in the sandpit and Jasmine knew that it was time to face things, that she and Jed could not keep skirting around the edges.

Here in her hands was the living proof of an exceptionally difficult relationship, here was the baggage she carried, and yet it felt right in her arms.

She had to be able to talk about it with someone she trusted.

And she had to start trusting Jed.

He was still waiting for her when she headed outside.

'About six?'

'He'll still be up.'

'I don't mind, or I can come over around nine if that's what you'd prefer?' She longed to let Jed closer but she just couldn't take any chances with Simon.

'About nine.'

Simon wasn't at his sunniest and her mum dropped over too. It was just one of those disorganised evenings, not helped by a disorganised brain thanks to the day's events. Jasmine had just got Simon down and was sorting out his bag for the next day when she heard a knock at the door and looked up to see that it was already a quarter past nine.

'I wouldn't have got here at six anyway,' Jed said, following her through to the kitchen. 'I only just got away. It's still busy there.'

'Who's on?'

'Rex!' Jed rolled his eyes. 'And Penny's still hovering. I swear she never sleeps.'

'Do you want something to eat?'

'Are you going to cook for me?' Jed grinned.

'No,' Jasmine said, 'but if you're nice I might defrost something.'

Actually, she did cook. Well, she made some pasta and defrosted some sauce and it was possibly their most normal night together. He ate a large bowl while Jasmine got things ready for the next day. Perhaps realising she wasn't ready to talk yet, he chatted a bit more about himself, telling her a bit about his siblings and their families.

'Don't you miss them?'

'A lot.'

'So how come you moved down here?'

'Just…' Jed shrugged. He knew he had to tell her, but there would be time for all that later—he wasn't here for himself tonight. He could see that she was still upset, see her hands shake a little as she folded some washing and then finally joined him.

'You got upset in Resus today.'

'I didn't.'

'Jasmine?'

'I just get annoyed when people don't check valuables properly,' she attempted. 'Everyone bangs on about how important it is and then if something goes missing…'

'People are busy.'

'I know that.'

'I heard you speaking to that paramedic,' Jed admitted, and he watched as she closed her eyes. 'Jasmine, did something happen at your old job?'

'No,' she broke in. 'Jed, please…' And then she started to cry. 'I found out that my husband was stealing from patients.' It was so awful to say it, to admit to it. She'd made it so huge in her mind that she half expected him to stand up and walk out, but of course he didn't. Instead, he took both her hands.

'Come on.' He was very kind and very firm but he wasn't going to leave it. 'Tell me what happened.'

'I don't know where to start,' she said. 'There was an unconscious patient apparently and there was a lot of money missing.' She knew she wasn't making much sense, so she just told him everything.

'Lloyd,' Jasmine said. 'Simon's father, he was a paramedic. We really got on, but then everyone did with Lloyd. He was very popular. We went out for about three months and—' she couldn't really look at that time properly '—I thought everything was fantastic at first,' she admitted. 'But I know now that it wasn't because I was being lied to even then. I didn't know but there had been a report put in about him.'

'You can't know if someone doesn't tell you,' Jed pointed out.

'I know that, but it wasn't just that he didn't tell me.' She took a deep breath, because if she was going to tell him some of it, then she had better tell him all. 'Remember I told you that I can't take the Pill?' She blushed as she had the first time she'd told him. 'Well, we were careless.' She went really red then, not with embarrassment, more with anger. 'Actually, no, we weren't. I know it takes two, but I think he was the one who was careless.'

'Jasmine.' Jed was completely honest. 'I nearly forgot our first time.'

'I know,' she admitted. 'But even if you had, I've got a coil now, so it wouldn't matter. It was more that I didn't forget.' She looked at Jed, she knew how they had lost it in bed together, but she never had till him. 'I reminded him, I tried to stop him. I don't know, I can't prove that, but there was an accident, and I found I was pregnant and not sure I wanted to be. I was just so confused and yet he was delighted. He insisted we get married and and then we took three months off to see Australia. As he said, to have loads of fun before the baby. I had lots of annual leave saved up.'

She couldn't even look at Jed as she went on. 'What Lloyd hadn't told me was that he was under investigation for stealing from a patient. It was all kept confidential so not even his colleagues knew, but another patient had come forward with a complaint and they'd placed Lloyd on three months' paid suspension. We were swanning around Australia and I had no idea.'

'When did he tell you?'

'He didn't,' Jasmine admitted. 'I went back to work. I was coming up for six months pregnant by then and he told me that he had another month off and then he started to talk about how, given I love my work, why didn't we think about him staying home to look after the baby? Every word that man said to me was a lie.' She could feel her anger rising as it did whenever she thought about him and wondered, as she often did, if he'd got her pregnant deliberately.

'So how did you find out?'

'The other paramedics were a bit cool with me,' Jasmine admitted. 'They're a pretty honourable lot, they don't take kindly to what Lloyd did and there was I, chatting with them like I used to, about our holiday, about things, and then one of my friends pulled me aside and said it might be better if I didn't rub things in.' She started to cry. 'She said it was fine if I could accept what he'd done, but it was a bit much for them to hear about us having fun with his suspension pay. He'd been fired by then and I didn't even know.'

'Oh, Jasmine.'

'He said that as his wife I should have supported him, but the fact is I wouldn't have married him had I known.' She looked at Jed. 'I wouldn't have. I'm not saying someone has to be perfect, I'm not saying you don't stick together through bad times, but I didn't even know that he was in the middle of bad times when we got married, when he made sure I was pregnant.' She was really crying now. 'I moved out and kept working right till the end of my pregnancy, but it was awful. I think my friends believed I had nothing to do with it, that I hadn't had a clue…'

'Of course they did.'

'No.' Jasmine shook her head. 'Not all of them—there was loads of gossip. It was just awful at the time.

'I see some of the paramedics now and we're starting to be friendly again,' she continued. 'I think they really do understand now that I simply didn't know. I'm just trying to get on with my life.'

'Do you speak to him at all?'

'Nothing,' Jasmine said. 'He came and saw Simon a couple of times when we were in the hospital, but there's been nothing since then. He's got a new girlfriend and so much for being a stay-home dad—he doesn't even have a thing to do with his son. He's working in the family business, they're all supporting him, as families do, and making sure it looks like he earns a dollar a week, so I don't get anything.'

'You can fight that.'

'I could, but I don't want to,' Jasmine said. 'I don't want any of his grubby money. I stayed close by for a year because, at the end of the day, I figured that he is Simon's dad and I should make it as easy for him as possible to have access to his son. But when he wanted nothing to do with him…' She was a little more honest than she'd expected to be. 'I was embarrassed to go back to work too. He just completely upended my life.'

And Jed got that, he got that so much, how one person could just walk into your life and shatter it, could make a normal world suddenly crazy, and he could have told her then, but Jed knew that now wasn't the time.

'And I'm the one left holding the baby.' She was the most honest she had been with another person. 'And I know if it hadn't happened then I wouldn't have Simon and I love him more than anything so I can't wish it had never happened, except sometimes I do.'

Of course she heard Simon crying then, just to ram home the guilt of her words.

'I need to go and settle him.'

'Sure.'

Simon didn't want settling, Simon wanted a drink and a play and a conversation.

'He's not going to settle.' She came back into the living room a good twenty minutes later.

'Do you want me to leave?'

'No,' Jasmine said. 'But I'm going to have to bring him in here.'

'Are you sure?' Jed checked.

'It's no big deal,' Jasmine said.

Except they both knew that it was. Jed hadn't seen Simon since that day on the beach when he'd helped get him into the water.

And Jed really didn't want to leave her.

Simon was delighted with the late night visitor, chatting away to him for as long as he could till his eyes were heavy and Jasmine put him back to bed.

'Cute,' Jed said. 'He looks like you—apart from the blond hair. Is his dad blond?'

'No,' Jasmine replied. Simon was a mini, male Penny.

'Have you told Lisa what happened?'

Jasmine shook her head.

'I think you might feel better if you did.' He was very practical. 'You did nothing wrong, but you know what rumours are like and it might be better to just tell Lisa up front what happened,' Jed said. 'And then you can stop worrying about it. If anyone does bring it up, Lisa will just blow them off.

'And…' he gave her a smile '…she might be a bit more understanding when patients land in the department with their life savings stuffed in a carrier bag.'

'I think I might,' Jasmine said. 'Thanks.' It was actually nice to have told someone and telling Lisa was a good idea.

'I'd better go,' Jed said. 'It's one thing having a friend over, but different me still being here in the morning. What are you on tomorrow?'

'I'm on a late,' Jasmine said. 'Ruby's picking Simon up from crèche.'

'How's that working out?'

'Good,' Jasmine admitted. 'She's really sensible and he seems to adore her. Simon's usually in bed by about seven so she gets her homework done.

'Stay if you like,' Jasmine said, 'I mean…'

'I know what you mean.' And he looked over at Jasmine and for the first time things were starting to get serious, and he didn't feel hemmed in. In fact, he wanted more of this and was sure that Jasmine was someone he could open up to about his past. She just didn't need it tonight. 'Are you sure?' Jed checked. 'He might wake up again.'

'He might.' Jasmine looked up at him. 'Look…' She didn't really know how to say it without sounding needy, but she had Simon to think of so she had to be brave. 'I want to see more of you, Jed.' His eyes never left her face. 'I'm the same as you. I don't want this to carry over to work, which means that if we are going to see more of each other… I'm not asking for for ever, but if you're thinking this isn't working out then say so now.'

'I think it is working out.'

'And I'd like to see you a bit more than a couple of hours once a week.'

'Me, too.'

'Stay, then,' she said.

It was all a bit different having Simon in the house with them.

Like at midnight when they were kissing on the sofa, instead of things leading to wherever they might lead, she had to check on Simon, who was whimpering with his teeth. By the time she'd given him some medicine and rubbed some gel on his gums, Jed was sitting up in her bed, reading his horoscope in one of her trashy magazines.

Except he put it down as she started undressing.

'Don't,' Jasmine said, because he had an unfair advantage, well, two actually. He was already in bed and also with a body like his there was no need to be embarrassed about stripping off in front of another person.

'Why are you shy now?'

'I don't know.' She actually wasn't shy, she felt guilty for what she had said. 'Thanks,' she said as she slipped into bed. 'For hearing me out and what I said about wishing it had never happened.'

'I'd be the same,' Jed said, shuddering at the thought of how much worse things might have been for him—and he closed his eyes for a moment, imagining the last couple of years with a baby added to the mix. And he turned and he almost told her, but he could see her eyes were still swollen from crying and it simply wouldn't be fair to her.

'Imagine if he hadn't stolen the money,' Jed said. 'You could have spent your life married to a guy who was crap in bed.'

He saw the start of a smile.

'Go on,' he said. 'Say it.'

'No.' Jasmine kicked him. 'Anyway, you don't know that he was.'

'Please.' Jed rolled his eyes.

'So much for not getting involved with anyone from work.' He looked down at her before he kissed her. 'I think we should keep it separate, though,' Jed said. 'I really mean that.'

She was incredibly glad to hear it. 'I'm the same.'

'Things are a bit sensitive at the moment,' he said.

'With the promotion?' It was an entirely innocent question, or at least she'd thought it was, but Jed stopped kissing her and frowned.

'You've heard about that?'

'Sorry.' She tried to play for time.

'How did you hear about that?'

She was glad for the lights being off for another reason now. Her face was on fire in the dark from her slip-up.

'I don't know,' she attempted. 'You know what that place is like, there's always talk.'

'I guess.' He let out a long sigh. 'Oh, well, if it's out there's nothing I can do about it. At least I know no one heard it from me.'

He forgot about it then but it took a while for Jasmine to.

He kissed her till she almost had, she kissed him back till she nearly did, but it was there at the back of her mind, just how complicated things were and he didn't even know.

'Are you all right?' He lifted his head.

'Just tense.'

She almost told him, she nearly did.

Except she'd promised her sister that she wouldn't.

'I can fix that.'

And he slid beneath the sheets and she lay there biting her lip, thrashing with her thoughts as his tongue urged her to give in.

He was incredibly patient.

Didn't seem to mind a jot how long it took.

And she tried to relax to the probe of his tongue. To forget her problems, forget Penny and Lloyd and everything really except…

'Jed?'

He didn't answer.

'Jed?' She had to tell him, had to tell him now. 'Things are complicated.'

'Not from where I am,' Jed said, lifting his head just a little. 'You worry too much.'

Maybe she did, Jasmine realised, closing her eyes to the mastery of his mouth.

He gave her no room to think about it anyway. His

hands lifted her buttocks so he could concentrate his efforts and he homed in, she pushed on his shoulders, because she should surely tell him, except he pushed back on the pressure she exerted and obliterated her thoughts with his tongue.

He was determined now, felt the shift in her, and it turned him on further. He loved feeling her unbend beneath him, loved the constant fight with her busy mind, and he would win this one and he felt her quiver as he worked on her most tender spot.

He felt her thighs start to tighten and the moans in her throat and he loved the wrestle within in her, loved how her hands moved from his shoulders and to his head, how her body begged him to continue while her mouth urged him to stop.

And then she gave in to him, shocked that he didn't stop there, that when he should surely abate he worked harder, and she throbbed into him and still his mouth cursed her restraint. Still his tongue told her there was more, and there was.

He rose over her in the dark, his hand moved to the bedside and it was hers that stopped him, stopped a man who, very kindly, never forgot.

'I told you,' she said. 'I've got the coil.'

And he smiled down at her as just once she said it. 'And, yes, as I've since found out—he was crap in bed.'

There was nothing to complicate or confuse right now, just the bliss of him sliding inside her, and for Jed he had never been closer to another, just lost himself in her. It was more than sex and they both knew it—it was the most intimate either had ever been. He thrust into her as he wanted to and she tightened her legs around him. He could hear the purr in her throat and feel the scratch of her nails on his back and she knew that, however they denied it, this was fast becoming serious.

And yet there were secrets between them.

For Jed there were no secrets, or there soon wouldn't be. He'd already made the decision to tell her, he just had to find the right time and tonight wasn't it. He felt her tighten around him, loved the intimacy and feeling her without the barrier of a sheath, loved the sob into his shoulder and the sudden demand within her that gave Jed permission to let go, which he did, but not fully. He lifted up on his arms and felt every beat of pleasure that shot out of him, he felt every flicker of hers, except he held back on the words that seemed most fitting right now.

He lay there afterwards and he should have been glad he hadn't said them. Neither of them were ready for love, but for Jed it was starting to feel like it.

And for Jasmine too, she felt as if they were on the edge of something, something that neither had seen, a place they had never intended to go. Except he was in bed beside her and it felt as if he should be, and she knew what to do now.

She wasn't waiting for the interviews, and Penny would just have to deal with it if it confused things.

Tomorrow, or at the very next opportunity, she would tell Penny.

Then she could be completely honest with Jed.

Then, Jasmine decided, there would be no holding back.

CHAPTER THIRTEEN

JED WAS GONE before Simon woke up, but her resolve was the same and once she'd given Simon his breakfast and got him dressed, Jasmine picked up the phone and rang Penny.

'What are you doing, ringing me at work?' Penny sounded irritated at the intrusion.

'It's the only chance I get to speak to you,' Jasmine said. 'Of course I can talk to you there if you prefer.'

'No, this is fine,' Penny sighed. 'What did you want?'

'I was hoping we could catch up away from work. There's something I'd like to talk about, something I need to check with you.'

'Fine,' Penny said.

'Tonight?' Jasmine asked.

'I'm going out tonight.' And she was working the next one. 'I'm going to Mum's on Sunday for dinner—how about then?'

Jasmine really didn't want to discuss this in front of their mother, but maybe they could go for a walk afterwards, or she could suggest that Penny go back to her place for a coffee?

'Sounds good.'

'So, when are you working again?' Penny asked.

'In a couple of hours' time.' Jasmine smiled. 'I promise to keep on ignoring you.'

As she dropped Simon off at crèche, Jasmine realised that things were starting to work out—she was starting to think that this was maybe doable and that nine-to-five job in the fracture clinic might not be necessary after all. Vanessa's mum was looking after Liam this evening, which meant that Ruby would pick Simon up from crèche and take him back to Jasmine's. Her babysitting arrangements were all under control, if a touch too expensive, but it was worth it to be doing a job she loved and for the first time since way before Simon's birth things were starting to look stable.

Well, not stable. Her heart leapt in her throat still at the sight of Jed and she was shaky with all the rush of a new romance, but the rest of her life seemed to be slotting together when just a few weeks ago it had seemed an impossible dream.

There was actually no chance to speak to Lisa about anything personal, or Jed, come to that. The department was incredibly busy and the late shift flew by, so much so that Jasmine blinked in surprise when Lisa caught her on the way up to the ward with a geriatric patient and lightly scolded her for not taking her breaks.

'I had no idea of the time,' Jasmine admitted, surprised to see it was already seven o'clock. 'I'll just take this one up to the ward.'

'Well, make sure that when you get back you take a break,' Lisa said. 'I don't care how busy the place is, I don't want my staff burning out.'

Lisa was always insistent that her staff take their allotted breaks, and often she would ring Admin and have a nurse sent down from the wards during particularly busy periods.

After handing her patient over, Jasmine realised she was actually hungry and stopped at the vending machine for chocolate to take to her break. 'It's crazy out there,' Vanessa greeted her when she got back to the staffroom. 'Did Lisa tell you off for not taking a break?'

'She did,' Jasmine said, slipping off her shoes. 'Maybe it's going to be a full moon tonight. I don't envy the night staff.'

'It will be your turn again soon.'

'I know,' Jasmine groaned.

'Did you speak to Ruby about staying over while you're on nights?'

'I did,' Jasmine said. 'She can do the first week. The problem is with the weekend on the second.'

'I can help you with that,' Vanessa said. 'If you can help out next month when it's my turn?' She gave Jasmine a nice smile. 'It all works out in the end.'

'I know,' Jasmine admitted. 'I think I've got to stop looking too far ahead and take things more day by day.'

'That's all you can do when you've got little ones.'

Right now, Jasmine was looking forward to it being nine o'clock so that she could go home. Jed got off duty at ten and had promised to bring food, which meant she had just enough time to chat with Ruby and then hopefully have a quick shower before Jed arrived.

Yes, she was starting to think that things might work out.

'Are you going to that?' Vanessa broke into her thoughts.

'Sorry?'

'It's the accident and emergency ball in a couple of weeks.' Vanessa pointed to the rather impressive poster up on the staff noticeboard. 'It's the big fundraiser for the department. Apparently there are still some spare tickets.'

Jasmine's eyes widened when she saw the price of the tickets and she wasn't surprised that there were still a few left.

'I doubt I'll be going.' Jasmine shook her head as she broke off some chocolate. Especially when she factored in the price of the new dress, hair, shoes and paying a babysitter. 'Are we expected to go?'

'Not really,' Vanessa said. 'It's really more for the bigwigs. Mind you, it will be a fun night—there's always loads of gossip whizzing around after an emergency do—we can have our fun with that afterwards, even if we can't be there.' Vanessa gave a mischievous smile. 'Still, it's a shame that we won't get to watch Jed and Penny studiously avoiding each other and trying to pretend that they're not together.'

Jasmine felt her blood run cold. She couldn't quite believe what she was hearing. 'Jed and Penny?'

'Didn't you know?' Vanessa was idly watching the television as she spoke and didn't see Jasmine's appalled expression and carried on chatting, blissfully unaware of the impact of her words. 'They've been on and off since Jed started here, not that they would ever admit to it, of course. Heaven forbid that Penny brings her personal life into work and be so reckless as to display human tendencies.' Vanessa's words dripped sarcasm. 'God knows what he sees in her.'

'Maybe he doesn't.' Jasmine was having great trouble speaking, let alone sounding normal. 'Maybe he doesn't see anything in her. It's probably just gossip—you know what this place can be like.'

'I wish,' Vanessa sighed. 'Jed is just gorgeous. He's wasted on that cold fish. But I'm afraid that this time the hospital grapevine is right—Greg walked in on them once and you can hardly miss the tension between them.' She turned and looked at Jasmine. 'I can't believe you haven't noticed. It's an open secret, everyone knows.' Vanessa stood up. 'Come on, we'd better get back out there.'

Except Jasmine couldn't move.

'I'll be along in a moment,' Jasmine said. 'I shan't be long.'

Her hand was clenched around the chocolate so tightly it had all melted, not that she noticed till Vanessa had gone and Jasmine stood up. She headed for the bathrooms—she didn't just feel sick, she actually thought she might vomit as she washed the mess off her hands. She held onto the sink and tried to drag in air and calm her racing thoughts before heading back out there.

Not once had it entered her head that Penny and Jed might be together.

Not one single time.

And Penny had never so much as hinted that she was seeing someone.

But, then, why would she?

Penny never told Jasmine what was going on in her life. Her engagement had ended and Penny had said nothing about it other than it was over. She certainly never invited discussion. Jasmine, in turn, had never confided in Penny. Even when her marriage had been on the rocks, Jasmine had dealt with it herself—telling her mum and Penny that it was over only when her decision had already been made.

She should have listened to Penny, Jasmine realised.

She should never have worked in the same department as her sister.

Jasmine scooped water from the sink into her hand and drank it, tried to calm herself down. Somehow she had to get through the rest of her shift.

Jed was coming round tonight.

Jasmine spun in panic at the thought.

She would talk to him… And say what?

If there was anything between him and Penny she would just end it and move to the fracture clinic.

Or back to Melbourne Central, because that sounded quite a good option right now. And if that sounded a lot like running away from her problems, well, at that moment Jasmine truly didn't care. As much as she and Penny didn't get on very well, never in a million years would she do that her sister.

Except it would seem that she already had.

'You seem in a hurry to escape the place,' Penny commented.

'For once, yes,' Jed said. 'It's all yours.'

He had more on his mind tonight than a busy department.

Tonight he was going to tell Jasmine the truth about what had happened with Samantha.

It was an unfamiliar route Jed was considering taking and one he was not entirely comfortable with. He was way too used to keeping things in. He'd avoided anything serious since his last break-up. Sure, he'd had the occasional date, but as soon as it had started to be anything more than that, Jed had found himself backing away. And as if to prove him right, the texts and tears that had invariably followed had only strengthened his resolve not to get attached and to step away. Except for the first time he felt as if he could trust another person. After all, Jasmine had opened up to him.

Jed wasn't stepping away now.

Instead, he was stepping forward.

He rang ahead to his favourite restaurant and ordered a meal for two, but despite confidence in his decision there was more than a touch of nerves as he paid for his takeaway and headed back to the car, as he built himself up to do what he said had sworn he would never do—share what had happened, not just with someone he was starting to get close to…but with someone he was starting to get close to from work.

'Hi.'

Jasmine opened the door and let him in, still unsure what she should say, how best to broach it. Did she really want to know that he was with her sister? Did she really want Jed to find out the truth?

Surely it would better to end it neatly?

To get out before they got in too deep?

Except she was in too deep already.

'I bought Italian,' Jed said, moving in for a kiss, 'but to tell the truth I'm not actually that hungry.'

She'd meant to carry on normally, to sit down and discuss things like adults while they were eating, but as he moved in to kiss her, just the thought that he might have been with Penny had Jasmine move her head away.

'Jasmine?' She saw him frown, heard the question in his voice about her less-than-effusive greeting, but she didn't know how to answer him. Despite three hours trying to work out what she might say to him, how best to approach this, she still didn't know how and in the end settled for the first thing that came into her head.

'I'm not sure that you ought to be here.'

'Sorry?'

'I don't think this is working, Jed.'

'It would seem not.'

Of all the things he had been expecting tonight, this wasn't one of them. Sideswiped, Jed walked through to the lounge and put the takeaway down on her coffee table, completely taken aback by the change in Jasmine. They'd made love that morning, he'd left her smiling and happy, with no hint of what was to come. 'Can I ask what has changed between this morning and tonight?'

'I just think things have moved too fast.'

'And could you not have decided this before you introduced me to Simon?' He didn't get it and he knew she was lying when he saw her blush. 'What's going on, Jasmine?'

'I heard something at work today,' Jasmine admitted. 'Something about you.'

'So it's gospel, then?' was Jed's sarcastic response. 'And while you were listening to this gossip, did you not consider running it by me first, before deciding we that weren't working?'

'Of course I did,' Jasmine attempted. 'That's what I'm doing now.'

'Is it even worth asking?' Jed said. 'Because it sounds to me as if the jury is already in. So, what is it that I'm supposed to have done?'

'I heard...' Jasmine swallowed because it sounded so pathetic, especially with how good he had been with her secret last night, but still she had to find out for sure. 'I heard that you and Penny...'

'Penny?'

'Someone told me that you and Penny...' She couldn't

even bring herself to say it, but the implication was clear and Jed stood there and shook his head.

'Jasmine, we agreed from the start that as erratic as things may be for us you and I wouldn't see anybody else so, no, I'm not seeing Penny.'

'But have you?' Jasmine asked. 'Have you dated Penny in the past?'

'What on earth…?' He just looked at her, looked at her as if he'd suddenly put glasses on and was seeing her for the first time and not particularly liking the view. 'I'm being dumped because the hospital grapevine states that I might be or in the past might have slept with a colleague?' He shook his head. 'I never took you for the jealous kind, Jasmine.'

'I just need to know.'

But Jed wasn't about to explain himself. 'Look, I don't need this.' He didn't confirm it and he didn't deny it and she honestly didn't know what to do. She could feel tears pouring down her cheek.

'Jed, please,' she said. 'Just tell me. I need to know if there's ever been anything between you and Penny.' She was starting to cry and she knew she had to tell him, no matter how awkward it made things for them, no matter the hurt to Penny, she just had to come right out and say it, and she was about to, except Jed didn't give her a chance.

'You want a complete itinerary of my past?' Jed said. 'What do you want, a full list of anyone I've ever dated so you can check them out online?'

'Jed, please,' Jasmine attempted, but he wasn't listening to her now.

'You're the one with the past, Jasmine. You're the one who's just had her divorce certificate stamped and has a baby sleeping in the bedroom and an ex who stole from patients. Did I ask for a written statement, did I ask for facts and details?' He turned to go and then changed his mind, but he didn't walk back to her. He picked up his takeaway and took it. 'I'm hungry all of a sudden.'

He headed out to his car and drove off, but only as far as the next street, and it was there that Jed pulled over and buried his head in his hands.

He couldn't believe it.

Could not believe the change in her—the second they'd started to get serious, the moment he'd actually thought this might work, he'd been greeted with a list of questions and accusations and for Jed it all felt terribly familiar.

After all, he'd been through it before.

CHAPTER FOURTEEN

THE WEEK HAD been awful.

Jed was back to being aloof, not just with her but with everyone, and on the occasions they had to work together he said as little as he could to her.

And now, when she'd rather be anywhere else, she sat at her mother's, eating Sunday lunch with Penny and wondering how on earth she could ever tell her and if it would simply be better if Penny never found out.

Which sounded to Jasmine an awful lot like lying.

'You wanted to talk to me.'

'I just wanted a chat,' Jasmine said. 'We haven't caught up lately.'

'Well, there's not really much to catch up on,' Penny said. 'It's just work, work, work.'

'It's your interview soon,' Louise reminded her.

'You haven't mentioned it to anyone?' Penny frowned at Jasmine. 'I told you about that in confidence. I shouldn't have said anything.'

'I haven't,' Jasmine said, but her face burnt as she lied.

'Well, I've heard that there are rumours going around, and if I find out that it's you…' Penny gave a tight shrug. 'Sorry, that was uncalled for. I just hate how gossip spreads in that place.'

'Are you going to the A and E ball?' Jasmine tried to change the subject, attempting to find out what she simply had to know.

Not that it would change anything between her and Jed.

Not just because of the possibility that he and Penny had once been an item, more the way he had been when they'd had a row. He hadn't given her a chance to explain, had just thrown everything she had confided to him back in her face and then walked out.

She didn't need someone like that in her life and certainly not in Simon's—still, she did want to know if the rumours were true, which was why she pushed on with Penny, dancing around the subject of the A and E ball in the hope it might lead to something more revealing.

'I've been asked to put in an appearance,' Penny said, helping herself to another piece of lamb. 'Why?' she asked. 'Are you thinking of going?'

'Not at that price,' Jasmine said. 'I just wondered if you were, that's all.'

'I have to, really. Jed and I will probably take it in turns—someone has to hold the fort and all the consultants will want to be there.'

'Jed?' Louise asked.

'The other senior reg,' Penny explained.

'The one who's going for the same position?' Louise checked, and Penny gave a curt nod.

'You and Jed…' The lovely moist lamb was like burnt toast in Jasmine's mouth and she swallowed it down with a long drink of water. 'Are you two…?' Her voice trailed off as Penny frowned.

'What?'

She should just ask her really, Jasmine reasoned. It

was her sister after all—any normal sisters would have this conversation.

Except they weren't like normal sisters.

Still, Jasmine pushed on.

She simply had to know.

'Is there anything between you and Jed?'

'If you're hoping for some gossip, you won't get it from me. I don't feed the grapevine,' Penny said, mopping the last of her gravy from her plate. 'So, what did you want to talk about?'

And really the answer didn't matter.

She and Jed were over. If he had slept with Penny she just wanted to be as far away from them both as possible when the truth came out. 'I'm thinking of taking the job in the fracture clinic.'

Penny looked up.

'Why?'

'Because…' Jasmine shrugged '…it's not working, is it?'

'Actually, I thought it was,' Penny said. 'I was worried at first, thought you'd be rushing to my defence every five minutes or calling me out, but apart from that morning with the baby…' She thought for a moment before she spoke. 'Well, seeing you work, you'd have said the same to any doctor.' She gave her sister a brief smile. 'You don't have to leave on my account. So long as you can keep your mouth shut.'

Her mum had made trifle—a vast mango one with piles of cream—and normally Jasmine would have dived into it, but she'd lost her appetite of late and Penny ate like a bird at the best of times. Louise took one spoonful and then changed her mind.

'I must have eaten too fast,' Louise said. 'I've got terrible indigestion.'

'I'll put it back in the fridge,' Jasmine said, clearing the table.

'Take some home,' her mum suggested. 'I don't fancy it.' She smiled to Simon, who was the only one tucking in. 'He can have some for breakfast.'

'Jasmine.' Penny caught her as she was heading out of the front door. 'Look, I know I kicked up when I found out you were going to be working in Emergency.' Penny actually went a bit pink. 'I think that I went a bit far. I just didn't think we could keep things separate, but things seem to be working out fine.'

'What if you get the consultant's position?' Jasmine checked. 'Wouldn't that just make things more difficult?'

'Maybe,' Penny said. 'But I don't think it's fair that you have to change your career just because of me. You're good at what you do.'

It was the closest she had ever come to a compliment from her sister.

'Look,' Penny said, 'I do want to talk to you if that's okay—not here…not yet.' She closed her eyes. 'It's…' She blew out a breath. 'Look, you know how I bang on about work and keeping things separate? Well, maybe I've being a bit of a hypocrite.'

'Are you seeing someone?'

'It's a bit more complicated than that.' Penny shook her head. 'Let me just get the interview over with. I mustn't lose focus now.' She let out a wry laugh. 'Who knows, I might not even get the job and then there won't be a problem.'

'Sorry?' Jasmine didn't get it. 'I thought you were desperate to be a consultant.'

'Yes, well, maybe someone else might want the role more than I do,' Penny said. 'Forget I said anything. We'll catch up soon.'

And as Jasmine lay in bed that night, she was quite sure she knew what the problem was.

Penny was worried that if she got the position it might hurt Jed.

For the first time in a long time Penny was actually putting another person before herself. She actually cared about another person.

The same person her younger sister had been sleeping with.

Monday morning was busy—it always was, with patients left over from a busy weekend still waiting for beds to clear on the ward, and all the patients who had left things till the weekend had passed seemed to arrive on Emergency's doorstep all the worse for the wait. Jed didn't arrive in the department till eleven and was wearing a suit that was, for once, not crumpled. He was very clean-shaven and she knew he wasn't making any effort on her behalf, especially when Penny came back from a meeting in Admin and her always immaculately turned-out sister was looking just that touch more so.

Clearly it was interview day.

She had to leave.

It really was a no-brainer—she could hardly even bear to look at Penny. She made the mistake of telling Vanessa on their coffee break that she was going to apply for the fracture clinic job.

'You'd be bored senseless in the fracture clinic.' Vanessa laughed as they shifted trolleys to try to make space for a new patient that was being brought over. Unfortunately, though, Vanessa said it at a time when Lisa and Jed were moving a two-year-old who had had a febrile convulsion from a cubicle into Resus.

'I'd be glad of the peace,' Jasmine said, and she would be, she told herself, because she couldn't go on like this. It wasn't about the workload, more about having to face Jed and Penny every day and waiting for the bomb to drop when he found out that she and Penny were sisters.

She could not face her sister if she ever found out that she and Jed had been together, even if it had been over for ages.

But then she looked over and saw that Lisa and Jed were there and, more, that they must have heard her talking about the fracture clinic job.

She wasn't so much worried about Jed's reaction—no doubt he was privately relieved—but Lisa gave her a less-than-impressed look and inwardly Jasmine kicked herself.

'Sorry,' Vanessa winced. 'Me and my mouth.'

'It's my fault for saying anything,' Jasmine said, but there wasn't time to worry about it now. Instead, she took over from Lisa.

'Aiden Wilkins. His temp is forty point two,' Lisa said. 'He had a seizure while Jed was examining him. He's never had one before. He's already had rectal paracetamol.'

'Thanks.'

'He's seizing again.' Just as Lisa got to the Resus door, Aidan started to have another convulsion. Jed gave him some diazepam and told Jasmine to ring the paediatrician, which she did, but as she came off the phone

Jed gave another order. 'Fast-page him now, also the anaesthetist.'

'Everything okay?' Penny stopped at the foot of the bed as Vanessa took the mum away because she was growing increasingly upset, understandably so.

'Prolonged seizure,' Jed said. 'He's just stopped, but I've just noticed a petechial rash on his abdomen.' Penny looked closely as Jed bought her up to speed. 'That wasn't there fifteen minutes ago when I first examined him.'

'Okay, let's get some penicillin into him,' Penny said, but Jed shook his head.

'I want to do a spinal. Jasmine, can you hold him?'

Speed really was of the essence. Aiden needed the antibiotics, but Jed needed to get some cultures so that the lab would be able to work out the best drugs to give the toddler in the coming days. Thankfully he was used to doing the delicate procedure and in no time had three vials of spinal fluid. Worryingly, Jed noted it was cloudy.

Jasmine wheeled over the crash trolley and started to pull up the drugs when, as so often happened in Resus, Penny was called away as the paramedics sped another patient in.

'Penny!' came Lisa's calm but urgent voice. 'Can I have a hand now, please?'

'Go,' Jed said. 'I've got this.'

The place just exploded then. The paediatrician and anaesthetist arrived just as an emergency page for a cardiac arrest for the new patient was put out.

'Jed!' Penny's voice was shrill from behind the curtain. 'Can I have a hand here?'

'I'm kind of busy now, Penny.' Jed stated the obvious and Lisa dashed out, seeing that Jed was working on the small toddler and picked up the phone. 'I'm fast-paging Mr Dean…' She called out to the anaesthetist, whose pager was trilling. 'We need you over here.'

'Call the second on.' Jed was very calm. 'He's stopped seizing, but I want him here just in case.'

'You call the second on,' Lisa uncharacteristically snapped and looked over at the anaesthetist. 'We need you in here now.'

It was incredibly busy. Jed took bloods and every cubicle in Resus seemed to be calling for a porter to rush bloods and gasses up to the lab. Jed was speaking with the paediatrician about transferring Aiden to the children's hospital and calling for the helicopter when Lisa came in to check things were okay.

'We're going to transfer him,' Jasmine explained.

'I'll sort that,' Lisa said. 'Jasmine, can you go on your break?'

'I'm fine,' Jasmine said. After all, the place was steaming.

'I don't want the breaks left till midday this time. Let's get the breaks started. I'm sending in Greg to take over from you.'

Jasmine loathed being stuck in the staffroom when she knew how busy things were out there, but Lisa was a stickler for breaks and really did look after her staff. That didn't stop her feeling guilty about sitting down and having a coffee when she knew the bedlam that was going on.

'There you are.' Lisa popped her head in at the same time her pager went off. 'I just need to answer this and then, Jasmine, I need a word with you—can you go into my office?'

Oh, God.

Jasmine felt sick. Lisa must have heard her say she was thinking of handing her notice in. She should never have said anything to Vanessa; she should have at least spoken to Lisa first.

Pouring her coffee down the sink, Jasmine was torn. She didn't want to leave, except she felt she had to, and, she told herself, it would be easier all round, but she loved working in Emergency.

Would Lisa want a decision this morning? Surely this could wait.

She turned into the offices, ready for a brusque lecture or even a telling-off, ready for anything, except what she saw.

The registrar's office door was open and there was Penny.

Or rather there was Penny, with Jed's arms around her, oblivious that they had been seen.

He was holding her so tenderly, his arms wrapped tightly around her, both unaware that Jasmine was standing there. Blinded with tears, she headed for Lisa's office.

Her mind made up.

She had to leave.

CHAPTER FIFTEEN

'I'M SORRY!' LISA walked in just as Jasmine was blowing her nose and doing her best to stave off tears. 'I really tried to speak to you first before you found out.'

So Lisa knew too?

'How are you feeling?' Lisa asked gently. 'I know it's a huge shock, but things are a lot more stable now…' She paused as Jasmine frowned.

'Stable?'

'Critical, but stable,' Lisa said, and Jasmine felt her stomach turn, started to realise that she and Lisa were having two entirely separate conversations.

'I've no idea what you're talking about,' Jasmine admitted. 'Lisa, what am I here for?

'You don't know?' Lisa checked. 'You seemed upset… just then, when I came in.'

'Because…' Because I just saw my sister in Jed's arms, Jasmine thought, and then she wasn't thinking anymore, she was panicking, this horrible internal panic that was building as she realised that something was terribly wrong, that maybe what she had seen with Penny and Jed hadn't been a passionate clinch after all. 'What's going on, Lisa?' Jasmine stood up, more in panic, ready to rush to the door.

'Sit down, Jasmine.' Lisa was firm.

'Is it Simon?' Her mind raced to the childcare centre. Had something happened and she hadn't been informed? Was he out there now, being worked on?

'Simon's fine,' Lisa said, and without stopping for breath, realising the panic that not knowing the situation was causing, she told Jasmine, 'Your mum's been brought into the department.'

Jasmine shook her head.

'She's very sick, Jasmine, but at the moment she's stable. She was brought in in full cardiac arrest.'

'When?' She stood to rush out there.

'Just hold on a minute, Jasmine. You need to be calm before you speak to your mum. We're stabilising her, but she needs to go up to the cath lab urgently and will most likely need a stent or bypass.'

'When?' Jasmine couldn't take it in. She'd only been gone twenty minutes, and then she remembered the patient being whizzed in, Lisa taking over and calling Mr Dean, Penny calling for Jed's assistance.

'Penny?' Her mind flew to her sister. 'Did Penny see her when she came in?'

'She had to work on your mum.' Lisa explained what had happened as gently as she could. 'Jed was caught up with the meningococcal child and I didn't want you finding out that way either—unfortunately, I needed you to be working.'

Jasmine nodded. That much she understood. The last thing she would have needed at that critical time in Resus was a doctor and a nurse breaking down before help had been summoned.

'And Penny told me to get you out of the way.' Jasmine looked up. 'She told me you were her younger sister and that you were not to find out the same way she had… She was amazing,' Lisa said. 'Once she got over the initial shock, she just…' Lisa gave a wide-eyed look of admiration. 'She worked on your mother the same way she would any patient—she gave her the very best of care. Your mum was in VF and she was defibrillated twice. By the time Mr Dean took over, your mum was back with us.'

'Oh, God,' Jasmine moaned and this time when she stood, nothing would have stopped her. It wasn't to her mother she raced but to next door, where Penny sat slumped in a chair. Jed was holding a drink of water for her. And to think she'd begrudged her sister that embrace. No wonder Jed had been holding her, and Jasmine rushed to do the same.

'I'm so sorry, Penny.'

She cuddled her sister, who just sat there, clearly still in shock. 'It must have been a nightmare.'

Penny nodded. 'I didn't want you to see her like that.'

She had always been in awe of Penny, always felt slightly less, but she looked at her sister through different eyes, saw the brave, strong woman she was, who had shielded the more sensitive one from their parents' rows, had always told her things would be okay.

That she'd deal with it.

And she had. Again.

'It's my fault,' Penny grimaced. 'Yesterday she was ever so quiet and she said she had indigestion. It must have been chest pain.'

'Penny.' Jasmine had been thinking the same, but hearing her sister say it made her realise there and then what a pointless route that was. 'I had indigestion yesterday. We all did. You know what Mum's Sunday dinners are like.'

'I know.'

Jasmine looked up at Jed. His face was pale and he gave her a very thin smile. 'I'm sorry to hear about your mum,' he said, and then he looked from Jasmine to Penny and then back again. 'I had no idea.'

'Well, how could you have?' Penny said, and then turned to Jasmine. 'Can you go and see Mum? I can't face it just yet, but one of us should be there.'

'Of course.'

'She'll be scared,' Penny warned. 'Not that she'll show it.'

'Come on,' Jed said. 'I'll take you round to her.'

Once they walked out of the door he asked what he had to. 'Jasmine, why didn't you say?'

'She'd made me promise not to.'

'But even so…'

'I can't think about that now, Jed.'

'Come on.' He put his arm round her and led her into her mum's room, and even if it was what he would do with any colleague, even if she no longer wanted him, she was glad to have him there strong and firm beside her as she saw her mum, the strongest, most independent person she knew, with possibly the exception of her elder sister, strapped to machines and looking very small and fragile under a white sheet.

'Hey, Mum.'

Jasmine took her hand.

'I'm sorry,' Louise said, but for once her voice was very weak and thin.

'It's hardly your fault. Don't be daft.'

'No.' She was impatient, despite the morphine, desperate to get everything in order before she went to surgery. 'I haven't been much support.'

'Mum!' Jasmine shook her head. 'You've been wonderful.'

'No.' She could see tears in her mum's eyes. 'Most grandmothers drop everything to help with their grandchildren.'

'Mum,' Jasmine interrupted. 'You can stop right there. I'm glad you're not like most mums, I'm glad Penny is the way that she is, because otherwise I'd be living at home even now. I'd be dumping everything onto you and not sorting my own stuff out, which I have,' Jasmine said firmly, and then wavered. 'Well, almost.' She smiled at her mum. 'And that's thanks to you. I don't want a mum who fixes everything. I want a mum who helps me fix myself.'

'Can I see Simon?' She felt her mum squeeze her hand. 'Or will I scare him?'

'I'll go now and get him.' Before she left, Jasmine looked at Jed.

'I'll stay.'

And it meant a lot that he was with her.

Oh, she knew Mr Dean was around and Vanessa was watching her mother like a hawk, but it wasn't just for medical reasons it helped to have Jed there.

She couldn't think of that now.

The childcare staff were wonderful when Jasmine told them what was going on. 'Bring him back when you're ready.'

'Thanks.'

Jasmine really didn't know if it would terrify Simon or how he'd react when he saw his nanny, but she knew that the calmer she was the better it would be for Simon.

'Nanny's tired,' Jasmine said as they walked back to the department. 'She's having a rest, so we'll go and give her a kiss.'

He seemed delighted at the prospect.

Especially when he saw Penny standing at the bed. Then he turned and saw Jed there and a smile lit up his face.

'Jed!'

He said it so clearly, there was absolutely no mistake, and Penny's eyes were wide for a second as she looked at Jed, who stood, and then back at Penny.

'I'll have to put in a complaint,' Penny said. 'The hospital grapevine is getting terribly slack.'

'Tell me about it,' Jed said, but whatever was going on, whatever questions needed answers, it was all put aside as Simon gave his nanny a kiss and a cuddle. He was amazing, not bothered at all by the tubes and machines, more fascinated by them, if anything, pointing to the cardiac monitor and turning as every drip bleeped. But of course after a few moments he grew restless.

'We're going to take your mum up to the catheter lab soon,' Vanessa said. The cardiac surgeon had spoken to them in more detail and her mum had signed the consent form, and it was all too quick and too soon. Jasmine had just got used to the idea that she was terribly ill and now there was surgery to face.

'Can I just take Simon back?'

'Of course.' And in the few weeks she'd been here, Jasmine found out just how many friends she had made, just how well she was actually doing, thanks to her mum. 'Tell the crèche that I'll pick up Simon tonight. He can stay at my place.'

'You're sure?' Jasmine checked. 'I can ring Ruby.'

'It's fine tonight. You'll probably be needing Ruby a lot over the next few days. Let me help when I can.'

The crèche was marvellous too and told Jasmine that she could put Simon in full time for the next couple of weeks, and somehow, *somehow* Jasmine knew she was coping with a family emergency and single motherhood and work combined.

And she didn't want to lose her job, no matter how hard it would be, working alongside Jed.

Except she couldn't think about it now.

Right now, her heart was with her mum, who was being wheeled out of Emergency, a brusque and efficient Penny beside her, telling the porter to go ahead and hold the lifts, snapping at Vanessa for not securing the IV pole properly, barking at everyone and giving out orders as she did each and every day, while still managing to hold her mum's hand as she did so.

And her heart wasn't just with her mum.

It was with her big sister too.

The time sitting in the Theatre waiting room brought them possibly the closest they had ever been.

'Is that why you were asking about Jed and I?'

They were two hours into waiting for the surgery to finish, an hour of panic, ringing around friends and family, and then an hour of angst-filled silence, and then, because you could only sit on a knife edge for so long, because sometimes you needed distracting, Penny asked the question that was starting to filter into both their minds.

'For all the good it did me.' Jasmine smiled. 'How come we don't gossip?'

'I never gossip,' Penny said. 'I don't do the girly thing and…' Her voice trailed off and she thought for a moment, realising perhaps how impossible for her sister this had been. 'You could have asked me, Jasmine.'

'What if I didn't like the answer?' Jasmine's eyes filled with tears and she couldn't start crying again. She'd shed more tears since her mother had gone to Theatre than she had in a long time.

'You're still not asking me.'

Jasmine shook her head, because if the truth were known she was scared to. Not just for what it would do to her but what the truth might mean for her sister.

'Nothing has ever happened between Jed and I.'

Jasmine felt as if a chest drain had been inserted, or what she imagined it must feel like, because it felt as if for the first time in days, for the first time since Vanessa had inadvertently dropped the bomb, her lungs expanded fully, the shallow breaths of guilt and fear replaced by a deep breath in.

'Nothing,' Penny said. 'Not a single kiss, I promise you.' And Jasmine could now breathe out. 'Who said that there was something going on between us?'

'It's common knowledge apparently, though I only heard this week. My friend couldn't believe that I hadn't notice the tension between you two.'

'The only tension between us,' Penny continued, 'is who might get the promotion.'

'I thought you were worried about getting it and upsetting Jed.'

Penny just laughed. 'Worrying about upsetting or upstaging Jed Devlin is the furthest thing from my mind—believe me. Do I look like someone who would step aside from a promotion for a man?' She actually laughed at the very thought.

'No,' Jasmine admitted. 'But you did say you weren't sure if you wanted the job…'

'Right now I'm not even thinking about work, I just want Mum to get well, that's as far as I can think today. You have nothing to worry about with Jed and I.'

'It doesn't matter.'

'It clearly did.'

But Jasmine shook her head. 'I'm just glad I haven't hurt you—Jed and I are finished.'

'Jasmine!'

But Jasmine was through worrying about Jed. She didn't have the head space to even think about him right now. 'Let's just worry about Mum for now, huh?'

'How is she?' Lisa asked when an extremely weary Jasmine made her way down to Emergency the next morning.

'She's had a really good night,' Jasmine said. 'They're going to get her out of bed for a little while this morning, can you believe?'

'They don't waste any time these days.' Lisa smiled. 'How are you?'

'Tired,' Jasmine admitted. 'I'm sorry to mess you around with the roster.'

'Well, you can hardly help what happened. Have you got time to go through it now—did you want the rest of the week off?'

Jasmine shook her head. 'I was actually hoping to come in to work tomorrow—Penny's going to stay with her today and I'll come back this evening, but I'd rather start back at work as soon as possible. I might need some time off when she comes out, though.'

'We'll sort something out,' Lisa said. 'We're very

accommodating here, not like the fracture clinic.' Lisa winked.

'Sorry about that.'

'Don't worry about it for now. We'll have a chat when you're up to it.'

'Actually,' Jasmine said, 'do you have time for a chat now?'

She sat in Lisa's office and, because she'd got a lot of her crying out when she'd told Jed, Jasmine managed to tell Lisa what had happened with her ex-husband without too many tears, and was actually incredibly relieved when she had.

'You didn't need to tell me this,' Lisa said. 'But I'm very glad that you did. I'd rather hear it from you first and it's a good lesson to us all about being less careless with patients' property. I can see why you panicked now. Anyway…' she smiled, '…you can stop worrying about it now.'

Finally she could, and only then did Jasmine fully realise how much it had been eating at her, how much energy she had put towards worrying about it, running from it.

'Go home to bed,' Lisa said.

'I will. But I just need to have a quick word with Vanessa, if that's okay?'

Vanessa was one burning blush when they met. 'Simon's been fantastic. He's tucked up in the crèche now and I can have him again tonight if you like.'

'I'll be fine tonight.'

'Well, why don't I pick him when my shift's finished and bring him home to you?' Vanessa offered, and as Jasmine thanked her she suddenly cringed. 'Jasmine, I am so embarrassed.'

'Why?'

'All the terrible things I said about Penny. I could just die. I keep going over and over them and then I remember another awful thing I said.'

Jasmine laughed. 'Believe me, you weren't the only one, and you told me nothing about Penny that I didn't already know—Penny too, for that matter. It's fine, I promise.'

'Me and my mouth!' Vanessa grimaced.

'Forget it.' Jasmine smiled. 'Anyway, I'm going to go home to bed, and thank you so much for your help with Simon. I'm just going to pop in and give him a kiss.'

'Jasmine.' Just as he had on the first day they had met, Jed called her as she went to head out of the department. 'Can I have a word?'

'I'm really tired, Jed.'

'Five minutes.'

'Sure.'

'Somewhere private.'

They settled for one of the interview rooms.

'How is your mum?'

'Getting there.'

'How are you?'

'A lot better than yesterday,' Jasmine said. 'I'm really tired, though.'

'Of course.' He took a breath. 'You should have told me that you and Penny were sisters,' Jed said.

'You didn't exactly give me much chance.'

'Before that.'

'I was working up to it. But if we weren't serious there didn't seem any point.' She gave a tight shrug. 'I told you from the start I was trying to keep work and things separate—you were the same.' She turned to go. 'Anyway, it doesn't matter now.'

'We need to talk.'

'No,' Jasmine said. 'I don't think we do.'

'Nothing happened between Penny and I,' Jed said. 'Absolutely nothing. I can see now why you were upset, why you felt you couldn't ask.'

And now it was, Jasmine realised, time to face things properly, not make an excuse about being tired and scuttle off. 'It's actually not about whether or not you slept with Penny.' Jasmine swallowed. 'I mean, had you, of course it would have mattered.' He saw the hurt that burnt in her eyes as she looked up at him.

'You gave me no chance to explain,' Jasmine said. 'I was struggling—really struggling to tell you something, and you just talked over me, just decided I was too much hard work. You didn't even answer my question. You just threw everything back in my face.'

She would not cry, she would not. 'It took guts to leave my marriage,' Jasmine said. 'But it just took common sense to end things with you. In any relationship there are arguments, Jed.' She looked right at him as she said it. 'And from the little I've witnessed, you don't fight fair!'

She saw him open his mouth to argue, but got in first. 'That's a no in my book.'

CHAPTER SIXTEEN

HE RANG AND Jasmine didn't answer.

And she stayed at her mum's, ringing and answering the phone to various aunts and uncles so even if he went over to her place, she wouldn't know and more to the point she wasn't there.

'Cold tea bags help,' Penny said when she dropped around that evening and saw her puffy eyes. 'You don't want him to see that you've been crying.'

'I could be crying because Mum's in ICU.'

'She's been moved to Coronary Care,' Penny said, 'so you don't have that excuse.'

'They've moved her already?'

'Yes. Great, isn't it? And you've got the night off from visiting. She was sound asleep when I left her. Still, if you want to go in I can watch Simon.' She must have seen Jasmine's blink of surprise. 'I *am* capable.'

'I'm sure you are.' Jasmine grinned. 'I might just pop in, if you're sure.'

'Of course.'

'He's asleep,' Jasmine said. 'You won't have to do anything.'

'I'm sure I'll cope if he wakes,' Penny said. 'And if you are going to see Mum then you need to put on some make-up.'

It didn't help much, not that her mum would have noticed. She was, as Penny had said, asleep. Still, Jasmine felt better for seeing her, but that feeling faded about five minutes after visiting when she saw Jed coming out of X-Ray.

'Hi,' he said.

'Hi.'

'I tried to call,' Jed said, but Jasmine wasn't interested in talking.

'I need to get home.'

'Run off, then,' Jed said, and Jasmine halted for a second.

'Sorry?'

'You said you had to go.'

She opened her mouth to argue. Had he just accused her of running off? But instead of challenging him, she threw him a very disparaging look, and as she marched off, Jasmine knew she didn't need cold tea bags on her eyes—she was through crying.

Her mum was right—it was completely hereditary.

The Masters women had terrible taste in men!

Still, even if she would have liked to avoid him it was impossible at work. Everywhere she went she seemed to be landed with him, but she refused to let him get to her, refused to give him the satisfaction that she was running off.

But worse than the department being busy was the times it was quiet and though she had no idea who knew what, she nearly bit on her gums when Lisa gave her a very sweet smile.

'Could you give Jed a hand, please?' Lisa said, even

though there were five other nurses sitting around. 'He's stitching a hand and she won't stay still on the trolley.'

'Her name's Ethel,' Lisa added. 'You'll get to know her soon, she's one of our regulars.'

'Sure.'

She painted on a smile and walked into Theatre.

'Hi, there, Ethel, I'm Jasmine.'

'Who?'

She was an angry old thing, fuelled on sherry and conspiracy theories, and she made Jasmine laugh.

'Why would they knock the hospital down?' Jasmine asked patiently, when Ethel told her the plans were already in and had been approved by the council.

'Prime real estate,' Ethel said. 'Imagine how many townhouses they could put up here.'

'Have you been talking to my mum?' Jasmine grinned.

'All money, isn't it?' Ethel grumbled for a while and then spoke about her children, who, from the age of Ethel, must be in their sixties at least. 'They're just waiting for me to go,' Ethel said bitterly. 'Worried I'm spending their inheritance.' She peered at Jasmine. 'Have you got children?' she asked.

'None,' Jasmine happily lied.

'Husband?'

'Nope.'

'Good for you,' Ethel said. 'Dating?'

'Nope.'

'Quite right, too.' Ethel said. 'They're no good, the lot of them.' And she ranted for a few minutes about her late husband. 'They're all liars and cheats and if they're not now then they're just waiting to be. Nasty, the lot of them—except for the lovely doctor here.'

She caught Jed's eye and they actually managed a slightly wry smile.

'No, we're all horrible, Ethel,' Jed said. 'You're quite right not to listen to their sorry excuses.'

And if he'd looked up then he'd have seen Jasmine poke her tongue out.

'How's your mum?' Jed asked, when Ethel gave in and started snoring.

'Doing well,' Jasmine said. 'She should be home on Monday.'

'How are you?'

'Good,' Jasmine said, and hopped off the stool. 'It looks like she's sleeping. Just call out if you need a hand.'

'Sure,' Jed said, and carried on stitching as Jasmine went to wash her hands.

She knew he was just trying to irritate her as he started humming, knew he was just trying to prove he was completely unbothered working alongside her.

And then she realised what he was humming.

A little song that was familiar, a little song about a little runaway, and when he looked up at her furious face he had the audacity to laugh.

'You'd better go,' Jed said. 'It sounds busy out there.'

There were maybe five patients it the department.

'Or do you need to pop up to visit your mum?'

He teased her with every excuse she had ever made over the last couple of days whenever he had tried to talk to her.

'Or is it time to pick up Simon?'

And then he got back to humming his song.

'I'm not avoiding you or running away.'

'Good,' Jed said. 'Then I'll be over about eight.'

* * *

'I don't want to argue.'

As soon as she opened the door to him, Jasmine said it. 'I don't want raised voices…'

'I didn't come here for that,' Jed said. 'And I wouldn't do that to Simon and I certainly wouldn't do that to you.' He saw her frown of confusion as she let him in. 'You are right, though—I didn't fight fair.' He said it the moment he was inside. 'And I'm not proud of that. I didn't give you a chance to explain. I didn't give us a chance.'

He took a seat. 'And I get it that there were things that you couldn't talk about easily. I've thought about it a lot and I can see how impossible it was for you—after all, if you and Penny had agreed not to tell anyone…' He looked up at her. 'You could have told me—I would never have let on.'

'Perhaps not,' Jasmine said, 'but when I thought you two might have been seeing each other…' She looked at him. 'Penny insists nothing ever happened.'

'It didn't.'

'Apparently Greg walked in on you two once?' She wanted to believe her sister, but deep down she was still worried that it was Penny protecting her all over again.

'Greg walked in on us?' Jed gave a confused shake of his head, raked his fingers through his hair and pulled on it for a moment, then he gave a small smile as realisation hit. 'We had words once.'

'Words.'

'A lot of words. It was a couple of months ago,' Jed said, 'before you were around. In fact…' he frowned in recall, '…it was the same day as your interview. We had a busy afternoon and there was a multi-trauma that

I was dealing with and Penny just marched in and tried to take over.'

'I can imagine.' Jasmine gave a tight smile.

'And then she questioned an investigation I was running—Mr Dean was there and I think she was trying to…' he shrugged, '…score points, I guess. I don't do that.' Jasmine knew already that he didn't. 'And I don't mind being questioned if it's merited, but, as I told Penny, she's never to question me like that in front of a patient again or try and take over unless she thinks I'm putting a patient at risk.' Jed looked up at her. 'Which I certainly wasn't and I told her that.'

'Oh!'

'And I asked her to explain her thought process, her rationale behind questioning me,' Jed said. 'Which Penny didn't take to too well.'

'She wouldn't.'

'Your sister's lousy at confrontation, too.' Jed smiled.

'I don't think so.'

'Oh, she is,' Jed assured her. 'She only likes confrontation when it's on her terms. You should remember that next time she starts.'

And Jasmine found she was smiling.

'Greg walked in on us, actually, we were in the IV room, and, yes, I guess he picked up something was going on, but it certainly wasn't that.'

'So why wouldn't you answer me that day?' Jasmine asked. 'Why couldn't you just say that there was nothing going on between the two of you?'

'Because I've spent the last two years convincing myself I'd be mad to get involved with anyone at work.'

'Especially a single mum?'

'You could come with ten kids,' Jed said. 'It was never about that.'

'Then why?'

'Jasmine, please.' He put up his hand. 'This is difficult.' And she knew then he had something to tell her, that she was as guilty as he'd been that night, because she was the one now not letting him speak.

'I left my last job, not because…' He really was struggling with it. 'I got involved with a colleague,' Jed said. 'And there's no big deal about that, or there wasn't then. She worked in the labs in research and, honestly, for a couple of months it was great.' He blew out a breath. 'Then she started talking about children…'

Jasmine opened her mouth and then closed it.

'I wasn't sure. I mean, it was early days, but it wasn't even on the agenda. I told her that. She got upset and that weekend I went out with some friends. I was supposed to go over to hers on the Sunday and I didn't, no excuse, I just was out and got called into work and I forgot.' Jasmine nodded. She completely got it—she forgot things all the time.

'She went *crazy*,' Jed said. And it wasn't so much what he said but the way that he said it, his eyes imploring her to understand that this was no idle statement he was making. 'I got home that night and she was sitting outside my flat and she went berserk—she said that I was lying to her, that I'd met someone else.' He took a long breath.

'She hit me,' Jed said. 'But we're not talking a slap. She scratched my face, bit my hand.' He looked at Jasmine. 'I'm six-foot-two, she's shorter than you and there was nothing I could do. I could have hit her back, but I wouldn't do that, though, looking back, I think that was exactly what she wanted me to do.'

'Did you report it?'

He shook his head. 'What? Walk into a police station and say I'd been beaten up? It was a few scratches.'

'Jed?'

'I thought that was it. Obviously, I told her that we were done. She rang and said sorry, said that she'd just lost her head, but I told her it was over and for a little while it seemed that it was, but then she started following me.'

'Stalking?'

Jed nodded. 'One evening I was talking to a friend in the car park, nothing in it, just talking. The next day I caught up with her in the canteen and she'd had her car keyed—there were scratches all down the side. I can't say for sure that it was Samantha…'

'What did you do?'

'Nothing for a bit,' Jed said. 'Then my flat got broken into and then the phone calls started. It was hell.'

He had never been more honest, had been so matter-of-fact about it when he'd discussed it with others, but he wasn't feeling matter-of-fact now, because for the first time he was properly reliving that time. The flat tyres he'd come out to, the phone ringing in the night, that he didn't even want to think of dating, not because he didn't want to but because of what she might do to any woman he went out with.

'It all went from bad to worse. In the end she just unravelled—she ended up being admitted to Psych and nearly lost her job.'

'It's not your fault.' She saw the doubt in his expression. 'Jed, the same way I wasn't responsible for what my ex did.'

'That doesn't stop you looking back,' Jed said. 'I go over and over the time we were together and maybe I did let her think I was more serious than I felt.'

'Oh, come on, Jed. She clearly had issues. If it hadn't been you it would have been the next guy.'

'But it *was* me,' Jed said. 'I had more than a year of it. She's getting help now, apparently, but I just couldn't stay around,' Jed admitted. 'I don't think it was helping either of us to work in the same hospital and in the end I didn't want to even be in the same city. That's why I moved.'

'That's awful.'

'It was,' Jed said. 'I wasn't scared for myself, I could stop her physically, but when she started messing with people I knew, that was enough. And,' Jed added, 'I was scared for her too. It was awful to see someone who was basically nice just going to pieces.' He managed his first smile since he'd arrived that evening. 'Do you believe me now when I say I had no intention of getting involved with anyone at work?'

'Yes.'

'And do you understand why, when you got so upset that I might have once dated Penny, I thought it was all just happening again? I mean, the second we got serious, and we did get serious, you know that we did…' He waited till she nodded. 'Well, the next night I come round and you're standing there, crying and begging to know if I've ever hooked up with Penny, if anything, *anything* had ever happened between us.'

'I get it.' Jasmine even managed to laugh. 'I'd have freaked too, if I were you.' She went over to him and he pulled her onto his knee. 'I promise not to stalk you when we break up.'

'Maybe we won't.'

'We'll see,' Jasmine said.

'I know that you wouldn't now, anyway. You handled the break-up brilliantly,' Jed added. 'I mean, a couple of late night phone calls wouldn't have gone amiss—a few tears…'

Jasmine held her finger and thumb together. 'Just a smidge of obsession?'

'Careful what you wish for, huh?' Jed smiled back. 'I think I dreaded a break-up more than a relationship—and you…' He smiled at her. 'You just carried right on.'

'Not on the inside.'

She'd never admitted it to anyone, not just about Jed but about her fears and her thoughts and how more than anyone in the world she hated confrontation, hated rows, and that, yes, she had been running away. 'I've got to stop avoiding rows…'

'I think it's nice that you do.'

But Jasmine shook her head.

'You're a lot stronger than you think.'

She didn't feel very strong sometimes and she told him a little of how it felt to be related to two very strong women who were so accomplished in everything they did.

'Jasmine,' Jed asked. 'What do you want?'

'Meaning?'

'What do you want?'

She thought for a moment, about Simon safe and warm and sleeping in his cot and her job that she loved and her little home right on the beach and a relationship that looked like it might be working.

'What I've got,' Jasmine said.

'And you've worked for it,' Jed pointed out. 'You could have listened to your mum and sister and been some high-powered lawyer or doctor and hating every minute of it, or you could be working in the fracture clinic because the hours are better, but instead you've stood your ground and you do a job you love… And,' Jed added, 'despite a lousy relationship you've got an amazing son and your heart's back out there. I'd say you're pretty strong.'

And he was right. She had everything she wanted, even if wasn't what her mother or sister might choose. She did, even if it was misguided at times, follow her heart.

'I do want a little bit more,' Jasmine said.

'What?' He moved in for a kiss.

'White walls,' Jasmine whispered. 'I'm on my fourth coat.'

And he looked at walls that were still green tinged and he started to laugh. 'Did you put on an undercoat?'

He saw her frown.

'Jasmine,' he groaned. 'I'll do it at the weekend. But for now…'

It was bliss to be kissed by him again, bliss to be back in his arms and to know there were no secrets between them now, nothing more to know.

Except…

'How did your interview go?' She wriggled out of his kiss—there was so much she had missed out on.

'Don't worry about that now.'

'But how did it go?'

'Very well,' Jed said. 'I should know tomorrow.'

'How did Penny go?'

'Just leave it, huh? Suffice it to say I'm quietly confident but I'll be fine if it doesn't come off.'

'Sure?'

'Sure.'

And then he got back to kissing her and this time she didn't halt him with questions. This time it was just about them, at least until Simon woke up. This time she didn't hesitate, and brought him straight through.

'Jed!' Simon smiled when he saw him.

'You outed us to Penny!' Jed grinned and then he looked at Jasmine. 'We need to go out.'

'I know,' she said. 'I'll speak to Ruby. I can't just...'

'I didn't mean it like that,' Jed said. 'I mean that we need to announce ourselves to the world before Simon does.'

'I think he already has,' Jasmine said. 'Can't you feel them all watching us?'

He just grinned and then he said what he was thinking and it was far nicer than having to censor every word and thought, so much better than having to hold back. 'Do you want to come to the A and E ball?'

'It's too soon.'

'Not for me,' Jed said. 'Though I will probably only be able to stay till ten, so you might be deposited home early, but I want people to know about us. It isn't too soon for me.'

'I meant...' Jasmine laughed '...that it's too soon for me to organise anything. The ball's tomorrow—and I'm working till four and I haven't got anything to wear.'

'You'll look lovely whatever you wear.'

'That's the most stupid thing I've ever heard...' Did he have not a clue as to how much went into getting ready for this sort of thing? Everyone who was going had the afternoon off and had been talking about dresses and shoes for weeks.

'I'm not going to argue with you.' Jed smiled. 'After all, I know how much you hate it. So I'm just going to tell you instead that we're going to the ball tomorrow and I expect you to be ready when I get here.'

CHAPTER SEVENTEEN

A BIT MORE notice would have been nice.

Lisa and Penny were bright orange, thanks to their spray tans, which they would shower off before their hairdresser appointments, Jasmine thought darkly, or after they'd picked up their thousand-dollar dresses from the dry cleaner's.

They were working on a head injury—their newly extended and painted nails hidden under plastic gloves. Penny wanted him admitted to ICU, except there weren't any beds at Peninsula, though they had been told there *might* be one available later on in the afternoon.

'Nope.' Penny shook her head. 'He'll have to be transferred.'

'Okay,' Lisa said. 'Do you want me to do a ring around?' She looked at Jasmine. 'You go and have your break.' As Jasmine opened her mouth to argue, Lisa overrode her. 'You might have to transfer him,' she pointed out, 'so go and have a break now.'

Jasmine didn't have time for a break.

Instead, she raced up to CCU. She was incredibly nervous about tonight and terribly aware of the lack of anything suitable in her wardrobe and she was determined to dash to the shops at lunchtime. She knew it might be her only chance to visit her mum but as she swept in to see her, Jasmine halted when she saw Jed standing there beside her bed.

'Hi, there.' Jasmine smiled, but it was a wary one, because Jed wasn't her mother's doctor. He hadn't even been involved in her admission. 'Is everything okay?'

'Everything's fine.' Louise smiled, but Jasmine was still cautious.

'Your mum's temperature was up a bit up this morning,' Jed explained. 'And Penny's stuck in with that head injury and insisted that I check things out…' He rolled his eyes. 'She's got a slight chest infection but they're onto it with antibiotics and your mum's physio has been increased.' He gave Louise a smile. 'Now that I've seen for myself that you'll live and have spoken to your doctor, I'd better get back down there and reassure your elder daughter.'

She hardly waited till he was out of the door and had she looked over her shoulder she would have seen Jed shake his head as Jasmine anxiously picked up her mother's charts and saw that her temperature had indeed been rather high but was on its way down.

'Jasmine.' Her mum was stern. 'I've got a chest infection.'

'I know.'

'It's not a big deal,' her mum said, and saw Jasmine's anxious eyes. 'Okay, it could be, but they're straight onto it. They've taken loads of bloods and they've got me up and walking and coughing on the hour. It's my own stupid fault,' Louise admitted. 'It hurt to take a deep breath and to cough and I didn't really listen when they said to increase my painkillers. I thought I was doing better by having less.'

'Mum.' Jasmine let out a frustrated sigh. 'You're so…'

'Stubborn.'

'I could think of a few other words,' Jasmine said. 'Why wouldn't you take the medication?'

'I just wanted to go home and I thought the sooner I got off the strong stuff the sooner they'd release me.'

'And because of that you'll probably be stuck here for another couple of days.'

'Well, we don't always do what's right for us, do we?' Louise admitted. 'But I am learning.' And to prove it she pushed her pain medication button and the little pump whirred into life. 'See?'

'I spoke with the insurance and the travel agent,' Jasmine said, 'and you shall have your cruise, but not for a few months.' She saw her mum rest back on the pillow. 'I brought in some brochures—you get to choose all over again.'

'That's such a relief,' Louise said. 'That means that I can help you out a bit more.'

'Mum, the only person you need to be concentrating on right now is you. I'm getting in the swing of things now. Vanessa and I are going to work out our nights and our late shifts, and we've got Ruby. I just needed you for the first few weeks.'

'And I made it hard to ask,' Louise said. 'I'm sorry.'

'Don't be sorry.'

'I am.'

'You gave me a push,' Jasmine said. 'I knew what I was going to get when I decided to come home—and you have helped. I couldn't have started back on shifts without you. But…' Jasmine took a deep breath, '…I'm not going to apply to work in the fracture clinic, I'm going to stay in Emergency. It's what I'm good at. And it might be a juggle, but…'

'You'll sort it.'

'I will,' Jasmine said, feeling far more positive.

'I don't remember much of my time in there, but…' she took her daughter's hand, '…I do know what was done for me and I've seen the nurses hard at it on ICU and in here. I'm proud of what you do, Jasmine, and I'm sorry I haven't been more supportive. I get it now.'

'Good.'

'And it breaks my heart what Penny had to go through, and I am so glad you were spared from that, but apart from that, I can't think of anyone I'd rather have looking after me than you. Don't let your career go.'

'I'm not going to.'

'No matter how easy it is to drop down to part time or—'

'Mum! I've got a one-year-old to support so dropping my hours down isn't even on the agenda. Not for the next seventeen years at least.'

'He seems nice.' Louise's head jerked to the door. 'Jed.'

'He is.'

'Penny said that you two have been seeing each other.'

'Mum!' Jasmine was firm. 'It's early days. Neither of us wants to rush into anything and there's Simon to think of. Still—' she couldn't help but share the news, '—I'm going to the A and E ball with him tonight.'

'What are you wearing?'

'I don't know yet.' Jasmine ignored her mother's horrified expression. 'I'm going to look at lunchtime.'

'In the village?'

Jasmine closed her eyes. There were about two clothes

shops near enough to get to in her lunch break and, no, she didn't think they would have a massive selection of ballgowns to choose from.

'I'd lend you something, but...'

'I'm not borrowing something from my mum!'

'I've got very good taste,' Louise said, 'and a black dress is a black dress, but...' she ran an eye over Jasmine '...it wouldn't fit.'

'Just keep pushing that pain medication button, Mum.' Jasmine smiled. 'You might need it soon.'

'What about your wedding dress?'

'Please.'

'Well, it's not really a wedding dress, is it?' Louise pointed out. 'It would look lovely.'

'No.' Jasmine gave her mum a kiss. 'I have to get back.'

'Are you getting your hair done?'

'Yes!' Jasmine lied. 'Don't worry, I'm not going to let the side down.'

'I know. Can you drop by on your way?'

'Mum!' That was too cringy for words.

'Penny is.'

'Oh, Mum,' Jasmine said. 'I think I preferred the old you.'

'Tough.' Louise smiled. 'You've got a new mum now. Right, you have a lovely day and I'll look forward to seeing you this evening.'

Jasmine headed back down to Emergency and gave a brief nod to Penny, who was sitting at the nursing station writing up notes, and beside her was Jed.

'Have you seen Mum?'

Jasmine blinked in surprise. 'I've just been,' Jasmine said. 'She looks well.'

'What's her temp?'

'Down to thirty-seven point five.'

'Good.'

'Well, she's certainly changed her tune,' Jasmine said to Jed as Penny was called back into Resus. 'I'm actually being acknowledged.' She made sure no one was listening. 'Have you heard?'

'What?'

'Jed!' He was so annoying sometimes. 'About the job,' she mouthed.

'Not yet!' he mouthed back. And then she remembered something. 'This is too embarrassing for words, but on the way to the ball Mum wants me to pop in.'

'No problem.'

'For two minutes.'

'It's no big deal,' Jed assured her.

'For you maybe,' Jasmine grumbled. 'I think they bypassed the old mum when they did surgery.'

'Jasmine.' She heard a rather familiar call from Greg and, jumping off her seat, she dashed into Resus to see the head injury Penny had been working on looking significantly worse. His arms were extending to painful stimuli and Penny was sedating him and getting ready to intubate.

Penny was marvellous, barking out her orders as always, but she actually called for Jed's help when the anaesthetist didn't arrive. Whatever way you looked at it, she was fantastic at her job, just a cow around the staff. That was to say, all the staff, so she didn't deliberately take it personally when Penny told her none too politely to hurry up as Jasmine loaded a syringe with propofol, an oily drug that was a bit slow to draw up. And she really was confident in her work. Penny's hands weren't even shaking as she intubated the patient, Jasmine noticed.

And then Lisa spoke and as Jasmine pulled up some more medication she noticed that her own hands were shaking.

'There's an ICU bed at Melbourne Central. The chopper is already out so I've called for MICA and a police escort.' She told the anaesthetist the same when he arrived and then she told Jasmine to prepare the patient and get herself ready.

'It will be fine,' Jed said just a little while later when Mark and his colleague arrived and transferred the patient to the stretcher. 'Jasmine, it will be.'

'I know.'

'No one's going to say anything.'

'And if they do?'

'They won't,' Jed said. 'But if they do, just tell them to mind their own business.'

He gave her shoulder a squeeze. 'If I don't see you before, I'll pick you up about six-thirty.'

Oh, God… Jasmine would have closed her eyes, except she had to move now, had to follow the stretcher into the ambulance. No, she wasn't going to be buying a dress this lunchtime, neither would she be sorting out her hair.

Instead she was going back to Melbourne Central.

With a police escort they practically flew down the freeway. The patient was stable throughout and Craig, the anaesthetist, was very calm, as were the paramedics. It was Jasmine whose heart was hammering as they approached the hospital she had loved and the place it had hurt so much to leave.

'Are you okay, Jasmine?' Mark asked, before they climbed out.

'Sure.'

'No one's going to eat you.'

'I know.'

Of course, it was a bit of an anticlimax. The hospital didn't suddenly stop just because she was back. In fact, she didn't recognise any of the staff on ICU as she handed the patient over.

The paramedics were going to be taking Jasmine and Craig back to Peninsula, but Mark wanted to take a break before the return journey.

'We'll just grab some lunch at the canteen,' Mark told her.

'I'll meet you back at the ambulance,' Jasmine told him. Tempting as it was to hide out in the canteen, Jasmine decided that she was tired of running away from things, tired of feeling guilty over mistakes that weren't even hers, so feeling nervous but brave she walked into Emergency.

'Hi.' She smiled at a face she didn't recognise. 'I was wondering—'

'Jasmine!' She never got to finish her sentence as Hannah, the charge nurse, came rushing over. 'Where have you been?'

'I moved back home.'

'You never even let us know you'd had your baby. Martha said that she heard it was a boy.'

And she was back and her friends were crowding around her, looking at pictures of Simon on her phone. Hearing their enthusiasm, she realised just how badly she had misjudged her friendships and she started crying.

'He was a bastard,' Hannah said when Jasmine told her why. 'Of course nobody thought you were involved.'

'Everybody was so weird around me.'

'We were embarrassed,' Martha said. 'Upset for you.' She gave Jasmine a hug. 'You're better off without him, you know.'

'Oh, God, do I know.'

'Does that mean you're coming back?' Hannah asked.

She thought for a moment, because she could come back and part of her wanted to come back except, Jasmine realised then, just as she had told Jed, she was very happy with what she had now.

'Maybe one day.' Jasmine smiled and then of course they asked if she was seeing anyone and she was through with covering things up and so she said yes.

'His name's Jed,' Jasmine said. 'Jed Devlin.'

'I know that name.' Hannah frowned. 'Where do I know that name from?'

'He came for an interview here,' Jasmine said.

'That's right.' Hannah nodded and then waved in direction of the door. 'I think your transport's ready.' Jasmine turned and there were the paramedics. 'Don't be a stranger,' Hannah warned. Then she laughed. 'Well, I guess you won't be now.'

Jasmine had no idea what Hannah meant, but she was on too much of a high to think about it, and then when she realised she still had nothing to wear tonight and she wasn't going to get to the shops, she was far too panicked to dwell on Hannah's words, especially when they hit traffic on the way home.

'Can't you put on the sirens?' Jasmine grumbled, but the paramedics just laughed. 'Some of us are going out tonight.'

CHAPTER EIGHTEEN

THANK GOD FOR heated rollers and quick-dry nail varnish, Jasmine thought as somehow she cobbled herself together, cringing as she pulled her old wedding dress on.

It didn't look remotely like a wedding dress.

It was a dark blue silk that her mother had said matched her eyes, and the strange thing was, as she looked in the mirror, she looked better in it than she had on the big day.

Then she had been sixteen weeks pregnant and bloated and miserable and not particularly sure that she wasn't making the biggest mistake of her life, and, no, she hadn't been particularly excited at the prospect of her wedding night.

Now she had curves and a smile and couldn't wait for the formalities to be over just to get Jed into bed!

'Wow,' Ruby said when she opened the door. 'You look gorgeous. I love the dress.'

'Thanks.' Jasmine smiled.

'Where did you get it?'

'I've had it for ages.' Jasmine blushed and mumbled something about a boutique in the city as she stuffed her bag with lipstick and keys. 'I don't think I'll be late back,' she told Ruby. 'Jed has to go into work and cover for Penny.'

'All you have to worry about is enjoying yourself,' Ruby said. 'He'll be fine.'

She knew that Simon would be fine.

It was two other people she was more worried about tonight.

Surely they wouldn't tell them about the job today, Jasmine reasoned. It was the A and E ball tonight so they would no doubt wait till next week to give the verdict.

Oh, God, Jasmine thought, putting in her earrings, she was torn.

Family first, she told herself, except she knew about the delays that had been caused in Jed's career. He was older than Penny and he wasn't where he thought he should be in his career.

And here he was at her door.

Her heart was hammering for different reasons when she first saw him in a tux.

'Wow.' Jed gave a whistle of appreciation. 'I told you you'd look lovely.'

'Wow to you too,' Jasmine said.

'I thought you said you had nothing to wear. Jasmine, you didn't go spending a fortune, did you?'

'No, no,' Jasmine said. 'I've had this for ages. I didn't know if it would fit!' Quickly she tried to change the subject. 'Have you heard about the job?'

'We'll talk about it later.' He sort of nodded his head in the direction of Ruby. 'We ought to go, especially if you want to drop in to see your mum.'

'I feel stupid walking through the hospital dressed like this.'

'It will be nice for her,' Jed said. 'And knowing that place, Penny will get called just as she gets into her dress and have to do something urgent and be swanning around Resus in pink satin.'

'I guess,' Jasmine said. 'Though I can't see her in pink satin.' Jed smiled, but she could tell he was a little on edge. Maybe he was having second thoughts about them being seen out together so soon and she told him so.

'You're being daft.'

It was worth going in just to see the smile on her mum's face.

'You look great.' Louise smiled. 'You both do.'

'I'm just going to go and ring the unit and check it's okay,' Jed said, and she knew it was because staff were a bit thin on the ground, but it also gave her a chance for a little bit longer with her mum.

'You look so much better.'

'I feel it,' Louise said. 'I told you your wedding dress would be perfect!'

'Shhh!' Jasmine warned. 'I don't want him knowing.'

'Now.' Louise was back to practical. 'Your sister's got something to tell you, some big news.' And her heart should have surged for Penny, except first it sank for Jed and then it surged back up because she was truly torn. 'It's big news and even if it's a bit hard to hear it, I think it's really important that you be pleased for her.'

'Of course I'll be pleased.'

'I know,' Louise said. 'I can't say anything, I don't want to spoil things for her, and I guess that it's her news to share, but just keep that smile fixed on.'

'I will.'

She gave her mum a kiss and then walked out to where Jed was just hanging up the phone.

'Let's get going.'

He was quiet on the car ride there and if he was just

a touch tense, at least Jasmine knew why, but he took her hand and they walked in together and she knew that if he was being a bit quiet it had nothing to do with her.

'Hi, there!' Penny came over all smiles, and kissed Jed's cheek and then Jasmine's too.

'You look amazing,' Jasmine said, because Penny did. There was a glow in her cheeks and a smile that was just a little bit smug, and she didn't blame Jed when he excused himself to have a word with Mr Dean.

'Why are you wearing your wedding dress?' Penny asked the second he was out of earshot.

'Because I had about ten minutes' warning about tonight,' Jasmine said. 'And don't tell anyone.'

'Isn't that a bit twisted?' Penny wrinkled her nose. 'Doesn't that make you a bit of a saddo?'

'Stop it!' Jasmine said, but she started to laugh. Penny was such a cow at times, but she was also very funny.

'Any news?' Jasmine asked.

'Not here, Jasmine,' Penny warned.

'Oh, stop it,' Jasmine said. 'No one can read my lips. You got the job, didn't you? I know you did.' She looked at her sister. 'I thought we were going to be more honest from now on.'

'Jasmine,' Penny warned.

'Well, I'm thrilled for you.' She really was. 'Honestly.'

'Jasmine, will you please shut up?' Penny gave a sigh of irritation then beckoned her towards the ladies. Of course it was crowded, so they went outside and Penny waited till they were about twenty metres from anyone before she spoke,

'I did get offered the job,' Penny said, 'and before you jump up and down on the spot and get all emotional and then start worrying about Jed...'

Jasmine took a deep breath.

'I withdrew my application.'

Jasmine literally felt her jaw drop. 'Why would you do that?'

'Because,' Jasmine said, 'and I never thought I'd hear myself say this, but some things are more important in life.'

'Your career is…' Jasmine buttoned her lip but Penny just laughed.

'Exactly,' she said. 'There needs to be more. I've been a terrible aunt,' Penny said, 'and an appalling sister, because I've been so incredibly jealous of you. I always have been. And I guess I still am. I want what you have.' And she smiled as Jasmine frowned. 'Not Jed, you idiot. The other guy in your life.'

'A baby?'

'It seems Mr Dean was right. They train you up and what do you go and do…?'

'You're pregnant?'

'Not yet,' Penny said. 'But I'm hoping to be in the not-too-distant future, and from everything I've heard about IVF, well, I'm not going to be the sunniest person.'

'Penny!' Jasmine was stunned.

'I'm in my mid-thirties and I just…' Penny gave a tight shrug. 'At the moment I have about sixty-three minutes a week to devote to a relationship. There are not many men who would put up with that.'

'There might be.'

'Well, I want my baby,' Penny said. 'And I've thought long and hard and I'll work right up to the last minute and then—'

'But IVF?' Jasmine queried. 'Don't you just need a donor?'

'I tried for a baby with Vince.' Jasmine watched her sister's eyes, which were always so sharp, actually fill with tears. 'We had a few problems.' She looked at her sister. 'Or rather I had a few problems in that department. It meant IVF and Vince and I...' She swallowed her tears down. 'Well, I think we weren't really up to the challenge.'

'Is that why you broke up?'

'In part.'

'Why couldn't you talk to me?'

'I am now,' Penny said, and Jasmine realised what her mum had meant about some big news. But, no, she didn't need to be told to keep her smile on, she was genuinely thrilled for her sister. 'You have to give me my injections, though.'

'I can't wait to stick another needle in you.' Jasmine grinned and gave Penny a hug.

'And I'm not giving up my career,' Penny said. 'I'm just not complicating things for now. I have no idea how I'm going to work things out.'

'You will,' Jasmine said.

'I think I'll have to get a nanny.'

'We can share one.' Jasmine grinned.

'I want this,' Penny said. 'And I'm not waiting around for Mr Right. Anyway, I've seen both you and mum stuff up—we have terrible taste in men.'

'I guess.'

'Not this time, though.' Penny smiled. 'Mind you, don't you go telling him I got offered the job.'

'Penny! I'm sick of lying.'

'I mean it. If he has got the job and that's what he's all worked up about, the last thing he needs is to be told

I turned it down. Just be all happy and celebrate when he gets the news.'

'Do you think he's got it?' Jasmine wasn't so sure—Jed seemed really tense.

'I'm pretty sure. There was an external applicant who was pretty impressive but I think Mr Dean wants to keep it in-house. He should hear any time soon.'

She had a terrible feeling that he already had.

Jed was lovely as they drove back from the ball a couple of hours later, but she could tell that he had something on his mind—it had stung when she had thought he had lost the job to Penny. She knew how his career had been sidetracked dealing with what he had, but losing it to an outsider would really hurt.

'Where are we going?'

Only then had she noticed they were driving to the city.

'Somewhere nice.'

'But you have to work.'

'Nope.' He grinned. 'Mr Dean arranged a locum, well, not really a locum—he's going to be working there in a few weeks so it's good if he gets a feel for the place.'

She looked over and tried to read his expression.

'Working there?'

'The new consultant.' He gave a small grimace.

'Oh, Jed.' She really didn't know what to say. 'I know it's hard for you…'

'Hard on me?' He turned and looked at Jasmine. 'It's hard on you, though Penny didn't look as upset as I thought she'd be,' Jed admitted. 'I thought she'd be savage.' He shook his head. 'She seemed fine.'

Jasmine looked out of the window to the bay. Penny had been right. Working in the same department was way too complicated. She could hardly tell Jed the real reason Penny was so delighted and she definitely didn't want to tell him that Penny had actually turned down the job.

They chatted about this and that but she could feel his tension and she was so irritated that they had told the applicants today of all days. Couldn't they just have enjoyed tonight?

'We can't stay out too long.' Jasmine glanced at her watch—half an hour really, if she was going to be back by midnight, though maybe she could stretch it till half past. It was hardly his fault. He just wanted to go out somewhere nice and wasn't used to factoring in a one-year-old and his babysitter.

'What are we doing here?' she asked as they pulled up at a very nice hotel.

'I told you I wanted to take you somewhere nice.'

'Just a drink at the bar, then.' She hoped he hadn't booked for dinner. He popped the boot and as Jasmine stepped out of the car, she frowned as he gave his name to park it and frowned even more at the sight of her rather tatty case being hauled out.

'Jed?'

'Ruby packed it,' Jed said. 'It's all sorted.'

'Oh.'

They went to check in. It was the nicest thing he could have done for her, but she felt terrible because surely he had been planning a celebration, or maybe he hadn't factored in that he'd know.

It was like holiday where it was raining and everyone was pretending it didn't matter, all grimly determined to enjoy themselves, and she would…she was. Jasmine was thrilled to have a night away with him, she just knew how hard this must be for him.

'Wow!' She stepped into the hotel room and tried not to notice the champagne and two glasses. Instead, she stared out at the view but Jed poured two glasses and it tasted fantastic and, yes, it was fantastic to be together.

'I am sorry about the job,' Jasmine said.

'Shhh,' he said. 'Let's just celebrate.'

'Cheers!'

'You don't know what we're celebrating,' Jed said.

'That we're here's good enough for me.'

'And me,' Jed said, and then he smiled. '"Oh, ye of little faith".'

She didn't understand. 'Sorry?'

He pulled back one of the curtains. 'Have a look over there. What do you see?' It was just a busy city. 'Over there.' He pointed to a tall building. 'That's where I'm going to be working. I got offered a consultant's position on Thursday, so I withdrew my application.'

'Oh!' She could have thumped him. 'You let me drive all that way thinking you were disappointed!'

'No,' Jed said. 'I knew that you *were* disappointed—it's awful for Penny. I really thought when I took the position at Melbourne Central that Penny was a certainty for the job. I think Mr Dean's really got it wrong. The new guy seems great by all accounts, but it's going to be tough on your sister.'

'No, you don't understand.' She opened her mouth, but again she couldn't say anything.

'What?'

Jasmine shook her head. 'Leave it.'

'I can't.'

'You can.'

'I can't.'

Jasmine was firm. 'She's my sister.'

She looked over to where he'd be working. 'I thought you were happy at Peninsula.'

'I've been incredibly happy,' Jed said. 'I applied to a few hospitals when I first thought of moving here and it was a close-run thing. I love big city hospitals but when Mr Dean hinted at a consultancy… Anyway, Central rang me last week and asked if I'd be interested in a more senior position than the one I interviewed for last year, and given the tension at work, given a lot of things, the choice was actually easy.'

'That's good,' Jasmine said, trying to mask the little edge of disappointment in her voice, that just when they were finding each other he was upping sticks, but, still, it was just an hour or so away.

'I like to keep work and home separate,' Jed said.

'I know that.'

'And I haven't been doing a very good job of it of late.'

He started to kiss her and then pulled his head back. 'You're sulking.'

'No.' She looked up at him and she was too scared to admit it, because he meant so much more than she dared reveal. They'd agreed they were going to take things slowly and, yes, they were back on track, but maybe once he got to a big hospital, maybe when things were more difficult, when Simon was sick and he was on call and it all became too hard to have a single mum as a girlfriend who lived a good hour away, maybe then things would go wrong for them.

'It's been a hell of a week.'

'And now it's over,' Jed said. 'Now you can enjoy being spoiled.' He gave her a smile. 'Come on, tell me, how come Penny's looking so pleased if she didn't get the job.'

Jasmine closed her eyes. 'Actually, come to think of it, it's a good job that you're going to Melbourne Central. I'm not breaking my sister's confidence.' She looked at him.

'Fair enough.'

'She's family.'

'I'm not arguing.' Jed grinned. 'I think you want to, though.'

'I don't.'

Jasmine didn't. She didn't want anything to spoil this night. 'So…' She forced her voice to be upbeat. 'When do you start?'

'Four weeks,' Jed said. 'It's going to be fantastic—it's a great hospital.'

'Good.'

'It's everything I want.'

He pulled her into his arms and he was smiling. She would not ruin this night, would not nit-pick, but how come he was so happy to be leaving? How come he had been so tense all night? Though he wasn't tense now, he was *delighted* with his good news, thrilled to be moving an hour away, and she swallowed down her tears.

'I can't wait to start,' Jed said. 'And tomorrow I thought I might go and look for somewhere to live.'

Some bachelor city apartment, Jasmine thought bitterly, but she kept her smile there.

'The staff there seem really friendly,' he added.

She thought of Hannah, who was gorgeous and flirted like crazy, and Martha, and the wild parties they often had, and he would be there and she would be home with Simon.

'And I can't wait…'

'Okay.' Her lips were taut with smiling. 'I'm thrilled for you.'

She reached for her glass as she did not want to argue; she took a sip of champagne and swallowed down a row, but it was fizzing. Yes, she was happy for him, yes, she was thrilled, but… 'Do you have to keep rubbing it in?'

She didn't get why he was smiling.

'Sorry?'

'Do you have to keep telling me how *thrilled* you are to be leaving, how fantastic it is to be moving away?'

'Come on, Jasmine.' He grinned. 'Don't spoil tonight with a row.'

'I want one!' She did. For the first time in her life she wanted her row and stuff it if it was an expensive one. So what if she was spoiling a wonderful night? Did he have to be quite so insensitive?

'Go for it.'

'I will,' Jasmine said. 'I'm thrilled for you. I really am, but do you have to keep going on about it?' She just said it. 'Do you have to keep telling me how delighted you are to be going away and all the parties…'

'I never said anything about parties.'

'Oh, but there will be.'

And he just grinned.

'And I'll be home with Simon and you'll be an hour away and, yes, I am happy for you and, no, I didn't expect you to take Simon and me into consideration, but I can't keep grinning like an idiot when the fact is you're moving away.' She started to cry. 'And I don't understand why you're laughing.'

'Because I love how you row.'

And he pulled her into him. 'I've been goading you.'

'Why?'

'Because.'

'Because what?'

'I want just a smidge of obsession.'

'Well, you've got it.' And he kissed her and it was lovely. She'd said what she thought, had had a good row and no one was any the worse for it. Then he stopped kissing her and looked at her for a very long time.

'I am pleased for you. I honestly am. I know you'll love it there.' And she realised then what Hannah had meant when she'd said that she'd see her around. If she was going out with Jed she'd be with him at times. 'I'm just sad you're leaving, that's all.'

'I have to,' Jed said. 'Because I'm not working alongside a woman who turned down my proposal.' And he took out a box containing a ring but she didn't even look at it properly, just looked straight back at him. 'And if she doesn't turn it down then I'm working in the same department as my wife and sister-in-law. That would be way too complicated and I already have trouble enough concentrating on work when you're around. So which one is it?'

'The complicated one,' Jasmine said, and watched as he put a ring on her finger.

'It won't be complicated for long,' he assured her. 'I'm taking time off before I start my new job and for the next few weeks I'm going to take some time to get to know that son of yours and you're going to get to know me properly. We'll go to Sydney and meet my family. We'll just take some time. I don't want you to feel you're being rushed into anything again. We'll wait as long as it takes for you to feel okay with it.'

'I already am.' She had never been more sure of anything in her life. 'And I don't feel as if I'm rushing into things this time. I know.'

'I know too,' Jed said. 'And you're coming to look for somewhere to live with me. Midway, maybe? Or we can just carry on as we are and I'll sort out the travel, but I promise you that you and Simon will always be my first consideration.'

She believed him, she really did, and her heart filled not just for her own happiness but because her son was going to have such an amazing man to help raise him, for all the happy times to come.

'Mum's going to have another heart attack when she finds out.'

'She already knows,' Jed said. 'What, do you think I'd ask you to marry me without asking for her permission?'

'You asked her?' So that was what her mum had been banging on about not dropping her hours or losing her career—she already knew.

'Of course I asked her.'

'You're an old-fashioned thing, aren't you?'

'Yep,' Jed said. 'But I'm filthy-minded too. I want to do you in your wedding dress.'

She blinked.

'I'm sure you will.'

'I mean this one.'

She just about died of embarrassment, right there on the spot. 'You knew?'

'Your mum told me.' He smiled, and then pulled her back into his arms. 'And now, seeing as I'm almost family, you can tell me what's going on with Penny.' She started to, but he stopped her.

'Not yet.' He was kissing her face, kissing her mouth, and making her feel wanted and beautiful in her wedding dress for the very first time, as he told her just how much the future was theirs. 'We've got ages.'

* * * * *

THE TAMING OF DR ALEX DRAYCOTT

JOANNA NEIL

CHAPTER ONE

'LOOK how many strawberries I picked,' seven-year-old Sarah announced, coming into the kitchen. She placed a wicker basket on the table, filled to the brim with fruit. 'There's loads,' she said, her blue eyes bright with excitement. 'Can we have some for breakfast?'

Alex looked at the lush fruit. 'Yes,' she murmured, 'of course...and as there's such a lot, perhaps we ought to take some round to Mrs Marchant next door? I've noticed she's usually up and about at this time of the morning.'

Sarah nodded. 'I'll go, if you like.' She smiled. 'I like Mrs Marchant. She's kind...but I think she must be quite old, you know, or poorly? She always looks a bit tired and sometimes she says she has to go and sit down for a while...but she's always nice. She gave me some toffees when I took the magazine round there yesterday.'

'I want to take the strawberries,' five-year-old James chimed in, his eyes lighting up at the mention of toffees. 'You went last time.' He glared at his sister and began to tug at the basket.

Sensing impending disaster, Alex intervened. 'We'll all go,' she said, taking hold of the basket and moving it from harm's way. 'Now, finish your breakfast, both of you. We don't have much time before we have to leave for school. And you need to go back upstairs to your bedroom and find your PE kit, James.'

'I don't like that bedroom,' James complained, scowling at Alex across the kitchen table, a lock of brown hair falling across his forehead. 'It's too small. Why can't I have the room with the window seat?'

'Because we talked about this...' Alex murmured. 'And you chose the one that looked out over the orchard.' She inspected the contents of his lunch box and then clipped the lid in place.

'So?' He hunched his shoulders. 'That doesn't matter, does it? I changed my mind. I can swap with Sarah.'

'No, you can't.' His sister batted that one away before the idea could take root, her fair hair quivering with indignation. 'I want the one where I can see the garden... I chose it...and I picked the colours and Auntie Alex has already started painting the walls for me. So it's mine.'

'Perhaps we can rearrange the furniture in your room to make it better for you,' Alex said, glancing at James. She pushed his lunch box into his school bag and closed the zipper. 'I made you egg mayonnaise sandwiches, and there are cracker biscuits with ham and cheese. And don't forget to screw the lid tight on your drink bottle when you use it, or we'll have another mess in your bag like the one we had last week.'

'I don't like egg maynaze.' James's chin jutted and his grey eyes took on a mutinous glint.

Alex held back the sigh that had started to build up in her chest. She raised dark brows. 'You told me it was your favourite.'

He gave her a disdainful glance. 'That was yesterday. Today I like peanut butter.'

'Well, I'm sorry about that, James, but I really don't

have time to start over.' Alex flicked back her long chestnut hair so that it settled in a gentle flurry across her shoulders, and handed him the bag. 'We have to get you and Sarah to school, and I have to go to work.' She checked her watch. 'Do you remember what I told you? This is my first day in the new job, and I need to be at the hospital on time.'

'Will you be in trouble if you're late?' Sarah's anxiety sounded in her voice. 'Mummy said she always got an ear bending from the boss if she wasn't at work for nine o'clock.' She frowned. 'I think that must hurt a lot. I wouldn't like it if it anyone pulled my ears.'

'How could that happen to Auntie Alex?' James said in a scornful tone. 'She's the boss. She can do what she likes.'

Alex smiled. 'Not exactly, James. There are several bosses in my department...but the fact is, if you're in charge you need to lead by example...show people the right way of doing things...so it's even more important that I get there on time.'

Sarah's face still bore a worried expression, so she added gently, 'Ear bending just means the boss would talk to your mother about where she was going wrong.'

'Really?' Sarah's blue eyes brightened. 'Well, I think he must be sorry, anyway, 'cos he sent Mummy some flowers. There was a card, and it said, *Get well soon.*'

She frowned again, and Alex gave her a hug. 'We all hope for that, Sarah. At least your mum and dad are in good hands. They're being looked after by the very best doctors.'

For once, James had nothing to say, and Alex sent him a quick, thoughtful glance. He seemed to be coping well enough in the aftermath of his parents' accident, but she suspected his newfound belligerence was all tied up with what had been going on in his life this last few weeks. She would have to keep a keen eye on both children for the foreseeable future.

A few minutes later they left the house and went next door. It was a minute or so before Jane Marchant answered Alex's knock, but when she did her smile was welcoming and she invited them inside.

'We can only stop for a minute or two,' Alex said, following her neighbour into the neat, pine kitchen. 'We just wanted to bring you these strawberries, and to make sure that you're all right.'

Jane stared at the fruit, her mouth dropping open in awe. 'Just look at that fruit—so ripe and juicy.' Her eyes glimmered with appreciation. 'I'll enjoy those with my tea—and I could make a lovely strawberry sponge cake. You'll have to come and share it with me.' She looked at the children, who nodded with enthusiasm at the suggestion. 'Thank you for this,' she said, embracing all three of them with her smile. 'It was very thoughtful of you.'

'Just don't go overdoing it,' Alex warned her. 'I know what you're like when you get started with the baking. I've been worried about you just lately, especially after that dizzy spell you had the other day. Are you still getting the headaches?'

Jane nodded. 'But you don't need to worry yourself over me, love. I'll be fine. Like I said, the doctor's been trying me with different tablets to see if we can calm things down. I probably just need to take things more slowly, that's all. I've perhaps done too much in the garden. I've been trying to tackle the weeds—you know yourself what a job that can be when you have an acre or so to look after.'

'I do.' Alex's lips made a downward curve. 'I'm still wondering what possessed me to take on that rundown house next door, with its dilapidated orchard and all those outbuildings.' Her mouth flattened. 'It just seemed like a good idea at the time.'

'I love it,' Sarah said. 'The garden's all wild and raggedy, and there's lots of fruit bushes all tangled up. And there's masses of strawberries…' she made a wide circle with her arms '…just spreading out all over the place.'

'It's like a jungle,' James put in, ignoring Alex's faintly amused groan. 'We can play explorers, hunting the bad people.' He began to make swashbuckling moves with an imaginary sword.

Sarah looked at Jane once more. 'I can help you with the garden,' she offered. 'Any time you like.'

'Thank you, sweetheart.' Jane beamed at the little girl. 'You're a treasure. Alex must be so happy to have you with her.'

'It's true,' Alex agreed. 'Both she and James have been good as gold, helping with the move.' She frowned. 'But as far as your tablets are concerned, I'm not so sure that they're doing the job.' She glanced at Jane. Her neighbour was in her early sixties, a slender woman with brown, wavy hair and pale features. As Sarah had pointed out in her innocent way, she didn't look at all well. 'I really think you ought to go back to your doctor and ask him to do some tests to find out if there's a specific cause of the high blood pressure that might have been overlooked—especially since you're having other symptoms, like the back pain and the muscle spasms.'

Jane looked doubtful. 'I really don't like to bother the doctor any more. I've already been back several times and he's doing what he can to keep everything in check.'

'Even so,' Alex commented, 'as a doctor myself, I think your symptoms need to be looked into a bit more. I worry about leaving you on your own during the day while I'm at work. Is there no one in the family who can come and look out for you?'

Jane shook her head. 'There's only my nephew. We're very close—in fact, he's more like a son to me. His parents, my brother and his wife, are out of the country, working on various projects.' Her features softened. 'He's such a lovely young man. I think the world of him…and he comes to visit whenever he's able. We often talk on the phone. I'm sure he'd do anything for me, but I know he's busy and I don't want to burden him with my problems.'

Alex's brows drew together. 'Maybe you should think twice about that—after all, he'd want to know if you were ill, wouldn't he?'

'Of course, but it won't come to that. I'll be fine. Besides, he has enough troubles of his own to deal with right now…' She pulled a face 'There's to be some kind of audit at work, apparently, and he has to figure out how to keep the chiefs off his back. He says they've appointed a new manager to whip the department into shape, and the last thing he needs is some busybody poking his nose into all the corners to see how they do things and then use it against him to turn all his carefully organised systems upside down.'

Alex's eyes widened a fraction, and she let out a small breath. Managers were never popular. 'I see what you mean…he does seem to have a lot on his plate at the moment, doesn't he? But I think you're more important than any of that. I wonder if he could find time to help occasionally...with the garden, maybe?'

'Oh, he does what he can.'

James was beginning to show signs of restlessness, wandering about the room, peering at all the fine porcelain plates and glassware on display. He ran his fingers over the smooth lines of a ceramic cookie jar and then began to reach for a chicken-shaped timer, intent on examining its flamboyant red comb and wattles.

'I think it's time we made tracks,' Alex murmured, stopping to give Jane a quick hug. She'd only known this woman for a couple of weeks, but already it was as though they'd been friends for a lifetime.

'Let's go,' she said, handing Sarah her school bag. 'With any luck we'll get to school before the first whistle goes.'

Jane went with them into the hall. 'See you later,' she said.

'I don't like school,' James began as Alex shepherded them out through the front door. 'Mrs Coleman won't let me do painting. She made me sit in the reading corner instead. I don't like reading...'

He was still complaining as Alex bundled them into the car. 'It's a shame you're not happy, James, but it's nearly the end of term, you know, and you'll be able to look forward to the summer holidays.' She glanced at him. 'Fasten your seat belt. You know, if you want to paint, you have to remember to keep your brushes to yourself and resist the temptation to daub the other children. Mrs Coleman said she'd explained it to you. Perhaps you could tell her that you'll be sensible if she'll let you have another go.'

'Yes—well, I don't like her, either.' James clamped

his lips together and squinted at the road ahead through narrowed eyes.

Alex checked that Sarah was safely installed in the back seat with a good space between her and her brother, and then drove towards the school. It was about a mile away from the house, along a winding country lane, and the drive was a pleasant one, though even that was not enough to calm her increasingly stretched nerves.

Had she taken on too much, making the decision to look after her brother's children? In itself, it shouldn't have been too difficult, but alongside the new job at Oakdale Hospital, and adding in the fact that she'd had to move to Somerset to be close to where they used to live, the stress was beginning to pile up. Her once calm and orderly life had been turned upside down. Everything was chaotic.

Not that there was much she could do about any of it. The car accident that had injured her brother and his wife had wreaked havoc with all their lives.

'Bye,' she said when they arrived at the school. 'Take care. Be good.' She kissed the children and hugged them and then watched for a minute or two as they met up with friends and went to stand in line for their teachers.

Then she headed back along the main road to town and her new place of work. The hospital was a few miles inland from the sea, and she drove towards it now, past the soft, rolling hills of the Quantocks, their slopes richly carpeted with heather and occasional dark oases of green woodland.

At the hospital, she parked in her designated place, and then made her way to the A and E department. She pulled in a deep breath, straightened her shoulders and walked into the main reception area. This was a new challenge, a difficult task that she'd been assigned, and she would need to have her wits about her. She was a little apprehensive about what lay in store, but she was determined to make the best effort she could.

Her first impression of the unit was a pleasant one. Everything seemed relatively calm in there. The treatment rooms were occupied, with patients being tended by medical staff, and the whiteboard showed the status of admissions and stage of treatment.

Across the room, a doctor was standing by the desk, chatting to nurses, until, after a moment or two, he noticed Alex and came over to her. He was good looking, long and lean, immaculately dressed in dark trousers and a white, self-striped shirt, finished off with a muted tie in a pale shade of blue.

'Hi, there,' he said. 'Can I help you? I guess you're not a patient, or you'd have been directed to the waiting room.' His voice was easy on the ear, deep and well modulated, and there was a warmth about him that made it seem as though he was genuinely interested in her. He had black hair, cut short to frame his angular features, and his eyes were a vivid blue, alert and enquiring.

'That's right. Yes, thank you, I'm looking for...' she checked his name badge '...Dr Brooksby.' She smiled. 'I believe I've found the very man I want.'

He laughed. 'Well, that's not something I get to hear every day...but more than welcome, all the same, coming from someone who looks as good as you.' His glance shimmered over her, taking in the tailored, dove-grey suit she was wearing, with the pencil-slim skirt and the jacket that nipped in at her slender waist. His gaze came to rest on the burnished, silky swathe of her hair, lingering there for a while longer than was absolutely necessary.

'Anything I can do for you, you only have to say.' His manner was open and friendly, his blue eyes quizzical, inviting her to offload any worries or problems she might have.

'That's very kind of you.' She let her glance roam fleetingly around the department. 'I must say, it's good to come to an A and E unit and find the atmosphere so relaxed and easygoing. That must be quite unusual, or perhaps I've come at a particularly quiet time? Either way, I imagine your bosses must be pleased with the way you run things around here.'

'You'd think so, but actually they're bringing in new management. And as to being quiet, it only appears that way—we've just finished dealing with the aftermath of a road accident, and now we're taking a breather and making the most of things...before the new manager comes along to sort us out and tell us where we've been going wrong.' His mouth made a rueful slant. 'Sorry to offload that way. It's a sore point. He's supposed to put in an appearance some time today so we're all on tenterhooks.'

A small ripple of dismay ran through her. This was definitely not going to be an easy ride, judging by his comments. 'Oh, I see.' She reflected on what he'd said for a second or two, before venturing, 'Maybe he'll find that everything's perfectly in order?'

'What a refreshing idea.' He gave a wry smile. 'Unfortunately, I very much doubt it. He's a bean-counter, sent to trim us to the bone. This is the NHS, after all.' He pressed his well-shaped lips together briefly. 'Enough of my problems, though. What can I do for you, Miss...?'

'It's Dr,' she answered carefully. 'Dr Draycott. Alex.'

He stared at her, his mouth dropping open a little until he recovered himself. 'Alex Draycott?' he repeated, cautiously.

She nodded. 'That's right.' She studied him. 'You look as though you're taken aback by that. Is something wrong?'

Slowly, he shook his head. 'No, not at all. It's just that...well...you're a woman.'

She smiled. 'That's very observant of you.'

He was still staring, and she prompted gently, 'Is that likely to be a problem for you?'

'Uh... No, of course not. It's just that, well, Alex is a man's name, isn't it? We were expecting a man.' He frowned, looking at her in a slightly accusatory fashion. 'And I thought you were maybe a relative concerned about one of our patients.'

'I'm not.'

'No, I see that now.' His frown deepened. 'So you're the new doctor/manager who's come to join the unit?'

She hesitated. 'Um...bean-counter was how you put it, I think.' She gave him a wryly amused look, her grey eyes taking in his obvious unease. 'It's odd how defensive people become whenever managers arrive on the scene, isn't it? And it's totally unnecessary, you know—after all, we're all in this together, aren't we, working for the greater good of the hospital? I have a job to do, but it doesn't have to put us at odds with one another.'

'Doesn't it?' He appeared sceptical. 'Perhaps you aren't aware that your reputation has gone before you? We've all heard how you wielded the axe at your last hospital. There were job cuts and ward closures.'

She sent him a quick look, her grey eyes troubled. 'Sometimes, no matter how you try to preserve what's already in place, it becomes impossible in the end, if budget restrictions are too tight. But in all fairness to me, I did manage to keep the department open, I kept the job losses down to natural wastage, and I put new measures in place so that some patients could be tended to elsewhere.'

'You didn't stay around, though, did you, once your job was done?' His blue gaze was flint sharp. 'Was that because you found the atmosphere suddenly less friendly?'

The attack was swift and unexpected and Alex felt a knot tighten in her stomach. 'I left for personal reasons,' she said, a catch in her voice. 'It was nothing to do with the job. My circumstances changed, and my contract had come to an end anyway. I chose not to renew it.' Even the memory of that time, when she had first heard about her brother's accident, was enough to make the blood drain from her face.

He studied her thoughtfully, and perhaps he realised that he had touched a nerve, because he said softly, 'I'm sorry. That was uncalled-for on my part. Put it down to tension, if you will. We're all a little on edge here, uncertain about what the future holds for us and for the department. Of course, you were just doing your job.'

He laid a hand lightly on her elbow. 'Perhaps I should take you along to the doctors' lounge and offer you a cup of coffee? It was thoughtless of me not to suggest it before. It's just that your arrival threw me off balance for a minute or two. We weren't expecting you until later this morning.'

'No, I realise that…but I thought it would be as well to come in early and get the feel of the place.'

'I expect I would have done the same,' he said, leading the way along the corridor to the lounge. 'I think you'll like it here. Everyone's very friendly, and we work well together for the most part. The only real problem is the one that faces all hospital trusts. We're struggling with budget deficits and the department is under threat of being closed down. Dr Langton, the chief executive, has been warning us that it's a possibility.'

Alex frowned as they entered the room. 'I was appointed by the board to try to make sure that doesn't happen.'

His mouth made a wry twist. 'Well, let's hope you can work wonders. It's a difficult job you've taken on, and in some ways management can turn out to be a poisoned chalice. Not many would want to do it.'

'I suppose not.' She was thoughtful for a moment or two. 'But in all the years I've worked as a doctor, I've come across things that aren't working as well as they should, and over time I began to think that perhaps if I went into management, I might be able to make a difference.'

'You've obviously put a lot of thought into it. For myself, I prefer hands-on medicine one hundred per cent of the time.'

'And I'm sure that must be the reason you've done so well for yourself. I've heard nothing but good things about you, from the occasional article in the press and the medical journals, as well as from Dr Langton. You've been at Oakdale for some time, haven't you?'

'Yes, for several years. I came here originally as a registrar and then I was offered the post of consultant. I love it here…it's like a home from home for me.' He grinned. 'Mind you, I think medicine's in my blood. It's been there ever since I was a child, pretending to be an army surgeon to my wounded toy soldiers.'

She laughed softly, trying to imagine him as a youngster. 'I can see you in my mind's eye,' she said, 'bandaging your action figures. Though I expect most boys wouldn't bother too much with those who'd been invalided out.' Still, even James had made a crutch for a toy soldier that had lost its plastic leg, painstakingly taping the wooden stick to its hand.

He made a wry smile. 'Maybe not.' He went over to the coffee machine to one side of the room and poured hot liquid into two mugs. 'Do you take milk and sugar?' he asked, and she nodded.

'Both, thanks.' She sniffed the air appreciatively. 'That smells good.'

He nodded. 'It's one thing I look forward to around here. Decent coffee.' He waved her to a chair. 'Have a seat and make yourself comfortable.' He came to sit close to her and swallowed his coffee, savouring the taste and taking a moment to relax. 'So, tell me about yourself,' he said quietly, his glance moving over her and coming to rest briefly on the smooth shapeliness of her long legs. 'From what I heard, you've moved here from Herefordshire? I suppose that means this job must have had some special appeal for you?'

'I thought it would give me the best of both worlds, the chance to work in paediatric emergency, which is what I like doing best—it's what I specialised in—and at the same time it allows me to take on a managerial role.' She clasped her cup in both hands, feeling the comforting warmth spread slowly through her. 'But the main reason I'm here is because I have family who have settled in Somerset.'

'Your parents?'

She shook her head. 'My brother and his family. My parents do have a home here, but they're away at the moment, because of my father's job. He's a trouble-shooter for an oil company, so he tends to travel a lot.'

He gave a brief smile. 'That's something we have in common, then. My parents have always travelled far and wide, as far back as I can remember.' A fleeting sadness came into his eyes and she studied him thoughtfully for a moment or two. Had that been a problem for him?

'Perhaps I've been lucky,' she murmured. 'My parents were always there for me while I was growing up. It was only when I started work as a doctor that they began to travel further afield.' She would have liked to ask him about his family, but something warned her that this might be the wrong time to do that. She didn't want to blunder into areas that might cause problems, especially on her first day. Perhaps when she knew him a little better...

'It must have been difficult for you, uprooting yourself,' he said. 'Did you manage to find a place of your own, or are you renting while you look around?'

'I thought about renting. Back in Herefordshire I'd taken out a lease on a flat, but it ran out—another reason why it seemed feasible to make the move to Somerset. I planned to do the same down here, but then I saw this big, old house on the market, going for a song, and I decided to snap it up. It was purely an impulsive action—not like me at all, but something about it appealed to me. Of course, the reason it was going so cheap is because it needs a lot of work...' She pulled a face. 'And the owner wanted a quick sale.'

'But things are working out fairly well for you, overall?'

She nodded. 'I think so. I hope so.' She drank her coffee and looked around. 'As I see it right now, though, my biggest challenge is going to be this job. According to Dr Langton, the hospital is deep in debt and the accident and emergency department is at risk. I want to do all I can to keep it safe, but it means taking some measures that might not be all that popular.'

She braced herself. 'In fact, I think I ought to make

a start on getting to grips with the job right now—it's been good to spend a few minutes in here, and I appreciate you taking a break and having coffee with me, but perhaps now I should start to familiarise myself with the way things work around here.' She glanced at him. 'Mr Langton suggested you might be available this morning to give me an insight into the way you run things—where and when you use agency staff, for instance—and perhaps you could let me see your drugs list, so I can gain some idea of expenditure in that area?'

He frowned. 'Are you sure you want to do that on your first day? Wouldn't you prefer to take a general look around and get to know some of the staff? I'm sure they're all anxious to meet their new colleague.'

She nodded. 'Of course, and I want to meet them, but I don't want to intrude on them while they're busy. I'll definitely make time to introduce myself to them through the course of the day. For the moment, though, I think it would be better if I were to spend time with you...going through the workings of the department.'

'Hmm...yes...' He seemed to be distracted all at once, and glanced at the watch on his wrist. 'Unfortunately, I have an emergency to attend,' he said, getting to his feet. 'So I'm afraid you'll have to forgive me. Maybe we could get together some other time?'

She frowned. 'But I understood that you would be free from clinical duties this morning for a couple of hours. Is that not so?'

He nodded. 'But then this emergency came up...a thoracic injury, flail chest. He should be coming back from Radiology any time now.'

Alex stood up. 'But I was really hoping to make a start...'

'Of course. I appreciate that, but, you know, I don't

actually have the figures you want right at this moment… you've caught me on the hop a bit there, and I really do have to go and check on my patient.' He gave her an encouraging smile. 'Perhaps it would be best if you go and find our registrar. He'll help guide you around the department. Ask him anything you want to know. He'll be only too happy to help you.'

'But I…' Alex gazed at him in confusion.

'I'm sure you'll soon have all the information you want.' He laid his hands on her shoulders, his grasp gentle, his fingers warm and strong, causing a ripple of heat to flow through her. It was odd, but all at once, as he held her, she became strangely conscious of her femininity. It was confusing. She was so used to taking charge, of being in control, and yet with just one simple act he had made her overwhelmingly conscious of his powerful masculinity.

'Take time to ease yourself into the job,' he said. 'It will all work out, you'll see.' Then he smiled, his blue eyes homing in on her face, taking in the faint line that creased her brow and the look of uncertainty that hovered around her eyes and mouth. 'You'll be fine, Alex,' he murmured. 'It's good to have you here.'

Then he released her and strode briskly away, leaving Alex to stare after him in a bewildered fashion. Somehow, she couldn't help thinking he was fobbing her off, albeit in a kind and gentle manner, and if he was an example of what she might expect from the staff here, it was clear she was in for a tricky time from the outset. His easy charm had befuddled her senses and she was finding it hard to come to terms with that. It knocked her off track, and she wasn't used to that at all.

CHAPTER TWO

'IT CAN never be easy, can it, seeing your loved ones this way...even if you're a doctor?' The nurse was sympathetic, sensing Alex's distress. 'All I can say is that your brother's condition is stable at the moment. I hope that might be some comfort to you.'

'It is. Thank you.' Alex dragged her gaze away from the hospital bed. It was heart-rending to see her younger brother lying there, looking so fragile. He was deathly pale, his hair dark against his pillow, various tubes and drains coming from his body, and there were cables linking him to monitors. Ross, who had always been so vigorous and who could be relied on to brighten any room with his presence, was just a shadow of his former self.

'It was a nasty accident,' the nurse added, 'and there was a considerable amount of lung damage because of the broken ribs he suffered. That's why he's still on the ventilator, but he's receiving pain medication, so at least he should be fairly comfortable.'

Alex nodded. 'I know you're all doing everything you can for him.'

The nurse made a note of Ross's heart rate and blood-oxygen levels. 'Have you been to see his wife? I know she was badly injured, too.'

'Yes, I make a point of looking in on her every day. The doctors are treating her for a laceration to her liver, but they found there was some damage to her kidney as well. She's been through surgery, and she's in much the same situation as Ross, reliant on tubes and drips and monitors. Even so, she's fretting over the children.'

'I'm sorry.' The nurse laid a hand on Alex's arm. 'It must be very worrying for you, especially with the youngsters to consider. I think it's good that you've been bringing them in to see their parents, though.'

Alex sucked in a deep breath. 'Better for them to see what's happening, I thought. Otherwise their imaginations might cause them to worry even more. Their grandparents will be coming over at the weekend, so that should help to cheer them up a little.' Her mouth flattened. 'My parents have found it hard, being so far away when it happened. But they've worked out a schedule so that one or other of them will be over here to spend time with Ross for a good part of the week.'

'You said they were working abroad, is that right?'

Alex nodded. 'My father works for an oil company. It's a really difficult time for him right now, but all he can think about is Ross.'

'That's understandable.'

Alex spent a few more minutes by her brother's bedside until she finally had to acknowledge that time was getting on. She had taken a late lunch, but now she needed to go back to work. Reluctantly, she made her way to the ground floor of the hospital, heading for A and E.

Things were no easier in that department, either. Her work colleagues were uneasy, doubtful about her intentions in her role as manager, and worried regarding their job security.

Alex tried not to let it unsettle her. She would try to put their minds at ease, and she would do the best she could for the department. After all, she was her father's daughter, wasn't she, strong, determined, willing to put in every effort for a cause she felt to be worthwhile? And in these difficult times keeping the A and E department viable and open for business was surely the best outcome for everyone?

Today, though, she was here in her role as doctor, and now she glanced at the whiteboard as she walked over to the main desk. 'Katie, I'll take the three-year-old with fever in treatment room two.'

'Okay.' The triage nurse handed her the child's admission notes.

Alex headed for the treatment room. As she had told Callum, landing this job had given her the best of both worlds—management took up fifty per cent of her time, and working as a consultant emergency paediatrician took up the rest.

She glanced at the triage nurse once more as she passed by the desk. 'Is Dr Brooksby about?' She'd been on the lookout for him all morning.

Katie hesitated, tucking a strand of glossy black hair behind one ear. 'Um…last I saw of him he was in Resus.'

'Hmm.' Alex had already checked, and he certainly wasn't there now. 'Thanks, Katie. I'm sure I'll manage to hunt him out.'

She found him a minute or two later in the treatment room next to hers. He was checking an ECG printout, while at the same time assuring his patient that he was in safe hands.

'You've had a minor heart attack,' he told the middle-aged man lying on the bed, 'but we have things under control now. The medication should help to open up your blood vessels, and things should soon start to feel a lot easier. Just keep pulling on the oxygen.'

He glanced across the room as Alex put her head round the door. 'So there you are,' she said. 'I'm glad I've run into you at last. I've been searching everywhere for you.'

'What it is to be popular,' he murmured, winking at his patient. He adjusted the settings on the medication pump and checked the drip. 'What could be better than having a gorgeous young woman seeking you out?'

Alex pulled a face. He obviously knew how to charm the birds out of the trees. 'I know you've a lot on,' she murmured, 'but I really need you to go over the drug expenditure figures with me some time soon—and I noticed your casualty cards aren't up to date. We need to get them filled in so that we can check waiting times.'

'Yes, of course.' He nodded agreeably. 'I've been working on it. We always try to fill these things in on time, you know, but it can get pretty frantic around here, and it isn't always easy to keep up with the admin paperwork.' He sent her an engaging smile, inviting her to agree with him, his blue gaze shimmering over her so that she found herself unwillingly caught up in his masculine magnetism and his easygoing manner.

'Yes, well…um…' She blinked. It was thoroughly disconcerting, the way he managed to tip her off balance. What was she thinking? She made an effort to pull herself together. 'Maybe we could get together for a few minutes as soon as you've finished here and go through a few of the items we need to get to grips with? I'll be next door in the paediatric bay, working with a patient.'

'Sounds like a good idea. I'll see what I can do.'

He was totally relaxed, completely unfazed by her request.

'Good. That's encouraging.' She slanted him a brief, searching glance. 'See you in a few minutes, then,' she murmured.

She left the room, with a friendly nod to the patient, who was looking much better than he had done a short time ago, and went to see the toddler next door.

The infant was lying on a trolley bed, clearly feeling too wretched and uncomfortable to be held in his mother's arms. A nurse was cooling him by holding a damp cloth to his forehead, but as Alex entered, she went to step aside.

'That's all right, Charlotte,' Alex said. 'You go on with what you're doing. I'm sure he'll feel much better for it.'

Alex smiled at the boy's mother. 'Mrs Stanhope, I understand Tom has been poorly for several days?'

The woman nodded. 'It's horrible to see him like this. He won't eat, he keeps being sick, and now he has a temperature. I'm really worried about him.'

'Of course you are.' She looked at Tom. 'The poor little chap looks really miserable.' She spoke gently to the boy. 'I'm going to try to make you feel a bit more comfortable, Tom,' she murmured, 'but I need to listen to your chest first...and maybe look at your tummy. Is that all right?'

The toddler looked uncertain, his lower lip trembling, and the nurse attempted to distract him by producing a teddy bear from a basket at the side of the bed. 'Look,' she said, 'Teddy's feeling poorly, too. His tummy hurts.'

Tom's eyes widened and he gazed at the toy, putting out a hand to feel his silky fur. Alex sent the nurse a grateful glance and gently began her examination. When she had finished, she said softly, 'That's all done now, Tom. You were very brave.'

The boy clutched the teddy to him. 'Teddy hurting,' he said. 'He feels sick.' Suddenly all the colour left his face and the nurse promptly moved forward with a kidney dish, holding it in place as he began to retch.

Alex went to sit next to the child's mother. 'We tested Tom's urine earlier,' she told her, 'and it looks as though he has a urinary infection of some kind. It's quite possible that his kidneys are inflamed, so I'm going to start him on a course of antibiotics. I'll give him the first dose by injection so that it will start to act quicker, but the rest we'll give by mouth.' She glanced at Charlotte and gave instructions about the medications. 'And that includes something to ease the pain and bring down his temperature.'

'Thank you.' Mrs Stanhope seemed anxious. 'How long will it be before he's better?'

'It could be two or three weeks... I feel we should admit him to hospital so that we can keep an eye on him—I know that's probably worrying for you, but we have to make sure we deal with this properly, right from the start, and of course that way he'll be on hand when we get the results of his urine culture back from the lab.'

Mrs Stanhope nodded. 'It's all right. I just want what's best for him.'

'That's good. I'll make the arrangements.' Alex stood up and went back to her small patient. 'Just a tiny jab,' she told him, preparing the antibiotic injection. 'It will all be over in a second or two.'

A few minutes later, she left the infant and his mother in Charlotte's capable hands, and went to look for Callum. He was nowhere to be found, not in any of the treatment rooms, or in Resus, or even out by the ambulance bay. She checked the quadrangle where staff sometimes took a breath of fresh air between seeing patients, but he wasn't there either.

She frowned. 'Any sign of Dr Brooksby?' she asked Katie as the nurse walked towards the reception area.

'None at all.' Katie shrugged lightly. 'I expect he's gone back to Resus.'

Alex suppressed a sigh. 'Not to worry,' she said. 'I dare say I'll catch up with him sooner or later.'

Katie nodded. 'That's how it is down here, unfortunately. Everyone's so busy.'

Alex's mouth made a flat line. Busy or not, they all had to work together to help streamline the department, or before too long the trust board would be calling for closures. One way or another they had to find time to co-operate with her. 'If anyone needs me, I'm heading over to Pathology,' she said.

She would take Tom's sample over to the lab herself for culture, and ask if the results could be hurried up. Once they knew the bacterial culprit, they could choose the most appropriate treatment for the child. The wide-spectrum antibiotic she had used was a catch-all for the most likely bacteria, but given the severity of the infection it was possible that they needed to use something more specific to counteract it.

She walked into the lab a few minutes later, shooting a quick glance around the room. Over to one side, by the workbenches, she saw a by-now familiar figure huddled over a rack of test tubes.

'So here you are,' she murmured, after handing over the specimen to the lab technician. 'I never would have thought to find you here, Dr Brooksby.'

He straightened, turning to look at her. 'I'm checking on some samples I sent for testing. I want to see how things are coming along, you know.'

'Really?' She inspected the label of the sample he was studying. 'Since when were you working with the staff on the geriatric ward? Was your patient sent there from A and E?'

He frowned. 'It's the wrong sample,' he said. 'My patient's elderly, but not geriatric.'

She sent him a cautious look, her grey eyes doubtful. 'You wouldn't be deliberately trying to avoid me, would you, Dr Brooksby?'

'Callum, please. Now, why on earth would I want to do that?'

'That's what I'm wondering. Only I was under the impression we were going to meet up in the treatment room a while ago. Didn't you agree to that?'

'Of course—though I believe what I actually said was that it was a good idea, which is not necessarily the same thing as saying I'd be there. You can't guarantee anything in the hectic atmosphere of the A and E department.' He searched among the papers in a wire tray and grasped one in triumph. 'Found it,' he said. He held it up to her. 'My patient's results.'

She stared at him in frustration. 'Why is it that I have the feeling you're playing games with me?' she asked. 'You haven't actually completed the drug lists, have you? Or tried to catch up on filling in the waiting times on your casualty cards?'

He leaned back against the workbench, his long legs crossed at the ankles. 'Actually…uh…no, you're right. I haven't.' His mouth made a rueful shape. 'As I said before, I'm much more of a hands-on medic than someone who concentrates on keeping his paperwork up to date.'

His gaze ran over her, appreciation lighting his eyes as he took in the shapeliness of her figure outlined by her classically styled dress. 'I know you want to get on with updating your numbers and counting the financial cost of everything, but is it so essential that it's done right this minute? You've only been here a short time. Surely you need to take some time to settle in? And how about giving everyone a bit of leeway? Give them a chance to get used to the idea of you being around. That way people would be so much more on your side.'

She sighed. 'That would be so satisfying, wouldn't it…just to let everything hang easy for a while, gain a little popularity and then sit back and enjoy the ride?' There was amusement in her tone. 'I hardly think that's going to happen.' Her grey glance meshed with his.

'You don't?' He frowned.

'I don't. Why do you imagine I was brought in here? The executives were hardly going to appoint a pussycat to monitor things, were they?' She didn't wait for an answer. 'The hospital budget is badly overdrawn and the trust has to make drastic cuts if the services the public want and expect are to survive.' She drew in a deep breath. 'So that's where I come in. I have the task of auditing the department to find out where savings can be made…and if I don't come up with the right answers, the whole emergency unit is at risk—so it's not just my job on the line, but those of everyone who works here.' She studied him. 'You do understand that, don't you?'

He lifted his shoulders. 'Of course I do…it's just that I don't see why you can't hold fire for a while. The trust has been overspending for years—a few weeks isn't going to make much difference to the grand scheme of things, is it?'

She shook her head, causing her chestnut curls to swirl and shimmer under the overhead lights. 'That's where you're wrong, I'm afraid. I have to report back to the board at the end of each month. They aren't going to look kindly on me or the department if I show them an empty file.'

He watched the cloud of burnished hair drift and settle. 'You realise, don't you,' he countered, 'that the board will do what it wants, no matter what facts and figures you manage to produce? If they're set on closing the department, then ultimately that's what they'll do. They just need you to give them the firepower.'

She regarded him steadily. 'Well, I don't think that way about it at all. I believe that I can make a difference. I believe we can make savings in lots of ways. In fact, going on my experience with a young patient this morning, I've decided I want to start a separate audit into the treatment of children with urinary infections...let's see if we can't cut down on the number of ultrasound scans, and choose our drugs more wisely, so that we're not prescribing expensive ones where generic drugs will do better.'

She warmed to her theme. 'It's just a question of devising the forms for people to fill in whenever they treat a child—and at the end we'll collate all the information and see what savings we can come up with.'

He looked at her, aghast. 'Good grief, woman...don't you have enough to do without getting started on audits that aren't even part of your remit?'

'But it all comes down to the same thing in the end, don't you see? Savings are at the heart of everything.'

He relaxed, beginning to smile at her. 'I can see

why you got the job…and I have to admire your persistence. You're so full of energy and enthusiasm—but there's more to life than work, you know. Where do you find time in all that for a social life—that thing called 'fun'—boyfriends, and so on?'

His glance drifted over her. 'You're a very attractive woman, and I'd have thought men would be queuing up to ask you out. Yet from what I've heard you don't have a significant other, you don't join the staff at the local pub—or even share lunch breaks with them. Isn't there something missing from your life?' His gaze became thoughtful. 'Or perhaps you've been hurt…' he said softly. 'Maybe someone let you down?'

She stared at him blankly for a moment or two. So he thought she was attractive? He'd said it before, but even so, it gave her a warm, fuzzy feeling, hearing him say it again. But as to the rest, when did she have time to socialise? Any spare time she had at work was spent on visiting her brother and his wife, and after work she needed to take care of the children.

'I see the hospital grapevine has been busy,' she murmured. 'Is nobody's life private around here?' She frowned. 'Though I could say the same for you. Snatches of gossip I've heard tell me you don't ever settle to a relationship—fear of commitment is how they put it, I think.'

He laughed. 'I don't see fear coming into it. Life's too short, and I'm having a good time just as I am—being footloose and fancy-free. Why would I want to change things?'

'Why indeed?' She smiled wryly. 'And much the same goes for me. I'm far too busy to even contemplate getting involved with anyone right now. Let the gossipmongers make of it what they will.'

'And they will, believe me.' He studied her. 'Why don't we fox them all and make a date for dinner—this evening, maybe? You should take time out, let yourself unwind a little.'

Unwind, with him? The thought had a dizzying effect on her. 'Thanks, but I really can't do that right now.' All the same, she conjured up a vision of the two of them together, taking a walk in the moonlight after a romantic meal at a restaurant, and all at once heat began to pool in her abdomen.

She couldn't let the idea take hold. It was impossible. She wasn't about to get involved with anyone, especially him, a man who seemed so laid back he made it seem as though she was positively racing through life in contrast. Anyway, she had far too much on her plate. The children relied on her to be there for them, her family life was chaotic, and, besides, he was simply trying to divert her, possibly even disarm her into the bargain, wasn't he?

His gaze flicked over her. 'That's a shame. Maybe some other time, then? I'm sure you'll feel all the better for a little rest and relaxation.'

She had the idea this was something he wouldn't give up on easily. 'I'll feel a whole lot better when I have your drug expenditure forms laid out on my desk,' she retorted swiftly. 'Along with a list of agency staff employed by the department over the last three months.'

She ignored his muffled groan as she made her way to the door. 'Any time in the next twenty-four hours will be fine.'

She was still debating how best to deal with Callum Brooksby when she made her way home later that day at the end of her shift. He was a thorn in her side, a devious, happy-go-lucky, aggravating man who gave the impression of being as difficult to catch as thistledown.

Every time she had him within her sights, he somehow managed to whisk himself away, out of reach.

'Look what we've found,' Sarah said excitedly, greeting Alex as she went to collect the children from her neighbour's house later that day. Sarah led the way into the kitchen. 'Auntie Jane showed us how to collect honey from the beehives in the orchard. We've been putting it into jars. It smells of flowers.'

Alex sniffed at the glass pot Sarah thrust under her nose. 'So it does,' she said. 'I expect the bees have been visiting the apple blossom and the bramble bushes. That should make for good fruit later on in the season.'

She looked at Jane, who was standing by the fridge, looking pale and tired. 'You've been busy. Are you sure you should be taking on all this work? I feel bad enough that I'm asking you to watch the children for me.'

'Oh, I like having them around. Anyway, I volunteered to have them after school, and it's no trouble to collect a bit of honey.' Jane smiled. 'I expect you had no idea what a wealth of treasures you were gaining when you bought the property next door. Of course, I didn't let the children go near the hives when I collected the honeycombs, but they loved seeing the end result. They were fascinated.'

'It tastes funny,' James said, screwing up his nose. 'Yuk.'

'I like it,' Sarah said happily. 'We had some on pancakes and they were scrumptious.'

'It sounds as though you had a lot of fun.' Alex watched the children as they carefully spooned the golden honey into scrupulously clean jars. Jane sat down by the table and let them get on with it for a while.

'How have you been feeling, Jane?' Alex asked,

giving her a long, thoughtful look. 'Have you been back to see your doctor?'

'Not yet.' Jane shook her head, and at Alex's small murmur of protestation she added, 'I know...I keep putting it off, and I shouldn't, but what's he going to do for me but give me more tablets? Nothing's working, so I might as well put up with things as they are.' As she spoke, she absently rubbed her back. 'The only that really gets to me is this pain, but I suppose I can take painkillers for that.' She sighed. 'But I guess that's old age creeping up on me.'

'I don't think so, Jane. I think it's something that needs to be investigated.'

She might have said more, but there was a brief tap on the kitchen door just then, and a moment later it opened, as a visitor stepped into the kitchen.

Alex pulled in a sharp breath.

'Hi, Aunt Jane,' Callum Brooksby said, going over to Jane and giving her a hug. 'How's my favourite aunt?'

'Oh, it's so good to see you,' Jane said, smiling. She looked at him with genuine affection. 'I was hoping you'd come round.'

He nodded. 'I know I've left it a little bit longer than usual. It's been a busy time lately, what with work and overseeing the builders at home.' Then he straightened and looked around, interested in seeing who had come to take tea with her.

His gaze met Alex's and they both stared at one another in shock.

'Alex?'

'Callum?' She blinked.

Callum frowned, his dark brows drawing together in a straight line. 'What on earth are you doing here?'

'I...I bought the house next door,' she said, stumbling

a little over the words, still in shock. 'That's how I came to know your aunt—she's been good to me, looking after the children while I'm at work.'

'Children?' His expression became incredulous as he turned his attention to James and Sarah, happily spilling honey over the scrubbed pine table and the assembled jars. 'Good grief.' He looked back at Alex. 'I don't know you at all, do I?'

Jane looked from one to the other, a puzzled expression on her face. 'So you two have met before this?' She frowned. 'Of course, it must be the hospital—it didn't occur to me. I knew you were in Paediatrics, Alex, and, Callum, you're in Emergency, but of course you must meet up on occasion.'

'All the while, Aunt Jane,' Callum agreed, a look of wonder coming over his face. 'We work in the same department.'

Alex was still trying to get over the shock. She studied him carefully. 'So you're the nephew?'

His head went back. 'Nephew? Why, who's been talking about me?' He looked at Jane, a glimmer of amusement coming into his eyes. 'It has to be you, doesn't it? You've only told her good things, I hope?'

'As if I'd do anything else,' Jane answered cheerfully.

Callum put an arm around her in a gesture of affection. 'She practically brought me up,' he told Alex. 'She's been like a mother to me.'

Jane patted his hand.

'Auntie Jane, can we go and play in the garden?' James asked, coming over to her and beginning to tug on her skirt.

'Yes, of course.' Jane's glance ran over him, and a line

indented her brow. 'Perhaps we'd better get you cleaned up a bit first, though.'

James looked down at the honey trails that streaked his T-shirt. 'It's all right,' he said. 'I can do that.' He pulled his shirt up to his mouth and began to lick the sticky patches.

Sarah pulled a face. 'You are so gross,' she said in disgust.

'Why?' James responded, astonished. 'Am not.'

Callum began to laugh. 'Was I ever like that?' he asked his aunt, and she nodded. 'All the time.' She turned her attention back to the boy. 'I'll get a cloth.'

'No, don't do that. I'll see to everything,' Alex said, intervening when Jane would have stood up. 'You stay there and rest. You've done enough for one day.' She helped the children to wash their hands, before sending them outside, and then she began to clear up the mess on the kitchen table.

Jane tried to lend a hand, gathering up spoons and honeycombs, but Alex gently took them from her. 'You're already hurting,' she remonstrated softly. 'Let me do it.'

Callum frowned, looking at his aunt. 'What's this about you hurting? Is it your back again?'

Jane nodded. 'It's nothing for you to worry about,' she said. 'I'll be fine.'

'Hmm. Why don't you go and sit down in the living room, and I'll bring you a cup of tea? I'm sure you'll be much more comfortable in there.'

His aunt smiled. 'You're probably right. What a good idea.' She looked from one to the other. 'Anyway, I expect you young things have plenty to say to one another.'

She left the room, and a moment later, still frowning,

Callum began to help with the clearing up. He placed sticky jars on the drainer, and flicked the switch on the kettle.

'I still can't get over seeing you here,' he said, looking at Alex. 'It's a small world, isn't it?'

'It certainly seems that way.'

He began to prepare a tray, setting out a cup and saucer, along with a plate of home-made biscuits. He smiled as he peered into the cookie jar. 'She's always loved baking,' he said, helping himself to an oat biscuit. He offered the jar to Alex. 'She let me help her when I was a child, but I'm not sure my efforts were all that brilliant. They tended to be misshapen, and a bit cracked around the edges.'

'Much like mine, then,' Alex said, helping herself to a biscuit, and they both chuckled. She looked at him, trying to imagine him as a child, mixing cookie dough or playing outside in the long garden. 'You said she was like a mother to you...does that mean you lived here with her?'

He nodded. 'For a good deal of the time, anyway.' He looked around. 'I love this house. It feels like home to me. In fact, I love the whole area.'

'And your parents? Where were they?'

'Mostly abroad, either in Africa or South America. I didn't see a lot of them in my teen years because they were off working on projects to improve the health of the underprivileged children out there. Things are much the same nowadays.'

'That must have been difficult for you.' Her grey eyes were sympathetic. She remembered how sad he'd been when he'd first mentioned his parents. 'You must have missed them.'

'I suppose so.' He frowned. 'But my aunt and uncle

made up for it. They gave me a decent home life and showed me what it was like to be part of a loving family. Until then, nothing had ever been stable. My parents were always busy, working all hours, and we moved around constantly. There was no chance of putting down any roots.'

Alex was sad for him. He'd obviously not known what a loving family was like in his earlier years.

'You were lucky, then, that your aunt was able to take you in.'

'Yes, I was.' He poured tea into the cup. 'I'd better go and check on her, and take her the tea.'

Alex glanced at him and hesitated a second or two before saying, 'You know she's having problems with her blood pressure, don't you?'

He nodded. 'It was diagnosed some time ago. She's been prescribed a number of different medications over the past year or so.'

'Yes, that's what she said. But it seems to me that whatever her GP's giving her isn't working, and I suspect that's because he hasn't yet found the root cause of her problem. I'm wondering if she ought to have some tests done at the hospital. She's suffering from a number of symptoms that need to be investigated…headaches, dizziness, pain in her back.'

A line etched itself into his brow. 'Her doctor's been taking care of her for years, though. She trusts him, and it's no easy thing to get her to go along to see anyone else.'

Alex's mouth flattened. 'Even so…I don't see how she can go on this way. She doesn't look at all well. Something needs to be done. In fact, I feel really guilty that I took her up on her offer to look after the children. It worries me that I'm putting too much on her.' She pulled in a deep breath. 'And I don't believe she's coping too well with the house and garden either. The weeds are beginning to overtake the borders, and it's all much more than she can manage.'

Callum gave Alex a perplexed stare. 'I mended the fence and tidied up the rockery a couple of weeks ago.'

Alex finished wiping the table with a flourish. 'I'm sure the stress of keeping up with the maintenance is taking a toll of her. Is there any chance you could arrange a more regular schedule? Find a local gardener who will come along and tidy things up, perhaps?'

He didn't say a word for a moment or two, but simply studied her as though he was deep in thought.

'You're very good at this sort of thing, aren't you?' he said at last, a note of wonder in his voice.

'This sort of thing?' She frowned. 'I'm afraid I'm not following you.'

'Organising people…deciding what needs to be done. I get the strongest feeling that not only am I being audited at work, but now you're taking stock of how I conduct my personal life as well.' He turned his blue gaze on her. 'I'm obviously done for. Maybe I should give in, here and now?'

Alex felt warm colour fill her cheeks. 'Well, that would be a good idea,' she said, giving a self-conscious laugh. 'That would make things easier all round, wouldn't it?'

He gave a wry smile. 'You'll find I don't surrender that easily.'

CHAPTER THREE

'I'M ALL done disturbing you, angel,' Callum murmured as the two-year-old girl fretted and tossed restlessly on the bed. 'No more horrible needles and stethoscopes and all that palaver.' He adjusted the medication drip, and then drew an ink line around the perimeter of the reddened area on the infant's leg. 'Let's hope that rash starts to shrink very soon,' he commented to the nurse who was assisting him. 'We'll make arrangements to admit her.'

He gave his attention back to the child. 'I think you'll be feeling a lot better before too long. I'm going to come back later to take a look at you, and I hope I'll find that nasty red area is beginning to disappear.' He carefully adjusted the bedcovers around the child, and gently brushed away the flaxen curls that massed around her hot cheeks. 'Just you go to sleep and let the medicine do its work. We'll have you right as rain in no time at all.'

Alex stood in the doorway of the treatment room, following his movements as he briefly checked the monitors. She had slipped into the room quietly, not wanting to disturb him, so he hadn't realised she was there, and for a moment or two she was able to watch him at work, undisturbed. It gave her a fascinating glimpse of the man behind the professional mask, and though she felt guilty at not announcing her presence, the compulsion to feast her gaze on him somehow overcame everything else.

He might well be a constant source of frustration to her where her budget schedule was concerned, but there was no doubting his commitment to the patients in his care. And even though paediatrics wasn't his specialty, she could see he had a sure instinct for dealing with children. This wasn't the first time she'd seen him tending to a youngster in A and E. It was clear that he had a genuine concern for his young charges, and the tenderness that she saw in him as he leaned over the cot brought an unexpected lump to her throat.

It made it all the more difficult that she had to confront him right now, but she had a job to do, regardless, and so she stiffened her shoulders and quietly claimed his attention. 'Might I have a word with you, please, Callum?' she said.

'Uh-oh...' Callum glanced at her, and then moved away from his young patient's bedside, giving final instructions to the nurse before walking towards the door where Alex waited, chart in hand. 'I've heard you use that tone of voice before...' he said under his breath, as he went out into the corridor. 'Quiet but insistent.' He frowned. 'It generally means I'm in trouble of some kind.'

'Not at all,' Alex murmured, following him and adding sweetly, 'You're obviously developing a persecution complex of some sort.'

He nodded, a faint grin tugging at his mouth. 'True. Funnily enough, it seemed to happen right about the time you joined the department.'

She tilted her head to one side. 'Guilty conscience, perhaps?'

He shook his head. 'Not true. I'm innocent as the day...at least, I think I am.' He glanced at the chart she was carrying. 'I expect that's one of mine, or you wouldn't be here. So what have I done this time?'

'It isn't just you,' Alex said in a sympathetic tone. 'I'm not singling you out. Please don't think that. I'm checking everyone's lab work to see if we can cut down on unnecessary testing...and here, looking at yours, I find you've ordered blood cultures, urine samples, swabs, to name just a few, for one small patient. Are you sure all these are really needed? Apart from the cost, we're laying a great strain on the laboratory facilities.'

He put on a stern face. 'If I hadn't needed them, I wouldn't have ordered them.'

'For a simple fever?'

'For a not-so-simple fever. The child was burning up, there was the beginning of a rash, and I suspect an insect bite of some sort that has led to a generalised infection which could lead to septicaemia.' He studied her. 'Do you really expect me to treat my patients without the proper diagnostic tools in place?'

'Of course not.' She smiled. 'I'm just checking, that's all. There's nothing wrong in making sure everyone keeps efficiency and cost awareness in the forefront of their mind, is there?'

He gave her a sour look. 'I'd appreciate it if you would take your checks elsewhere. I'm a consultant, remember, like yourself. I didn't get to this position by not knowing what I'm doing.'

'And I'm not suggesting otherwise. I see no reason why you should be so uptight about the situation,' she commented in a soothing tone, trying to placate him. 'We all want to do our best for our patients, and all I'm saying is that it's only natural that sometimes we might be a little over-zealous in our efforts.'

'I was not being over-zealous...I was being thorough. The child needs admission to hospital and treatment with an intravenous antibiotic. And if that doesn't meet with your approval, then I'm afraid it's too bad. That's how it's going to be.'

She put up a hand as though to ward him off. 'I'm not stopping you from doing anything. All I'm saying is that we all have to be responsible and think carefully about the tests we order. It's easy to slip into lax ways when you're not the one counting the cost. Unfortunately, that's down to me, and ultimately I have the job of making sure everyone complies with the new, stringent measures.'

He gave her a long look. 'It never ceases to amaze me how very single-minded you are. Don't you ever relax and watch the world go by without wanting to leap on its back and wrestle it into shape?'

She gave him a bewildered glance. 'I've a job to do. What do you expect?'

'I expect you to take a breather every once in a while.' He checked the gold watch on his wrist, and as he moved she noticed the sprinkling of dark hairs that ran along his bare forearm. His shirtsleeves were rolled back, to show an expanse of skin that was lightly bronzed. His arms were muscular, his wrists strong, giving the impression of overwhelming masculinity, and for a second or two she felt a sudden tide of awareness that surged throughout her body and left her momentarily breathless.

He began to speak again, his voice cutting into her thoughts, and she reluctantly dragged her gaze away. It was strange, these weird sensations of being out of control that had afflicted her of late. She wasn't used to feeling this way. Perhaps she was overworked, stressed, and the sheer amount of changes that were taking place in her life right now was making her unduly sensitive.

'It's getting late,' he said, 'and I don't suppose you've had a break since lunchtime. I certainly haven't. Why don't we take a few minutes to go and get a cup of coffee—in my office, perhaps?'

She shook her head. 'I'm sorry,' she answered abruptly, struggling to get a grip on herself, 'but I don't have time. I have to finish this data chart by the end of my shift, and I'm already running late.'

'We could use the time to go over the budget cuts you had in mind,' he suggested silkily, a glint coming into his blue eyes. 'Of course, if you'd rather leave it until another day, that's fine by me.' He started to turn away.

Alex was suspicious of his sudden apparent willingness to work with her, but his offer was one she could hardly refuse, was it? 'Uh…maybe I was a little hasty. I dare say I could spare a few minutes, since you appear to have had a change of heart.'

'Change of heart? Me? I've always been happy to go along with your suggestions.'

She gave him a withering look. 'Let's not push it, shall we?'

He laughed softly, and stopped for a moment to sign off his patient's treatment chart before dropping it into a tray on the reception desk. 'Are there any casualty cards for me to fill in?' he asked the girl behind the counter.

She checked, but then a moment later shook her head. 'Seems you're all up to date,' she told him.

Callum gave Alex a smug glance. 'See?' he said. 'Didn't I say I was only too happy to work with you?'

She made a wry smile. 'I heard you'd shut yourself in your office and barred all callers after your shift yesterday so that you could catch up with things.' He hadn't been in the best of moods, by all accounts. 'Amazing what a little gentle badgering will do, isn't it?'

He huffed, and gently but firmly took her by the arm, and ushered her into his office. He shut the door.

'Oh my!' she exclaimed softly, looking around. 'You've done well for yourself, landing a prize room like this, haven't you? It's much bigger than mine.' She gazed out of the large, Georgian-style window onto a wooded landscape to the side of the hospital. 'What a beautiful view.' After a moment, she turned back to face him. 'I'd find it really hard to work in here—I'd be so distracted by that lovely scenery.'

'I was going to say, hands off,' he said thoughtfully, 'but maybe we should do a swap—it might help to slow you down a bit. I've never met anyone before who was so driven—well, maybe one, but she was an exception, like you.'

'You'd give up your room for me?' She seized on his words and stared at him, wide-eyed, ready to tease him mercilessly. 'What a lovely idea.' She gazed around the room once more, her glance taking in the glass-fronted bookcase and luxuriously upholstered leather chair. She ran her fingers lightly over the polished surface of his desk. 'I could really see me making myself at home in here.'

'Yes, so can I.' He watched her float dreamily about the room, stopping only to perch on the corner of the desk, draping herself possessively over it, one hand flat on the shiny top, the other resting lightly on her hip, her long legs crossed at the knee and showing a hint of creamy thigh. He looked at her abstractedly for a moment or two and appeared to be struggling to pull himself together.

'On second thoughts, forget it,' he said, going over to the other side of the room and setting out a bowl of sugar on the worktop. He retrieved a small jug of cream from the fridge. A coffee jug had been simmering gently on its base since they'd entered the room, but now he lifted it and began to pour the liquid into two mugs. 'I can just imagine,' he added in a droll tone, 'once you get yourself established in here, you'd be so invigorated you'll end up doing twice the amount of work you're doing now.'

She chuckled. 'You think so?'

'I know it.' He waved her to a padded leather chair by the side of the desk, and pushed the mug of coffee towards her. 'Help yourself to cream and sugar.'

'Thanks. Mmm…this is good.' She sniffed the aroma appreciatively and then went to sit down. 'Much better than the stuff in the machines out there.' She waved a hand towards the corridor outside and then frowned. 'But I'm a little concerned about your opinion of me. Where did you learn to be so mistrustful?'

His mouth quirked. 'At my mother's knee. And through dealing with people like you who prod and poke and instigate changes until what was once a smooth-running organisation becomes a mere sliver of what it was before.' He lifted his mug to his lips and swallowed the hot coffee. 'What is it that makes you so focussed and determined?'

She shrugged lightly, adding cream to her coffee and stirring it slowly. 'I suppose I've always had a strong work ethic. It probably comes from my father. He believes in hard work, sticking to a task—for him there's no such word as "can't". He says there's always a solution and we have to keep going until we find it.'

'And you live by his rules, even now, even though you're a grown woman, with a mind of your own?'

'Why wouldn't I?' She met his gaze full on. 'It seems a reasonable enough philosophy to me. Besides, I've worked hard to get where I am today, and I'm not about to let it all slide. I always wanted to be a doctor…ever since I was little and I saw my friend being struck down by appendicitis, I knew it was the career for me. Now I've reached the point where I can see things that would be better for being changed, and I'm glad I'm in a position to do something about it.'

He sighed. 'Lord save us from a woman on a mission,' he murmured, his gaze sweeping over her. 'Does it never occur to you to stop for a while and look at things from someone else's viewpoint?'

'Like yours, you mean?' She shook her head. 'I've a feeling you think everything can stay the same, and you go ploughing on, regardless of the warnings from all around you. There'll come a time when the plough will break down and there will be no money to replace it. What will you do then?'

'Get a spade and start digging.' He frowned, studying her closely. 'I must say you seem to be very clinical in your attitude, and strangely unemotional.'

She shrugged. 'Someone has to be.' She took another sip of her coffee and looked him over. His dark hair was a perfect foil for his rugged good looks and his eyes had that quality of being able to see right into your soul. It was disturbing, to say the least.

'Anyway,' she said, 'I've noticed the same work ethic in you. You put in a lot of hours, you're very dedicated to the job, and you must have been ambitious to get as far as you have in this profession. There aren't too many consultants around who are in their mid-thirties.' Her glance ran over him, gliding over the strong line of his jaw, coming to rest on the firmly moulded mouth that hinted at hidden sensuality. Dreamily, she wondered what it would be like to kiss him… Then she brought herself up sharply, veering away from the errant path her thoughts would have taken her. What on earth was wrong with her?

'I suppose that's true.' He looked at her oddly, as though he was trying to fathom what was going on in her mind, and a wave of heat ran through her body. Heaven forbid he should work it out!

'So what made you decide to become a doctor?' she asked. 'Are your parents in the same line of work? You said they were working with underprivileged children.'

He nodded. 'In a manner of speaking, they are. They're part of the World Health Organization, so mostly their work involves organising medical care. They generally manage to collaborate with one another on various projects.'

'So I guess you don't see much of them?'

'That's true. Of course, they come home on vacation, and they have a fairly generous span of time off, but they're dedicated to what they do, especially my mother. The job is very important to her.'

He gave a faint smile but didn't comment any further, and Alex was prompted to ask, 'Would I be right in thinking your mother is the other person you know who is "driven", as you put it?'

'I guess so.' He pressed his lips together briefly. 'She's a very fierce believer in getting things done. Once she sets her mind on doing something, it becomes the be-all and end-all…there's no stopping her. Of course, that's great, if you've a project that needs to be up and running, but it doesn't bode well for anyone who would hanker after a cosy home life.'

'Like you?' She was frowning a little, wondering what it must have been like for him as a young child to live with parents who were constantly travelling the world. 'I expect you must have seen more than your fair share of countries.'

'That's right. I always went with them in the beginning, but there came a time when I was due to start my secondary education, and I wanted stability. So that's where my aunt and uncle came in…although my uncle passed away a few years ago. My parents kept in touch by phone and email—we even have a video link set up now.' He smiled. 'My mother was anxious about leaving me, but Aunt Jane is a home bird and she more than made up for any sense of loss I might be feeling. My uncle and aunt didn't have any children of their own, and so I think they were glad of the chance to look after me.'

'She's a lovely woman,' Alex said. 'I took to her straight away—and the minute she saw that I had children she offered to help out. I still feel anxious about letting her take that on, especially with the school holidays coming up soon…but she seemed like a godsend at the time.'

He nodded. 'Strange, that,' he murmured. 'I'd no idea that you had children.' He stood up then to go and fetch biscuits from a cupboard on the wall. 'We have bourbons, sandwich creams, plain, ginger…' he said, rummaging through the various packets. 'Or there are fruited tea buns left over from yesterday afternoon.' He pressed the packaging to test their freshness, and his features lit up. 'They seem fine. Would you like one?'

She grinned at his boyish pleasure. 'Thanks, that would be great.'

He set them out on plates, and added a selection of biscuits. 'I'm starving,' he told her with a hint of apology. 'My lunch was interrupted today—an emergency cropped up. It's always happening—that's why I keep a stash of goodies on hand in here.'

He came to sit back down, and pushed a plate towards her before biting into a tea bun. 'You'll be pleased to know that I made an appointment for my aunt to see a specialist friend of mine—I managed to arrange it for next week, so we should soon know the score about what's causing the high blood pressure. Like you, I've been worried about her.'

'I'm glad you did that.' Alex smiled, and he looked at her, almost as though he was seeing her for the first time, his gaze lingering on her features for a while.

Then he seemed to pull himself together and said cautiously, 'As I said, it was a bit of a shock to find that you had children. It must make things difficult for you, doing a high-powered job like this one and still having to maintain a family life.'

'It isn't easy, I grant you.' Alex took a bite from the remaining bun, and chewed thoughtfully for a moment or two. 'First there was the move down here to Somerset, that was an ordeal in itself, for me, at least, and it was a bit of a challenge for the children, having to settle into a new house.'

He glanced at the fingers of her left hand, and then frowned. 'And your husband? I don't see a ring. Are you and he divorced...separated?'

'Neither. I've never been married.' She finished off the bun.

He drew in a deep breath and looked faintly puzzled. 'But the children's father...'

'Is in hospital. He's my brother.' She took pity on his bewilderment and went on, 'He and my sister-in-law were involved in a bad motorway accident. They were travelling back from a reception organised by his firm when it happened, so, in one way, perhaps it was fortunate that they were on their own in the car. The children were staying with friends.'

'I'm so sorry, Alex.' He reached for her hand, covering it with his palm. 'That must have been a terrible shock for you.'

'Yes, it was.' She tried not to think about the way his gentle touch evoked warm ripples of sensation and sent them coursing along the length of her arm. 'I suppose, in the end, I'm just thankful that they survived. It was bad, but it could have been worse.'

'Yes, it could. But at least the children were safe. I suppose that became the immediate priority.'

She nodded. She was finding it hard to concentrate with his long fingers clasping hers. It was a gesture of comfort and support, and it made her feel good inside, as though he was letting her know he was there for her and that she need not be alone in all this. It had been a long while since she'd felt that way.

'There was no one to look after the children, and Beth was desperate that they shouldn't go into care, so I stepped in. I love my family and I want to do the best for them.'

'Of course you do.' He frowned. 'So what was the reason for you buying the house?' he asked in a puzzled tone. 'Didn't they have a place of their own?'

'They did. They'd all moved into rented accommodation some six months ago when Ross took up a new job in the area, but the lease expired and the landlord didn't want to renew it. So I had to look for a place with enough room for all of us.'

He shook his head. 'It sounds as though you had a hefty task on your hands. I can't imagine having to juggle all those problems at once. You must have worked wonders to hold it all together.'

She gave him a faint smile. 'I don't know about holding it all together. Sometimes I worry that I've taken on too much, especially with the house. But at least the children were already settled at school. That was one less problem to sort out.' Her brows drew together. 'All I have to worry about now are the school holidays. I'm going to have to sort out some full-time care for them. I don't want to ask Jane, because she seems so unwell.'

'That's true, but I'm sure you'll find someone very capable and willing to look after them. Obviously it will be better if it's someone you know.' He frowned. 'And this job must be an extra worry for you. You've taken on a big responsibility.'

She sighed. 'Yes, but I'm sure things could work out well if we just put our heads together and try to sort things out…' she sucked in a breath '…which reminds me, weren't we going to discuss those budget cuts?'

'It's true, we were.' He straightened up, reluctantly sliding his hand away from her. Then he swallowed the remains of his coffee and glanced down at his pager. 'But it appears that I'm wanted in Resus.' He glanced at her. 'Sorry to have to break things up, but I must go.'

Alex stared at him. 'I didn't hear your pager go off.'

'No,' he said, 'you wouldn't. I set it to silent alarm.'

He showed her the text message that was displayed on the pager's screen and then gave her an encouraging smile. 'But not to worry, perhaps we can do this another day? I'll come up with all the figures you want, I promise. Meanwhile, why don't you stay here and finish your coffee? It's been good to see you relax for a while. I'm sure a little longer will do you the world of good.'

He stood up and made for the door, and Alex was filled with frustration as she watched his disappearing back. It seemed that all her efforts to get the job done were fated where he was concerned.

CHAPTER FOUR

'IF ONE more ball goes flying over the fence into next door's garden, I shall stop you from playing football out there.' Alex abandoned her battle with the ancient Aga and went to remonstrate with James in the garden. 'Auntie Jane has better things to do than to keep throwing them back, and sooner or later you're going to damage something.'

'Oops.' The warning came too late. James pulled a face as his favourite football went sailing over the fence and was followed a second or two later by an ominous thudding sound. 'I didn't mean it,' he said, with a bemused expression. 'It was an accident.'

Alex sighed. 'You'd better go round there and apologise,' she told him. Turning to his sister, she said, 'Will you go with him, Sarah, please? Find out if there's been any damage. I have to stay here and keep an eye on the pizza in the oven.'

'Okay.' Sarah took James by the hand and led him away.

'Why do we have to go?' James complained. 'I didn't do it on purpose. I just tapped it and it went over.'

'Yeah, like always,' Sarah said. 'That's 'cos you keep trying to see how high you can kick it.'

'No...I was just aiming for the goal. You wanna see

how Rooney does it,' James said, warming to his theme. 'See how they did it in the match on telly? You have to run and shoot, get it in there quick.'

'Yeah, but they lost the game,' Sarah pointed out in a blunt tone. 'Didn't do them any good, did it?'

'Well, they'll do it next time.' James scowled at his sister as they went out of the back gate.

Alex could still hear them bickering as they walked along the path to her neighbour's property. A wave of guilt swamped her. There was no doubt about it, she ought to have gone with them, but there was just so much to do…lunch to prepare, laundry to finish, ironing, and that was before she made a start on tackling the endless round of decorating that was needed to spruce up this old farmhouse property.

And now the Aga was playing up. The pizza, which should have been cooked several minutes ago, was still pale looking, and Alex guessed that meant she would soon be paying out for a new thermostat for the oven.

She left it to bake some more and started to gather together the ingredients for a salad. And what of the football game that had gone wrong out there? Was she going to have to fork out for damage to Jane's property as well?

The children came back a few minutes later. 'Auntie Jane made us a cake,' Sarah said excitedly, bursting into the kitchen.

'Goodness! A reward for causing her all that trouble? Auntie Jane must be a saint.'

'It's all covered with strawberries and cream.' James was licking his lips in anticipation. 'I'm hungry,' he said. 'Can we have some now?'

'After you've eaten your lunch,' Alex murmured.

'Isn't that just typical of adults?' a familiar, deep

voice commented, and Alex was startled to see Callum follow the children into the kitchen. 'There are never any goodies to be had till after the main course, are there?' He peered around the door. 'Is it all right if I come in?' His glance slid warmly over her, moving from head to toe and taking in her slender shape, outlined by the snug-fitting jeans and the stretchy cotton top she wore.

'Of course.' She studied him in return, flummoxed for a moment, seeing him here, in her kitchen. He looked good, dressed in casual clothes, dark chinos teamed with a loose cotton shirt, a strong contrast to the smart, formal suits he wore for work.

She waved him to a seat by the table. 'Come and sit down.' She frowned, and then added hesitantly, 'I was just about to serve up lunch. You're welcome to stay and eat with us, if you like.'

He smiled, seeming surprised by the invitation, and she was back-footed all over again by the way the smile softened his angular features. 'Are you sure? Thanks. That would be great...if you're positive it's no trouble?'

'None at all...though I won't guarantee the state of the pizza.' She frowned. 'It started out with all the promise of a healthy, home-made meal, but it's a bit of a sorry effort now, given that the Aga's putting on a go-slow.' She took the pizza from the oven and set it out on the worktop.

Callum studied it. 'Looks fine to me. Lovely golden melted cheese...with ham, tomato and salami... Definitely a winner.' He sniffed the air appreciatively. 'Smells good, too. This reminds me of being in my aunt's kitchen when I was young. Lots of lovely baking smells.'

'Talking of which...' He held out a large, round

plastic container and placed it on the table. 'Aunt Jane asked me to give you this...it's her famous Somerset pound cake. Apparently it's a mix of butter, sugar, flour and a whole basket full of eggs.' He grinned. 'I can tell you from experience that it's a mouth-watering concoction, anyway.'

Alex looked at the cake. 'It's wonderful,' she said. 'She's too good to us—we really don't deserve it after the trouble we've been to her. I've lost count of the number of times the ball has landed in her vegetable patch—and last time it went over, we heard this awful thud...was anything broken?'

He shook his head. 'The shed took a strong hit, but it's a solid, sturdy piece of workmanship. She says not to worry about it.'

'That's easier said than done. I'd be getting stressed out if the neighbours kept doing it to me.'

His mouth made an odd quirk. 'Yes, but you seem to be constantly under pressure, what with work and keeping up with this place. Aunt Jane tells me you're finding all sorts of problems here—you need to have some of the roof tiles replaced, she says. That must be a hassle you can do without.'

'And the rest.' She pulled a face. 'I didn't realise this place needed quite so much work, when I took it on.' She glanced at him as she set out plates on the table. 'But you must be having problems of your own—didn't you say you had builders working on your house? It was why you hadn't been able to get around to seeing your aunt, you said.'

'That's right. I was having work done on the garage and in the garden. The work's all finished now, though. Obviously, it was nothing compared with what you have to do here.'

Alex nodded. 'I keep asking myself why I bought this place.' She broke off to tell James and Sarah to go and wash their hands at the sink. 'Originally, I'd no intention of buying such a rambling place, but it sort of drew me in… It looked like a dream house, with its lovely, honey-coloured Somerset stone and the sloping roofs at all angles, and once I set eyes on it, I was hooked. I've never owned a house before…I've always lived in small, rented accommodation. Nothing else seemed necessary.'

'But suddenly you wanted to put down roots?'

She nodded. 'I think so. I don't know why. I really don't know what came over me. Up to now, I've been so busy with work that I didn't need anything more than a place to rest my head. Then I came here…' She frowned. 'Perhaps I thought it was time for a change. I had visions of this old farmhouse being lovingly renovated, and the orchard bursting with fruit—a kind of rural paradise, if you like.' She grinned. 'Now I'm beginning to wonder if I might have bitten off more than I can chew.'

Callum opened his mouth to answer, but he was interrupted by a horrible clanking and groaning sound coming from the water pipes as the children turned on the kitchen tap. No water came out.

'Where's the spanner?' James asked, his face serious as he began to hunt around in the cupboard underneath the sink.

'Isn't it there?' Alex frowned. 'I must have moved it. Look on the shelf by the fridge.'

Callum looked from one to the other, clearly puzzled. 'He's not going to try to fix it, is he? Surely he's too young?'

'Nah…it's easy,' James told him, putting on his man-of-the-house expression. He found the spanner and bent down inside the cupboard, concentrating deeply on the task in hand. Then he gave the pipe a couple of hard whacks. 'Try it now,' he instructed Sarah.

She did as he told her, and obligingly water spurted from the tap.

Callum watched in wonder. 'I'm impressed. Who needs a tradesman when you can do it yourself?'

Alex's mouth curved. 'It is annoying, though,' she said. 'The water pipes creak and groan and make an almighty noise a lot of the time. I'm going to have to do something about it, because one of these days banging on the pipe just won't do the trick.'

The children finished washing and came to sit at the table. 'I love pizza,' James said, trying to cram a whole portion into his mouth at once.

'That's great, but slow down,' Alex warned him. 'I don't want to see you choking on your food.'

James grinned amiably, and he and Sarah compared slices before James began to show his sister how to make faces with pieces he arranged carefully on his plate. 'You just cut it with your knife, like this,' he explained.

Alex turned her attention to Callum. 'So how is Jane?' she asked. 'I looked in on her this morning, but it seemed as though she'd been overdoing things again. Her cheeks were very flushed, and I guessed her blood pressure was up. Has there been any news from the hospital?'

'Yes, I talked to the specialist yesterday, and I gave her the news this afternoon. She said it was okay to let you know the result.'

'And that is?'

'She has Conn's syndrome. It's very rare, and that's perhaps why it wasn't picked up before, but the CT scan showed a tumour on her adrenal gland. It's causing the gland to produce too much aldosterone, and that's pushing up her blood pressure.'

Alex pressed her lips together briefly. 'That must have come as a huge shock to her. Is she all right?'

'I think so. She went to lie down for a while, but she seemed to take it well enough.'

'And what about you? How do you feel about it? It must be a real worry for you.'

His mouth straightened. 'I'm not sure. Generally these things turn out to be benign, so I'm trying to stay calm about it. I tried to paint a positive picture for my aunt, too…but she's a hardy woman, generally. I think she'll be all right. Things don't normally knock her back for long.'

Alex pulled in a quick breath. 'I'll make sure to give her any help and support she needs,' she vowed. 'When will she be having the surgery? Is your friend going to operate?'

He nodded. 'He said he'd do it next week. One of his patients postponed, because of unexpected travel plans, so he'll fit my aunt in then.'

'That's brilliant news. She's healthy enough otherwise, isn't she, so there shouldn't be any problem?'

'Let's hope so.' He helped himself to salad, and then sent a cautious glance in the children's direction before asking quietly, 'How are your family doing? You said they were involved in a nasty accident and they must already have been in hospital for quite a while.'

Her eyes clouded. 'It's going to take some time before they're back on their feet. Ross is still on a ventilator, but Beth is doing a little better. Even so, there were broken bones that need to heal, as well as the internal injuries.'

She shot a look at the children. Thankfully, they were

both still engrossed in seeing who could make the best pattern with what was left of the pizza. Sarah had added cherry tomatoes to her effort, along with a curved slice of red pepper for a mouth, and now she pronounced that she had made the best face.

'She has curly hair, too,' she said proudly, showing off the adornment of pasta spirals.

James pursed his lips. 'Faces are easy,' he said. 'I'm making a tractor.'

'Oh, is that what it is?' Sarah squinted at his effort, tilting her head sideways so as to see it from a different angle. 'You need some salami rings for the wheels.'

'Yes, but I ate them,' James said, frowning. He inspected her plate. 'Can I have yours?'

'No, you can't.' Sarah moved her plate out of reach when he would have swooped with his fork, and Alex closed her eyes fleetingly.

'Try eating your food instead of playing with it. And when you've finished, you can go outside and play on the swing for a while. Get rid of some of that energy,' Alex said to both of them.

'I want to play football,' James said, his grey eyes challenging her.

'No more football today,' she answered. 'We talked about that.'

'Well, then, why can't we go to the seaside instead? You keep saying we'll go, but we never do.'

'Yes, but we've only been here a few weeks, James, and we've been busy. There's been a lot to do, moving in here and getting everything shipshape.'

'It isn't a ship!' James retorted, his brows shooting upwards. 'I want to go to the seaside.' He glowered. 'Mum would have taken us.'

Alex hid a groan, and Callum's mouth twitched a

fraction. 'They know how to hit where it hurts, don't they?'

'Too right they do.' She glanced at the children, but by now James was making another attempt to steal salami from Sarah's plate, and she decided it was time to intervene.

She picked up James's plate and held it aloft. 'Have you finished with this?' she asked. 'Do you want me to put this out for the birds?'

James scowled, but shook his head.

'All right, then. Eat up. Any more messing about and I'll take it away, and then there'll be no strawberry cake.'

Both children began to eat, and Alex gave a faint sigh. 'They're like this all the while,' she told Callum, with a shake of her head. 'I don't know how their mother used to cope. I feel as though I'm run ragged half the time, sorting out their disputes.'

'I expect she lets them get on with it,' he said, smiling. 'By the time you've come around to playing referee, they'll have moved on to something else.'

'That's true enough,' she said with a laugh.

He glanced at the youngsters, who had begun to argue over which one of them had more cheese than the other, and added softly, 'Of course, James does have a point about the seaside, you know. To a child, a day can seem a long while to wait for something, let alone several weeks—and the coast is only a few miles from here.'

A small line creased her brow. 'I know I should have taken them—it's just that the weekends are so full, and they haven't really mentioned it much.'

'Perhaps they were waiting for you to arrange it. Anyway, I can't help sympathising with youngsters who want to spend time at the seaside...especially when their parents aren't around to take them there.'

'I know.' She frowned. 'I kept thinking we'd wait until I have some time off from work, in the summer holidays. As it is, I have a mass of work to do here. I'm halfway through painting the living room, I have to do something about the blocked-up chimney in the dining room, and the kitchen cupboards need stripping down to bare wood so that they can be restored to what they once were. And that's not counting the roof tiles that need replacing and the plumbing that needs to be fixed. I just don't know when I'm supposed to do all this.'

'Later,' he said. 'All those things can wait. You need to get your priorities sorted out.'

'Do I?' She made a soft sound of exasperation. 'That's easy for you to say, isn't it? You're not involved. As far as I can tell, everything's going smoothly for you, and all you have to do is make sure your aunt is safe and secure.'

'Maybe, but I'd like to do what I can to help you. I'm sure we can find a solution.'

'What do you mean?'

'I mean how about I take a look at the plumbing, while you clear the table and get everyone ready for a trip to the coast? I know a lovely little cove not far from here, where the children can fish in the rock pools.'

'Yes!'

'Yes!'

Alex looked round in astonishment as James and Sarah both shouted gleefully, whooping with delight. 'Say yes, Auntie Alex...please say yes.' Sarah turned pleading blue eyes on Alex, and James's face was lit up with joyful expectation.

Alex was stunned to find that they had both been

listening to her conversation with Callum. She turned to him. 'Now look what you've done.'

Callum's expression was bland. 'Who? Me? I didn't do anything. I just offered to try and fix the taps for you. If you want me to leave it, that's fine by me.'

'No, no...Auntie Alex, don't let him leave it...' Sarah was beside herself with dismay. 'You keep saying how you're going to...knock that pipe into next week if it doesn't stop playing up. Now you don't have to. I know he can fix it for us...or at least he can try.'

'And then we can go to the seaside,' James finished.

'Yeah!' They both added the chorus.

Alex melted at the sight of the children's eager faces. 'I don't see how I have any choice.' She looked at Callum and gave a faint shake of her head. 'There are a thousand and one jobs I should be doing, but now it looks as though I'll be spending the afternoon by the sea.' She gave him a mischievous look. 'Maybe you could help out in other ways,' she suggested with a wry smile. 'Perhaps you'd like to come and do my laundry while you're about it, and mop the floors?'

His mouth twisted. 'Sorry, but I don't do domestic. I come from a household steeped in tradition—Aunt Jane did all the homely things, and my uncle ran the show from his study. He always had lots of advice on how things should be done...but leave it to the women, he used to say.'

Her mouth curved. 'Well, let's hope at least you can fix the plumbing,' she said. 'That would be a definite bonus.'

He nodded. 'I'll need a carrier bag and a sponge of some sort if you have one?'

She stared at him blankly. 'Those aren't the usual

plumbing tools, are they? I can offer you spanners, a wrench, hammers…pliers or grips…'

'A carrier bag and sponge will be just fine, thanks… and some plastic adhesive tape if you have it.'

She frowned. 'Okay.' She studied him briefly. 'Are you quite sure you know what you're doing?'

He nodded. 'I hope so.'

She went to fetch him what he needed, and then sent the children upstairs to get ready for their outing. 'You'll need a spare set of clothes in case anything gets wet,' she told them. 'And you'd better hunt out your swimsuit and trunks.'

'Seaside! Yay!' James ran up the stairs, followed swiftly by Sarah. 'Can we take the fishing nets?' he called back.

'I'll get them,' Alex told him. She stopped to think about that for a moment or two. Last time she'd seen them, they'd been at the back of the shed, along with buckets and spades from previous years…years when they'd gone with their parents to spend time by the sea, digging in the sand and making spectacular sandcastles, with moats and drawbridges, and all sorts of embellishments made from shells and pebbles that they'd found lying about. She'd seen the photos, and heard all about it from Ross and Beth.

The memories brought sudden tears to her eyes. How could she ever hope to replace all that love and commitment, even for a short time? Would things be the same for them ever again?

'Are you all right?' Callum was looking at her oddly, and Alex blinked, trying to stem the tears that threatened.

'I'm fine,' she said, her voice a little choked. 'I was just thinking about Ross and Beth…it caught me unawares. I suppose I've been a bit wound up lately, trying to work out how to deal with everything.'

He wrapped his arms around her and drew her close. 'You're bound to feel that way,' he said softly. 'So much has happened in such a short time.' He ran his hands over her shoulders, her back, gently soothing her.

'I'm just afraid I've let them down.' Her voice faltered. 'It's as though I've been suffering from tunnel vision lately, trying to form order out of chaos. I've concentrated so hard on dealing with day-to-day life… it all seemed so important at the time.'

He rested his cheek against hers. 'Perhaps it was the only way you could cope. But what really matters is that they should be happy. You can't make up for this awful thing that has struck down their parents, but you can do something to help the children.'

She nodded. 'You're right. I know you're right.'

He smiled. 'Anyway, you could do with a break yourself. It's time to step off the treadmill—so, if you'll pass me the sponge and tape, I'll get on.'

He carefully released her, easing back from her a little, and she took a moment to get used to being on her own once again. She missed his warm embrace. She missed his closeness.

But she needed to pull herself together, so she went to find the things he needed.

She handed them to him a minute or so later, and then watched curiously as he placed the sponge inside the carrier bag and taped it firmly beneath the outlet of the tap.

'First we switch on the cold tap,' he said, 'then the hot. Wait for the gurgling to stop… then turn off the hot tap.' He waited a moment or two, leaving the cold tap running, and then abruptly removed the bag and sponge. Water spurted out.

'We'll try that one or two times more,' he murmured, 'and see if it does the trick. It's just an airlock that's causing the trouble.'

A minute or two later, the water was running freely, and Alex watched and marvelled. 'Thank you for that,' she said. 'I would never have guessed it was something so simple. I can see I'm going to have to get myself a book on how to fix things around the house…or find a decent internet site that explains everything in layman's terms.'

'As opposed to having a man around the place?' He sent her an oblique glance, a smile playing around his lips. 'Are you sure you wouldn't prefer your own handyman on the premises?'

Her mouth curved. 'Are you putting yourself forward for the job?'

'Oh, yes.' His glimmering gaze skimmed over her. 'With perks, of course…'

'Oh?' She looked at him warily. 'And they would be?'

'Well, let's see…you could pay me with tea and pizza, or maybe a slice of strawberry cream cake…'

'That sounds reasonable enough,' she said with a smile. 'I think we could manage both of those.'

'Hmm.' He dried his hands on a tea towel and then turned to face her once more. 'Though there are other far more interesting ways I could think of.' His gaze lingered on the pink fullness of her mouth, and she simply stood there for a moment, lured by the sheer invitation in those incredible blue eyes and wondering what it would be like to be kissed by him. Somehow he was so close that it would only take a breath of movement, and his lips would be touching hers. She felt heady with the intensity of the moment, lulled by the spell he was weaving around her.

'James wants to take his snorkel and flippers,' Sarah said, coming into the kitchen at that moment. 'I told him we're not going swimming, but he won't listen. And he thinks we're going to take the dinghy and his wooden boat as well as the beach ball.'

Alex came back down to earth with a bump. She gave Callum one last, cautious glance, and saw that his mouth had curved into a resigned smile. 'Tell him the beach ball and his wooden boat are fine,' she said, trying to keep her voice on an even keel. 'And we'd better get a move on if we're to have plenty of time at the beach.'

She turned to Callum, breathing in deeply to calm herself. 'Will your aunt be okay while we're out? It seems like the wrong time to leave her.'

'I'm sure she'll be fine. Martha from across the way is coming over to visit her this afternoon, so at least she'll have company. Anyway, she knows to ring me if there's a problem…but I'll go and have a word with her right now, and then we'll set off.' He paused a moment, then added, 'You might want to ask Martha about looking after the children during the school holidays, if my aunt's going to be out of action for a while. She used to foster children, so I know she'd like the opportunity.'

'Really? That's great. I'll talk to her about it.' She marvelled at his thoughtfulness. She'd been trying to work out what to do for the best, and he had come up with a solution. Having him around was turning out to be a boon.

'Good. And as to what we were saying before…I'll come round and give you a hand with some of the jobs you have to do around here. I'm quite handy with a paintbrush and I'm not too bad on fixing roof tiles either. Between us, we should soon have this place looking good.'

'Oh…that's really thoughtful of you.' The words left her on a soft breath of surprise and, impulsively, she reached out to touch his arm. 'That's a wonderful offer, but you don't need to do that. I took it on, and it's my problem. I'm the one who should deal with it.'

'I don't see it as a problem. I see it as a project. I'll be really glad of the chance to help you renovate this place on my days off. It'll be good to have something to do that's completely different from work at the hospital.' He smiled as he walked towards the door. 'And it will give us the chance to spend more time together.'

She stared at him in shock, stunned by his offer. Did he really want to spend his weekends with her?

By the time he came back from Jane's house, they were all ready to set off. James was wearing his super-spy slimline shades, and Sarah had her favourite drinks bottle with the curly plastic straw.

Callum drove along the main road towards the coast, pointing out the various landmarks along the way. Soon, the rolling hills of the Quantocks gave way to Exmoor's rugged landscape, with majestic headlands, towering cliffs and beautiful bays. The sea was a perfect blue.

'I thought we'd stop at a little cove near here,' he said, as he turned the car onto a road leading towards the sea. 'It's sheltered by the cliffs, so you can get some shade from the sun, and when the tide's out, as it is now, it leaves behind lots of pools where you can find baby crabs.'

He parked the car and looked back at James. 'Did you bring a bucket?'

James nodded, holding up a huge blue bucket, shaped like a castle. 'For the crabs,' he said.

'Good. A boy after my own heart,' Callum said. He glanced at Sarah. 'Are you all right with crabbing? Not squeamish, are you?'

Sarah shook her head. 'But Auntie Alex isn't too keen. She doesn't like their little pincers.'

He laughed. 'I might have guessed.' He sent Alex a sympathetic look. 'Not to worry. You can collect shells and seaweed instead, if you like.'

'Thank you so much,' Alex answered, her tone dry. 'I can't think of anything I'd like more.'

He nodded. 'You will, once you get the hang of this "taking things easy" exercise.'

'Of course I will,' she murmured. 'I have vague memories of it, from when I was in my teens, I think.'

'What it is to be focussed,' he said softly. 'Is your career really the be-all and end-all of everything?'

They climbed out of the car, unloading rubber rings, a huge beach ball, the bag with towels and a change of clothes, and another bag with camera, drinks bottles and assorted paraphernalia.

'Do you remember good times by the sea with your parents?' Alex asked Callum as they walked down the cliff path to the sand below.

'Some,' he said. 'But mostly I went with Aunt Jane and my uncle. They'd let me bring a friend along, sometimes a couple of friends, and we had some great times.' He looked around. 'This was a favourite haunt.'

She nodded, looking around for a place where they could settle down when they reached the sandy beach. 'I can see why. It has everything you could want.'

She handed out buckets and spades, and the children set to work, digging in the sand. 'I'm going to make a fort,' James announced, 'with battlements and a moat.'

Alex gazed out over the sparkling waters of the Bristol Channel, and then looked back at the cliffs, layered with strata of shale, and blue, yellow and brown limestone. 'This place is fantastic.'

'It is,' Callum agreed. 'I used to hunt for fossils in those rocks. It was great fun.'

'I can imagine.'

They spent the next hour digging in the sand and fetching water from the sea so that James and Sarah could complete their grand castle. That done, they set off to explore the cove, treading carefully over flat rocks and peering down into rocky inlets where the tide had washed up all manner of seaweed and sea creatures.

James filled his bucket with baby crabs, while Sarah collected shells, looking for perfect specimens. 'I want to take them to the hospital to show Mum,' she said.

Alex watched as they padded over the damp sand. Callum bent to look at James's latest find, and the two males engaged in a deep discussion about how the creature moved and whether it could live out of water. Then Callum turned to Sarah and admired the perfectly intact cockleshell she had discovered.

He was good with both of them, Alex acknowledged. He spoke to them quietly, interested in everything they had to say, and every now and then his gentle laughter floated on the air.

Eventually, they returned to the sandcastle where they had started off, and Alex hunted out drinks from the depths of one of the bags. Satisfied after quenching his thirst, James wanted to go down to the water's edge to paddle in the surf.

'Okay, but stay where I can see you,' Alex told him. 'No further than that wooden marker.'

Sarah went with him, and Alex watched their progress, anxious in case they should wander too far into the water.

'It's a safe beach,' Callum told her. 'They'll be okay... and we'll both keep an eye on them.'

She nodded. 'This is really lovely, being out here. It seems so long since I last sat on a beach and looked at the sea. I didn't realise how much I missed it.'

'Didn't you take holidays?'

She shook her head. 'I haven't done recently. Somehow I just don't seem to have found time for a proper break these last few years. I've been studying for specialist exams, taking on high-profile jobs and generally letting myself be swamped with work.'

'I suppose you must get an adrenaline buzz from all that, otherwise you wouldn't do it.'

'Maybe.' Her eyes clouded. Why was it that her life's work suddenly seemed nothing compared to these stolen moments in a sandy cove where the only sounds were the gentle swish of the sea lapping at the shore and the call of the gulls overhead? What had she been missing all these years?

Callum leaned back against a rock and studied her with a quizzical expression. 'And where do men friends fit into all this hard work and dedication to the job in hand? You said you were too busy to be involved with anyone right now, but there must have been someone in the past?'

'Maybe.' She wasn't going to fill him in on her skirmishes with romance, and anyway it seemed odd to say that no man had ever featured greatly in her life. There had been opportunity enough, if she'd wanted to take it, but somehow no one had ever lit that spark in her that would make her fall head over heels in love. There had been good men, rugged men, men who'd made her laugh and promised her the world, but none had made her want to give up her career or turn her back on ambition. Perhaps there was something wrong with her. Perhaps she was expecting too much.

'I see...dark secrets, eh?' Callum tilted his head on one side to study her. 'I heard there was a doctor in Men's Surgical who lost his heart to you for quite a while. A couple of years, at least, but it was unrequited love, people said. They say you think more about the job than you do about your love life.' His glance meshed with hers. 'That's quite a challenge for any man.'

'Is it?' She saw his gaze drop to her mouth, and felt a sudden flood of heat in her abdomen. 'I don't know what to do about that, because the truth is I mean it when I say I don't have time for a relationship right now.' Her mouth made a brief quirk. 'Heavens, I don't even have time to do my ironing. At this rate, the children will be wearing crumpled T-shirts to school in the morning.'

He laughed. 'I don't suppose anyone will mind. You'll be the only one who notices.' He leaned over her and smoothed back a tendril of hair that had fallen across her cheek.

'Maybe. But that's the problem I'm wrestling with, isn't it? I notice all these things and I care about them, and I want to put them right. Not T-shirts so much, but generally taking care of the children and making sure everything runs smoothly.'

'It could be that these things aren't so important as you imagine.'

'But they matter to me.'

Perhaps that was the reason none of her relationships

had worked out right in the past. She had her own set of priorities, and the men she had known had without fail wanted to override them with their own concerns. Callum was probably much the same.

She gazed out to sea, to where the children were splashing one another and jumping with each wave that rolled onto the shore. 'The tide's coming in,' she said. 'I think we'll have to make a move.'

'Yes.' There was a note of regret in his voice. 'I think you're probably right.'

CHAPTER FIVE

'YES, I understand perfectly, Dr Langton...we're looking for cuts right across the board.' Alex frowned. 'Of course, you realise, don't you, that it isn't as simple as cutting back on nursing staff and putting the cleaning contract out to tender? Either of those measures could mean that the emergency department will function less well.' Alex adopted a gentle, coaxing tone. 'I was hoping rather that we might make savings through using low-priced generic drugs and altering practices within the unit so that we're more cost-efficient.'

Dr Langton shook his head. 'My dear, that simply won't be enough. From the figures you've shown me, those measures will take far too long to bring results. Unfortunately, this job's all about tough decisions. We need to do something now...and reducing staff numbers is top priority, along with putting a stop on any new equipment being ordered. Some departments are quite irresponsible in thinking they can demand all the latest equipment...we simply don't have the budget for it.' He frowned. 'Make sure they know that in A and E, won't you? Out of all the departments, that one has the highest expenditure for the last six months.'

'I've already done that,' she said. 'I've put a stop to any new orders.'

'Good.' He gave her a benign smile. 'We need to show the board that we've made dramatic headway at the next meeting...but I know you can pull this off, Alex. I've every faith in you.'

Alex nodded. 'I'll do my best. At least with all these measures in place we should be able to keep the A and E department up and running. I've looked closely at the figures and everything seems to be on course.'

He nodded. 'That's what it's all about.'

She left the chief executive's office a short time later, deep in thought, and made her way to A and E. Things were going from bad to worse. Right from the beginning, this day had started out wrong.

First of all she had visited Ross and Beth, only to find that her brother had suffered a setback. His breathing had deteriorated, and the doctors were worried about an infection in his lungs. They were initiating more tests and thinking about changing his medication...all of it bad news. How was she to explain things to the children? And on top of that, this was the day that Jane was having surgery to remove the tumour on her adrenal gland... one more thing to play on her mind.

For now, though, she tried to concentrate on the job in hand. She didn't have to look too far to find the culprit behind some of the so-called irresponsible ordering that had annoyed the chief executive.

Callum was determined that A and E should have the best equipment for the job, and although he was aware that the budget was restricted, he'd been determinedly pushing for those things he felt necessary.

And as for staff cuts, those wouldn't go down well at all, would they? It was a disturbing situation. Even though Dr Langton was the boss, she couldn't help thinking he was being short-sighted in ordering them.

'There you are...I'm glad you're back from your meeting,' Katie greeted her as she entered the unit. 'We've a three-year-old in treatment room two—he has a foreign body in his ear, and so far Dr Henderson hasn't been able to remove it. The boy's getting quite distressed, and his mother's becoming agitated, too. Dr Henderson's tried irrigation and now he's having a go with forceps. He doesn't like to admit defeat and he's doing his level best, but I think it's a difficult one for him. He asked for a second opinion.'

'Okay, I'll go and see the boy. It's not easy dealing with youngsters when they're fractious, and it's amazing how deep into the ear canal they can push things.' She glanced at Katie. 'Is there a nurse assisting?'

Katie shook her head. 'No, everyone's busy at the moment, but I could go along if you like. I've finished here for the moment.'

'That would be great, if you would. He might need help to calm the infant.'

Callum came up to the desk as she was speaking. He looked purposeful and energetic, as though he meant business, immaculately dressed in dark trousers, a navy-blue shirt and a subtly patterned grey-blue tie. He was so different from the casually dressed man she'd spent time with on the beach, and yet either way he managed to set her pulse racing.

'Did I hear you talking about Simon Henderson's patient—the three-year-old who thinks it's fun to stick things in his ear?'

Alex nodded.

'I would have had a look at the boy myself,' he said with a frown, 'but I have a patient waiting—I suspect she's had a mini-stroke.' He gave Alex a smile that warmed her through and through. 'You've just come from seeing Dr Langton, I take it? What was it today? Cut back on the use of surgical gloves and paper towels and make do with cheap coffee in the staff lounge?'

She shook her head. 'No, nothing like that. I'm afraid it was much more serious.' She hesitated. He probably wasn't going to like what she had to say, but she gave him a wry smile and tacked on, 'As far as you're concerned, it means ordering any new equipment is definitely off limits for the foreseeable future.'

His brows drew together. 'I might have guessed. Still, let's look on the bright side—that can't apply to stuff already on order.' He pulled a face. 'I don't suppose there's any news on the transcranial Doppler ultrasound machine I requested, is there?'

Alex sucked in a breath and laid a hand lightly on his arm as though to soften the blow. 'Callum, you know as well as I do that it's not a piece of equipment that would normally be used in the emergency room. You're setting your expectations way too high in this economic climate. You don't have a chance. You know the board won't sanction any undue expenditure.'

Perhaps it was a mistake, touching him. It made her recall all too vividly the way they had sat close together on the beach. A wave of nostalgia hit her. Those few short hours had seemed like stolen moments, and she longed to experience them all over again…but it seemed as though she was wishing on a moonbeam. Her life was complicated enough, without hankering after something that was out of reach. And she and Callum had nothing in common, did they? Their personalities were totally different, and even at work they managed to clash. She let her hand drop to her side.

He laid an arm around her shoulders and looked into her eyes. 'That's as maybe, but refusing to even look at it shows a complete lack of forward thinking on the part of the board.' He grinned. 'I'm pretty sure you could sweet-talk them into changing their minds. With the right diagnostic equipment in place we could save several days of waiting for test results. That way, we could avert imminent strokes, and by taking quick action we could save the hospital money by not having to keep patients in hospital for long periods. You could say it's false economy to avoid having one.'

Alex's mouth made a crooked shape. 'You could say that, and I can see your point, but I'm not at all sure Dr Langton will be convinced by that argument. He's not into long-term solutions right now. All he wants is to see immediate cost-cutting.' She liked having his arm around her. It might not mean anything...it might simply be his way of trying to wheedle her into doing what he wanted, but it still felt good.

'Hmph. So I guess all this means you won't be putting a rush on my order for another bedside X-ray machine, will you?'

She shook her head. 'You already know the answer to that one. No, I won't...not for the foreseeable future. I did warn you.'

He nodded. 'It's as I thought...but it's a very misguided attitude. The repair bills for the one we're using are getting beyond a joke.' He was thoughtful for a second or two, before adding mischievously, 'And I suppose I'm right in thinking there's going to be a bit of a wait for my new ECMO machine?'

Alex laughed out loud at that. 'An extracorporeal membrane oxygenating machine at around a hundred thousand pounds with running costs? I should think so, Callum. That's a very expensive pipe dream.'

His mouth twitched, before turning down at the

corners in mock dismay. 'But one we could do with—after all, we're near the coast, and drowning is just one other way in which a patient might need bypass support for the heart and lungs. Children have been known to recover from drowning in cold water, and with one of those machines on hand to gently warm their blood supply, their chances of survival would be so much greater.'

'I'm with you all the way on that one,' she acknowledged with a smile, 'but it isn't going to happen, I'm afraid. Why don't you get back to the real world and go and save your mini-stroke patient from imminent disaster by giving her the standard treatment?'

'A couple of aspirin, you mean, while I wait for the MRI scanner to be freed up—not likely to be very soon, given the waiting list—or until I can gain access to CT in a few days' time, given that the patient isn't on the critical list?' He made a face. 'A transcranial Doppler ultrasound machine would have given me an accurate diagnosis in a fraction of the time.' He sighed, releasing her, and Alex immediately felt the loss of his comforting arm around her. 'What it is to be working in modern medicine.'

He went on his way and Alex watched his confident stride. How was it that he had found his way into her affections so easily? She had always been careful about the men she let into her life, and yet he seemed to have invited himself, and was completely at ease.

She made an effort to shake off these distracting thoughts, and hurried along to see Dr Henderson's patient in the treatment room.

She could hear the child squealing before she even reached the room, and when she pushed open the door and looked inside, she saw a tearful, red-faced infant rubbing his eyes with his knuckles and glowering at the unfortunate junior doctor. Dr Henderson had relinquished the forceps and was trying unsuccessfully to pacify both the child and his mother. Katie was doing all she could to divert the boy's attention, offering him toys to cuddle and talking to him in a soothing voice, all to no avail.

'Poor Harry,' Alex murmured, going over to the boy after introducing herself to his mother. 'Is your ear hurting?'

The boy stopped sobbing long enough to nod and stare at her. 'Oh, dear, I'm sorry about that,' she said softly. 'This has all been a bit too much for you, hasn't it? I think we'll give you something to calm you down a bit, and then you'll feel much better.'

She turned to the boy's mother. 'Sometimes these foreign bodies in the ears can slip much further down than we can easily reach and it's obviously troubling him now—but not to worry, I'll give Harry an injection of a sedative and something for the pain, and then we can try again, using suction.'

The woman nodded. 'Thank you. I hate seeing him this way. It's really upsetting.'

'Of course it is. Do you know what it was he put into his ear?'

'A wooden bead. I've told him time and time again not to put things in his ears. He wasn't supposed to play with the beads, but his sister got them out, and he was straight in there. He's into everything these days, like a tornado around the house.'

'It happens a lot, especially with boys,' Alex said in sympathy. She shuddered to think about all the things James got up to… Beth had told her about the time he'd dismantled his toy car and swallowed the button battery.

That had meant a swift visit to A and E after it had stuck in his throat.

She prepared the injection and gently explained to the boy what she was about to do. 'Just a scratch,' she said, signalling with a nod of her head to Katie, who was ready to divert him with a toy train.

They waited for the injection to take effect, and when Harry finally appeared to relax and began to take an interest in the toys, Alex showed him the light on the otoscope and explained to him that she was going to use it to look in his ear. 'It's a bit like a torch,' she said.

He seemed happy to go along with that. 'I'll seek out the position of the bead, Simon,' she told the young doctor, 'and then I'll introduce the catheter through the otoscope and apply suction.'

She reached for the catheter that was attached to a wall suction device and after a few fraught seconds carefully located the object that was lodged deep in the child's ear canal. A short time later, she withdrew the catheter along with the bead, which she dropped into a kidney dish. 'There you are,' she told the boy. 'All done.'

Harry's mother smiled, and Simon looked relieved and embarrassed at the same time. 'I hate having to remove these things,' he admitted under his breath. 'It can be such a tricky procedure, and the children are always fractious. You make it look so easy.'

'It just takes practice,' she said lightly, adding with a grin, 'From now on, we'll make sure to give you all the cases that come in when you're on duty.'

Simon looked horrified. 'You don't mean that?'

'Well, maybe one or two...just so you get used to doing it,' she said in a cheerful, placating tone. 'Don't worry...you'll always have help on hand.'

He grimaced, but seemed resigned to his fate, and a few minutes later she left him with the mother and child, and started back towards the main desk.

'Alex…' Katie called her name and fell into step beside her. 'I heard you telling Callum about Dr Langton putting a stop on ordering new equipment. Is that all he's asking for…along with the cost-saving measures you've already put into place?'

Alex shook her head. 'I'm afraid not, Katie. He thinks we should cut staffing levels.'

'By staff, you mean nurses, don't you?' Katie's brow furrowed.

'Yes, but I don't want you to start worrying about that just yet. I'm not planning on making any cuts amongst the general staff. I'll see what I can do by stopping all agency work to begin with. That should make a big difference.'

Katie was still concerned. 'But it will make our jobs harder, too, won't it? How are we to cover for people who are off sick, or cope when we're inundated with patients in A and E? What if we have a major incident to handle?'

'I'm sorry, Katie, I do understand what you're saying, but I'm afraid that's the way it has to be. We're going through hard times. There just isn't enough money available to cover everything.'

'It's worrying.' Katie frowned.

'Yes, it is. But I promise you I'll do everything I can to keep things running as smoothly as possible. If you have any major problems, let me know and we'll see if we can find a way around things.'

Alex talked to Katie for a little while longer and then went to find her next patient. She worked solidly for the next few hours, and when she had made some headway through the mass of patients on her list, she stopped and stretched her aching limbs and began to think about lunch. Perhaps now that things were a little quieter in the waiting room, it would be a good time to go and grab something to eat. Maybe she could even drop in on Jane for a few minutes, to find out how she was doing.

She left the department, and walked towards the delivery bay close by the open quadrangle where staff sometimes took their lunch. She caught sight of Callum there, talking to a man in uniform while he cheerfully signed a paper attached to a clipboard. She brightened a little. Perhaps they could have lunch together.

She went over to the two men, nodding towards the deliveryman before turning to look directly at Callum. 'Hi,' she said. 'I wondered if we might have lunch together?'

'Ah… there you are,' Callum said quickly, pulling in a sharp breath. He seemed to be distracted by her sudden appearance. 'That sounds like a good idea…though I thought you might already have gone for lunch by now. You're a bit later than usual, aren't you?'

'Yes, I had a heavy workload.'

'Ah.'

She frowned. His manner was definitely a little odd, and she was beginning to wonder why he was so preoccupied. She looked around, wondering what it was that the man in uniform was delivering. Behind him, on a trolley, half-sheltered by the two men, was a huge package, as big as a man and twice as wide. Then it occurred to her that something highly suspicious was going on.

'This looks interesting,' she murmured, peering behind them to glance at the box once more. 'Is this something I should know about? Is this something that's destined for the A and E department?'

'Um...yes,' Callum answered quickly, 'but it's nothing at all for you to worry about.'

'Isn't it?' She lowered her voice, turning away so that the deliveryman wouldn't hear. 'We weren't expecting any deliveries, were we? I thought we'd agreed that any order for new equipment was to go through me first of all?'

'Yes, yes...that's quite true, but everything's in order, so you don't need to worry about it.' He moved her gently to one side, while at the same time saying to the man, 'I'll leave you to take it through to the department, then, Jim. You can leave it where we arranged.'

Jim nodded and Callum turned his attention back to Alex. 'Actually, I'm glad I bumped into you. I was thinking of going up to see Aunt Jane after I've eaten. Do you want to come along? She should be out of the recovery room by now.'

'Yes, of course, I planned to do that, but...' She looked around to see where Jim was taking the package, but the man had disappeared along with his trolley. She frowned. Callum was clearly trying to distract her. 'You're up to something, aren't you?' she said, her gaze thoughtful. 'I specifically said no new portable X-ray machine was to be ordered, and yet somehow you've managed to go behind my back and acquire one.'

'What makes you think it was an X-ray machine?' he said in surprise, raising dark brows. 'All I could see was plain brown packaging.'

'With the words, *Radiology equipment* written in black ink along the base,' she retorted in a laconic tone. 'I suppose you thought you'd sneak it into place while I wasn't looking, and make out it was the one we already have. Did you really think I wouldn't notice the difference?'

He winced. 'Something like that.' He looked her over. 'There's no getting anything past you, is there? You're like a hawk, keeping a beady eye on everything, ready to swoop without warning when you see something you don't approve of.'

'Is that so?' Unaccountably, his description of her stung, and she said crossly, 'Perhaps I wouldn't have to be like that if it wasn't for people like you...haven't you just shown yourself to be a devious, underhanded, sneaky kind of a man who has absolutely no respect for rules and regulations?' Her eyes narrowed on him. 'How could you deliberately flout the new policy that way?'

'I didn't.' He gently placed a hand beneath her elbow and started to lead her towards the quadrangle and the corridor that led to the hospital restaurant.

It was yet more diversion tactics, but she wasn't going to let him wriggle off the hook that easily. 'Didn't it occur to you that I would see the invoice? Or were you hoping to sneak that past me, too?'

He appeared to be giving it some thought. 'I suppose there was always the chance I'd get away with it, for a week or so at any rate. But you must agree with me that the old machine needs a thorough overhaul...it's always breaking down at inopportune moments and then we have to wait for the main X-ray room to be clear for use. And some patients are in too bad a way to be moved, so a bedside X-ray is really convenient...as well as quick and safe.' He looked at her closely, his gaze sweeping over her taut features. 'Surely you understand why I did it?'

She looked at him in frustration. 'Of course I understand, but you know as well as I do that things are tight around here these days and we have to be extra-careful with spending. But you don't seem to care about that. Why else would you spend money we don't have?'

He opened his mouth to answer and she cut him short. 'No, don't answer that. I'll tell you why. You did it because you thought you could get away with it…because that's the kind of man you are, a law unto yourself, totally oblivious to the wider picture, to how your actions will affect everyone else, let alone having any regard for the kind of example you're setting. As long as you get your own way, nothing else matters, does it?'

His dark brows rose. 'Phew!' He whistled softly under his breath and stared at her, his eyes widening. 'I didn't realise you had such a negative opinion of me. Are you quite sure there isn't anything you left out?'

'Oh, I'm sure there's more where that came from,' she said tersely. 'Give me time, and I'll come up with a list.'

He absently nodded agreement. 'I thought you might…' He studied her. 'I'd no idea I could rouse you so much…you're usually so calm and in control. You never lose your cool. It's what everyone says about you… you don't show what you're thinking. You just get on with the job and deal with everything and everyone efficiently, without any kind of sentiment.'

He studied the quick rise and fall of her chest, his glance roaming over her tense figure, drifting down over the cotton pin-tucked blouse she wore, with its self-coloured buttons, and the slim-fitting skirt that gently skimmed her hips and ended at the knee, to show shapely calves.

'Perhaps things are different now, though,' he murmured. 'Nothing's quite going the way you want it to now that Dr Langton's intervened, and you're having to fight to keep everything in order. You seem quite flushed with the exertion.' Light glimmered in his eyes. 'It makes a very appealing picture, you being all pink and agitated. I'm not at all used to seeing that, though I have to wonder why you're getting yourself so worked up…I might even say passionate…about what you imagine I've been up to.'

'I'm not getting myself worked up.' She ground the words out through her teeth and sent him a stony look. 'I'm just pointing out the error of your ways.'

'Yes, I appreciate that. But I'm still intrigued. This is so unlike you. You never vent your spleen, no matter how provoked you might be.' His expression was quizzical, his glance trailing over the firm jut of her chin and coming to rest on the soft fullness of her mouth. 'I wonder if you'd have reacted the same way if it was any other colleague who had been implicated?' He shook his head. 'Somehow, I doubt it. I have the notion that I'm the only one who can bring out such strong feelings in you.' His eyes glinted. 'Now, there's food for thought.'

She pulled in a shocked breath. 'That's complete nonsense.'

'Is it?'

They went out through the glass doors and into the deserted quadrangle. From here, they would be able to reach the restaurant, which was situated just beyond the dense screen of trees and herbaceous plants.

Alex was deep in thought. He was talking rubbish, wasn't he? Of course she wasn't getting herself all stirred up about him…it was the situation that disturbed her, wasn't it? It couldn't be that he had managed to fire up some spark that lay dormant within her…could it?

She couldn't fathom it out. Why *was* she so het up? Was it really true that he, alone, was able to provoke her to such a wild and deeply emotional response, one that started up in the very core of her being? Surely not? The idea was unthinkable. She sent him a surreptitious glance, at the same time giving an imperceptible shake of her head, as though she was trying to rid herself of the notion, but just at that moment he turned towards her and caught her troubled glance.

'Thinking it over?' he asked, an amused note coming into his voice. 'You're having doubts, aren't you?' He reflected on that. 'Perhaps we should put the theory to the test.'

She looked at him suspiciously. 'What do you mean?'

'I mean, maybe we should find out just how deep your feelings go.' He placed a hand lightly under her elbow, and before she realised what he was doing, he had managed to manoeuvre her into the shelter of a privet hedge. 'Perhaps you're not so cool and unemotional as you make out, and it's all welling up inside you, but you just don't know how to handle those instincts that you've buried deep down.'

She shook her head. 'You're way off beam. Why would I...?' Her voice trailed off in uncertainty as his arms gently slid around her waist.

'Why would you get yourself into a state over me?' he finished for her. He drew her close, so that the softness of her breasts was crushed against the hard wall of his chest and her legs encountered the pressure of his strong thighs. 'Well, let's see now...could it be that you're not quite as immune to normal, human emotions as you think you are?' He lowered his head so that his mouth was just a breath away from hers, and Alex suddenly found that she couldn't think straight any more. She knew that she ought to pull away from him, but although her head told her one thing, her treacherous body was telling her something altogether different. His hands were warm on the gentle slope of her hips and she was discovering that she liked the feeling.

'I don't know what happened to me, why I reacted the way I did,' she said cautiously, trying to keep herself on an even keel. She hesitated, doubts clouding her brain. 'I don't know what came over me.' She frowned, confusion settling on her, so that she was torn between wanting to berate him for his misguided actions, and yet, at the same time, she was conscious of her own shortcomings holding her back and undermining her confidence. And all the while he was holding her, setting her senses on fire with his gently stroking hands and somehow managing to befuddle her wits.

'It's not surprising you feel this way,' he said in a soothing tone. 'You're stressed and overworked. You've taken on far too much…your brother and his wife are seriously ill, you have the children to care for, the house is a work in itself, and on top of all that, you have a difficult job to do. You shouldn't blame yourself. Anyone would bend under the strain.' He ran his hand over the length of her, letting it glide slowly over her back, her hip, her thigh. 'But I can make things easier for you. I can show you how to forget your worries for a while.'

He rested his cheek against hers, his hand lightly caressing her, smoothing over the small of her back, and drawing her into the shelter of his body. 'You just have to let me help you.'

For some reason, she didn't even think of resisting, wanting only to lean into him and take comfort in his nearness…and that was strange, because no man had ever had quite that effect on her before this. Perhaps he sensed that inherent need in her, because after a moment or two he moved even closer, brushing his lips over hers and delicately testing the soft contours of her mouth.

Involuntarily, her lips parted, tantalised by his sweet exploration, and she gave herself up to his kiss, loving the way he moulded her to him and wrapped his arms around her. Somehow, just by holding her and cherishing her this way, he made her feel that she was all woman. For just these few moments she felt utterly feminine and desirable, and she realised that it was a feeling that she had lost over these last few months. She had been so bound up in her work, her problems, that she had forgotten there was more to living than being an automaton. It had taken Callum to bring her to life and show her that she couldn't stay locked up in her ivory castle. Why was it that she let her work and the chaotic demands of family and household chores rule her everyday life?

'Alex?' He lifted his head and looked down at her, reaching up with his hand to smooth away the creases that had formed on her brow. 'You're thinking again. I can feel you thinking… I thought we'd established you should take time out from that?'

'I…I don't know… I didn't realise…' She could feel herself tensing up all over again. 'That's all very well for you to say, isn't it? You seem to sail through life without worrying about anything. I'm the one who has to explain to the bosses when things go wrong. I'm the one who has to come up with answers. I can't just cast it off as though it's nothing.'

He sighed, leaning his head against her forehead. 'This is about the X-ray machine again, isn't it? There's no way you're going to relax until you've resolved it in your mind.'

'You know me so well, don't you?' It was a question

tinged with regret. Why couldn't she simply let go, and cast her worries to one side?

'Would it help if I told you that it isn't a new machine?' He frowned. 'It's a reconditioned model—what they euphemistically call "pre-loved". And as to the money to pay for it, I've been raising funds for some time now, through various fun runs and dinner dances, raffles and so on. Now we're reaping the rewards.' He ran his fingers through the silk of her hair. 'So you see, you had no reason to worry. I didn't go against you. In fact, I told you that in the first place.'

'Oh!' She looked at him, aghast. 'And you let me go on…'

'And on…' He chuckled. 'I'd have stopped you, but it occurred to me that you needed to get it off your chest. You've been wound up for days, weeks. All you think about is the job, cost-cutting, and whether or not everyone is toeing the line.'

She stiffened. 'But that's what I'm here for. It's the reason I was set on.'

'But you're not alone in any of this. I'll be there for you. I'm working with you, not against you. I appreciate how difficult the job is for you, and I'll do whatever I can to help you. Together we can sort this out. Believe me.'

She closed her eyes briefly. She wanted to believe him. But in the past those men she had thought she could rely on had always let her down. They didn't want to know about the hassles of the job. All that mattered to them was to take life as it came and if things went wrong, so be it.

She couldn't live like that. She wanted to relax and enjoy life, but she couldn't let it toss her about on a whim, like flotsam and jetsam on a beach. Somehow, if it was in her power, she wanted to make a difference.

Could she trust him? Those few moments of inner peace, when he had held her in his arms and shown her that another side to life was possible had been so fleeting. Deep down, she recognised that they were two different people, opposites in every way, and yet she was drawn to him, as though by some invisible, magnetic thread.

Now she was more confused than ever.

CHAPTER SIX

'Do you think Mummy will like this?' Sarah asked, adding petals made out of red tissue paper to the flowers that decorated the front of the card she was making. 'It's a vase, see, with lots of flowers in it.'

'I'm sure she'll love it,' Alex said, admiring her efforts. 'It's very pretty, and I know your mother loves flowers.'

'I made a sailboat picture for Daddy,' James put in, waving his card in the air. 'He likes boats. He takes me to sail mine in the brook sometimes.' He frowned, his grey eyes troubled, and Alex wondered if he was thinking about those special times spent with his father, which had come to an abrupt end after the accident.

'You're right, it's perfect for him...and we'll put it on his bedside table at the hospital, so that he can see it as soon as he's feeling a bit better.'

'He's really poorly, isn't he?' Sarah's eyes clouded, and Alex wished there was some way she could comfort her. The children missed their parents and as time went on it was becoming more and more difficult for her to soothe their worries. 'The nurse said he wasn't well enough to see us. She said he had to rest.'

'When are we going to see him again?' James asked.

'I want him to come back home. I want Mummy to come home.'

'I know... It's very difficult for both of you, isn't it?' Alex laid her arms around the children's shoulders as they stood close to one another by the kitchen table. 'But your mother is getting stronger every day, and perhaps it won't be too long before she's able to come home.'

'And Daddy?' Sarah's gaze was almost pleading and it wrenched at Alex's heart not to be able to give her the answer she wanted.

'I don't know. The doctors and nurses are doing what they can to make him more comfortable. We just have to wait, and hope that soon he'll be stronger.'

James's bottom lip trembled, but he didn't say anything more, and Alex gave him a hug. 'Why don't you finish making your cards for Auntie Jane?' she suggested. 'If you can finish them off in the next few minutes, before I drop you both off at Martha's house, I'll be able to give them to Jane when I go in to work today.'

'She's going to be home soon, isn't she?' Sarah brightened a little. 'You said she had her operation and she was all right.'

Alex nodded. 'She just has to stay in hospital for a couple of days, so the doctors can make sure she's healing up nicely.' Jane's operation had been done with minimally invasive surgery, which meant that the surgeon had made several small incisions and used a laparascope to help with the procedure.

'I don't want to go to Martha's,' James grumbled, his bottom lip jutting. 'I want to stay here with you.'

She knelt down and put her arms around him. 'But I have to go to work, James. You know that, don't you?'

'Yes, but I want you to stay at home. I want you to stay here, with us.'

Alex shook her head. 'I'd like to do that. I wish I could, sweetheart, but it just isn't possible right now. I have to go to work to earn money so that I can pay all the bills. I'd love to stay here with you, but I can't.' Alex frowned. 'Anyway, I thought you liked being with Martha? You have a good time at her house, don't you?'

James didn't answer, but Sarah said quietly, 'She's okay. She takes us to the park—but it's not the same. We like it here with you. The only thing better would be for Mummy and Daddy to come home.'

Alex kissed both of them, wanting to comfort them and reassure them at the same time. 'If I could wave a magic wand and make it happen for you, I would, but for now, we all have to make the best of things.'

She got to her feet and glanced at the table, littered with glue sticks, cards and coloured tissue paper. 'Like I said, if you want me to give the cards to Auntie Jane, you'd better get a move on, because we have to leave here in twenty minutes.'

She arrived at the hospital some time later, feeling harassed and dejected. James had begun to play up as she'd dropped him off at her neighbour's house, and it had taken all her ingenuity and powers of reasoning to soothe him and help him to settle down. It also meant that she was a few minutes late for work, and that added to her stress levels, leaving her flustered.

'We're short-handed,' Katie told her as she made her way to the main desk. 'The waiting room's full and we don't have enough nurses to cope with the workload. Charlotte's off sick, and Simon Henderson is away on a course.' She shook her head. 'I don't know how we're going to manage things.'

'I know it's difficult, but we'll just have to keep going

as best we can,' Alex told her, giving it some thought. 'Unfortunately, I can't bring in any locum doctors, and we won't be using the agency nurses any more. It means that your job, triage, is more important than ever, because we'll probably need to allocate nurses to the most serious cases. Waiting times will be stretched, of course, but there's nothing we can do about that in the circumstances.'

Katie sighed. 'We'll do what we can.'

'Thanks, Katie. You're all very good at what you do, and I'm just hoping that you'll be able to keep things together for as long as possible.'

She took a moment to glance at the status board. An infant was coming in by ambulance...something else to turn up her stress levels a notch. Very young, sick children were always a source of concern.

'Did I hear something about waiting times?' Callum came over to the desk. He placed a chart in the tray and picked out another one, just as Alex reached for a file. Their hands brushed against one another, sending small explosions of sensation to rocket through Alex's arm. She sucked in a breath. Why was it that her senses went on overdrive every time he came near? She stole a glance at him, but looked away when his gaze met hers. It didn't help that he always looked so good, either. Her heartbeat had quickened and there was a strange ache starting up inside her. He was way too distracting. He wore dark trousers and a shirt that moulded his body and showed off the flat plane of his stomach, hinting at the vital, energetic man within, a man who was always on the go and kept himself totally fit.

'Waiting times are getting longer,' Katie said. 'It's the budget cuts coming home to roost.' She moved away, heading towards the treatment room.

Callum's brows drew together. 'There's no easy answer, is there?' He glanced at Alex, who was trying to clear her head of errant thoughts by attempting to concentrate on her work schedule and make some sense of it. She was not going to let herself get worked up about him. It was her hormones that were bothering her, nothing else. 'No,' she said. 'The problem is, we need more money, not less.'

She frowned at her work schedule. How was she going to pull in her clinic time as well as take in another meeting with the executive board? Dr Langton seemed to forget that she had other priorities when he called these impromptu gatherings. And in the meantime, would it help to cheer up the nurses if she bought in pizzas and cookies to keep them going through the busy times when they weren't able to get away for a proper break? It was surely worth a try. She made a mental note to phone the local take-away food shop to arrange delivery.

'You look a little flushed,' Callum said, sending her a thoughtful glance. 'Is it the staffing problem, or something else? I saw you come flying in here a couple of minutes ago as though the hounds of hell were at your feet.'

Alex made a helpless gesture with her hands. He was looking at her so intently and she wanted so desperately to be close to him. She was trying not to think about the way he had kissed her not too long ago, or about the way it had felt to be wrapped in his arms.

'It's the children, mostly,' she murmured, 'James and Sarah. It's very worrying. They're both finding it difficult to cope with their parents in hospital, and I don't know what to tell them now that Ross has taken a turn for the worse. I'm becoming really anxious about him.

And now that school has broken up for the holidays they're saying that they want me to be there for them.' She gave a sigh. 'I feel as though I'm being torn all ways.'

'There's no perfect solution to any of those, is there? Given a choice, I suspect children are always going to want their parent or guardian close at hand...but in this day and age even in the best of circumstances I guess it isn't always possible.'

She shook her head. 'No, it isn't. I've been thinking about it, and maybe I'll try to get them enrolled in some play activities over the next few weeks. That might help to distract them a bit.'

'Good idea. That could work out well.'

A siren sounded in the distance, and they both turned towards the ambulance bay. 'This must be the two-year-old we've been expecting—the one with the high temperature and vomiting,' Callum said. 'Would you be able to work with me? I've a feeling we'll need your skills as a paediatrician with this one.'

She nodded, walking briskly alongside him. 'Do we know anything about her condition? The GP sent her to us, didn't he?'

'That's right. Apparently, she had chickenpox a few weeks ago, and since then she's been going rapidly downhill. She's been generally unwell, lethargic and showing signs of irritability. Her mother complains that she's gone off her food over the last few days, and now she's very poorly.'

They hurried to greet the ambulance technicians, who were wheeling the child into the department. 'This is Rachel Vernon,' the paramedic said. 'She's two years old. She had a couple of seizures in the ambulance, so we've given her medication to control them, but her condition's still unstable. There are signs of neck rigidity and photophobia.'

Callum nodded grimly. 'Thanks,' he said, taking over and accompanying the infant into the treatment room. He gently began to examine the child while Alex talked to the girl's parents.

'It's bad, isn't it?' the father said, his face taut with anxiety. 'She looks so ill. The GP said it might be meningitis.'

'It's a possibility,' Alex agreed. 'Meningitis means that the meninges, the brain's protective covering, are inflamed, but I'm concerned that the seizures are a sign that there's inflammation within her brain, too. We'll do tests to find out exactly what's causing her problems, though, and in the meantime we'll give her supportive treatment.'

She tried to reassure the parents that they would do everything possible to help their child. Then she turned to Callum, wanting to know the results of his examination.

'It's possible we're dealing with a viral infection,' he said, 'but if that's the case, it's more serious than usual. This little girl is very sick.' His expression was sad as he looked at the infant, but there was something else in his eyes that Alex had learned to recognise, a growing determination, perhaps, that he would do his utmost to pull the child through this distressing illness and get her back on her feet once more. He straightened. 'I'll get a CT scan done as soon as possible.'

Alex nodded. 'I agree. I'd recommend antibiotics as a cover, until we know what we're dealing with, along with medication to bring her temperature down and control her pain, and something to stop the vomiting. And we need to do a lumbar puncture as soon as she's stable.' A lumbar puncture would show them whether they were dealing with a bacterial or a viral infection, and once they knew the nature of it, they would be able to choose the most appropriate treatment.

He nodded and briefly addressed the nurse who was assisting. 'I'll give the child a corticosteroid to control the inflammation, along with an anticonvulsant, and at the same time we'll set up an EEG so that we can monitor any more seizures. Later on we may need to start an infusion of mannitol to control any rise in intracranial pressure. In the meantime, we'll take blood for testing, and I'm going to ask the lab to get back to us urgently with the results.'

'Okay, I'll organise a trolley.' The nurse hurried away to prepare the equipment.

Some time later, when they had done all they could to safeguard the child and make her more comfortable, Alex and Callum spoke once again to the parents, before finally turning their attention to their other patients.

'We'll look at the possibility of doing a lumbar puncture in a few hours,' Callum said. 'It all depends how well she responds to the initial treatment.'

'Waiting's always difficult,' Alex said, frowning. She could see that he was worried about his small patient, but their options were limited right now. They were doing everything possible to control the infection, but until they knew exactly what they were dealing with, they were working in the dark. 'Given that she's just suffered a bout of chickenpox, it's quite likely that we're dealing with a viral source…the abnormalities on the EEG certainly seem to point that way, but without the lab tests we can't know for sure.'

They both went their separate ways after that, treating

a variety of patients who had come in with all manner of problems from fractures to worrying chest infections.

Around lunchtime, Alex met up with Callum again as she was suturing a gash in a child's hand. He put his head around the door of the treatment room, and said quietly, 'Rachel hasn't had any more seizures since we last saw her, so I'm thinking we might do the spinal tap after lunch. Right now, though, I'm going up to see my aunt… I thought you might want to come with me as soon as you're free. I'll be in the staff lounge, grabbing a bite to eat.' He gave her a knowing wink. 'I heard some good fairy had pizza sent in, along with baguettes and cakes and other goodies.'

Her mouth curved. 'Just give me a minute to finish up in here.' She glanced at her young patient a short time later. 'That's it…we're all done, Lewis. The nurse will put a dressing on the hand for you, and then you're free to go home with your mum.' She smiled. 'You've been very brave,' she added, presenting him with a teddy-bear badge and a page to colour, and he left the room with a beaming smile on his face.

She found Callum in the lounge, tucking into a bacon-filled baguette. 'These are good,' he said, munching appreciatively. 'You want to try one?'

She nodded. 'Perhaps I will.' She could see from what was left in the boxes that her gesture had gone down well with the staff. Katie and a couple of the other nurses on their lunch break were tucking in.

'There's a rumour going around,' Katie said, swallowing the last dregs of her tea and rinsing her cup at the sink. 'People are saying that Dr Langton will use the reduction in staff as an excuse to cut down on the emergency department's hours.'

Alex frowned. 'I haven't heard anything like that.

When I told him that we were on budget to keep the department up and running, he agreed with me.'

Katie made a face. 'I wonder how much we can trust him. My friend worked at a hospital where he was an executive some time ago. He closed her unit down and transferred the services to the city hospital several miles away.'

Callum was thoughtful for a moment or two. 'I suppose, with the cuts in place, he could say that we don't have the people to man the unit, and therefore we'll no longer be able to provide a twenty-four-hour service.'

Alex's eyes widened. 'That isn't going to happen here. I'm making these changes for the good of the department. I'm not going to stand by and watch the A and E unit be disbanded.'

'Well, I thought it only right to warn you.' Katie made her way to the door. 'But thanks, anyway, for the food. It helps a lot. There's nothing like a full stomach to give people a boost.'

Alex watched her go out into the corridor, followed by the other nurses, leaving them alone in the room. Could there be some truth in what Katie had said? She brooded on the subject for a moment or two before going over to the table and picking out a slice of pizza.

'Try not to worry about it,' Callum said, studying her taut features. 'You're doing the best you can. I don't see how you can do any more.' He gave a crooked smile. 'As it is, you're like a whirlwind at the best of times, coming up with all these ideas for savings, starting new practices and setting up new audits. Since you arrived, no one's really had time to gather breath.'

'Oh.' The word came out on a faintly shocked exhalation. What was she to say to him? 'Is that really how you see me?'

'I think you believe in getting the job done. You don't think about failure…and that's a good thing.'

'Is it?' She nibbled at the pizza. 'Right now, if there's any truth in what Katie says, it looks as though failure's staring me in the face. It seems that whatever I do, Dr Langton will try to close us down.'

'But we won't let that happen, will we?' He smiled at her. 'I've been thinking about what you said—about the hospital needing more money, not less. Perhaps there's a way we can make that happen.'

'Oh?' She was intrigued. 'I'm not sure how we could do that, unless we offered paid services of some sort.' She finished the pizza and wiped her hands on a serviette.

He nodded. 'That's exactly what I was thinking. Maybe we could rent out facilities that aren't being used, if not full-time, then on a part-time basis…like the theatres and the scanner, for instance.'

She thought about it. 'You're right,' she said, her mouth curving. 'And maybe we could rent out some of the outpatient facilities that aren't used at weekends. That way, we could perhaps have a GP-run minor injuries unit to take some of the strain off A and E.'

'See? You're getting the idea.' He came and put his arms around her. 'I told you I would help.'

'And you have, brilliantly.' She tilted her face up to him, glad to have him hold her and keep her close. 'I could put those suggestions to the board. It would make such a difference—it's a whole new way of thinking.'

He ran his hands along her arms. 'So maybe now you'll be able to think less about work, and more about getting some much-needed rest and recuperation along the way. I was thinking of maybe a trip out somewhere… an afternoon in the hills, or a few more hours by the sea, or perhaps we could drive out to Cheddar some time?'

'Oh, what bliss.' She smiled up at him. 'You make it sound so tempting. And I did have such a good time the other day. It was so lovely to walk with you over the rocks and then sit with you and watch the waves break on the shore.'

He dropped a kiss lightly on her mouth, making her whole body tingle with pleasure. 'Then we'll do it again, soon.'

He moved away from her as the door opened and one of the junior doctors came in. Alex drew in a quick breath. How had she let herself be tempted into such a situation at work of all places? All sensible thoughts seemed to go out of her head the moment Callum touched her. Emotionally, she was all over the place at the moment, and it was so unlike her to be this way. What was happening to her?

Perhaps it was simply that she was of an age to be settling down and having children of her own. Up to now, she had bypassed that route, but thinking about it, a distinct pang of loss ran through her.

For an instant, as she tried to imagine how things might be, she could see herself quite clearly with a family of her own, living in the beautiful, sprawling, mellow house with the orchard and acres of land. Subconsciously, hadn't she chosen it because it was a place where she could put down roots?

She thought about it some more. All the children in her surreal vision would not be like her, she was sure of that. They would take after their father, a man who was laid-back, carefree, taking life as it came...the complete opposite of her...

It was odd how these images clamoured to be seen,

showing her two sides of a coin, almost as though she was fighting a battle within herself, and she tried to shake off the strange feelings that were assailing her. What was wrong with her? Perhaps she'd been overdoing things. That had to be the explanation.

Callum cut in on her thoughts. 'Perhaps we should go and see Jane while we have the chance?' he suggested.

She nodded, draining the last dregs of her coffee. 'She should be feeling a bit better by now, I expect.'

'Let's hope so. It's been twenty-four hours since the tumour was removed, and by all accounts the surgery went well. Her blood pressure is settling down nicely, too, according to the nurse on duty.'

'It all sounds positive, at any rate.' They left the lounge together and made their way up to the ward.

'It's good to see both of you,' Jane said with a smile as they entered the room. It was a small bay, with four beds, and she was sitting in a chair by the window, looking out over the hospital grounds. For the moment, she was the only occupant. 'The others have gone to the day room,' she told them, 'except for one lady, who's having physio.'

She caught her breath as she spoke, as though she was in pain, and began to rub absently at her side. Alex frowned. 'Are you all right? How are you feeling?'

'I'm okay,' Jane answered. 'A bit bruised, I think. It's gone a bit purple-looking around here.' She waved a hand vaguely over her upper abdomen. 'It hurts when I breathe, but that's probably only to be expected after the surgery.'

Callum was instantly alarmed. 'May I see? Has the doctor been to look at you since the operation?'

'Yes, dear.' She patted his hand, and allowed him

to check the bruising. 'I went to have an ultrasound scan this morning…' She paused to gather her breath. 'I think they were just checking everything's all right. They didn't say much to me about it. The technician said she has to send the results to the doctor, and I'll be seeing him again, later today, apparently.'

Callum stood up, tension evident in his whole body, and Alex understood his reaction perfectly. The purple bruised area was not what they should have expected to see. 'Why wasn't I told about this?' he asked, almost as though he was talking to himself.

'I'm telling you now,' Jane said.

'But the medical staff should have kept me informed.' He shook his head, frowning. 'I must go and find out about this. I need to know what's going on. Excuse me. I'll be back in a little while.'

He left the room and Jane sighed. 'Oh, dear. Now there's going to be trouble.'

'I'm sure he'll be very thoughtful in how he goes about things.' Alex gave her a reassuring smile, keeping her own anxieties about Jane's condition to herself. Jane was looking worried, and perhaps the best thing she could do was wait until Callum returned with details of what was actually wrong before she made any comment.

'He loves you dearly, you know,' she said. 'He won't rest until he knows you're up and about and feeling strong again.' She gave her the get-well-soon cards the children had made for her. 'And you've made a lasting impression on James and Sarah, too.'

'Bless them. These are lovely.' Jane looked at the cards, Sarah's bright with a basket full of paper flowers, and James's a mouth-watering design of a delicious-looking cherry cake.

'James is looking forward to you being home and filling the house with the smell of baking,' Alex told her. 'He says it's the best thing in the world. Of course, to be fair to him, his instincts aren't entirely selfish. He's really fond of you...but he just loves your cooking, too.'

'Oh, he's a treasure.' Jane chuckled. 'He does so remind me of Callum when he was a youngster. He was always up to something, and he could wind me around his little finger when he wanted.' She paused to rest for a while, lightly rubbing at the ache in her side. Then she glanced at Alex and said, 'So, how are things with you? Are you managing with the children? I know it must be difficult for you, especially with your brother taking a turn for the worse.'

'We're coping,' Alex said. 'Martha's been a great help. I'm really glad you put us in touch with each other.'

'Well, I knew you would need some help.' Jane was quiet for a moment, studying her features. 'Something's wrong, though, isn't it? I could tell as soon as you walked in. You're not yourself. Is it the job? Or Callum? Have you two been fighting?'

'Me...fight with Callum?' Alex gave a self-conscious laugh. 'Heaven forbid! I'd never win... I thought I was strong-minded and on the ball, but he runs rings around me without even trying.'

Jane was very perceptive. Nothing much escaped her, did it? Even when she was ill. 'I think he feels I'm a workaholic.' She gave a faint sigh. 'I don't see how I can do things differently. I was given a job to do, and I'm getting on with it as best I can.'

'Ah, well, you shouldn't mind him too much. Most likely, he's speaking from personal experience there. His feelings go way back to his childhood, and it was always a bone of contention for him that his mother was so often away from home. Of course, she had an important job to do. He always understood that, and she always tried to make up for it once she was back with him. I dare say he has mixed feelings about the whole business of career women. I think that's why he's never settled down. I have the feeling he was put off by his parents' way of life—he saw how the idea of parents and family could go wrong and he doesn't want to risk that for himself.'

Alex frowned. He'd told her once, some time ago, that he preferred to be footloose and fancy-free, and she'd taken it to mean that it was just a temporary state of mind. But perhaps the hospital grapevine had it right after all…he was afraid of commitment.

Callum pushed open the door just then and came to join them. He was still frowning. 'I just had a word with the doctor,' he said, going over to his aunt and sitting down beside her. 'It's nothing to worry about, but the reason you're feeling so uncomfortable is that during the keyhole surgery the space for manoeuvre was limited, and it seems that one of the instruments caused a blood clot to form on your liver. It's building up slowly, and that's why you're feeling so uncomfortable.' He glanced at her to make sure that she understood what he was saying.

Jane was puzzled. 'Are they going to do something about it? Or will it go away on its own?'

'The surgeon's going to drain it for you this afternoon, in an hour or so. He's going to come and talk to you about it in a while. It's not a difficult procedure, and he'll do it with the aid of the ultrasound monitor to guide him. He'll anaesthetise the area and give you a sedative, so you won't feel anything, and afterwards you'll be much more comfortable.'

'Oh, I see.' Jane fell silent after that, but there was tension in her shoulders, and Callum gave her a gentle hug. 'I'll stay with you throughout the procedure, if you like. I'll be there to make sure everything's all right.'

'Are you sure you'll be able to do that? Won't you be too busy with your work in A and E?'

'You're more important to me than my work,' he said simply, putting his arm around her. 'If it will make you feel better, then I want to be with you.'

She nodded, and relaxed a little, some of the stiffness leaving her shoulders, and Alex guessed she was more worried than she appeared. She wanted Callum to be with her. He was a comfort to her, and she thought the world of him, as though he was the son she never had. Watching them, Alex almost envied them their closeness. He thought the world of his aunt, and Alex could see that it was a bond that would never be severed.

They stayed and talked to her for a little while longer, and then Callum said reluctantly, 'We have to go back down to A and E to look in on a little girl, but I'll be back with you before you know it. Don't worry about anything.'

'I won't.' She clasped his hand as he lightly kissed her cheek, and then she waved them to the door. 'Go and see to your work,' she said. 'I'll be fine.'

Callum didn't say anything as he and Alex went down to the emergency department. Alex wanted to talk to him, she even opened her mouth to ask him how he was feeling, but he shook his head, cutting her off. His features were shuttered, as though he was working something out within himself, and she just had to accept that this was the wrong time, that she would be intruding if she pushed him to speak.

Just a few minutes later, they worked together to prepare the little girl for the lumbar puncture. She was still very poorly, and Alex was anxious to see that they made the procedure as painless and unobtrusive as possible for her.

'We'll give her a sedative first,' Alex told the nurse, 'and it would be better for her if her mother could come and be with her.'

The nurse nodded. 'I'll make sure we have some toys on hand in case we need to distract her.'

As soon as everything was in place, Callum injected the girl with anaesthetic around the area where they were to do the spinal tap. He waited for it to take effect, and then inserted a needle to withdraw some of the spinal fluid.

Alex labelled the vials and gave them to the nurse to take to the lab. 'We need the results urgently,' she told her.

Once they had finished, they made sure that Rachel was sedated enough so that she would lie still for the next hour or so. Callum checked her medication and made certain that everything was in order, before finally checking his watch.

'I should go,' he said, glancing at Alex. 'Would you take over for me while I'm away?'

'Of course,' Alex said quietly as they left the treatment room. 'You're worried about your aunt, aren't you?' She frowned. 'It's not a difficult procedure, to remove the haematoma, you know. I'm sure she'll be all right.'

He nodded. 'I'm not really concerned about that side of things.' His expression was bleak, his mouth flattening a little as they walked along the corridor. 'It's just that she has always been so strong in every way. Up to now, she's always been there for me whenever I needed her, she would look after me and comfort me when I was ill as a child, and now that the positions are reversed it hurts to see her looking so frail.'

His eyes darkened. 'She won't give any sign that she's worried or upset, but I know that deep down she's afraid and uncertain. And who can blame her? To think that these last few years she's been suffering all these symptoms of high blood pressure and I did nothing about it. I let the doctor go on treating her with tablets that were doing no good whatsoever. I should have spotted that something was wrong sooner and arranged for her to have tests.'

Alex laid her hand on his, causing him to come to a stop by the lift bay. 'As things turned out, you couldn't have done any more than you did,' she murmured, running her fingers along his arm in a gentle caress. 'It was normal procedure to treat her with medication in the first instance, and none of the tests would have shown the presence of a tumour until this late stage. Her condition is really very rare. You can't blame yourself.'

He wasn't convinced. 'You're very sweet, Alex,' he said softly, lifting a hand to gently cup her face. His fingers traced the line of her cheekbone and slid along the angle of her jaw. 'Thank you for trying to make me feel better...but I'm okay, you know. I can handle it. I just have to make sure that she knows I'll be there for her, come what may.'

The lift doors swung open, and they parted company as Callum headed back up to his aunt's ward. Alex turned away to go and seek out her next patient. She could still feel the light touch of his fingers on her cheek, and somehow that made her incredibly sad, and at first she didn't know the reason for that. Perhaps it was because it made her yearn for what she could not have.

Because there was no way she could allow herself to fall for Callum, was there? So far, he hadn't shown that he was the kind of man who was ready to settle down, and for her part, there was far too much going on in her life right now for her to even think of getting involved.

Why, then, was the temptation so irresistible? Right now was the worst possible time for her to be even thinking of starting a relationship, especially one with a colleague…and yet there was no getting away from the fact that she was filled with a longing that couldn't possibly be assuaged.

CHAPTER SEVEN

'IT'S good to see you finally taking time out to relax,' Callum said, sitting down on one of the comfortable patio chairs that Alex had set out on the raised wooden decking just beyond the back of the house. It stood amongst landscaped gardens, with rustic arbours and pergolas that were covered with rambling roses.

'I don't recall you giving me much choice,' Alex said grumpily. The sun was shining down on them from a clear blue sky and she was overheated and becoming conscious that she would have done better to wear a cotton skirt with her loose, sleeveless top, rather than her jeans. 'One minute I was repairing the boundary fence, and the next you'd taken over and sent me to make cold drinks.' She was still hot with indignation at being moved bodily out of the way and relegated to the kitchen. She had one day off this weekend to get things done, and he had come along and thwarted her plans.

'You have to admit, though, you weren't getting on too well, were you?' Callum gave her an amused look. 'If I hadn't stopped by to pick up some fresh clothes for Aunt Jane, you'd still be struggling with it now. Anyway, before that you were busy in the kitchen making goodies to take into hospital for her—that was very thoughtful of you, so I figured the least I could do was to help you out.'

He'd already helped her out a good deal over the last few days, coming along to fix the tiles on the roof and lend a hand with the painting. 'Well, I felt it was the right thing to do. She was looking so much better yesterday, so I thought she'd be in a mood to appreciate some cookies. And the children enjoyed helping to make them.' She could hear their voices now, coming from the orchard as they played amongst the trees that were burgeoning with fruit.

He nodded. 'I was worried about her, but everything went well, and it's beginning to look as though she'll make a full recovery. And the tumour was benign, so that was the best news of all.'

'Oh, it was such a relief to hear that. Now all she has to do is rest for a couple of days and then with any luck she'll be able to come home.'

'Let's hope so.' He looked at her, his mouth making a crooked line. 'That might work for you, too,' he said. 'You've been looking quite stressed lately, and I can't help feeling that you could do with some days off.'

'Well, don't hope for too much, because it isn't likely to happen.' She shook her head. They both knew they were miles apart when it came to the demands of her job. 'Though I suppose in the end I *am* glad you came along and stopped me today,' she admitted with a rueful smile. 'That fence has been bothering me for ages, and I was struggling a bit with the wood, where it had rotted.'

'Well, there are new planks in position now, so everything's secure and looking good once more.' He gazed around at the colourful, flower-filled garden and then looked beyond it to the meadow that bordered the apple orchard.

'You certainly picked a gem when you bought this place,' he said on a thoughtful note. 'And all your hard work is paying off at last. You've tidied everything up, the garden, the orchard...and after a lick of fresh paint the house looks like a beautiful, rambling old cottage. It's like something on a picture postcard, with the wisteria round the door and the natural stone wall with the plants growing in the crevices.' He frowned. 'And yet I bet you hardly have time to sit back and enjoy it.'

Alex was wistful. 'I certainly haven't until now. When I took it on, I wasn't at all sure I was doing the right thing—it was rundown and I knew it would be difficult to sort out, but I couldn't help myself—something told me it had potential.' She nodded towards him. 'You're right, it has been hard work, but with your help, we're gradually restoring it to its original state. Things are beginning to come together now really well.'

'I've been surprised how much I've enjoyed helping out.' He smiled. 'I think house renovation could become a new hobby for me.'

'You're certainly good at it. The old inglenook fireplace in the lounge looks great after being spruced up. I hadn't realised the house held so many treasures.'

She lifted the jug from the centre of the table and started to pour out glasses of chilled Sangria. Ice cubes clinked and mingled with slices of melon, apple, orange and lemon. She handed him a glass.

'Thanks.' He took a sip of the bright red liquid, and savoured the taste on his tongue for the moment. 'This is good,' he said, shooting her a quick glance. 'Is there some subtle ingredient I don't know about?'

'That depends on how you usually make it,' she answered. 'I put in red wine, orange juice and ginger ale, and then topped it up with fruit. I added a few cinnamon sticks, too.'

'It's delicious.' He peered at the slices of apple. 'It won't be too long before you're harvesting your own apples,' he mused. 'Have you thought about what you'll do with them? From the looks of things there are going to be masses.'

She shook her head. 'Apart from eating the dessert apples and making pies with the rest? No, I haven't. Though I suppose I could look into the whole business of cider making. At one time it was made here, on the premises, apparently, in all those old outbuildings.'

He smiled. 'And that will mean even more work for you. You're a glutton for punishment, aren't you? I suppose you wouldn't even consider the easy option, selling them to the local shops, would you?'

'I don't know.' She shrugged. 'Maybe. Though the idea of cider making is sort of intriguing—and it's what Somerset's all about, isn't it? So if I did decide to have a go at making my own, I would be part of it, wouldn't I?'

She leaned back in her chair, studying him through her lashes. He was probably right in what he was saying. It was in her nature to take on too much. As it was, she had been working frantically from early that morning, trying to catch up with her chores, baking and then tackling some of the repairs to the property, and it had taken Callum's determined efforts to make her stop. That had annoyed her. She had a limited time scale, and she'd been so intent on getting everything done, on ticking all the boxes and making sure things were in order, that when he had intervened she had put up a strenuous fight, only to lose out.

She was fast discovering that in his casual,

unconcerned way he was every bit as strong-willed as she was. He was her opposing force, the common-sense counterpart to her frenetic power hub.

And yet, for all that, in the end, she was thankful for these few moments of peace and tranquillity that he'd given her. For all her misgivings, she felt better for sitting here, letting the sun warm her bare arms, and she had him to thank for that.

She liked the fact that he was close by, too, sitting back in his chair appearing calm and perfectly relaxed. And he was as heart-stoppingly good-looking as ever. He was dressed in casual clothes, stone-coloured chinos and a dark cotton shirt that emphasised his broad shoulders and brought out the intense blue of his eyes…eyes that were looking at her now and making her go hot all over. It was strange how just with a look he could make her heart quicken and cause the blood to surge through her veins like wildfire.

The sound of children's voices cut in on her reverie. 'We want to pick flowers for Mummy and Auntie Jane,' Sarah shouted up to her from the garden. 'Can we cut the sweet peas down by the fence?'

Alex stood up and went over to the deck rail. 'That's okay,' she said. 'Just make sure James is careful with the scissors.'

'I will.' Sarah's fair curls quivered with excitement. 'We want to decorate some flower baskets. Can we use the ones out of the greenhouse?'

'Yes, that will be fine. I'll help you with them later.' She'd have to, otherwise the sweet peas would probably end up bedraggled, with broken stems and crushed petals, and the flower basket displays would be haphazard and lopsided.

Callum came to join her by the rail. 'Flower baskets?'

he queried. 'They won't be content with anything so simple as a bunch of flowers, then?'

She smiled. 'You don't know these children, do you? They don't do anything by halves. Next thing, I'll be sorting out flower-arranging plastic foam and helping them create something special in a wicker basket. They're always coming up with ideas for something or other.'

He laughed. 'They obviously take after you. Perhaps it runs in the family. Is your brother as doggedly determined and resourceful as you?'

A shadow touched her features. 'He was,' she said quietly, 'until he had the accident.' She shook her head. 'I just don't know how he's going to come through it. I don't know what to say to the children any more. I try to shield them from what's happening, but all the time I'm afraid for the worst.'

He put his arm around her. 'I'm sorry. That was thoughtless of me. You must be sick with worry.'

'I'm okay.' Her tone was flat. 'I'm just trying to take things one day at a time.'

'I suppose that's all you can do for now.' He held her close, letting his head rest against hers. 'You amaze me, Alex, the way you get on and cope with life. You don't let anything faze you for too long, do you? You have this marvellous ability to forge ahead and get through things, no matter what.'

She gave a faint smile. 'Some people simply say I'm stubborn and don't listen to reason, but that I keep on going regardless.'

He shook his head. 'I don't see it that way. I have nothing but respect for the way you deal with everything that comes along. Given what you've had to cope with, I suspect a good many women would have given up by now and settled for the easy life…a rented property, an undemanding job, keep the children quiet with videos and a selection of DVDs…but you've done the opposite. You've grabbed life head on and given it a good shake. I think that's remarkable.'

'I'm glad you think so,' she murmured. 'I just wish I felt as strong as you imagine I am. For myself, most of the time, I feel bewildered, lost, under pressure, a little scared about what's to happen.'

He drew her into his arms and held her close. 'You don't have to feel that way,' he said softly. 'I'm here for you. Remember that. I'll do whatever I can for you.'

She lifted her face to him. He looked as though he meant it, as though his words were heartfelt, and it warmed her to think that he would want to be by her side in this, to help her through it. It was comforting to feel that she could rely on him to take some of the burden from her. 'Thank you,' she whispered. 'That means a lot to me.'

His head lowered a fraction, until his lips gently brushed hers, and in the next moment he was kissing her, slowly, with infinite care, as though she was the most precious thing in all the world. Alex gave herself up to that kiss, revelling in the feel of his long body next to hers, loving the way his hands moved over her and lightly shaped her body.

This was more than just a kiss. It was an expression of tenderness, of warmth, of wanting to take care of her, and yet, soon, it became much more than that. There was a growing passion, a sudden heated desire that started as a flicker and developed into an all-consuming blaze.

He deepened the kiss and his body moved to pressure hers, almost as though he would meld with her and claim possession. His breathing became ragged, and Alex clung to him, wanting more, overcome by the frenzied outpouring of sensuality that had overtaken both of them.

'I want you so much, Alex,' he said in a roughened voice. 'You drive me wild with wanting you. Somehow, when I'm with you like this, it's all I can do to hold back. You've put some kind of spell on me. I don't know what it is that you do to me to make me feel this way.'

She cupped his face with her hands, and then slid them down over the hard wall of his chest. She felt the same way. She wanted him, and it was an overpowering feeling, something that she'd never felt before with such intensity.

'This is madness,' she murmured huskily, her breathing coming in quick, short bursts. 'We're worlds apart, you and I.' But it was a madness that devoured her all the same, one that took over her soul. She returned his kisses with feverish abandon, running her hands over his arms, his shoulders, wanting more than this, needing him to show her that he cared enough to be there for her for ever. She was stunned by the intensity of her feelings. She had never before felt this way about any man.

It was an earth-shattering moment of realisation for her. Because, for all their differences, and despite all her guarded emotions, she realised she was falling for him. How had it happened? She was filled with doubts. Was it simply an overwhelming desire that had crept up on her out of the blue? She didn't know. She couldn't tell. She had never experienced anything like it before.

'Auntie Alex, come and see how many flowers we've collected.'

James's childish voice registered on Alex's consciousness like a bolt of electricity. It startled her and pulled her back into the reality of where she was and what was going on. She stared up at Callum and laid her fingers shakily against his chest.

'I have to talk to them,' she said in an unsteady voice. 'I have to see to the children.'

She eased herself away from him, and he let her go, reluctantly, watching her as she turned to look over the deck rail once more. 'You've been very busy, haven't you?' she managed, trying to keep her voice even. James's grey eyes were bright with enthusiasm, and Sarah was bursting with energy and eager to get on. The children had filled both baskets with the delicate flowers, more than enough to make a couple of gift presentations. 'Take them into the house and put the stems in some cold water in the sink. I'll be there in a minute or two.'

James nodded gleefully and ran off towards the house, leaving Sarah to follow.

'Are you all right?' Callum wound his arms around her once more and looked at her cautiously.

'I don't know,' she said. It was one thing for her to be taken up with the heat of the moment and to have given way to her emotions, but what was really going on inside his head? How did he actually feel about her? 'I feel a bit strange to be honest. I'm not sure I understand what just happened… I think I need to get my head straight.'

He smiled ruefully. 'That goes both ways, I guess. I can't say I was expecting to feel the way I do. Perhaps it's the midafternoon sun that's getting to both of us.'

She frowned, trying to gather her thoughts together. Was he regretting what he'd said just a few moments ago and trying to find a way out? Perhaps it was just as well that they'd been interrupted.

'Maybe.' She looked at him, her gaze troubled. 'I should go and see what the children are up to,' she said.

He nodded acknowledgement of that, and slowly released her. 'I know.'

She added hesitantly, 'Do you want to stay and have some tea with us?' She wasn't altogether sure how she would cope, having him close by for the rest of the afternoon. She was already overwhelmed and confused.

He shook his head. 'I think I'd better go,' he said with some reluctance. 'I promised I would take some clean nightwear into hospital for my aunt, along with a few bits and pieces she asked for, magazines and so on.'

'Okay. You could take the cookies in to her, if you like.'

'Will do.'

She saw him off a few minutes later, feeling sad to see him go, as though she was losing something special. Then she went back into the house and tried to push those thoughts aside and give all her attention to the children. She spent the rest of the afternoon making flower baskets with them. With any luck, they would stay fresh until they could take them along to the hospital.

'Can we go and see Mummy tomorrow?' Sarah asked. 'I want to see if she can come home soon.'

Alex nodded. 'I have to work, but Martha said she would take you there. She wants to go and see Auntie Jane.'

Alex's weekend break came to an end all too soon, and she was left feeling frustrated at not having achieved all she wanted, as well as being slightly out of synch. There were never enough hours in the day to do everything that was necessary, and it left her irritable and out of sorts. Perhaps the workload was beginning to get to her.

Worrying about her brother didn't help the situation. She pulled in her visits to Ross, Beth and Jane first thing next morning, before she started work, and that only added to her anxieties. Ross was in a bad way. He was breathless, breathing fast and he was complaining of chest pain.

'We're going to get an X-ray of his chest,' the nurse on duty told her. 'And, depending what that shows, the doctor might order a CT scan. There was a lot of trauma to his chest, initially, but after surgery we thought he was on the mend. This is a complication he could do without.'

Alex nodded. 'Will you let me know what happens? I'll be down in A and E, but you can page me at any time or use my mobile number.'

'I will.'

Things were no more settled down in the emergency unit. In fact, when Alex walked towards the department a few minutes later, she found her way to the main doors was blocked by a throng of news reporters, all shouting questions towards a small group of doctors and nurses.

'So how do you feel about the threatened closures?' one man asked. He thrust his recording device towards Katie, who was obviously the spokeswoman for the nurses.

'I believe it will do irreparable harm to patients,' Katie told him. 'They will be diverted to the new hospital some fifteen miles away, and that means treatment will be delayed for precious minutes. People who live locally are being denied the services they need.'

The reporter turned to the others and began asking

more questions. 'Why is the board considering making this move?'

'It's all about budget cuts,' Simon Henderson answered. 'The hospital is running out of money.'

Alex worked her way to the fringes of the group. 'What's going on here?' she said urgently, keeping her voice low as she drew Katie to one side.

'Oh, you won't have heard, will you? You weren't here.' Katie frowned. 'Dr Langton's threatening to close the A and E department down at night. He laid the plans out in a circular he distributed to the staff late yesterday. He thinks we can save money by staying open for fewer hours, but it makes us think that will just be the beginning.'

'Is it actually going to happen, or is it just a threat?' Alex was bewildered by the news. 'Why have the press been called in? How did they get to hear about it?'

'As soon as we read the circular, we thought they should be kept informed. Maybe if the public know that their emergency department could be lost to them, they'll be able to influence the hospital board and persuade them to drop their plans. That's what Callum believes, anyway. He thought our idea of bringing in the press was a good one.'

'Callum? He's part of this?'

'Very much so.' Katie nodded. 'He's over there, speaking to a journalist from one of the nationals.'

Alex pulled in a sharp breath. 'I'll go and talk to him.'

Involving the press was a bad move, bad for everyone. It meant that people would be tense and antagonistic and much less likely to listen to reason, and it would probably irritate the members of the board and cause them to react in a negative fashion. This whole thing was wrong.

She turned to look back at the reporters as Callum's voice suddenly sounded loud and clear. 'If Oakdale's services are moved to the new city hospital, lives could be put in danger. We have to fight this. Asthmatics, patients with heart conditions or kidney disease—all these could suffer if they have to travel long distances for emergency treatment. This is a bad policy. It will be a bad day for the people who live locally if this plan is allowed to go ahead.'

Alex's expression was bleak as she watched him. He had the attention of everyone present. They were hanging on his every word, eager to capture his thoughts and take the story back to their newsrooms. How could he do such a thing without talking to her first? He knew how hard she'd worked to keep the unit viable by making savings, and he knew how much it meant to her to succeed.

She moved towards him, only to be waylaid by one of the reporters who read her name badge and thrust his tape recorder towards her. 'You're one of the managers here, Dr Draycott? What do you have to say about the proposed closure?'

She took a deep breath. 'I'd say that's all it is…a proposed measure. Nothing has been decided, and there are other options still to be considered. We've already made substantial changes to ensure the smooth running of the emergency department, whilst still being able to work within a limited budget—but there are other steps we can take. It's my opinion that services should continue to be provided here at Oakdale, and I shall be talking to the members of the board with suggestions as to how we can do that.'

The reporters threw a barrage of questions at her, but

she stepped back, saying briefly, 'Excuse me, please. I have to go to work. As soon as there are any detailed announcements, please be assured you'll be the first to hear them.'

She pushed through the main doors and went into the A and E department. She pulled in a deep breath. How could she have been pushed into defending her ground like that? How could Callum have let it happen?

'You stood your corner well, back there,' he said, coming up alongside her a minute or so later. 'It must have come as a shock to you, to walk into that.'

'It certainly did.' She sent him a troubled glance. 'Why on earth would you want the press involved? And how do you imagine I feel, when you know how hard I've worked to keep things running smoothly? It's as though you've pulled the rug out from under my feet. You know Dr Langton can't make a move without the approval of the board—this was all unnecessary. I'd expected more from you. I'd hoped you would support me.'

'I do support you, and if you'd been here yesterday I would have brought you in on what we were planning—but, believe me, Dr Langton would have gone to the press sooner or later. As soon as we saw the circular, we realised he'd reverted to his old style. It's what he did when he worked at the other hospital, and we felt we had to gain the upper hand, one way or another. The new hospital building in the city is his pet project. It's beginning to look as though he has no loyalty to Oakdale. He thinks services should be centralised and that's what he's pushing for.'

'But Dr Langton doesn't have the final say in this.' She frowned. 'He's just one member of the board, and if the rest of them disagree he'll have to go along with the majority decision. You're all assuming it's a done deal. It isn't, and I'm just so disappointed that you could throw away everything I've done as if it was of no account, and that you have so little faith in me.'

'Alex, you're putting the wrong interpretation on this. It isn't that we don't appreciate what you've done. You've done your very best in a difficult situation. But going on past history, Langton is a law unto himself. He's totally single-minded, and once he's decided on something, he's not easily diverted.'

'We'll have to see about that, won't we? All I know is that you kept me out of the loop and went ahead without talking to me. I feel so let down.' She started to move away from him, her shoulders stiff, her whole body tense.

'This isn't about you, Alex, or the way you've done your job.' He caught up with her and laid his hands on her shoulders, his grasp warm and firm. 'It's about Dr Langton and his policies. You're overreacting.'

She was stunned by his comment. 'You think I'm overreacting?' She shook her head. 'How exactly would you expect me to react? You're handing Dr Langton a publicity coup—how do you think he's going to respond to this? He'll bring out all the arguments for placing the new foundation hospital at the centre of things. Oakdale will become yesterday's news. Well, let me tell you—that's not going to happen if I have anything to do with it.'

'Alex, you need to listen—'

'No, I don't think so.' She started to walk briskly away from him, and didn't stop when he called after her. She was going straight up to Dr Langton's office to deal with this matter at its heart.

'I'm sorry, but Dr Langton is not seeing anyone at

the moment,' his secretary told her when she walked into his office a short time later.

'I believe he'll see me.' Alex walked across the room and knocked on the inner door. Then she opened it and went in.

'Alex...' Dr Langton was startled.

His secretary followed Alex into the room. 'I'm sorry Dr Langton...' She hesitated, appearing flustered. 'I told her that you were busy and not free to see people this morning.'

'It's all right, Natalie.' He waved her away. 'You can leave us alone...just hold my calls for a few minutes, will you?'

Natalie withdrew, shutting the door behind her, and Dr Langton sent Alex a cautious look. 'You seem upset, my dear,' he said. 'Is there something I can do for you?'

'Yes, I'm upset.' Her glance ran over him. 'And, yes, there is something you can do for me. Perhaps you can explain to me why you've circulated plans to close down the A and E department without even consulting with me first of all. Wouldn't it have been a professional courtesy to keep me informed of what you had in mind? And perhaps you can tell me why are you even considering closure when there are so many alternatives available to us?'

'Ah...so you've heard about that?'

'Oh, yes. There's a gaggle of press outside the main doors, all clamouring for information, and I was caught up in it without having any warning or knowledge of what it was all about.'

'The press?'

'The press,' she confirmed. 'Did you not expect word to get out?'

'Well, maybe not so soon...'

'The thing is, Dr Langton, I feel you should have kept me informed of your plans regarding A and E. You put me in a difficult position, having to defend management strategies. As I understand it, you think we can cut down on the hours that the department is open and gradually divert services elsewhere. Am I right in thinking that way?'

She waited for him to answer.

He cleared his throat. 'Ahem... It does seem to me that the community might be better served if services were more centralised. I felt that by putting out a circular we might put forward the ideas for change and at the same time gauge the reaction of the staff.'

'But you didn't consult with me first. I'm saddened that you didn't feel able to share your ideas with me—it might have saved a lot of distress if you'd done that—because unfortunately your circular has upset a lot of people.'

'I would have included you, of course, my dear, but the timing seemed right, with the board meeting coming up shortly. It was all a bit rushed, I have to confess, but I think the board members will most likely agree with my proposals.'

'Yes, it was rushed. And as you've said, the whole matter still has to go before the board. I have to disagree with your notion about the outcome. I don't believe the closure of the A and E department, at night or permanently, is a foregone conclusion at all. And I do feel that there are still so many proposals to lay before them so that they will think twice about any reduction in the A and E services.'

He spread his hands in an open gesture. 'Of course, you're entitled to your opinion. I know you've worked tremendously hard, but we have to think of these things on a larger scale. We have to think what would best serve the wider community.'

Alex's mouth firmed. 'We also have to think of the local community. Oakdale has a great reputation for being one of the best hospitals around, and its A and E unit is second to none. I won't see it obliterated in order to justify the expense of a foundation hospital. A good many people who live around here owe their lives to this emergency department, as do the tourists who come to the area every summer. Believe me, Dr Langton, I won't stand by and see it fall by the wayside.'

She left his office in a flurry of determination. After all the meetings she'd had with him, all the different ways she'd come up with to pare down expenses, he'd turned his back on her and gone his own way. Well, he would regret that. The board would hear of her ideas for boosting the hospital budget and there would be no more going through Dr Langton first—he hadn't been considerate enough to consult with her. Instead, she'd email her suggestions to them and follow them up at the next board meeting. She was on good terms with the other executive members and she would see what they had to say about all this.

She was still disturbed by the whole business when she went back to her office in A and E. She sat down at her desk and rattled off a round-robin email, pressing the 'send' button just as Callum knocked on her door and walked in.

'Is it safe for me to come in or are you likely to throw things at me?' he asked, making a show of protecting himself with his hands.

'I don't find any of this the least bit funny,' she said in a dry tone.

'No, actually, neither do I.' He glanced at the computer monitor. 'I should say, though, it might not be wise to send off emails while you're upset.'

'Are you saying you don't trust my judgement?'

'I didn't say that.' He came and perched on the edge of her desk and she shot him a cool glance. 'I'm just warning you, that's all,' he murmured, 'in case you might do something you come to regret.'

'I don't regret any of my actions. Perhaps Dr Langton will think things through, though, after my visit to his office.'

Callum winced. 'You've been to see Dr Langton?'

'I have.'

'Was that wise?'

'I've no idea. It felt pretty good to me at the time.' She sent him a thoughtful glance. 'Have you come here to discuss my actions, or are you looking for a rundown on the latest management diktats and offerings?'

He frowned. 'And what would they be?'

She braced her shoulders. 'Here, I have a list. Perhaps you'd like to give me your opinion.' She pushed a piece of paper across the table to him. 'From now on, the pharmacist is going to pass to me any requests for prescription drugs that don't fit the criteria of generic or are expensive where cheaper versions are available. No more trying to sneak around the protocol and think it won't be noticed.'

He had the grace to look uncomfortable at that and she gave him a wry smile before going on. 'Another change that's about to happen—the cleaning contract was put out to tender, and a new team will be starting next week. I'm hoping everyone will do their best to make them welcome. And the cafeteria and restaurant likewise—they are being operated under new budgetary restrictions. But I'm sure people will find the meals just as nutritious and satisfying as before.'

She hesitated briefly, letting her words sink in. 'So, what do you think?'

He studied the paper in silence for a moment or two, and then said flatly, 'And those are just the tip of the iceberg. There are several more items written down here.'

'True.'

He raised dark brows. 'I hardly know what to say. I think you're formidable...like a steamroller.'

'Well, that's good, isn't it?' She made a fleeting smile. 'I think I'm quite pleased about that.'

His mouth twisted. 'It wasn't intended as a compliment.'

She shrugged and made a face. 'Perhaps it's all in the eye of the beholder. Was there anything else I can help you with?'

He put up his hands as though to ward her off. 'I don't think so. I can see that you're not in an altogether receptive mood, and I guess this is quite enough for me to be going on with.'

He left the room and Alex slumped back in her chair. She stared at the door long after he had gone. She felt as though all the air had left her body, and now she was thoroughly deflated.

She was utterly alone. The one man who had promised to support her, to be there for her, had gone and left her to her own devices. It all came down to a question of loyalty, didn't it? And it was beginning to look as though that was something that was distinctly lacking in their relationship.

CHAPTER EIGHT

ALEX stayed in her office for another half an hour, ostensibly dealing with managerial tasks, until the sounds of activity beyond her door intruded on her and drew her back into the mainstream of activity. She started working her way through the list of paediatric admissions, and when she was satisfied that their treatment was under way and all the necessary tests had been done, she went over to the reception desk.

'This has just arrived with the latest batch of lab reports,' Callum said, passing her a sheet of paper. He looked at her cautiously, as though trying to assess her mood. 'It's the test results for young Rachel.'

'It's about time,' Alex acknowledged. 'When I checked on her in the assessment ward first thing, she was still very poorly. The antibiotics don't seem to have done much to help, but at least her temperature's down and she's had no more seizures.'

He nodded. 'According to this report she has viral meningitis and encephalitis, but at least now we can start her on antiviral medication. I'm proposing to use acyclovir.' He gave her a wry smile. 'Does that meet with your approval, or will the pharmacist be blacklisting me?'

She scowled. 'Let's not resort to childishness, shall we?'

His mouth twitched. 'Sorry, obviously you need a little longer to get yourself back in the right frame of mind. Maybe coffee would help?'

'Or perhaps getting on with the task in hand would do the trick.' Her grey eyes flashed with renewed vigour. She wasn't going to let him ply her with coffee and coax her into submission. 'Isn't there a patient waiting in treatment room three? A small child, so I guess that's probably one of mine.'

He nodded. 'I looked in on him earlier, and sent him for an X-ray. He should be back from there by now.'

She shot him a quick glance. 'Do you want to keep this case?'

He shook his head. 'I have to see a cardiac patient. Anyway, I'd better not get any more involved with young Kyle. His parents were bickering about the ruination of their holiday... I could feel myself getting hot under the collar at their attitude, so perhaps it would be better if you take over. I wouldn't trust myself not to say something untoward.'

Alex was astonished. 'Hot under the collar—you? That doesn't sound like the man I know. You're always calm and relaxed, no matter what happens.'

'Not this time. In fact, I may already have gone too far.'

She gave a wry smile. 'It looks as though we're both having one of those days.'

He nodded, and threw her a quick glance. 'It must be something in the air.' He picked up a chart. 'But, seriously, you have a different way of looking at things, and maybe you'll manage the situation better. Perhaps

I could look in on you later, and see how things are going?'

'Okay.' She was glad to be able to get back to work. It was what she knew best, and while she was with her patients at least she didn't have time to think about annoying administrators or wonder about how Callum managed to get under her skin and cause her emotions to ebb and flow like mercury.

Her patient was a young boy, six years old, tousle haired, with tearful blue eyes. A nurse had placed a supportive sling around his arm, but he looked thoroughly miserable.

'I don't know what we're doing here,' his father told her. 'There's nothing wrong with him. He just had a bit of a fall, that's all. He should have been looking where he was going, and then he wouldn't have tripped over. Anyway, he's done it before, and he's been fine afterwards. His mother's mollycoddling him, insisting on bringing him here.'

'A bit of a fall that has left him unable to use his arm,' Alex remarked in a blunt tone. 'I believe that's something that needs investigating.' She glanced at the boy and saw that a single tear was sliding down his cheek. 'And I have to ask you to think carefully about what you're saying, Mr Dunbar,' she added quietly. 'Your son is obviously very upset. I'd prefer we keep things calm and try to soothe him as best we can while we find out what is wrong.'

'More mollycoddling.' He strode across the room and stood by the window as though to distance himself from proceedings.

Alex went over to the boy. 'Hello, Kyle,' she greeted him. 'I'm Dr Draycott, and I'm going to have a look at you and see what we can do to make you feel better.'

She gave him a reassuring smile. 'Has the nurse given you something for the pain?'

He nodded. 'She gave me some tablets.'

'And are they helping?'

'Yes, a bit.'

'Hmm.' She gently examined his arm, frowning when she discovered she couldn't feel the distal pulse. It was possible that a major artery was being constricted. 'There's quite a bit of swelling there,' she said, 'so I think we'll give you some medicine to help bring that down. Just excuse me for a moment, while I go and find a nurse to organise it.' Once the inflammation had settled down, it was quite possible that the pulse would be restored. If not, she would have to apply forearm traction as an emergency measure.

Katie was with another patient, but she agreed to bring the medication as soon as she had finished. 'I'll be with you in a few minutes,' she said. 'We're rushed off our feet here.'

'I know. I appreciate what you're up against.'

Going back to Kyle, she found his father pacing the room impatiently. 'We've been here for hours,' he complained.

Alex checked the waiting-time log. 'An hour and a half, to be exact,' she murmured. 'And in that time Kyle has been assessed by the triage nurse, looked at by a doctor, received painkillers and has been to Radiology for an X-ray.'

His mouth flattened. 'We were supposed to be setting out to meet up with relatives,' he said, 'my brother and his wife and their children. We were already late to begin with. They're coming all the way from London. Can't you just give him some more painkillers that we can take along with us? He's got his arm in a sling. Why do we have to hang around? What's the problem?'

Alex brought the image of the X-ray film up on the computer monitor. 'There's the problem,' she said, pointing to an area of bone around the elbow. 'It isn't very clear on this film, but I believe it's what we call a supracondylar fracture. These things can be quite complicated, and need careful attention.'

She examined the boy once more, worried that there might have been damage to nerves in the arm, or vascular injuries. She looked up as Katie came into the room, and smiled in acknowledgement before turning back to her patient. 'I'm going to ask another doctor to come and take a look at you, Kyle,' she said gently. 'He's a doctor who knows all about bones and joints and how to put them right.'

Kyle's father made an explosive sound of exasperation. 'Another doctor? What's going on here? You're a qualified doctor, aren't you? Or aren't you capable of deciding what to do about it yourself? It's not that difficult, is it? He's always falling over or getting into scrapes. It's never anything serious. It's just how he is. He's clumsy.'

Kyle's bottom lip began to tremble, and tears washed his eyes once more. Alex stood up. Enough was enough. 'I can see this is a trying time for you, Mr Dunbar,' she said, 'so I'm going to ask you to leave. Kyle is obviously upset and I'm afraid your attitude is not helping. Perhaps you would care to go and get a cup of coffee in the waiting room just across the corridor?'

'No, I wouldn't.' He glowered at her.

'No? Then I'm afraid you leave me no option but to call Security and have you removed,' she said, stepping closer to him and speaking quietly so that Kyle would not hear. 'Your son is in a great deal of discomfort, he has a broken elbow, which may require surgery, and I need to be able to concentrate on my work. I'm sure, when you've had time to think things over, you'll come to realise that your child's health and well-being is far more important than you being late for a meeting.' She studied him for a moment or two. 'So, have you made your decision? Which is it to be? Do I call Security?'

He face was a rigid mask as he turned away from her and walked briskly out of the door. He didn't even look back to see if his wife was following.

'I must apologise for my husband,' Mrs Dunbar said, hurriedly. She was a thin, fair-haired woman, with blue eyes and features that closely resembled those of her son. 'He's been under a lot of pressure lately, but I'm sure he'll calm down before too long. A whole lot of things have gone wrong today, and he's a little uptight about this meeting with his brother and his family. They haven't seen each other for some time.' She gave Alex a quick look. 'I hope it's all right if I stay?'

'Of course. I'm sure Kyle will be glad of it.'

Alex went over to the phone at the side of the room to call for an orthopaedic surgeon to come and look at Kyle's arm. Katie was smiling, and as she came alongside her to prepare the boy's medication, she said softly, 'That was very well done, Alex. You and Callum must be two of a kind. The only difference is that Callum wasn't going to call Security, he was going to do the job himself until the man backed down.' She shook her head. 'It makes you wonder why some people bother to have children.'

'That's true.' So Callum had squared up to him? She couldn't imagine him doing anything so aggressive. It was so unlike him.

Alex went back to her young patient. 'It looks as though you've broken a bone in your elbow, Kyle,' she told him, 'and things are a bit out of place there, so a doctor needs to put them right for you. I think what will probably happen is that Mr Adams will come along and fix things for you. He'll give you something to make you go to sleep, so that you won't feel anything while he does it.' She looked at him. 'Is there anything you'd like to ask me?'

He shook his head. 'I don't think so.'

'Okay.' She turned to his mother. 'What about you, Mrs Dunbar? Do you have any questions?'

'Only one, really...do you have any idea how long will it be before his arm is better?'

'I couldn't say for certain...it really depends what Mr Adams, the surgeon, makes of it...but it's a longish job. It could be up to twelve weeks before function is restored, and overall it might take six months before things are completely back to normal.'

'Oh, dear.' Mrs Dunbar put an arm gently around her son. 'Not to worry, Kyle. Everyone's going to take good care of you here.'

'But Dad doesn't believe me.' Kyle hiccupped and chewed at his lower lip, still distressed. 'He thinks I'm making it up.'

'And your dad's going to be very sorry when he realises that you've really hurt your arm.'

Callum came to see how things were going some time later when Mr Adams was making his assessment.

'Luckily, he's had nothing to eat or drink for a few hours,' the surgeon said, taking Alex and Callum to one side after he had spoken to Kyle's mother, 'so I'll see him up in Theatre in about half an hour. And we'll admit him for observation. I don't foresee any problems, but you never know with these things.'

'Thanks,' Alex said. 'I'll make the preparations.'

She left the room with Callum some time later, leaving the boy in Katie's capable hands.

Callum checked his watch. 'It's getting late. Shall we go and get some lunch? There's nothing urgent going on here, and you look as though you could do with getting away from the hospital for a while.' He glanced at her. 'You're a bit pale, and I guess being here isn't helping very much. I know a pub not too far from here where they do a great lasagne—their honey-glazed ham is delicious, too. What do you say?'

She thought it over, but prevaricated. 'It sounds good, but I'm waiting for news about my brother. He took a turn for the worse this morning, and I want to be on hand in case they get back to me.'

He sucked in a sharp breath, his blue gaze running over her features. 'Alex, I'm sorry. You didn't say a word… I wish you'd told me, instead of trying to cope on your own. What is it…his lungs? You said the doctors thought he was fighting an infection, didn't you?'

She nodded. 'But I think this is something more. The nurse said they were worried about him. She's going to let me know if there's any news.'

His mouth firmed. 'This is all the more reason for you to get away for a while. I think you've had about as much as you can handle for one morning. The pub is only a ten-minute drive away. We'll come back the instant we hear anything.'

'And what about A and E? Oughtn't we to stay around?'

'You're entitled to a proper break. There's another consultant on duty, plus the registrar, and in any case, we can be reached by phone. Katie will let us know if she hears of anything major coming in. Besides, you're not even supposed to be on clinical duty this afternoon, are you? This is one of your management days, isn't it?'

'Yes, it's true.' She sighed. 'You know, I think you're right, I could really do with getting away for a while, but I can't help thinking it would be unwise to leave the hospital grounds right now. At the same time, I feel as though I'm on a roller-coaster ride, going up and down and round and round, and now, all of a sudden, I just want to get off.'

'Then that's exactly what you'll do.' He took hold of her arm and led the way along the corridor to the main doors, stopping off on the way at the main desk to tell the clerk where they were going. Alex felt a strange sense of relief that he was taking charge.

They walked out to the car park. 'You're positive it isn't far away?' she said, a frown creasing her brow.

'I am.' He held open the car door for her, and she slid into the passenger seat, leaning back against the soft leather upholstery, relaxing in the sheer opulence of this luxurious vehicle. It even smelled new, and she closed her eyes and breathed in the subtle fragrance of expensive leather and wax polish.

They drove for a while through the Quantocks, past heather-clad moorland and rolling hills, where sparkling streams meandered by scattered villages and small hamlets. Soon they reached a charming country inn, and Callum drew the car to a halt on the forecourt.

'It's lovely,' Alex said, stepping out of the car and gazing around in wonder. 'Just look at that open countryside. It's so peaceful.'

'I thought you'd like it. Come inside, and we'll see if we can find a table by the window. The service is pretty good here. You don't usually have to wait too long for your meal.'

Alex chose seared breast of chicken wrapped in bacon and served with a tangy sauce, creamed potatoes and vegetables, while Callum opted for the lasagne.

'They make the sauce for the lasagne with red wine, tomato and Italian seasoning, as well as onion and mushrooms,' he told her. 'It's delicious.' He dipped a fork into the lasagne and offered it to her. 'Here, have a taste. Tell me what you think.'

He slid the food into her mouth and she savoured it for a moment or two, conscious all the while of his gaze centred on the ripe curve of her mouth before it moved along the slender column of her throat.

'Mmm...you're right, it's lovely.' She sent him a quick, mischievous glance. 'You just did that to make me doubt my choice, didn't you?' She made a weighing action with her hands. 'Chicken and bacon on the one hand...lasagne on the other... What to do...what to do?'

'You've changed your mind?' He smiled. 'That's all right, I'll swap you, if you like. It really doesn't matter to me.' He began to push his plate towards her.

'No...no, really, I was just kidding.' She held up a hand to stop him. 'Keep it, please. I'm perfectly happy with what I've chosen.' She sent him a quizzical glance. 'Trouble is, you're not used to seeing me in a teasing mood, are you? You see me as straightforward, always concentrating on work. I expect you think I'm not capable of letting my hair down.'

He shook his head. 'I don't know about that. I think you could be absolutely fabulous at letting your hair down, given half a chance.' His eyes glinted, his gaze moving slowly over her, taking in the smooth line of her dress that clung where it touched. His glance lingered. 'That's definitely something I'd love to see…but unfortunately I get the feeling it's highly unlikely.'

Alex felt her cheeks flush with heat. She could imagine spending time with Callum, getting close to him, experiencing the thrill of being in his arms, knowing the touch of his hands on her body…but she was coming to realise that she wanted much more from him than just a passionate fling.

It had never happened to her before. There had never been anyone who had made her feel this way, but now she knew she wanted a relationship that would last.

But where Callum was concerned, wasn't that just a flight of fancy? She couldn't help feeling that in the long term she simply wasn't his kind of woman. He would never choose to spend his life with a career woman. His soul mate would be someone who was relaxed and tranquil, someone who could share his philosophy on life, instead of a woman who caused him problems on a daily basis.

'The trouble is,' he said, bringing her back to the present with a jolt, 'you never have time to simply be yourself.' He tasted the lasagne and was thoughtful for a moment. 'There are always too many demands on you… like this morning, for instance. You were plunged into that press conference out of the blue, and that's probably why you—'

He broke off, and Alex finished for him. 'That's probably why I reacted the way I did this morning.' She gave an awkward smile. 'I'm sorry about that. You were just doing what you felt to be right.'

'Still, it's perhaps just as well that we showed Dr Langton we wouldn't let him get his own way without a fight. He'll keep pushing it.' Callum paused, his fork halfway to his mouth. 'Anyway, what did you say to him? Did you ask him about the circular?'

She nodded. 'I told him that I had some proposals of my own to put before the board.'

'Good.' He frowned. 'In fact, just before we came away, I heard he's organising a meeting with the board for tomorrow to bring it to a vote. That could turn out to be a turning point for all of us...but with you there to back our cause, I imagine we stand a better chance.'

'Maybe. Though, going on what we talked about the other day—renting out services, and so on—I've already put forward some money-spinning suggestions to the board in the emails I sent out. They won't be popular with everyone, but I'm hoping they'll at least have time to think about them.' She took a sip of her iced drink, a pure fruit juice topped up with lemonade. 'It all depends whether they agree with my way of thinking...but either way, I don't see how we can do any more.'

He curled some creamy strands of cheese around his fork. 'We could try to get a licence to run a lottery. That should bring in quite a bit of money for the department, and there are always raffles to be run every now and again. I'm on the fundraising committee and we have some good people who are willing to put in a lot of time and effort for the cause.'

'They get results, too, judging by the new portable X-ray machine we've just acquired.' Her mouth curved. 'You're not at all what you seem, are you? You appear to be quiet and unassuming and altogether laid-back, but one way and another you achieve an awful lot behind the scenes, don't you? I'm thinking about the way the doctors and nurses look up to you and respect your decisions...and then there are those seriously ill patients you manage to edge higher up the waiting lists, not to mention the way you handle the press.'

He made a dismissive movement with his hands. 'What's the point of being in high places if you can't manipulate the odds from time to time?'

She chuckled and finished off her chicken and bacon, laying down her knife and fork.

'Would you like dessert and coffee?' he asked, and she nodded.

'Oh, yes, please. I've had my eye on the toffee pudding they have in the glass-fronted display case over there. And coffee would be great, thanks.' She toyed with her serviette while he called the waitress over to take their order.

'I'll have the apple pie,' he said, handing the girl the menus. She nodded, giving him a dimpled smile, and he responded with a gentle curve of his lips.

Watching them, Alex felt an immediate, involuntary stab of jealousy. The force of it shocked her to the core. What was wrong with her? Why did it matter that he smiled at a girl in a restaurant? She frowned. The truth was, she was beginning to care for him deeply, but how could she ever compete with all those pretty girls who knew how to take life as it came and simply enjoy being around a good-looking, easygoing man?

She didn't know how to be his type of woman. She was here with him now, enjoying a wonderful meal in a romantic country inn, and hadn't she spent most of the time talking about work?

Callum glanced at her, a small line indenting his brow. 'Is everything all right? You look anxious all at once.'

'I'm fine.' She tried to get a grip on herself. He was too perceptive by half and it wouldn't do to have him know what she was thinking. 'I'm glad you brought me here,' she said. 'It's good to be able to relax and enjoy the comfort, and the great food, as well as to look out over the hills. It just makes me wish I could do it more often. Of course, it's difficult with the children.'

He nodded. 'You could always bring them with you… except I don't suppose you'd be able to relax too much, knowing how those two get into everything.' He sent her a crooked grin. 'They certainly keep you on your toes.'

'True.'

He shot her a quick look. 'You must be really pleased with the way things are shaping up at home. The trees in the orchard look healthy and strong, and it looks as though it will be a good crop. But I still can't imagine how you settled on such a place. I could see you in a small, executive-type home, with all the mod-cons, something easy to manage, with no fripperies, but I've never picked out a rambling farmhouse with acres of land, in a month of Sundays.'

'You see me living a very orderly life, don't you?' She smiled. 'I must say, nothing's been straightforward these last few months. Far from it. I've had to come to terms with a whole new way of life, but I've found that I'm actually enjoying the farmhouse side of it. It's the one place where I feel contented. I think the children are happier for being there, too.'

'Where will they live when your brother and his wife come home from hospital? Didn't you say they used to rent a place before the accident?'

'That's right. Ross had relocated because of his job, and was renting while he looked around for something suitable. I expect they'll do the same again.'

She studied him. 'But what about you? I haven't seen

your house, but I imagine you living in something like a barn conversion, with lots of books and a plasma TV and music centre.'

He laughed. 'Completely wrong, I'm afraid. I have what they call a studio apartment not too far from the hospital. I don't need anything grand, because it's just me living there. It's basically open plan, with a mezzanine floor where I have my bed…and my books. There are definitely lots of books.'

'And the building work you mentioned a while back?'

'I had the garage extended, and a wall built around the back of the garden. It's only small piece of land, but it goes with the apartment, and I wanted to keep it secluded.'

She shook her head, trying to imagine how he lived. 'That's not at all what I expected,' she said. 'You drive a fantastic car, you wear expensive, beautifully tailored clothes, and I expected your house would be equally grand.'

He shrugged. 'When I bought it, some years back, I didn't see the point in owning anything more than a bachelor pad. Not that it's under par in any way… I've been told it has the wow factor that everyone goes on about these days. But the fact is, I was young and I didn't see any reason to settle down, start a family and so on. I suppose I looked at the way my parents lived their lives and decided that maybe marriage and commitment weren't for me. My parents were never in one place for long and, no matter how they tried, they weren't able to look after me properly.'

'Not all families are like that.'

'No.' He winced. 'But you see those like the Dunbars, where everything is supposedly normal and yet beneath the surface there are all those tensions bubbling away…a father who thinks more of his own agenda, rather than caring for his son. I wonder sometimes if they're representative of a good many families. I don't know. I just see so many broken relationships, children left without steady parenting, and it makes me think that's not the sort of thing I would want for myself.'

Alex didn't comment on that. She didn't know what to say. Instead, she dipped her spoon into her toffee pudding and let it rest there for a moment or two. Callum had said he didn't want marriage or commitment—or at least, that's how he had felt when he'd first bought the apartment, and yet she'd come to realise that those were the very things she wanted. All these years, she'd been relaxed about how she viewed relationships, but things had changed. She'd met Callum, and she'd discovered that for her, it was all or nothing.

If he was still keen on the bachelor way of life, it seemed that she had been right to be cautious about getting involved. Trouble was, it was way too late for that now.

CHAPTER NINE

'OH, GOOD, you're back.' Katie greeted Alex and Callum as they walked into A and E after spending their lunch break. 'Your niece and nephew arrived a few minutes ago with your neighbour, Alex—she said her name was Martha. I'm afraid the children are a bit upset—they've been asking for you. I suggested they might like to wait in the staff lounge. I thought it would be a bit more comfortable for them in there.'

'Thanks, Katie. That was thoughtful of you.' Alex's heart had started hammering, going into alarm mode at the news, but she tried to stay calm as she asked, 'Do you happen to know what they're upset about? Is it my brother?'

Katie nodded. 'I think so. It sounds as though he's in a bad way and they weren't expecting to see him like that. The nurse didn't realise they'd gone in to see him until it was too late.'

Alex took a steadying breath. 'I'll go and see if I can smooth things over. Thanks again, Katie.'

'You're welcome. I found them some paper and coloured pencils, and one or two toys to try to keep them occupied for a while, but I don't think they can settle to anything.'

Alex nodded. 'I knew I should have stayed here,' she

said under her breath. 'I just knew something would go wrong.'

Callum laid a restraining hand on her arm. 'Don't start blaming yourself,' he advised her. 'Take a deep breath and stay calm. You had lunch, nothing more, and they've only been here for a few minutes. You can't be at everyone's beck and call every minute of the day. They'll come through this. You'll all come through it.'

'I'm all right.' She was beginning to feel increasingly agitated. 'I must go.'

'I'd like to come with you. Is that okay? I might be able to help in some way.'

She nodded, and they hurried along to the staff lounge.

They found Sarah in tears, sitting on one of the sofas, while James was trying to keep a stiff upper lip but was unable to disguise his shaky, ragged intakes of breath. He looked at Alex with bewildered eyes, not really knowing what was going on but sensing the tense, unhappy atmosphere in the room.

'I feel terrible about this,' Martha said, coming to meet Alex. She was a sensible woman, middle-aged, with gently waving brown hair and grey eyes that were troubled. 'I'd no idea Ross was in such a bad way or I'd never have taken them to see him.'

'What happened?' Alex tried to suppress her anxiety, wanting to stay calm and composed for the sake of the children. 'Did the nurse tell you what was going on?'

Martha shook her head. 'She wouldn't tell me anything about his condition, because I'm not a relative.' She lowered her voice. 'But he looked terrible...pale, with beads of sweat on his face, not breathing properly. He was very weak.'

'Daddy couldn't talk to me,' Sarah said, the tears

welling up in her eyes and spilling over. 'He couldn't sit up in bed or do anything. And the nurse had to help him lean back against his pillows.' Her voice began to wobble. 'I tried to talk to him, but he couldn't answer me. His mouth moved but nothing came out and then the nurse put a mask on his face.' She began to sob.

Alex went to sit down on the sofa between the two children. She put her arms around Sarah and held her close. 'I'm sorry you had to see your dad looking so poorly,' she said softly. 'I know the doctors and nurses are doing everything they can to make him better.'

Sarah's sobs became louder. 'But it's not working.'

Alex hugged her, and laid an arm around James's shoulders, squeezing him gently. He, too, had given way to tears. 'Have you been to see your mother?' she asked.

James nodded. 'We gave her the flower basket.' He pulled in a shuddery breath. 'She said she thought it was lovely.'

'That's good, isn't it? You know, she's doing so well, I expect she'll be coming home soon. You'll like that, won't you?'

'Yes. She said she'd be home in a few days. She wants to come and live at your house for a bit.' He looked up at her. 'Can she?'

'Yes, of course.' She glanced at Sarah to see if any of their conversation had managed to divert her, but the little girl was locked into a cycle of misery.

'I think I should take them home,' Martha said quietly. 'They wanted to stay here and see you, or we would have gone earlier.'

'I know. Thanks, Martha.'

Sarah turned tear-drenched eyes on Alex. 'I want you to come home with us.'

'I'll come in a little while, Sarah.' She glanced at her watch. 'I have to finish my shift here, just another couple of hours, and then I'll be home with you.'

It wasn't what she wanted to hear, and Sarah started to cry all over again.

Callum went down on his haunches beside her. 'You know, Sarah,' he said in a quiet voice, 'your mother wouldn't want you to be upset like this. She'd want you to be strong, so that you can take care of your little brother. He doesn't really understand what's going on, but if he sees you being all grown up and getting on with things, it will be better for all of you.' He paused, waiting to see what effect his words were having on her. 'Maybe you could go home and start preparing a room for your mother. Put some flowers in it, perhaps make up a fruit basket, or make something for her that she'll enjoy when she comes home.'

'Like a little box for her rings?' James's eyes lit up with enthusiasm. 'We did some paper curling at school… we could make a lid with some decorations on it.'

'They call it quilling, I think,' Martha said. 'I've some coloured paper we can use. Shall we go home and give it a try?'

James nodded, wanting to go right away and get started, but Sarah was still reticent. 'I don't want you to stay at work,' she said, looking earnestly at Alex. 'I want you to come home with us.'

Callum stood up, laying a gentle hand on her shoulder. 'She won't be long.'

'I'll be there before you know it,' Alex told her. 'Go home with Martha now, and I'll follow in my car. I won't be long, I promise.'

They left a few minutes later, with James full of ideas about the box he was going to make and Sarah still subdued. Alex watched them go and then, as the strength drained out of her body, she reached for a chair and sank down into it.

'You know, you could have gone with them,' Callum murmured. 'You don't have to stay here, and it's obvious they need you. Sarah must have been very shocked by what she saw, and she clearly needs reassurance—perhaps that's something only you can give her. Martha's doing her best, but she isn't a relative. The children have already gone through the distress of knowing their parents were injured in a road accident, and now this is an added stressor.'

'Do you think I don't know that?' She resented his implied criticism. 'Do you imagine all I ever think about is work? I want to be with them, I want to make all this go away, but I can't.'

Perhaps she had been too sharp in her retort, because his head went back a fraction, light flaring in his blue eyes, his mouth making a straight line, and she was instantly conscious of the fact that he was only trying to help. The last thing she needed right now was to get into an argument with Callum.

'I have to go and see my brother and find out what's gone wrong,' she said. She felt as though she was caught up in the middle of a whirlwind. These last few months had been a nightmare and she was about at the end of her tether. Her brother was dangerously ill and she needed to go to him. He was her priority right now.

'Of course you do.' He frowned. 'But I don't think you should be on your own right now. I want to be there with you.'

A feeling of relief shot through her at his understanding. She gave a faint, almost imperceptible nod, and they left the room together.

When they arrived at the intensive care unit Alex found that her brother was every bit as ill as Martha had said.

'He looks so much worse than he did this morning,' she said in a whisper, and Callum laid a comforting arm around her shoulders. It was plain to see that Ross was in a bad way. He was deathly pale, and the constant bleeping of the monitors around him warned of a galloping heart rate and a worrying lack of oxygen in his blood.

'We've been doing tests all morning,' the nurse told her, 'but Dr Allingham looked at the CT scan a little while ago and said he has a pulmonary embolism. I was just about to page you.'

Alex pulled in a shaky breath. A blood clot on the lung was a dreadful diagnosis. Depending on its severity, it could mean the difference between life and death, and, judging by Ross's condition, this was the worst news she could have received. A blood clot in one of the main arteries could cause his circulation to fail, and the damage to his lungs would mean he couldn't get enough oxygen to his tissues.

'What is Dr Allingham going to do?'

'He started him straight away on anticoagulants, and he's prescribed thrombolytic therapy. It will take a while, of course, but he's hoping that we'll see initial results within the next twenty-four hours. After all Ross has been through, he wants to reserve surgery as a last option.'

'I can understand that.'

She looked at Callum, her eyes bright with tears, and he said softly, 'They're doing everything they can for him. At least they've found out what's wrong, and now they can do something about it.'

'I know.' It didn't make it any easier to bear, though. Who could say if the medication would work quickly enough? Anticoagulants would thin his blood and prevent any more clots from forming, while the thrombolytic therapy would begin to dissolve the clot, but this was a race against time.

Callum gently drew her head down into the crook of his shoulder, and she nestled against him for a moment or two, absorbing the comfort he offered. Tears trickled down her cheeks, but she was soothed by his steady support. He was strong and reliable, and by being with her right now he was showing her that he cared about her and her brother.

After a while she managed to gather herself together. She glanced at the nurse. 'I'd like to stay with him for a while, if that's all right?'

The girl nodded. 'Of course.'

She stayed with Ross for a few minutes, talking to him even though she couldn't be sure that he heard her. She told him how Beth was becoming stronger, day by day, and how the children were looking forward to him coming home. 'You've always been a fighter, Ross,' she said softly. 'You can do it. You can get through this.'

When she was ready to go, she walked with Callum to the car park. 'I could drive you home,' he said, but she shook her head.

'I'll be all right. Thank you for staying with me.'

'I wanted to be with you.' He hesitated. 'Maybe when your brother is better and things are going more smoothly for you, we could spend some time together... maybe take a trip somewhere. I think it will do you a world of good.'

She nodded. 'Maybe.'

The children were quiet when she picked them up

from Martha's house and took them home. James, being younger, was vaguely aware that something bad was happening, but it wasn't at the forefront of his mind. He could be distracted fairly easily. Sarah was much more difficult to handle. She was a sensitive, loving child, and intelligent enough to recognise that her father was in great danger. She'd always been Daddy's girl, and this was hard for her to take in. She knew there was a chance that he might not come through this latest setback.

'Shall we do some baking?' Alex suggested when they were back in the farmhouse kitchen. 'I thought we might make an apple-and-blackberry pie and take it round to Auntie Jane. She's only just home from hospital, so she's not up to doing very much for herself yet. I expect she'd be glad of some home cooking.'

Sarah nodded, and James went to fetch the pastry board and rolling pin. 'I love apple-and-blackberry pie,' he said. 'Do you think we'd better make two?'

'Definitely. That's a very good idea.'

By keeping them busy, Alex managed to calm them down over the next few hours, but she wasn't at all sure how she was going to handle things the next day. Instinct told her she should stay home with them, but she was supposed to be on duty at the hospital and Dr Langton had called a crucial meeting for the afternoon.

'Are you going to work today?' Sarah asked her at breakfast next morning. Her expression gave nothing away, but she didn't quite look Alex in the eye, and there was the merest flicker of a glance from under her lashes as she tried to gauge Alex's response.

Alex hesitated. 'I thought I'd stay here with you,' she said. 'We could go and see Auntie Jane this morning, and perhaps we might plant those dahlias for her—the ones that she bought before she went into hospital. And of course there will be a lot of weeding to do.'

'Yay! I want to do that,' James said, cramming a piece of buttered toast into his mouth.

Sarah relaxed visibly, her shoulders sloping as though a great weight had been lifted from her. She came over to Alex and gave her a hug. 'Can we phone Mummy later today? I want to tell her about the room we're getting ready for her and Daddy. She said Gran and Grandad were going to visit her this afternoon, so I might be able to talk to them as well.'

'Okay. That sounds like a good idea. It's good that your gran and grandad have been able to come to see them, isn't it?'

Sarah nodded. 'They said they wanted to see me and James as well. Grandad said his job was all done and they were coming back to stay at their house in Somerset.'

'That's good news, isn't it? I expect they'll come and see both of you very soon.'

In the meantime, Alex was still in a quandary about work. She wasn't sure what she was going to do about Dr Langton's meeting, but the least she could do was to warn Callum that she wouldn't be there. She called him after she had rung the hospital for an update on her brother.

'I'm going to stay at home with the children today, and probably tomorrow as well,' she told him. 'I think it's for the best.'

'I wondered what you would do,' he said. 'Is everything all right? Are they okay?'

'They seem to be,' she said. It was good to hear his deep voice. It was somehow reassuring, as though he was close to her even though the miles separated them.

'They're a lot more settled, having me here with them. Things are probably a lot better all round this way. Dr Langton seems to think so, anyway. That's the impression I had when I spoke to him on the phone a few minutes ago. I get the feeling he's pleased I won't be there to spike his guns.'

'Hmm. How do you feel about that?'

She was quiet for a moment. 'A bit deflated, really, and anxious because I might be letting people down. But I don't see any way round the situation. Sarah's not saying very much, but she's on the verge of tears a lot of the time, and what she's not saying is speaking volumes, if you know what I mean.'

'Yes, I think I do. I can understand why you've chosen to stay with them. As to the meeting, it's a pity I'm not on the committee, or I could stand in for you and state your case. Let me give it some thought, and I'll see if there's some way we can get round it.'

'Thanks, Callum.' She didn't think there was anything much he could do, but she was glad of his offer to help. He was without exception caring and thoughtful, ready to step in where he was needed, and she was coming to realise that he was someone she could rely on in her darkest hour.

'I'm happy to do what I can,' he said. 'Is there any news about Ross?'

'Only that his condition is much the same. At least he isn't any worse. I haven't told Beth yet. I didn't want to worry her, and I'm hoping Sarah won't say anything when she phones her this afternoon. I'd sooner tell her if and when he appears to be on the mend.'

'That sounds reasonable enough to me. Keep your chin up. Just remember I'm here for you if you need me.'

'I will. Thanks.' She was sad when he cut the call,

because she wanted to go on hearing his voice. It filled the empty void and made her feel that she was not alone, just for a few minutes. She wanted to be with him.

In truth though, wasn't she kidding herself? He was concerned about her and he was offering to help, but what did he really feel about her? Yes, he was caring and sympathetic, and he had shown her that he would be there for her, but how deep did his feelings go? He might be attracted to her, but that might be as far as it went.

And who was she to complain about that? Wasn't that how she had viewed things, to begin with? Her career meant everything to her, and there had never been much time for anything else. She had been reasonably content. There had been no one who might have persuaded her to set it all aside…until now, until she had met Callum. He had proved himself to be a man apart from all others. He was quiet, strong and steady, and he had tried to show her how to take herself less seriously.

And perhaps his efforts had achieved a result. After all, she had changed over these last few months. Perhaps looking after her brother's children had shown her a different way of life, had taught her that home and family could take precedence over ambition.

She sighed. Musing on all this wasn't getting her anywhere. For now, she had to put aside her thoughts about Callum and concentrate on the children. They needed her, and she ought to be keeping them occupied instead of standing here wool-gathering.

'We need the gardening tools,' she told them, calling them back into the kitchen a few minutes later. 'Gardening gloves, forks, trowels and the bag of plant food out of the greenhouse. We'll need compost, too.'

'I'll get the food,' James said. 'Sarah can bring the tools.'

'I'm not carrying all that lot on my own,' Sarah complained, scowling at her younger brother. 'You can help.'

'Nah.'

He threw her a mutinous, cheeky glance and ran off, leaving Sarah to say crossly, 'He's always doing that. Daddy says he... Daddy said—' She broke off, biting her lip to stop it from trembling, and Alex put her arms around her and gave her a hug.

'I'll help you with the tools. I'll talk to James in a little while—just as soon as I manage to catch him,' she said.

They spent the morning with Jane, planting dahlias in her sunny border, while she sat in a garden chair and offered them cold drinks from an iced jug.

'You look so much better than you did a while ago,' Alex told her, coming to sit beside her and take a break for a while. 'Has your blood pressure settled down yet?'

Jane nodded. 'Yes, it has. And I'm healing up nicely, too, so I'm beginning to feel as though I'm on the mend at last.'

'That's really good news.' Alex took a long swallow from her glass. 'That was a bit of a scare you had, back in the hospital, wasn't it? I know Callum was worried about you.'

'He's a good man. He's always looked out for me, and made sure that I was getting on all right.' Jane was quiet for a moment or two, and Alex guessed she was thinking about the way he had helped her over the years. 'I know he has a difficult job to do at the hospital, and sometimes he has a lot on his mind, with all the worries about patients, and so on. He cares about people, you see. And I know he's concerned about these threats to close the unit down. He said he'd written to the board members, telling them of the risks to patients if services were to be transferred to the city.'

'Has he?' Alex was surprised. 'He didn't mention that to me.'

'No, well, I think he feels you have enough to cope with already. He didn't want you worrying about what he was doing and saying.'

Perhaps he had been put off by her reaction when he'd gone to the press. Alex made a face. It was her own fault that he didn't confide in her. Just lately she had been edgy and out of sorts, and who could blame him for going it alone?

Still, he'd offered to try to sort something out before the meeting this afternoon. Would he be able to come up with anything? She wanted to put her views to the board, and it would have been much better to do that in person rather than through an email that some members might not even have read.

She took the children back home an hour or so later. 'Why don't you go and play in the orchard for a bit while I make lunch?' she suggested.

'I want to stay here, with you,' Sarah said quietly. 'I don't want to play. Do you think Daddy is all right?' Her voice quavered. 'I heard the nurse say that he might not make it without an operation.'

Alex frowned, and Sarah hurried to add, 'She didn't know I was there. She was talking to another nurse.'

Alex studied her thoughtfully. She had been clingy all morning, not wanting to stray far from her side, and that made her realise that it was probably a wise decision she had made to stay home with her. What was it Callum had said? The children needed a relative at a time like this. 'I'm sorry you heard that,' she said. 'It must have been upsetting for you, but the nurse said she would ring me if there was any news about your father—if he had taken a turn for the worse. Even so, I'm going to phone her now, to find out what's happening. After that, you can talk to your mum, if you like.'

Sarah nodded. James took himself off to the garden to play on the old rope swing, and Alex dialled the hospital number. Best to do it now, and hopefully put Sarah's mind at ease, along with her own.

'There's been no major change,' the nurse told her, 'but his blood oxygen level has risen very slightly. Dr Allingham thinks that could be a good sign, but he says Ross has quite a way to go yet.'

'Thanks.' Alex relayed the news to Sarah. 'It means we still have to wait and see, but at least it's not bad news.' It was difficult to know how to handle this kind of situation with a young child. She didn't want to be negative, but at the same time she didn't want to fill Sarah with false hope. The consequences of that could turn out to be disastrous.

She left Sarah talking to her mother and grandparents a few minutes later, and went into the kitchen to prepare a salad for lunch. Her mobile rang as she was slicing peppers, and she wiped her hands on a towel and went to answer it.

'Hi, there,' Callum said, and her heart warmed at the sound of his voice. 'How are things? Are you managing all right with the children? Are they coping?'

'James is fine,' she answered, 'but Sarah's finding things difficult. We just rang the hospital to see how Ross was doing and there's been no real change as yet.'

'These things take time. At least they've made the

diagnosis and started to act on it. A good many pulmonary embolisms go undetected until it's too late.'

'I know.'

'And how are you? Are you bearing up?'

'I'm okay.' She wasn't going to tell him how she really felt, her worries about her brother or her fears for the children's well-being. For the moment, it was enough for her that he had called. His voice was deep and soothing, like a balm to her overwrought senses.

If only he could be here with her right now. Suddenly, she wanted to see him, to be with him. She wanted to have him hold her and reassure her that everything was going to turn out all right. Just being in his arms would have given her the strength to go on.

'How about you?' she asked. 'Your aunt said you were concerned about what was going on at the hospital. She said you'd written to the board.'

'That's true. I thought it might help. Actually, I've been thinking about the meeting this afternoon, and I've a suggestion to put to you. You don't have to consider it...you might have other plans, or you might want to walk away from it all, given that you've so much on your plate right now.' She could hear the frown in his voice. 'Though I think you should know that most of the staff appreciate how hard you've worked ever since you started the job and they're all behind you in this.'

'I'm glad about that. What was it you wanted to ask me?'

'It occurred to me that you could still take part in the meeting if we set up a video link. I could fix it from the hospital end—it would give me an excuse to be in on the meeting if I have to monitor the link, so I could maybe add my twopenny worth to anyone who cares to listen. And anyway the executives have asked for one or two representatives from non-board members to be present—and you could set up the software and web-cam on your laptop from your end.'

She thought about it for a while. Having Callum take part in the meeting was another bonus point. 'It sounds feasible, but I don't know how well it would go down with the board if Sarah or James were to come and interrupt every few minutes.'

He chuckled. 'That's one of the hazards of working from home, I suppose. You could always bribe them to keep quiet with fizzy pop and cookies. Not very politically correct, but quite effective at times, I'm told.'

'Yes, you're probably right.' She came to a decision after a second or two. 'I dare say I'll think of something. Will you let me know when you've organised it at your end?'

'I will.' There was a smile in his voice. 'Thanks, Alex. I owe you one.'

'Let's just hope it goes well. I'll do my best, but I can't promise anyone will listen.'

He rang off, and Alex went on with her preparations for lunch, trying to think of ways to keep the children amused while she attended the virtual meeting.

'How about you look through the DVD collection and choose something to watch while I'm talking to the people at work?' she suggested, taking the easy way out. 'I really need you to promise not to interrupt me unless it's something very important. Do you think you can do that?'

'Yeah...if we can watch space aliens,' James announced eagerly.

'Space aliens are rubbish,' Sarah told him. 'We should watch the one about the animals who escape from the farm.'

'Nah…that's a girly film. I'm not watching a girly film.'

Alex intervened. 'You have five minutes to choose something you both agree on,' she said briskly, 'or I'll choose for you.'

Half an hour later, she was seated at her desk in the study, talking to the hospital executives. Callum's image appeared on her computer monitor, almost centrally on her screen, and it was a huge comfort to her to be able to see him, even if he was not there with her in the flesh.

'You already know of the many savings we've made in the A and E department,' she said, addressing the board in general. 'We've gone almost as far as we can down that route. Perhaps the time has come to think of the situation from another angle.'

'Another angle?' one of the executives challenged her. 'What are you suggesting?'

'I think we could look at ways to bring money into the hospital.'

He frowned. 'And how do you propose to do that?'

'There are some areas that are underused for one reason or another. I'm suggesting that we could rent out certain wards and theatres to the private sector. There's also the scanner—it isn't used from six o'clock in the evening unless there is an emergency—and it seems to me that's another opportunity for us to earn income from the private sector. Fee-paying patients will benefit from having treatment out of hours, and the hospital will gain by getting a badly needed cash boost.'

'This is the NHS,' Dr Langton said dismissively. 'The principle has always been that it is free for those in need of medical help. NHS treatment and private medicine don't mix. The two are incompatible.'

Alex nodded. 'I know some people find the idea of

private medicine unpalatable. I've always believed in the principle of the NHS, that treatment should be free for everyone who needs it. But the private sector serves a purpose for those who don't want to wait to see a specialist or be put on a long waiting list for surgery, and in these days of cash-strapped hospitals perhaps this is the time for radical thinking. A good many hospitals have already gone along this route, with great success. With the money earned from the private sector, we could keep the department open and make changes that would benefit other areas of the hospital.'

Callum intervened. 'I think Alex is right. With extra money we could streamline some of the services we already offer and make them more efficient. We could set up a minor injuries unit to be run by nurses and a doctor—maybe a GP—and we could add a new mini-stroke unit, which would have a preventative role and eventually save patients from progressing to major problems—which in themselves would cause further strain on our limited resources.'

The discussion went on for another hour before Dr Langton drew the meeting to a close.

'Thank you, everyone,' he said. 'Obviously, a lot of points have been made here today, and they will need some consideration. I suggest that the executive board meets again tomorrow to make its final decision.'

Alex gazed at the screen. She had done what she could and now they simply had to wait for the result.

Callum's glance meshed with hers. His expression mirrored her thoughts, saying, 'That's it for now. There's nothing more we can do.'

She looked for something extra in his eyes, something that would show her a hidden message, perhaps, a hint that he wanted to be with her...but there was nothing. He simply turned away as one of the executives began to speak to him, and a few minutes later the video link was cut.

CHAPTER TEN

ALEX wandered aimlessly about the house next day, trying to decide which job she ought to do next. Nothing appealed to her or filled her with enthusiasm. The trouble was, she didn't feel inclined to do anything. All she really wanted was to talk to Callum, to hear his voice. Better still, she would have liked to be with him.

She reached for the phone before she could change her mind. 'Hi, Callum,' she said. 'I hope you don't mind me disturbing you at work. Are you busy?'

'Alex...' She could hear the smile in his voice. 'You can call me at any time. In fact, I was about to call you myself. It's quiet here just now...no major accidents, just a waiting room full of the walking wounded. Of course, we're all waiting for news of the board meeting, but we won't get that until a little later.' Then he added on a concerned note, 'Anyway, how are you? Are you all right?'

'Yes, I'm fine. I just...' She let the words trail off. Perhaps it had been a mistake to call him—she never made the first move with any man, and she was acting completely out of character—but for once she had thrown caution to the wind. 'I'm on my own here,' she said, 'and I just wanted to talk to you for a while...not about anything in particular.'

'You're on your own? How did that come about?'

'My parents came over just before lunch and took the children out for the afternoon.'

'That's brilliant,' Callum said. 'You must be glad of the break.'

'Yes, it's lovely for the children to be able to go out with their grandparents. The thing is, Mum and Dad are back here to stay now, in Somerset, and they say they'll be around to help out from now on…which is great news. I just wasn't expecting it and, to be honest, I'm not used to having the place to myself. I'm feeling a little strange…a bit lost, somehow. I know that must sound odd.'

'It doesn't sound odd at all to me. You've been through a difficult time lately, and you're used to working at full stretch.' He chuckled. 'It isn't every day you get the chance to play hooky.'

'No.' She smiled. 'I suppose not.'

He sobered. 'Is there any news about Ross?'

'Yes,' she said brightly. 'They say they're cautiously optimistic. His oxygen levels are better and his breathing is a little easier. Actually, I was thinking of going in to see him in a while.'

'That's a good idea. It will cheer you up to see him looking better.' The smile was back in his voice. 'Maybe I could go with you? I could come and pick you up, and then we can play hooky together?'

She laughed. 'But you're at work…are you saying you're going to take time off? That isn't like you.'

'No, it isn't,' he agreed. 'But I have a half-day owing to me, and it seems to me that this is as good a time as any to take it. Besides, I want to make sure that you're all right.'

'I am, thanks.'

'Good. Well, perhaps after you've been to see Ross, we could go out for the afternoon and make the most of the sunshine. What do you say?'

'I'd like that...if you're sure you can get away.'

'I can. I'll come and pick you up in half an hour.'

She was glowing inside when she cut the call a second or two later. She looked around. It was only just dawning on her that everything she'd done, all the loving care she'd poured into this place was for nothing if she didn't have Callum by her side. And now her dreams were coming true because he was on his way home to her.

The doorbell rang some half an hour later, and she hurried to answer it.

'Hi,' Callum said, as she pulled open the door. He rested a hand against the doorpost and gave her an engaging grin.

She couldn't stop the smile from spreading across her face. 'I was half-afraid you would change your mind,' she said. 'I thought if an emergency cropped up you'd have to stay at the hospital.'

He shook his head. 'We've enough people on duty to cover this afternoon.' He sniffed the air. 'Is that coffee I can smell?'

'Yes, come in, and I'll get it for you.'

He followed her into the kitchen. He looked like perfection to her, long and lean and totally masculine, wearing dark trousers that moulded his long legs and a cotton shirt that was open at the neck to give a glimpse of lightly bronzed skin.

She passed him a mug, and he sipped the hot liquid as he glanced around. 'It's very quiet in here without the children. I don't know whether that's a good thing or a bad thing. I think I could get used to the sound of their banter.'

'Me, too. I've loved having them around.'

'Still, it gives us the chance to slip away, doesn't it? After we've called in at the hospital, I thought we might take a trip to Cheddar Gorge and see the sights if you want?'

She nodded, her spirits soaring. 'I'd like that.'

'Good. Maybe we'll have lunch when we get there, and then take a wander around the place? I don't know how you feel about exploring the caves, but the whole area is beautiful.'

'So I've heard.' It didn't really matter to her where they went. Just being with him was enough for now.

They called in at the hospital a short time later. Ross was still being given supplemental oxygen, and he was breathing faster than normal, but he was propped up against his pillows and he was able to talk to them, which filled Alex with hope.

'It's good to see you, Alex,' Ross said, taking his time with the words. His grey eyes were filled with warmth. 'I feel we owe you so much, Beth and I.'

'No, you don't.' She glanced at the monitors, glad to see that the readings were coming down to a more normal level. She could hardly believe that this was the man who had been so near to death a couple of days ago. 'I'm just so happy to see you looking so much better than before. Has Dr Allingham been in to see you today?'

'Yes, he came just about an hour ago. He seemed pleased.' He rested for a few moments, leaning his head back against his pillows, a lock of brown hair falling across his brow. Alex looked at him with affection. 'He said there was a chance I might go home in a couple of weeks if I go on making progress. I'll have to carry on with the medication for a few months, but he thinks I'll be able to build up my strength better at home.'

'That's brilliant news.' Alex gave him a hug. 'I told Beth you could all stay at my house until you find a place of your own. You haven't seen it yet, but I know you'll like it. There's plenty of room. It's an old farmhouse I bought, with extensions that have been added on over the years.'

'Thanks for that, Alex. You're a treasure.' He glanced at Callum, who was standing quietly by her side. 'I don't think I've seen you before, have I? You must be someone special… Alex is very cautious about who she lets into her life.'

Callum smiled. 'Yes, I've begun to realise that over this last couple of months. It hasn't been easy, getting to know her as well as I'd like.'

'Well, just as long as you do right by her. I love my sister. I don't want to see her hurt.'

'I'll take good care of her, you have my word,' Callum said.

Alex sent him an uncertain look. That sounded as though he meant it. Did it mean he was planning on staying around, being part of her life?

They left her brother a few minutes later so that he could get some rest. 'Sarah will be so happy when she hears the news,' Alex said as they walked out to the car park.

Callum nodded, laying a reassuring palm on the small of her back. 'You must be relieved. Perhaps now that your mind's at ease you'll be able to relax and enjoy the rest of the afternoon.'

'Definitely,' she said, looking up at him and drinking in his features. For the first time in ages she felt as though life held some very real promise.

Suddenly, the quiet was disturbed by the bleeping of Callum's phone. His mouth flattened. 'Sorry about this,' he said, gently releasing her so that he could answer the call.

He spoke to the person on the other end of the line for a minute or two. 'Thanks, Katie,' he said after a while, and Alex looked at him curiously. Why would Katie be phoning him?

'It's good news,' he said, cutting the call and putting his phone back into his pocket. 'The board has posted its decision—the A and E unit is safe. They're going to follow some of your suggestions to bring in money from outside. And it looks as though my mini-stroke unit is a go, as well.' He grinned. 'You realise, don't you, Miss Bean Counter, this means I'll probably get my Doppler ultrasound machine after all?'

'Oh, Callum, that's great news.' She flung her arms around him. 'I hardly dared hope they'd go for it.' Then she leaned back a fraction and looked him in the eyes. 'Bean Counter?' she said, lifting a brow. 'Is that going to be my title for evermore?'

'Hmm. I'll have to think about that. Maybe we could change it for something else.'

'I should hope so.'

He smiled. 'Perhaps we should be on our way. I'm starving, so I think we should find a place to eat first of all.' He pulled open the car door for her. 'I know this great place just as you come into Cheddar.'

'Another one? How come I don't know these places?'

'Probably because you've had your nose to the grindstone for way too long. It's high time you learned how to loosen up and enjoy life.'

'And you'll show me how to do that?'

'Oh, yes.' His blue gaze travelled over her, his eyes filled with promise. 'I'm making it my very next project.'

He set the car in motion, and headed for the main road that would take them towards the Mendip Hills and on to Cheddar. Alex watched as the landscape changed from gentle slopes to rugged hills and deep gorges. It felt strangely as though she was travelling towards some new destiny, but perhaps that was due to the sheer excitement of being with him on this glorious afternoon, free as a bird for once. She wasn't going to think about the future, she decided. She was just going to take life as it came.

They stopped at a pretty, stone-built inn, made colourful with window-boxes full of flowers and hanging baskets spilling over with bright surfinias and trailing silver-leaved ivy.

'We could sit outside, if you like,' Callum said, leading the way through the inn and showing her the gardens through the open glass doors. There were bench tables set out in a courtyard that had been decorated with foliage plants and tubs of scarlet begonias. Beyond that were landscaped gardens, where flowering shrubs bordered a wide sweep of lawn.

'Yes, please, that would be lovely.' She could feel the sun warm on her bare arms, and on her legs where her light cotton skirt flowed delicately and skimmed her calves.

For his meal, Callum chose fillets of sea bass, served on a bed of roasted vegetables, whilst Alex went for a pork steak, topped with an apple-and-cider relish, and finished off under the grill with Cheddar cheese.

'They make the cheese just along the road from here,' Callum murmured, as he watched her spear the topping with her fork. 'Have you heard the legend about how it came to be made?'

'No, I haven't.'

'Well, apparently a milkmaid left a pail of milk in one of the Cheddar caves, and returned some time later to find that it had turned into a tasty cheese. Whether that's true or not, I don't know, but even today they mature the cheeses in Gough's Cave, wrapped in muslin cheesecloth. They say the tangy taste is due to the rich grazing pastures around here.'

'So if we visit Gough's Cave, we'll see them?' She thought about that. 'And probably smell them.'

He chuckled and lifted his fork to taste the succulent fish. 'Among other things, yes.'

Some time later, full up and satisfied after a meal that had been finished off with fresh fruit salad and liqueur coffees, they set off in the car once again. Alex was relaxed and happy. Her only niggling desire was that Callum should put his arms around her, but of course he wouldn't do that. They were in a public place...and she couldn't help wishing that they could be somewhere else where they could be totally, utterly alone.

He sent her an oblique glance as they drove along the road towards Cheddar. 'You're very quiet. Is everything okay? You're not worried about your brother, are you?'

'No, I'm fine. I'm sure he's going to be okay. I'm having a great time. It's just good to be out here under a perfect blue sky, and it's taking me a while to get used to it.' It wasn't like her to be this way...hung up on getting close to a man...but Callum was different. He was gentle and thoughtful, and it was totally restful, being with him.

They were opposites, though. He was good for her,

but was she good for him? She'd always been ambitious, following her career, and by all accounts that was the kind of woman he would rather steer clear of in the long term.

It was some half an hour later when they reached Cheddar Gorge. The scenery was spectacular, and Alex marvelled at the ravine, and its sheer-sided cliffs, cut out of ancient limestone. The banks were rich with greenery, and there was the occasional crop of wildflowers here and there, adding tiny patches of colour.

'Have you been here before?' Callum asked as he parked the car.

She shook her head. 'I've heard all about it, though. They say it was formed by a river some three million years ago, and then the Ice Age came, and after that the meltwater carved out the gorge.'

'I think that's probably right. Shall we go and take a look at Gough's Cave? It's the biggest one, and it's well worth seeing.'

'It would be a shame not to, while we're here.'

'Good.' He clasped her hand in his and she felt the thrill of his touch glide along her arm like a ripple of warm silk. They walked to the cave and went inside, and before long Alex was marvelling at the weird and wonderful formations that had been brought about by water dripping through the limestone over millions of years.

It was awe-inspiring. In one chamber, impressive stalactites were reflected in a pool below, giving an impression of a village perched on a mountain top. In another chamber, huge stalagmites reached high up into the roof and water droplets were reflected in the cavern's lights so that they sparkled like crystal.

Alex shivered slightly in the cool atmosphere, and

Callum immediately took off his light jacket and wrapped it around her, drawing her close. 'We can't have you getting cold,' he said. 'We don't want you ending up like the man they found in here, do we?'

Alex was shocked. 'What man? What happened to him?'

Callum laughed softly. 'He was young, apparently, and he was buried here some nine thousand years ago. His skeleton was found intact, and they've even managed to extract DNA from his tooth cavity, to show that he still has relatives living in the area.'

'You're joking!'

'No, it's true, believe me.'

She smiled. 'That's some family history—if you were searching for your ancestors, you'd hardly expect to go so far back, would you?'

'You wouldn't.' He held her close, walking with her back through the caves, until they emerged out into the sunlight once more.

She handed him his jacket. 'Thanks for that,' she said. She was reluctant to let it go. It had been warm from his body, and it had bought her nearer to him than she had been for what seemed like a long time.

He slung it over his shoulder, holding it with one hand, while he clasped her fingers with the other. 'Shall we walk by the river for a while?' he suggested.

'Yes, that sounds good.' She looked up at him. 'Somehow, I don't want the day to end. I know it must, eventually, but it's been so good, I want it to go on and on.'

He laid his arm around her shoulders. 'That's how I feel, too, and I think it's done you a world of good. You needed a break after all that's been happening. You certainly look better for it. There's colour in your cheeks and your eyes are sparkling.'

They walked towards the fields and the river, taking their time, ambling along and enjoying the lushness of nature all around them. By the riverside, Alex spotted a kingfisher searching for prey in the water, and further on there were two white egrets, shuffling their feet in the shallows.

It was glorious and so peaceful, and they stopped and sat for a while on the grassy bank in the shade of a broad oak tree, watching the sunlight playing over the water.

Callum eased himself closer to her. He looked at her, his gaze wandering over her features, over the smooth line of her cheekbones and the soft curve of her cheek. Then he bent his head and dropped a kiss on to her soft mouth, surprising her and starting up an array of tingling sensations that ran from her lips right down to the soft centre of her abdomen.

'Oh,' she said huskily. 'What was that for?'

'Just because.'

'Because what?'

'Because it was something I just had to do. Because your lips are soft and inviting and it's all I can do to resist you.' His fingers caressed her cheek. 'Because I've been wanting to do that all day.'

'Oh.' She was finally speechless. She gazed up at him, loving the feeling of being close to him, of having his long body mesh with hers.

His blue eyes glinted, his gaze trailing over her as though he would absorb her features into his memory.

'It's been great to see you looking so relaxed. We'll have to find more opportunities to take time out and explore different places together. I want to spend a lot more time with you.'

'Funny, that...I was thinking the same thing.'

He nodded. 'It doesn't matter where...the beach, meadow walks, your place or mine...just as long as we're together.'

She smiled at him. 'It's what I want, too.' She was quiet for a moment. 'Strange, isn't it, that I've never seen your place? I was beginning to wonder if it was some kind of sacred bachelor pad...your very own sanctuary.' Her expression became wistful. 'You more or less said that's what you intended when you bought it.'

His mouth made a crooked shape. 'People change. I changed...at least, I changed when I met you.' His glance flicked over her. 'I'm not alone in that, am I? Hasn't the same thing happened to you? You used to live in a rented place, and then you came down here and bought that rambling old property. I always wondered why you took it on, especially at a time when you had so much else on your plate. I think your subconscious mind was telling you that you needed to settle down, to be part of a family unit, and that house would be the one place where you sensed could be truly happy.'

'You think so?'

'Mmm-hmm. Though it's going to be a little more crowded than you expected, quite soon, from the sound of things, when your brother and his wife move in with you. I think it's great that you're doing it, but are you going to be happy with that?' He tugged her closer to him as though he needed to feel the softness of her curves against his taut, masculine body. His hands stroked the small of her back, moving over the swell of her hips.

'I think so.' She snuggled up against him, cherishing

the moment. 'I want to see Ross and his family reunited, and they need somewhere to stay while they recover from their injuries. Beth's come on by leaps and bounds, and I'm sure she'll soon regain her strength. I think Ross will take a little longer, and he needs to be perfectly fit before they can go house-hunting…unless Beth does it for them. At least his job is being kept open for him. The company wants him back.'

Callum smiled. 'That's good.' He lowered his head to hers and kissed her once again, taking his time, exploring the softness of her lips, moving against her as though he couldn't get enough of her.

Alex was in seventh heaven. This was way more than she could have hoped for, to have him kiss her and hold her and make her feel that she was everything to him just then. She ran her hands over his shoulders, his arms, trailing her fingers over the length of his spine.

'That feels so good,' he murmured, his voice roughened as he dragged his mouth reluctantly from hers. 'But every time I hold you I think it's not nearly enough. I want us to be together.'

She gave him a cautious look from under her lashes. 'I'm not sure what you're asking.'

He laid his cheek against hers. 'Do you think you might want to move in with me for a while, once Ross and Beth are settled in your house? I know my apartment is a bit small, after what you're used to, but we can at least be together, alone, private.'

She hesitated, drawing back a little and laying her palms flatly against his chest as she looked up at him. 'You're suggesting we live together?' Was he saying he wanted just a casual fling, no strings attached? Her spirits plummeted. She wanted so much more than that.

He nodded. 'Just until Ross and Beth find a place

of their own. I mean, I really like the children, and it's great having them around, and I'm sure I'll get along fine with your brother and his wife…but I really would like to have you to myself for a while. I know it's a lot to ask of you, but once they find their own house, I can put my apartment on the market.'

She frowned. 'Why would you want to do that?'

'Like I said, I've changed. Why would I need a bachelor apartment any longer? I've fallen in love with a woman who has the perfect family home. We could spend a lifetime together there.'

Her mouth dropped open a little. 'Is this your way of telling me that you love me?'

He nodded. 'I do love you, Alex. We're like two opposite halves, but we fit together so well. I just know we could make it work…if you would agree to be my wife. After all, you said you didn't want to be Miss Bean Counter, didn't you? Mrs Brooksby has a nice ring to it, don't you think?'

A soft sigh escaped her. 'I thought you were asking me to move in with you, for us to live together without any kind of commitment.' She looked up at him, her expression quizzical. 'I thought you said you never felt the need to settle down, that marriage and commitment weren't for you?'

He nodded. 'That was all true…until I met you. Then after that everything was different. It took me a while to realise what was happening. I couldn't believe that I'd fallen for someone who was so strong and career minded—the very opposite of what I thought I wanted—but you showed me that you know instinctively what's more important. You showed it when you came down to Somerset to look after Sarah and James, and you showed it again when you took the time off work to be with them. I know things are going to work out just fine for us, Alex.' He looked at her intently. 'I just need you to tell me that you love me too, and that you want me as much as I want you.'

'I do.' She gave a soft sigh. 'I never knew that I could feel this way. I never met anyone who could make me feel the way you do. You're so calm and relaxed, you don't let things throw you, and you know exactly how to cajole me into seeing what really matters. And at the same time you're single-minded and so good at what you do. You're the perfect man for me...the only man for me.'

She tilted her face to his and kissed him tenderly. 'I love you,' she murmured. 'More than anything in the world. And I'd love to be your wife and move into your apartment...' her mouth curved '...just as long as we get back to the farmhouse as soon as possible.'

He breathed a sigh of relief. 'That's just wonderful. For a long while, I've felt as though there was something missing from my life, but now I feel complete. Just as long as I have you, life will be everything I ever wanted.'

'Funny, isn't it?' she said softly, reaching up to kiss him once more. 'That's exactly how I feel.'

PLAYBOY DOCTOR TO DOTING DAD

SUE MACKAY

To Louise Groarke,
my wonderful critique partner.

And to Iona Jones, Barb Jeffcott Geris,
Margie Stewart, Deborah Shattock and
Emily Gee – of the very supportive
Blenheim Writers group.

CHAPTER ONE

ABBY BROWN stared out of the window at the long, neat rows of nectarine trees with their small fruit that were just beginning to fill out. Her father's orchard: the one constant in her life. Each season brought its own routine and, with summer officially starting this week, December meant spraying and crop thinning.

Stop procrastinating. This had to be done. On a long, indrawn breath, she pressed redial. The one phone call she did not want to make, had tried making for two years. She knew the number off by heart she'd rung it so often. But this time she actually had to let the phone ring. Had to wait for Kieran to answer. This time she could not hang up in a panic. She could no longer put off telling him.

This was her third attempt to reach him tonight, and the only reason she kept trying was because having this particular conversation face to face with him would be worse. A whole lot worse.

The ringing stopped as the phone was picked up somewhere in Dublin. 'Kieran Flynn speaking.'

Words died on Abby's tongue. That sweet Irish lilt reminded her exactly why she'd got into this situation in the first place.

'Hello? Anyone there?' Kieran asked, a smile in his voice.

She couldn't do this.

She had to do it. Quickly, before she could slam the phone down, she answered, 'It's Abby Brown.'

'Abigail? Really? Where are you? I mean, are you here? Or are you calling from New Zealand?' Measured surprise lifted his voice.

'I'm at home.' How could she afford to travel to Ireland? 'I thought it was about time I made contact with you.'

'What a coincidence. I'm coming down your way in a few days.' Kieran paused then added, 'I'm working in your local hospital for two months, managing the emergency department.'

'I heard. The hospital grapevine is in good working order. I had hoped you'd have been in touch before coming out.'

'I thought I'd wait until I'd settled in, get to know my way around first, before giving you a call. I also wondered if I might possibly spend some time with Olivia.'

Yeah, sure. His niece. The little girl they had joint guardianship of. The child he barely remembered to send birthday and Christmas presents to. Had he really intended calling? Or did he think this was the right thing to say now that she'd contacted him? Obviously he hadn't realised he'd see her at the hospital. Heaven help her. It wasn't going to be easy if they didn't get past the news she had for him. 'We'll be working together.'

'We will? That's fantastic. For some reason I thought you were nursing in Paediatrics.' Charm thickened the lilt.

It also sent the muscles in her stomach into spasms, which was plain stupid because she didn't hold any special feelings for this man. Really? 'I transferred to ED nearly a year ago. I prefer it to Paediatrics.' These days she didn't like dealing with sick children all the time. It made her worry too much. At least in ED she worked with a variety of patients.

'Then we'll have plenty of time to see each other, and catch up on things. Should be fun.'

Things? A child was not a thing. 'That will be great. Olivia needs to get to know her Irish family.'

'I guess so.' He sounded unsure. Backing off already?

'Of course she does. It's an important part of her heritage. I think I'm right in believing you're the only living relative on her mother's side.'

'No, there is her grandfather, but I haven't a clue where he is these days. I don't think there's any hurry for Olivia to meet him. In fact, she's probably a whole lot better off never knowing him.'

'That's kind of sad.' She couldn't imagine not knowing where her father was, or any member of her family for that matter. 'Olivia adores her Kiwi grandfather.'

'Then she's very lucky and we should leave the situation as it stands.' His tone suggested she'd be wise not to argue.

Okay, so she could be patient, give him time to get to know Olivia better before raising the point again. But right now she was being sidetracked from the purpose of this call. Again a deep breath.

But Kieran spoke before she could gather the courage to tell him.

'Look, Abigail, I hate to rush you but I've got lots to do before I catch my plane out. Two months is a long time to be away from my job here. Did you ring for a specific reason? Or is this a welcoming call before I arrive in Nelson?'

Here it was, the moment she'd been dreading. 'I have to tell you something that I think it best you know before you get here.' Before she saw him again, and read the shock and anger that would surely fill those startling blue eyes that haunted her every day. Tell him, get it over. 'I have a son, Seamus. He's fifteen months old.' The words poured out in a torrent, her mouth dry.

'Oh, right. A playmate for Olivia, then. That must be good for her.'

He paused, and Abby waited, her stomach in a knot, her heart thumping in her chest.

Then she gasped, surprising hurt spiralling through her, when he said, 'Of course, I didn't know you were in a relationship. Have you married since we last saw each other?'

Didn't he get it? Come on, Kieran. Do the sum. Fifteen months plus nine? What had they been doing together two years ago? Had he forgotten that night they'd spent making love? A night that had never faded completely from her memory. But, then, he didn't have a young child running around his home to constantly remind him of that time, so he probably had forgotten. Strange how disappointed that made her feel.

She blurted, 'Seamus is your son.'

There, she'd told him. She couldn't take the words back. The truth was out. And the silence was deafening. Of course she'd been wrong not to have told him the moment she'd seen the blue line on the pregnancy testing strip. But his career was very demanding and he'd been afraid of having anything to do with Olivia. He'd told Abby bluntly that he believed the child would come a distant second to his job. He'd warned he'd probably send Olivia to boarding school as soon as she was old enough. Providing financial backing seemed to be his share of the guardianship issue. And Olivia was only his niece. What chance was there that he'd go the extra distance for their son? So Abby, concerned about the emotional damage Kieran believed he was capable of inflicting, had taken the easy option and kept quiet.

Huh. Easy? That'd be the day. She'd agonised over her decision every single day, knowing Kieran should be told about his child. All those aborted phone calls she'd made to him. And then there were the many letters she'd written and not posted. The photos of Seamus she'd taken and not sent. None of that counted for anything now.

'Kieran?' she finally whispered.

'Are you sure he's mine?' The charm had disappeared now, replaced by uncertainty.

Thanks a bunch. 'I don't make a habit of sleeping around.' But she had spent one passionate night with this man, a night that had been totally out of character for her. She'd been numb with grief for her brother and sister-in-law, and Kieran's arms had been warm and comforting. Too comforting.

He continued, 'What I meant was I used precautions each time.'

'Ah, well, there was once when, um, we kind of forgot.'

'I never forget. The last thing I have ever wanted is to be a parent. Because of that I make doubly sure something like this won't happen. Ever.' His voice snapped out that last word.

Sorry, buddy. I've got the evidence. 'Seamus is the spitting image of you. Your colouring, that slight lift of the right side of your mouth when you smile. I wouldn't be surprised if, when he starts talking, he has an Irish accent.'

Again silence fell between them. Abby twisted her hair around her fingers as she stared outside. Dusk was falling, softening the view. She'd told Kieran. At last. Even if he exploded at her, called her every miserable name he could think of, she felt as though a huge weight had finally been lifted. Not telling Kieran about Seamus had never sat comfortably with her. She mightn't trust him to do the right thing by his child, or by her. She might believe he'd back out of their lives so fast he'd be like a train without brakes; but it went against all she believed in not to have told him the truth. Sound reasons or not.

'Am I to understand that you're only telling me now because I'm coming out to Nelson this week?'

'Yes.' She waited for the explosion, shoulders tense, fingers white where they gripped the phone.

'There's an honest answer.' Were his teeth grinding? 'Why didn't you tell me the moment you knew you were pregnant?'

'What would you have done about it, if I had?'

'How do I know? I haven't got a clue what to say now, so as to what I'd have said or done two years ago is beyond me. But I would've had time to get used to the idea.' He didn't sound like he'd really grasped what she'd told him. As in really, truly, understood that he had a child. Too much to take in?

She tried to explain the inexcusable. 'You had made it abundantly clear how you felt about having a child of your own.' On two occasions. 'I'm talking about your reaction to becoming Olivia's guardian. You were so adamant you didn't want anything to do with her upbringing that I…' She faltered. 'I figured if you couldn't cope with helping bring up your niece, the last thing you'd want to deal with would be a child of your own.' Don't forget the financial side. 'I know you've provided well for Olivia, very well, but I didn't want you to think I was asking for that for Seamus.'

'That gave you the right to decide I shouldn't know about this boy? My son?' His words were like bullets, slamming into her with piercing sharpness. 'You made this choice? For me?'

She would not apologise. She'd seen the trepidation clouding his eyes at the thought that he might have to raise Olivia. Trepidation that in truth she'd never fully understood. Had she done the guy an injustice? Probably. The guilt twisted her gut. But what hope was there that he'd have been willing to become a father to Seamus? In his own words, no father at all was better than a random one, and he'd told her they didn't come more random than he'd be. 'Kieran, rightly or wrongly, I had my reasons. But now that you're coming here, you need to know.' Hopefully he'd have calmed down by the time she got to see him at work. 'And I want Seamus to know his father.'

There was a sharp intake of breath at the other end of the line. Had she gone too far?

If so, he didn't divulge his feelings. 'I won't have much spare time during my tenure at your hospital, so I hope you're not expecting a lot from me.'

Only some time with your niece, who really needs to get to know her mother's brother. Only an acknowledgement of your son, and maybe a softening of your heart towards him. Only your understanding and forgiveness. Too much to expect? Probably.

He continued, 'Spare time or not, we have a lot to discuss. I'll set up a meeting with you once I've settled in.'

Set up a meeting? Her shoulders slumped. That's not the way to go about this. But she'd leave it for now. 'I'm sorry you had to find out this way, Kieran.'

What happened to not apologising? The trouble with that notion was that she felt incredibly guilty. Not only had Kieran missed out on so much of his son's life, if he'd wanted to be a part of it, but Seamus had also missed out on too much. And right at this moment she suspected Seamus would continue losing out for a very long time to come. Maybe, when he was an adult, he'd be able to approach his father and see if they could establish a bond.

Unless she could patch things up with Kieran. She didn't like her chances.

Five days later

Abby blinked. Nelson Airport terminal already? It seemed only moments ago she'd pulled out of the hospital car park. Had she been speeding? Not when she didn't want to be here, surely? Not even running ten minutes late would've made her speed today. Meeting Kieran Flynn was right at the bottom of her 'want-to-do' list. Right there after going to the dentist.

But he'd emailed to ask, no, demand, that she meet his flight. Michael, the department head Kieran was temporarily replacing, had thought it an excellent idea. 'A friendly gesture,' he'd said. So why hadn't Michael thought of meeting the man? And saved her the anguish of being squeezed inside her car with a hostile Irishman?

She stopped her old Nissan Bluebird in the two-minute pick-up zone and shoved out into the searing mid-afternoon heat that not even the offshore breeze helped to cool. Her skin instantly prickled with perspiration as she slung her handbag over her shoulder. Sucking in her churning stomach, she locked the car door, all the while fighting the urge to leap back in and race away.

Gritting her teeth, she headed for the main entrance. As her sandals slapped the hot, sticky pavement she practised a welcoming smile. And failed. Miserably.

Today she would have to face Kieran for the first since telling him he was a father. The ramifications of what she'd done, or not done, were about to start. She'd thought the hardest part had been phoning him the other day, but now she had to actually see him. No doubt he'd have spent the thirty-plus hours flying to New Zealand, thinking up truckloads of horrible things to say to her. Unfortunately, she knew she probably deserved them.

The yoghurt she'd eaten for lunch curdled in her stomach and her mouth soured. She hesitated. It would be so easy to turn around and head back to work, bury herself in broken bones and chest pains.

Merely delaying tactics. Kieran would still catch up with her.

Dragging her feet through the main doors, her eyes scanned the noisy crowd for the tall, dark-haired Irishman who'd haunted her dreams for the past two years. No sign of him. A wave of relief engulfed her. Maybe he wasn't coming? Maybe he'd changed his mind.

But common sense prevailed. Of course he hadn't changed his mind. He'd made a commitment to the hospital and if she knew one thing about Kieran Flynn, it was that he didn't break commitments. Especially when they involved his work. But a commitment to a child? He hadn't broken one to Olivia because he'd never made one. Abby knew that Kieran's strong belief that he'd be an inadequate father had been behind his decision not to be a part of Olivia's upbringing. And behind her own decision not to tell him about Seamus. She rubbed a hand down her cheek as she remember the slap of his hand on the lawyer's desk as he had stated categorically that she should never expect him to be there for Olivia in any role other than a distant uncle who'd finance the child's education. Abby now realised that she needed to learn more about what was behind this, for both the children's sakes.

There would be plenty of time. Again she wondered why Kieran's stellar career as an emergency specialist had brought him to a small city way downunder in New Zealand. Could he have been thinking about Olivia when he'd applied? Was this his way of touching base with his niece without getting too involved? She doubted it. He hadn't exactly inundated the child with his attention since her parents had died. His communication over that time made a mute person seem verbose.

Abby tugged her blouse down over her hips and crossed to read the arrivals screen. Just where was this guy who had her little household all in a twitter? And who made her head spin with worry?

Kieran peered through the window down onto the glittering sea of horseshoe-shaped Tasman Bay. What a damned long way to come for two months' work. But he'd have gone to Siberia if that's what it took to please the chairman of the Board and further his own career. He sighed. He still didn't understand why the old boy thought it necessary for him to take a secondment overseas before he put in his application for head of the emergency department of Mercy Hospital in Dublin.

He'd been heading to Adelaide, Australia, for his secondment until this one in New Zealand had suddenly appeared. Adelaide had been the obvious choice. A much larger facility with higher patient numbers, which would look good on his CV. But Nelson required someone urgently as the current head of department had a very ill child needing care in Australia. Something about a liver transplant.

Even then Kieran had resisted, but whenever he'd glanced at the travel brochure on Nelson an image of a woman and one heated night of passion, the likes of which he'd never known before or since, had kept flicking across his mind.

Abigail. She lived in Nelson. Not that he intended picking up where they'd left off that night. No, thank you. That was a road to disaster. But the mental pictures of her and that one night had caused him to fill in the wrong set of papers.

Don't forget Olivia. It had broken his heart to watch her at the airport in Dublin, clinging to Abigail's hand as she had disappeared from his life through the bland doors of Immigration. Even knowing he'd done the best thing for Olivia hadn't made the pain any easier. He missed his sister, and Olivia was the only connection he had left to her. Two losses in one week had been horrendous. But no way would he change the arrangement. Olivia was far better off living with Abigail.

Kieran's hands clenched against his thighs as the plane

shook and bucked. Why couldn't the pilot fly it in a straight line? Sweat slithered down between his shoulder blades, plastering his shirt to his skin.

A gnarled hand tapped his forearm. 'It's a bit bumpy, isn't it, dear?'

Kieran flicked a glance sideways at the elderly lady sitting beside him, her crotchet momentarily still in her lap. She didn't seem at all fazed by the turbulence. A benevolent smile and sparkling, washed-out blue eyes focused on him.

'Just a little,' he concurred, dragging out a smile.

'We won't be long now.'

'I certainly hope not.' He peered out the window looking for a distraction. But his mind quickly turned back to Abigail.

Of course, if he'd known of the bombshell she had been about to drop on him he'd definitely have chosen Adelaide. His muscles tensed. Would he? Truly? He shrugged, trying to ignore the multitude of questions that had buzzed around his skull since that phone call from her. Now here he was, minutes away from landing in her town. He shivered. Nelson. Where a whole bundle of difficult issues and decisions awaited him. And none of them medical.

A son. Abigail said the lad looked like him. Some alien emotion stirred within his chest, a feeling he didn't recognise. Surely not curiosity? Or pride?

Was it the familiar fear that he'd let Olivia down? And now Seamus? But how did a man who'd never experienced love from his parents love his own child? As his father had said often enough, he'd make a terrible parent. He didn't have it in him to love and care for children. The sooner he explained so that Abigail understood, the sooner her expectations about his role in the children's lives would disappear. For ever.

Just grand. He'd been coming for work, and now that

had been pushed to the back of his mind with thoughts of Abigail and the children, making him feel rattled. Inadequate, even.

At least he'd be busy putting in long hours covering for staff on leave over Christmas and New Year. Apparently this was the time of year that Kiwis took their major holidays, spending weeks at the beaches, out in the mountains or following major sports events. At least there'd be time to get used to the idea of being a father and to decide how to deal with it.

'Don't bother. You'll make a mess of parenting, like you make a mess of most things in your life.' His father's voice slammed into his brain. The words that had spurred him to become an exceptional emergency specialist.

Bitterness soured his mouth as the old litany made its umpteenth rerun in his skull. He wasn't good at looking out for people he cared about. He'd known that since the day when Morag, his sister, had tripped and broken her ankle during a student party in his flat. She'd wrecked her chances at the European ski championships. In a blind fury their father had unfairly laid the blame firmly at Kieran's feet, telling him he was incapable of thinking of anyone except himself.

A fact his father had taken great delight in rubbing in again when Kieran's girlfriend at the time had miscarried. Kieran had been working late and hadn't had his cellphone switched on. His girlfriend had accused him of not being there when she'd needed him most. His father had added his taunt, saying that surely Kieran had finally learned his lesson and accepted he shouldn't get involved with anyone who would depend on him to look out for them.

Oh, he'd learned his lesson all right. He'd made a lifetime commitment to it. And nothing one little boy could do would change his mind.

Swallowing the bile rising in his throat, Kieran tried to focus on something brighter, less distressing. Abigail. Again.

Funny how she popped straight into his mind. It had never once occurred to him that she'd be working in the same department he was going to. What if she insisted on being overly friendly at work? Worse, what if everyone already knew he was the father of her child? He cringed. That would put him on the back foot straight away. He was the head of the department, albeit temporarily, and fraternising with the staff was not good for staff relations.

Too late, boyo. The fraternising has been done, can't be undone. Abigail has a child, your child. A boy named Seamus.

He would do his damnedest to keep that information under wraps. If he wasn't already too late.

'I'd better not be,' he muttered.

All his muscles tightened. As they had done a thousand times on this trip whenever he thought about the situation. He still couldn't believe he was a father.

Was that because he didn't want to believe it?

He'd always taken care to avoid an accident of this kind. That's why he bought condoms by the ton. But he knew the boy was his. He knew Abigail wasn't one of those women who went from one man's bed to the next without a care. Neither would she use something like pregnancy to snag a man into marriage. If that had been her intention, she wouldn't have kept Seamus's arrival a secret from him. No, Abigail was honesty personified.

Discomfort made him squirm as he remembered that night in Dublin two years ago. Both of them had been totally smothered in grief after the joint funeral of his sister and Abigail's brother. They'd turned to each other for comfort, and for a few hours had forgotten everything as they'd discovered each other. He knew her all right. Intimately.

The plane shuddered. So did Kieran. His tense fingers ached, bent like claws. He squeezed his eyes tight. God, he hated flying. Think of something else, anything else. Abigail again. Wrong focus. But her image burned his eyeballs. As it had at unexpected moments ever since they'd made love.

'Did I hear an Irish accent?' Beside him the metal hook flicked in and out of the cotton. 'What brings you out here?'

A hurricane of waist-length dark blonde hair, and long arms and legs. A quirky smile that challenged him, and piercing hazel eyes that devoured him. Abigail.

No. He hadn't endured this agony to see her. 'I'm working at the local hospital. I also have a three-year-old niece living here.' *And your son. What about him?* If he mentioned Seamus then he was acknowledging the boy was a part of him. *I'm not ready for that.*

'They're a bundle of fun and tricks at that age. My grandson is into gardening at the moment, much to his mother's consternation, digging being his favourite occupation.'

'I can see how that could be a problem.' What did Olivia enjoy doing? Damn it, who does Olivia look like? His sister? Or David? How tall was she? He didn't know anything about her.

Appalled, he leaned his head back and stared at the moulded-plastic ceiling. He'd barely acknowledged any correspondence from Abigail about Olivia. He had behaved dreadfully, deliberately keeping out of touch. Arranging a regular money transfer from Dublin for Abigail to use for Olivia had been easy, and had salved his conscience whenever he'd thought there might be something he should be doing for his niece. No wonder Abigail hadn't contacted him about Seamus. She must have a very low opinion of him. Would she be waiting at the airport with a bat to bludgeon him over the head so she could drag him home to see the children? He forced his fingers straight, loose. Expanded his lungs. He couldn't blame her if she did.

Beside him the lady asked, 'So, your niece, is she a Kiwi?'

'Yes, she is, but she's Irish as well. My sister married a doctor from here, a friend of mine.' Best friend he'd ever had. 'They were killed in a car accident in Dublin a couple of years ago.'

'I'm very sorry to hear that.' The woman glanced at him. 'So the little girl has come over here to live with her father's family?'

'It seemed the best place for her, surrounded with lots of aunts and her grandfather. There's only me available on her mother's side and I live in the middle of Dublin. Not at all suitable for a small child.' *Not at all suitable for him.* Thankfully, David and Morag had it written into their wills that if anything should ever happen to them, he and Abigail would be Olivia's guardians, and she'd live with Abigail unless there was a very good reason why not. Which, of course, there wasn't. Abigail was very caring; perfect for a small, bewildered child who'd just lost her parents.

His companion nodded at the window. 'There's Nelson City. We'll be on the ground in a minute or two so you can relax now.'

'You aren't by any chance a psychologist?' he asked her.

'Just a canny old lady.'

'What are you doing in early February? I could do with you distracting me again when I head home.'

'I'm sure you could find a young lady to do that.'

That was absolutely the last thing he wanted. Or needed. He had a very comfortable lifestyle back in Dublin, one that didn't allow for anyone else interfering with his comings and goings. He'd created a perfect life that didn't involve… anyone. Especially not a family. Not with his appalling credentials. Not even Olivia and Seamus could change his belief on that.

Seamus, a good Irish name. A clever move on Abigail's

part? Or a name she liked more than any other? What did it matter what she'd called the lad? His jaw tightened some more. It shouldn't, but the fact that she'd had his child and not mentioned it right up until he was days from leaving Dublin galled. Which wasn't being fair to her. He knew he had a lot to make up to her for. But did he want to? It would mean getting to know the children, getting close to them. He shivered at the thought.

The plane's wheels thumped onto the tarmac. On the ground again. The end of his journey at last. Something unfurled in the pit of his stomach. The knot caused by his fear of flying? No, this felt different. Like…excitement. *No way.* Did he even know what it felt like to be really excited? Abigail's face floated into his mind, and the truth exploded through him. These feelings were all about her. The woman he'd never quite vanquished from his mind, from his body. Suddenly he couldn't wait to see her, hug her, laugh with her.

Reason enough to stay aboard the plane and fly back the way he'd come.

CHAPTER TWO

ABBY's gaze was pulled to the plate-glass windows looking out over the tarmac and the disembarked passengers walking towards the terminal. Her nails dug painfully into her palms. One man towered above the rest of the passengers. Raven hair shining in the sun. A winning smile on a handsome face. He'd be exhausted after his long flight, but she'd never have guessed it from the way he carried himself. Shoulders back, legs swinging with confidence. As he came through the security door his gaze swept the terminal, searching. Then those twinkling eyes met hers and she saw the wariness in them. But then his smile broadened, oozing charm.

Her heart fluttered in her throat. That exact lopsided smile had once drawn her into bed with him. The urge to weep rose as unbidden memories teased at the fringes of her mind. Sweet memories of Kieran's face next to hers on a white pillow, of her fingers pushing through his dark curls as they'd lain entwined in the hotel's large bed, of his deep chuckle when she'd amused him.

It had been an unnatural time when emotions were raw, feelings bouncing all over the place. She'd be a fool to believe there was anything in those memories that could be rekindled now. She'd be a bigger fool to want anything close to that.

Remember, he's probably angry with you. As if she needed reminding. The ache in her stomach was testament to days of waiting and worrying about that. *This isn't some happy reunion of two friends. Kieran Flynn has come here to work. Not to see you. And to say they'd been friends would be stretching the facts a little.*

She gulped, tugged her shoulders back. Two children's happiness depended on her getting along with this man, who was now approaching her. But how to get around the fact that just seeing Kieran made her forget everything except him?

She studied Kieran. Sexy. The word banged into her head. Instantly she was back in that hotel bed with him. Her cheeks warmed. Her silly heart tripped. It wouldn't be easy, remaining neutral around Kieran. But she had to try. Starting right now.

'Hi, Kieran, welcome to Nelson.' Scintillating stuff, but her thought processes were mush. *Try to squash the longing. Hang on to the fact that you've deceived him.*

'Hello, Abigail.' And he dropped a light kiss on each cheek. Almost air kisses, kisses that meant absolutely nothing. Told her nothing. 'It's great to see you again.'

Oka-ay. The friendly approach. The friendly *playboy* approach. But, then, Kieran was known for his charm, so of course this would be second nature to him. She had to be careful not to be taken in by it all. She tried for a similar tone. 'Same. Good to see you, I mean.' Still making captivating conversation.

He stood, his arms hanging loosely at his sides. Aha. His fingers were tense. He wore a wary smile on his face. Waiting for something? A more welcoming response from her? What was she supposed to say to him? How was she supposed to greet him? She didn't know what he felt about the Seamus issue now that he'd had time to think about it. She hadn't a clue how he felt about her since her revelation.

His back was ramrod straight, his chin jutting out defensively. He lifted a hand towards her, let it drop. 'Thanks for coming to pick me up.'

Right, that helped. She knew exactly where she stood now. Not. Her hands fisted around her handbag strap. Then she got a whiff of that special Kieran scent of maleness and aftershave. She took a step back. A big step. That scent could undo all her resolve to remain neutral. It had lingered in the edges of her mind for two long, lonely years; teasing, annoying.

She forced a smile, worried he'd sense her unease. She hadn't forgotten how perceptive he could be. 'Kieran, I'm…' She sucked a breath, tried again. 'I'm really happy you've come. The family's looking forward to seeing you again.'

'How are they all? I guess the twins are out breaking the men's hearts these days.' This time he flashed a tired smile that had her feeling sympathetic towards him. Sympathy would draw her under his spell. That she couldn't afford. So ignore it.

'There have been a few casualties.' She straightened her back again, tried for a smile. 'Charlie and Steph have some parties lined up that you might like to go to.' Where there'd be plenty of single women for him to enjoy the company of. Abby felt a spurt of envy. She'd love to go to a party. With Kieran.

His black eyebrows rose. 'That's kind, but I'm going to have to disappoint them. I'm here to work, not socialise.'

'No one at the hospital expects you to spend the whole eight weeks tied to the A and E department. Dad's hoping you'll join the family for a meal on Friday night, and Olivia's so excited about you coming. And so is Seamus, although he doesn't really understand yet.' From few words to too many. Brain mush again.

He stepped back, looked around cautiously. 'They're not here? With you?' His glance settled on a little girl standing with a small group of people next to them.

Oh, my goodness, he doesn't know what Olivia looks like. 'They're at home with their nanny.'

As he turned back and gave her another cautious smile, she added, 'I've been working today. I was given time off to meet you, and take you to your apartment.'

'Thank you, I really appreciate it.' His smile tugged at her heart, made her momentarily forget why she'd been so nervous.

She found her mouth lifting in a return smile. 'You didn't give me much choice.'

'Bit abrupt, was I?' His blue eyes fixed her to the floor.

'Just a weensy bit.' She nodded, biting down on the smile. She looked up into his face, and again felt her stomach muscles tighten with apprehension. How would she survive having Kieran living in her home town? Working in the ED department as her boss? Visiting his niece and son in her cottage? If he visited them. Of course he'd visit them. He had to.

Right now she was stunned at the depth of feeling she had for this enigmatic man tripping her up at every turn. She hadn't expected that. Get back on track, the common-sense side of her brain warned. This was the day of reckoning, the day when she'd learn how Kieran intended dealing with the fact he was a father. It had been a long time coming, and yet she had always known it would come. Even if she'd had to wait another year, another five years, it would have come.

And she would never have been ready.

'You've cut your hair,' Kieran commented, feeling a pang of loss.

'Too hard to manage with small children and their sticky fingers.' She flashed him a half-smile.

She had beautiful hair. Even now. Cut in a soft style that tucked around her face Kieran wanted to reach out and touch the silky strands. He resisted with difficulty. Touching her would not help the situation.

Abigail's nervous with me. She was trying to hide it but her give-away facial expressions told the truth. Pique rippled through him. He wasn't used to being treated in such a deliberately offhand fashion. Of course she'd be apprehensive after shocking him about Seamus, but he'd just spent nearly two days travelling around the globe so he didn't appreciate being treated like something dragged up from the bottom of a deep pond. He was the one who had something to be upset about. And hadn't he been charming and friendly?

'I apologise for the brevity of my email, but there seemed to be hundreds of things to be organised before I left home.' He risked another smile. His smiles usually won him anything he wanted.

Abigail leaned closer, a whiff of some exotic flower tantalising him. She was no doubt only now recognising that she hadn't been very welcoming. How would she make up for that? A light kiss?

She said, 'Baggage claim's outside.'

Great. Getting warmer. His heart banged against his ribs. He'd have to polish his charm if the next two months were to be bearable. 'Right, let's grab my gear and get out of here.'

As he turned to follow her, the old lady who had sat next to him on the plane waved and called softly, 'You won't be needing me next trip.' Her head tilted at Abigail.

Oh, yes, he would. He might want to win a warm smile from the woman who'd shanghaied his brain but he couldn't imagine taking a long-haul flight with her and Olivia. And Seamus, a little voice piped up in the back of his head. He winked at the old lady. 'See you in February.'

Then he strode outside to the baggage claim area. As he did so he thought about the unexpected change in the warm, vibrant woman standing next to him. He'd first met her at his sister's marriage to David. Abigail seemed quieter, more uptight than he recalled. Guess being a mother did that.

He totted up other changes he'd begun noticing. Abigail didn't bounce on her toes any more. Her quick grin seemed to have flicked off permanently. Shadows lined the skin beneath her eyes. Life since they'd spent that wonderful night together had been harder on her than him.

A screech of tyres snapped through the air, followed by a thump. A woman screamed.

Another woman cried out, 'Quick. Someone, help.'

Kieran met Abigail's startled glance. 'That our cue?'

She nodded, 'I'd say so.'

'I'm a doctor.' Kieran squeezed past gaping faces and prodding elbows.

Abigail followed. 'Let me through. I'm a nurse.'

'He stepped right in front of me.' A male voice sounded defensive. 'I never had a chance to avoid him.'

Abigail dropped to her knees beside a prostrate man held down at his chest by the front wheel of a four-wheeled motorbike towing the baggage trailers.

Looking around, Kieran said, 'Someone, call an ambulance.'

'I'm onto it,' a man answered.

Urgency underlined Abigail's words. 'We need that bike lifted away.'

Kieran searched the closest faces, found the driver of the bike, an orange safety jacket and a white face the give-away. 'How many of us will it take to move this bike?'

'Six, I reckon. I'll unhook the luggage trailers.' The man's voice trembled as he stared down at the accident victim. 'Is he going to be all right?'

Kieran gripped the driver's shoulder. 'We can't say until we've had a proper look at him.'

'He kind of tripped. I never saw him coming.'

Tripped? Stepped out? Fainted? Heart attack? Kieran tossed up scenarios. The unconscious man appeared to be in his late forties, maybe early fifties, so cardiac malfunction couldn't be ruled out.

Turning to the pressing crowd, he spoke loudly and clearly. 'Step back, everyone. Give us some space, please.' He searched for strong men to help lift the quad bike away.

'Abigail, you'll have to move aside for a moment.' He didn't want her getting hurt if the lift went wrong and the bike toppled over.

She nodded. When their patient had been freed, she leaned close to him. 'You weren't meant to start work today.'

'If you mean, am I alert enough after thirty-six hours' flying? No, I'm probably not up to a full-scale emergency. But I think we can manage this between us.' At least the patient might be happier to have him around than she appeared to be.

A shadow crossed her eyes, darkening them to the colour of well-cooked toast. 'I only meant it's not much of a welcome to Nelson.'

He squeezed her hand, suddenly in need of contact with her. Any contact. He wanted to establish a connection that would get him over the hurdles of the coming weeks. 'Let's look at our man.'

They knelt, one each side of their patient, and Abigail lifted the man's wrist as he opened his eyes slowly, blinking in the bright daylight.

'What happened?' he croaked.

'You've been knocked down by a quad bike,' Kieran explained. 'I'm Dr Flynn, and this is Abby Brown, a nurse. Can you tell me your name and address, please?'

As he answered, Abigail counted his pulse rate.

'Paul Stokes, three Caper Drive, Richmond.'

Nothing wrong with the man's coherence. Kieran gently felt Paul's chest. 'I'm checking your ribs for fractures.'

He didn't add that if any ribs had been staved in a lung might be punctured. Pneumothorax was a distinct, and very serious, possibility.

His patient grunted through white lips, beads of perspiration covered his forehead. 'It hurts like hell. When I breathe in.'

Around them people jostled for a look at the unfortunate man while others quickly collected their bags and disappeared.

Abby placed Paul's wrist down at his side. 'Pulse is elevated. The paramedics can run an ECG when they arrive.'

Kieran nodded, and asked their patient, 'Do you remember feeling any chest pain before you were knocked down?'

Paul's voice was weakening. 'I felt odd. Like I couldn't quite get enough air into my lungs.' The words dragged out around his pain, his red face now grey.

'Did you notice the bike before it ran into you?' Kieran was aware of Abigail carefully checking their patient's legs for any injuries inflicted when the bike had rammed him.

'No. Just my weird breathing.'

Abigail muttered, 'There's swelling along the thigh, but no blood seepage. I'd like to remove these jeans and have a closer look at his right leg.'

'It'll have to wait,' Kieran replied. 'Okay, Paul, try to relax.' He asked Abigail quietly, 'Just how far away is the nearest hospital?'

A slow smile curved her lips and burned him with its warmth. At last, the Abigail he'd been looking for. 'Nearest hospital? The only hospital. You're not in Dublin now.' Her smile widened, taking away any sting he might've found in her words. 'The ambulance base is ten minutes from here if they get a clear run.'

Paul groaned, flapped his hands over his chest. 'Worse,' he gasped. His eyes closed, and his head rolled to the side.

Immediately Abigail located his neck pulse, shook her head. 'Nothing.'

Cardiac arrest. Just what they needed. Kieran fisted his hand and gave a hard thump to Paul's chest but the heart didn't restart. 'Compressions. Quick, or we'll lose him.'

Abigail tilted the man's head back to open his airway while Kieran placed his interlocked hands over Paul's heart. As he pressed down and began counting the compressions, his admiration for Abigail's efficiency crept through his mind. From the moment they'd first heard the dreadful thud of Paul taking a slam she'd been one step ahead of him. Now she held the man's head, no doubt ready to take over the compressions if required.

Kieran continued the compressions. 'Thirty.' At his nod Abby checked Paul's carotid pulse, shook her head. Kieran pressed down again. Thirty compressions. No pulse. Somewhere beyond the terminal a siren screamed. *Please let it be the ambulance.*

Abby placed her forefinger on the carotid artery. 'Come on, Paul, breathe for us.'

Kieran pressed down, heard Abby gasp, 'I think we have a pulse. Her mouth curved into a tender smile as she nodded. 'Yes, definitely.'

Kieran sagged in relief. 'Thank goodness for that.' He glanced up as the paramedics arrived. They would take over now. He grinned at Abigail. 'We make a great team.'

Her smile wavered. 'We do.' She placed a hand on his arm and leaned close. Then suddenly jerked backwards.

Had she been about to kiss him? Disappointment surged through his tired body. If only she had. He squashed the urge to haul her into his arms and kiss her. Properly. He had not come here to rekindle their fling. That had been a one-night, grief-blanking event. It had been absolutely magical, but never to be repeated. Sadness swamped him. Never? *Never.*

A sigh rippled across his bottom lip. 'At least we know we work well together.'

'We know more than that.' Then she slam-dunked him. 'We also made a beautiful little boy together.'

'So that's our new boss.' Sally stood behind the nurses' station in the emergency department, ogling Kieran as he chatted to two nurses. Two female nurses, who were having trouble keeping their jaws off the floor.

'Yep, that's him.' Abby sighed wistfully. He already looked as though he belonged there. Five minutes and he had the staff eating out of his hand.

Kieran had come in from the airport in the ambulance with Paul Stokes. It hadn't been necessary but he'd insisted, saying he'd feel happier about the situation. The female paramedics had acquiesced to his charm within seconds. Abby had screwed up the parking ticket she'd found under her windscreen wiper and followed the ambulance, her car filled with Kieran's luggage. If she hadn't known better she'd have thought he'd come for a year. But she did know better. Even if he finally accepted his son, Kieran wouldn't be staying. His career always came first. Why was that? Did he continuously have to prove himself, like someone else she'd known?

'Very tasty.' Sally almost drooled.

'You think so?' Abby glanced in the same direction as her friend and felt a hitch in her throat as Kieran bent over the cardiac monitoring equipment attached to his patient, stretching his trousers across a very tidy backside. But totally agreeing with her closest friend didn't mean she had to admit it out loud.

Happily married, Sally was in the business of finding Abby a husband, so far without success. Mainly because Abby had no interest in settling down with anyone ever again. She'd tried it once and had been scorched so badly she no longer trusted her own judgment.

'Whenever you speak in that so-who-gives-a-damn voice I know you're covering your real thoughts. Come on, what harm can it do to admit the guy's gorgeous?' A smug look settled over Sally's face. 'He's single, right?'

'Don't go there. I am not the slightest bit tempted. Believe me on this one.' Abby huffed out a breath and turned away from the intriguing sight. She had to stop Sally in her tracks. It didn't help that her friend didn't know who Seamus's father was. Abby had never divulged that information, and Sally had quickly learned not to mention it. 'I am definitely not interested.'

'Not interested in what?' asked the man himself from behind her.

Sheesh. Her hands fisted in her tunic pockets. She'd been so intent on getting the message through Sally's skull that she hadn't noticed Kieran leave his patient and cross over to them.

'Nothing,' she muttered.

'Are you sure?' Kieran's gaze scudded over her.

'Absolutely.' A shiver tickled her spine but she met his gaze head on, and gulped. His eyes, so bright, so perceptive, held her enthralled. She'd been expecting anger, not beguiling smiles and twinkling eyes. With an extreme effort she looked away, fully aware that Kieran was quite capable of seducing her into a false sense of ease before he delivered his attack about Seamus. She held no illusions that a diatribe would come. Why not? She'd behaved badly over this.

'Hello, Abby?' Kieran waved his hand before her. 'Where have you gone?'

She shook her head. Not very far at all. She seemed to have lost her grip on reality today. 'How's Paul Stokes?' She nodded in their patient's direction in the hope of deflecting Kieran. 'How's the latest ECG looking?'

Kieran continued to study her in that disturbing manner that made her want to check whether she had any clothes on. Finally, he replied to her query. 'Not good. Who's the duty cardiologist? How do I get hold of him?'

Sally took over. 'Hamish Harrington, and I'll track him down for you.'

'Has the patient's wife been called?'

When Sally nodded, Kieran turned back to Abby. 'Can you give me a quick tour of the department and introduce me to the staff? Paul's in good hands with the intern until the cardiologist gets here.'

With his hand firmly holding her elbow, she had little choice except to do as he'd asked. But as the nurse in charge of the department Sally should be the one to show him around. 'Sally? You want to do this?'

One wink from Sally and Abby knew there'd be no help from that quarter. Her friend would actively foster any interest that Kieran might show in her.

Tugging her arm free, Abby answered, 'It won't take long. It's not a huge department such as you'll be used to.'

'Makes an interesting change. There might be more time to get to know the staff than I have back home.'

Abby rolled her eyes. 'Unfortunately, we still get incredibly busy. As with any hospital board, finance rules. Staffing levels are usually at least one, if not two, people below what we require.'

'Typical.' Kieran shrugged. 'Dr Banning mentioned that this hospital services a huge rural area.'

It was Michael Banning's position as Head of Department that Kieran would be covering.

Abby filled Kieran in. 'The whole of the top of the South Island really, apart from Blenheim, which is more than a hundred kilometres away. There are small rural towns and plenty of farms, orchards and vineyards fanning out from here, plus major industries such as forestry and fishing.'

'Both those industries are susceptible to hideous accidents.'

'You're not wrong there.' Abby's lips pressed together and a flicker of despair cramped her stomach. Twice she'd nursed old school friends after logging accidents.

Kieran was right behind her when she pushed open the door to Michael's, soon to be Kieran's, office, the last stop on the tour. She felt so aware of him that her skin seemed to have a life of its own; a hot tingle touching the insides of her elbows, a searing on her neck just below her chin. She took a large step inside to put space between them, and turned to face Kieran.

The door clicked shut, and Kieran leaned back against it, his unfathomable eyes fixed on her. A shiver of trepidation chilled her. Was this it? Had the moment she'd been dreading arrived? Here? At work? Surely not.

She swallowed around the lump in her throat. 'It's a pity Michael couldn't be here to meet you but, of course, he's incredibly tied up at the moment and not expecting you to come in until Friday.'

'Abigail.' He stopped, shook his head. 'You're not comfortable with me being here, in the department, are you?' His bewilderment appeared genuine. His chin lifted and those blue eyes darkened as he waited for her reply.

'It's a little awkward, with what's between us. I—You...' She stopped. *Even today, every time he looks at me, I want to put my hands on his face, run my fingers along that strong jaw. I want one of his bone-bending kisses. No, I don't. I want to run away from the questions in those tired eyes.* 'We do need to talk about Seamus, but I don't think this is the place.

Right now you have a patient to hand over and then you should get out of here while you can. You're exhausted from your trip, and in need of a meal and a shower.'

For a long moment Kieran stared at her. Abby shoved her trembling fingers deep into her pockets as she waited for him to tell her what he really thought about her decision not tell him about his son.

Finally, Kieran jerked the handle to open the door. But his voice was surprisingly soft, almost sympathetic. 'We've not finished talking, but you're right, it'll have to wait until a more suitable time and place.'

'Thank goodness.' Relief whooshed through Abby.

Kieran raised a black eyebrow. 'There's nothing to be thankful for. We have one hell of a mess to sort out.'

'Mess?' That was not how she'd describe her family but, then, she wasn't the one terrified of raising children. 'Listen, Kieran. I love those kids and believe I'm giving them everything they need to grow into happy, responsible adults. Where's the mess in that?'

'I only have one...' He hesitated. 'Sorry, two relatives, and they both live on the opposite side of the world from me. I never know what is happening in their lives. Until a few days ago, I didn't even know there was a second child I should be aware of. This, to me, is a mess.'

He had a valid point. Despite the photos and Olivia's drawings she'd sent him, he didn't really know his niece. Whose fault was that? But they weren't really talking about Olivia. It was Seamus who hung between them, divided them.

'You wouldn't believe the number of times I tried to ring and tell you about Seamus. I even wrote letters to you, included photos in with some of them.'

'Odd I never got them.' Disbelief dripped off his tongue in great dollops.

Hurt, she cried out, 'I can give them to you any time you want. I've still got them all.'

'I don't see the point now.' He turned toward the door, the conversation over. At least the disbelief had abated. Then he looked over his shoulder at her. 'One thing. Do any of the staff here know I'm the father of your son?'

'Absolutely not.'

'There's something I can be grateful for, then.'

Raw pain gripped her. Was he ashamed of his son? In all the scenarios her mind had tossed up, not one had included Kieran feeling like that. Shame she could not cope with. 'You're not giving any of us a chance.'

His smile was professional; confident and cool. 'You think so? How's this for a chance? I'll visit you and the children later this afternoon. Will that suit you?'

And if it didn't? But she could see in his now chilly eyes that he wouldn't take no for an answer. Anyway, she wanted him to see the kids, meet his son. She wanted it over and done with. Her stomach couldn't take too much more tension. 'Come for dinner. Six o'clock.' Obviously he didn't want her to deliver him to his apartment.

'You eat dinner at six?'

'No, the children do. We'll eat after they go to bed.'

He pulled the door open, held it wide for her to pass through. 'You still live on the same road as when I was here for the wedding?'

She sighed. What did he know about any of them? 'Yes, but don't forget I'm in the cottage next to the orchard. David and Morag's place.'

'I'll see you at six, then.' He strode along to the nurses' station, leaving her shaking in his wake.

She stared at his ramrod back and wished him back in Ireland. Then she'd be able to go back to the simple problems of raising two small children while holding down a responsible job, of making her dollars go twice as far as they were intended to, of looking out for her father and high-maintenance twin sisters. Easy, compared to dealing with an angry, hurt man who had claim to her family.

CHAPTER THREE

KIERAN'S head pounded, and his eyes were gritty. He drove carefully, aware of the tiredness threatening to engulf him. That enormous bed back in the apartment arranged for his stay had been tempting but, given the state of his mind, sleep would've been impossible.

Why the hell had he said he'd go out to the cottage tonight? What had happened to the idea of getting settled before seeing the children? Abigail had happened, that's what. Damn, but she got to him so easily. So much for his renowned self-control.

HOPE. The green road sign drew his attention, and he eased his foot off the accelerator. If he remembered correctly, the turn-off to Abigail's place wasn't much further.

HOPE. The small community that boasted one store and a café, a cluster of houses, and orchards for as far as he could see. He swallowed as goose-bumps lifted his skin. A community. A place where families grew up. Families like Max Brown's. Max was Abigail's father and had raised four children in this district, had buried his wife here, lost his son in a tragic accident, welcomed his granddaughter. And his grandson. Don't forget Seamus, his brain nagged.

His son. As if he could forget the boy. Even when he tried to, the unsettling situation remained firmly fixed in his mind.

Kieran pulled off the road in front of the sign, the engine of his hired car idling. His hands were slick with sweat, and he rubbed them down his jeans. In a few minutes he'd meet his son for the first time. His gut clenched, his breathing became shallow. It wasn't too late to turn back to the apartment.

To be sure, Abigail would understand. Who was he fooling? A family girl through and through, she might think she understood his struggle with coming face to face with Seamus for the first time, but she'd be wide of the mark. Abby didn't know he had nothing to offer apart from money. For him to give unconditional love to a small child was the same as someone trying to breathe without lungs. Impossible.

No way would Abigail comprehend how different his life had been from hers. She had roots here, while, with his father in the diplomatic service, the world had been Kieran's community. Boarding schools and sterile apartments in countless cities hadn't given him a sense of belonging anywhere.

What had it been like for Abigail, growing up here? When she'd left home she'd crossed the orchard and moved into the cottage that used to belong to her brother and his wife and which was now held in trust for Olivia. A narrow life? Or a free, all-encompassing way to live? At least she knew where she belonged. She had somewhere to return to, people to turn to, whenever life went belly up.

Abigail. Twice at the airport while they had been administering to Stokes he'd called her Abby. He didn't know why but until then he'd always used her full name. Except that night when they'd made love. Then Abigail had seemed wrong for the passionate woman in his arms, stroking his body, revitalising his jaded outlook on life, and making him briefly question his lifestyle.

Kieran nodded at the sign. HOPE. Could that be the peculiar sensation tapping under his ribs? Did this place hold the answers to all those emotions he was afraid to face? Warmth trickled through him. Odd, when he should've been feeling a chill at the thought.

Checking the road was clear, he pulled out and headed towards Abigail's house. To his future? Or to trouble? Only time would tell. All he could be sure of was that he was about to meet his son.

As he turned into Abigail's road his stomach did such violent flips he thought he would be sick. A thin line of sweat rolled down past his jaw. His teeth clenched, aching.

Get a grip. He could not be seen to be failing at this first encounter. Damn it, he was thirty-five years old, a doctor, a man who'd stood up to drunken thugs on a Friday night in the emergency department. He would not be bested by a fifteen-month-old toddler.

Says who?

'Welcome to Rose Cottage.' Abigail opened the narrow gate at the end of a footpath leading to a small weatherboard house.

'Thank you. Were you waiting out here for me?' Kieran reached for the gate, his hand inadvertently brushing against hers. The brief touch sent a zing up his arm and into his already fried brain. One innocent little touch and he dropped further out of his depth.

'Not quite. Olivia's so excited about you coming and I caught her on the roadside, trying to look for you. I figured a game on the lawn might distract her.' Abby pointed to a little girl charging along the path in their direction. 'Here she comes now.'

Kieran let the gate slam behind him. Then promptly leaned against it for strength. Pain stabbed his chest as he watched this bundle of arms and legs and dark curls hurtling towards him. His sister as a child. Memories swamped him. Frightened him. It had been his fault Morag had had an accident and ruined her career. And this little girl was the spitting image of his sister. Was he a danger to her, too?

Shaking his head to dispel the stranglehold these thoughts had on him, he tried to move. Couldn't. Paralysed by memories evoked by a three-year-old. Him! Dr Flynn. Dr Cool, Calm and Collected. Mr Charming with the ladies. What could he possibly say to Olivia?

Olivia didn't suffer the same problem. 'Uncle Kieran, Uncle Kieran, here I am.'

Uncle. His mouth fell open. Uncle. He swallowed around the ache in his throat. He was an uncle. Here was the living proof.

Thump. She slammed into his knees, her arms reaching for him. Was he supposed to pick her up? Hug her? Hesitantly he leaned down and lifted her up to hold her warm body against his trembling frame, his arm muscles tense. She was warm and soft and unable to stay still. Her fingers touched his face and he jerked his head back, stunned at the unexpected contact. Slowly he let his head fall forward again. Thankfully Olivia was turning around in his arms, grabbing at his hands, still making him feel totally lost.

Abigail watched them in that enigmatic way of hers. Did she find him lacking? She'd have to give him time to become familiar with his role in Olivia's life. Would two months be enough to learn the art of being an uncle? A good uncle? Not to mention being a father. How did one go about being a father? He had no idea. And had no intention of learning.

Where was Seamus? Looking around, he couldn't see a toddler anywhere. He felt weird, disorientated, expecting to see his son. And now, with Olivia in his arms, everything as he knew it was unravelling. What used to be real for him had become a murky picture in his head. In the short space of time it had taken to get from his car to holding Olivia, his comfortable life seemed to be changing. That was plain scary. His mouth dried. Terrifying, really. He did not want his life to change. He loved it exactly as it had been until this moment.

Focus on Olivia. She, he might be able to handle. If he had a fairy godmother hovering overhead. 'Olivia's full of energy,' he said lamely.

'Amazing what the promise of a visit from Uncle Kieran does.' Abby finally gave him a full-blown, power-packed smile that sent all thoughts of children miles from his mind. Sweet longing for that special connection they'd once known shot down to his toes. He'd missed her. The knowledge slammed through him, rocked him back on his heels. *He had missed her.* It couldn't be possible after such a short liaison. But he found no other explanation for the hollow feeling in his chest. He'd missed Abby, and now he was with her he felt the ground rolling under his feet. Was it too late to pull out of his contract and return to Dublin?

Sticky hands again touched his face. 'Do you like me, Uncle Kieran?'

Kieran gulped, refocused on his niece. 'Absolutely, Princess.' And to his surprise he found he meant it. 'Absolutely.'

'Abby, he likes me.'

'Of course. Who wouldn't?'

Abby slipped past them, her hip brushing against him, tightening the longing that threatened to unravel his precarious rein on his emotions. Had to be the jet-lag. Or the shock of seeing Olivia after all this time. Or the apprehension about coming face to face with his son. This odd sensation of drowning in need-filled sweetness couldn't have anything to do with Abby. Abigail. Stick to calling her Abigail and he might be able to banish thoughts of that night they'd shared.

He followed her, his lively bundle twisting and turning in his arms as they walked down a path overgrown with roses.

As Abigail entered the house she turned back to him. 'Seamus is with Dad, having a ride on the tractor.'

Kieran swallowed a tug of disappointment. *Ha, gotcha. You were looking forward to seeing your son for the first time.* He gulped, checked to see if Abigail had noticed.

She winked at him. 'Seamus will be driving before he can talk at this rate. Dad spends hours taking him for rides on either the four-wheel bike or tractor.'

'But he's only one. Surely it's not very safe for someone that young.' Worry flared. This was his son they were talking about.

Abigail looked at him as though she knew exactly what he was thinking, and a triumphant smile lifted her mouth. 'Dad drives so slowly snails pass them. He also straps Seamus into a harness fitted to him, otherwise I'd be the first to stop them.'

'I guess you would.' He didn't doubt she'd be a very responsible parent. His concern ebbed. He shouldn't be worrying, that was Abigail's job.

She twisted away on her feet. 'Come inside. Make yourself at home.' Then she smiled over her shoulder at the girl he held. 'Bath time, missy.'

'I don't want one,' Olivia answered from the safety of his arms.

'Now, why doesn't that surprise me?' Abigail stood with one hand on her hip. 'The only time you like water is when it's in a muddy puddle.'

Kieran asked Olivia, 'Don't you want to be clean for me?'

'No.'

'Do you want Uncle Kieran to bath you?'

What? Did he get any say in this? He wouldn't know where to start when it came to bathing small children.

It was time he went back to town and the relative safety of

his apartment. A haven from his niece and her expectations of him.

'I want Abby to bath me.'

Relief poured through his tense muscles as he put Olivia down. Warily he followed her through the house. What would it be like to share bathtimes with your kids? It might be fun.

Whoa. Back up. Bathing a child meant getting involved and he didn't do involvement. Funny how his resolve seemed to be slipping away so fast within hours of arriving. If he had already started wondering about bathtime, what would he be doing by the end of his two-month spell here? He had to remain focused on the purpose of his visit, which was to run ED, not to become enmeshed in this family.

'If you want a glass of wine or a beer, you'll find some at the back of the fridge, top shelf.' Abby swung Olivia up into her arms in a graceful movement that drew his eyes to her curves.

Abigail. Her name was Abigail. So what if today she walked and talked more like an Abby? Looking nothing like the slim, almost anorexic women he usually dated, her height and voluptuousness fascinated him. The night of passion they'd shared in Dublin still slammed into his head at the most unexpected moments. Often in the middle of the night when he couldn't sleep he'd think of the Kiwi woman who'd shared his grief in the most intimate way imaginable. Her brother, his sister. Both gone, all because of a teenager who'd thought driving his mother's car would be easy. Abigail's big, sad eyes had drawn him to her and, like an alcoholic to the bottle, he'd had to have her.

It hadn't been enough. It should've been. He didn't do commitment. Commitment meant love, and Abigail was the kind of woman that eventually would want, would deserve, commitment and love. He couldn't give any woman love. Abigail hadn't grown up learning the hard lessons about relationships that he had got from his father. Thankfully, Morag, being the apple of their father's eye, hadn't suffered the knocks he had, hadn't grown the hard shell around her heart that he had.

Stop the thinking. Grab a beer and relax. As the cool liquid rolled across his tongue he looked around. Abby had created a cosy atmosphere, perfect for young children. The bright blues and apricots on the walls and in the furnishings were warm and vibrant. Just like the woman herself. The furniture had seen better days so she obviously didn't use the money he sent on anything other than Olivia. If she used it at all. It occurred to him that she mightn't have touched a single cent.

But this was all about the children. What about Abigail? Surely she got lonely for adult company at night? He was assuming she spent the nights alone, but was probably wrong.

Piercing giggles coming from somewhere along the short hallway drew his attention. Before he could think about what he was doing he followed the sound. Stopping in the bathroom doorway, he leaned against the doorjamb and watched Abby bath Olivia. He had to swallow hard to get the next mouthful of beer past the lump in his throat. The bath was filled with soap bubbles, and Abby wore her share of them on her cheeks and forehead. She looked gorgeous.

He cleared his throat. 'If Olivia gets this much fun out of a bath then I can't begin to imagine her excitement in those puddles you mentioned.'

'It gets fairly messy.' Abby tugged a towel from the rail and lifted a protesting Olivia out of the water. 'Let's get you dry, little missy. Seamus will be here in a minute and he'll need scrubbing from top to toe.'

Kieran gulped and returned to the kitchen, feeling useless and out of his depth. The door looked very tempting. A few strides and he could be at his car. His son would be here any minute. His heart felt oddly out of whack as he grappled with the enormity of that. The moment he'd been dreading since Abigail's phone call was racing towards him. He wasn't ready. He'd never be ready. He stared around, panic beginning to boil up. He needed something to occupy his brain. A bag of groceries lay on the bench. Peering inside, he found steak and salad vegetables. Some of the tension tightening his shoulders eased. Cooking steak and tossing together a salad he could do blindfolded.

Just then the back door flew open. A deep voice he recognised as Max Brown's was telling someone, presumably Seamus, to slow down or he'd trip. A little boy tumbled into the kitchen, his clothes covered in grass stains. His chubby face was red and he was chattering nonstop in gibberish.

Kieran's hand stopped halfway out of the grocery bag. His breath stuck in his lungs. The time had come. No getting out of this one. What if he got it all wrong? Said or did the wrong thing? Scared the boy off so they'd never get along? He dropped the packet of steak back in the bag. He was out of here. Now. Before Seamus came any closer, before the boy caught his eye and turned him into a complete blithering idiot. Damn it, he should've left when he'd had the chance instead of dithering around procrastinating.

Then Abigail was standing beside him, her hand reaching for his, and it was too late. He couldn't leave now. The tremor in her fingers surprised him. When he lifted his eyes to hers he saw his own fear and trepidation mirrored there. Her teeth were digging hard into her bottom lip. Turning his hand over, he twined his fingers through hers. Knowing this might be as hard for her as it was for him made everything just a little bit easier.

He whispered through his blocked throat, 'Introduce me to our son.'

She blinked. 'Sure.' But she didn't move a muscle.

'Come on, Abby, we can do this.' Really?

Another blink. Then, inclining her head in acknowledgement, she turned to face the man and toddler waiting expectantly. 'Hey, Dad. Seamus…' She dropped to her knees and lifted the dark-haired boy against her, hugged him tight for a moment, as though afraid to let him go. Afraid to share him? No, not Abby. She wanted this. Didn't she?

As the boy squirmed to be set free, Abby stood up and held him so Kieran could take a good look at him. 'Seamus, love, this is Uncle Kieran.' She raised troubled eyes to Kieran. 'Sorry, I'm not sure what you want to be called, and Olivia has been talking about her uncle all week.'

Kieran stood spellbound. This was his son. His own flesh and blood. There was no denying the wide, full mouth came from the Flynn side. Seamus had the black hair and blue eyes that all Flynns seemed to inherit, but the expression in those eyes gawping at him was pure Abby. Kieran could've wept. He felt his heart dissolving. The boy was beautiful. His boy. Was this how every father felt when he saw his child for the very first time? Frightened? Protective? Lungs all gummed up so he couldn't breathe?

The silence in the tiny kitchen was deafening. Kieran couldn't have spoken a single word if his life had depended on it. All the arguments he'd had for not wanting a part in this boy's life evaporated faster than ice cream in a desert. He lifted his arms to take Seamus and was rewarded with a toothless grin. Somewhere under his ribs he felt a sharp stab. Of love? Whoa. He was not ready for this. If this was unconditional love then he wasn't ready, wasn't capable of doing it. It frightened him. Like bungee-jumping without a cord.

Then his arms were filled with a wriggling toddler. He grasped Seamus with stiff fingers, held him awkwardly out from his chest. And stared down at him. Seamus. A huge lump blocked his throat, cut off his breathing. He drank in the sight of his son, aware of every wriggle, every thump of one tiny fist on his arm. He saw big eyes peering up at him, trusting him. He saw innocence so sweet it made his knees weak. His heart felt as though it would explode right out through his ribs. This was what it felt like to be a parent. This simple. This terrifying.

He couldn't do it. He wasn't father material. What if he harmed Seamus with his ineptitude? Seamus needed love and caring and twenty-four-hour attention. Not a dried-up shell of a man for whom the closest thing to love was sharing a bed with a warm woman for a night.

He turned to hand the boy back to Abigail, to put him aside, back to where he'd be loved. But Abigail took a step away. What? She wasn't going to rescue her child? The panic he'd felt earlier threatened to erupt. He clenched his muscles and Seamus wriggled against him in protest. See? Already he had made a mistake. *Suck in a breath. Deeply. Let it out, ride the panic. Another deep breath. I can't do this.*

'Grandad, Grandad.' Olivia's shouts filled the cottage, and Max leaned over to shake his hand, saying above the din, 'Welcome to Nelson, lad. It's great to have you here.'

Kieran shook his head in an attempt to clear away the overwhelming emotions engulfing him. The panic calmed. 'Thanks, Max.' He huffed the air from his lungs. 'It's good to see you, too.' Loosening his grip on Seamus and trying to hold him with one arm, he managed to return the handshake. He hadn't been called 'lad' since boarding-school days, and never in the friendly tone Abby's father had used.

So did Max know he was Seamus's father? If so, what did the older man think of him? Maybe Max had called him 'lad' to soften him up before getting him into a corner and telling him exactly what he expected from Kieran for his grandson. And for his daughter.

Abigail was very quiet. Kieran looked around, found

her regarding him steadily. Then she leaned close. 'Isn't he gorgeous?'

He stared down at Seamus, at the complete trust reflected in the young eyes looking back at him. Assessing *him*? Did Seamus see the fear? The emptiness? Gazing back, Kieran saw no sign of the crushing defeat of a child who strived, and failed, to be loved by his parent. With Abby for a mother it was unlikely he ever would. Thank goodness.

But the same couldn't be said about Seamus's father. The boy deserved better. Somewhere behind his ribs he felt something sharp, like he had a stitch from a long run. A painful stitch. Was he going to give away his chance with this child before he'd had time to get to know him? If he knew what was right for the boy he should. But…it wouldn't be easy to walk away now. It would've been better all round if he hadn't met the lad. Now he knew what Seamus looked like, knew how it felt to hold him.

'Kieran?' Abigail nudged him. 'Don't you think he's great?'

He could only manage, 'He's beautiful.' His eyes still focused on Seamus, his arms reluctant to let the boy go even when he knew he should. Before he became too involved.

Max told the room at large, 'I'll be off. I'm going out for dinner. Catch up with you at the weekend, Kieran, when you've had time to settle in.'

Kieran was vaguely aware of Max hugging his granddaughter before leaving. Then of Olivia turning on the TV, and Abby quietly telling her to turn the volume down. Kieran tugged out a chair from the kitchen table and dropped onto it, still holding his son, now very tenderly. *Almost as though afraid he'll break.*

As Seamus forced a thumb into his mouth Abby sauntered in and leaned against the bench, relief lightening her face. 'He's taken to you, no problems.'

'How can you be so sure this soon?' Kieran heard the edge in his voice, and cursed silently. Abby had been as nervous about this meeting as he had, and now she seemed to be handling it all right. Why couldn't he?

'You'd know if Seamus didn't want to go near you. He has a set of lungs on him you wouldn't believe. Must have got them from your side.'

'I can see he's a right little charmer, just like me.'

'Yep. You win that one, hands down.' Her smile sagged a little, and Kieran was reminded that it was his charm that had ultimately led to one night of passion and this little boy.

Seamus yawned, and Kieran felt his heart swell. Gently he cuddled his warm bundle against his chest. Shock banged through him. Whatever his feelings about love and fatherhood, he wouldn't be able to walk away from this family and never look back. It was way too late for that. He was going to be looking over his shoulder for the rest of his life.

CHAPTER FOUR

ABBY dropped onto the lumpy couch in the lounge, holding Seamus tight, as though for protection, though what from she had no idea. Earlier in the day, at the airport, she'd felt like she could trust him to do the right thing, that he wouldn't turn their world upside down. That had been in direct contrast to the way she'd reacted to him. The deep pull in her stomach toward him had stunned her. She'd always known she still cared about this man but never had she considered how explosive those feelings might be. No wonder she felt in need of protection. From Kieran? Or from herself?

She glanced across at him wiping down the kitchen benches. Hard to believe he'd cooked dinner. No one did that for her. Not even her father. But Kieran had taken charge, preparing their meal while she'd dealt with the kids' food. She knew he'd needed something to keep himself occupied and avoid getting too involved in the children's night-time rituals. He'd watched her feeding Seamus from a safe distance, grimacing when mushy food had ended up on her T-shirt. He had a lot to learn. She called softly, 'Thanks for dinner, and especially thanks for cleaning up.'

He turned and gazed at her, that bewildered look that had appeared when he had first held Seamus still there. 'I don't know how you do this all the time.'

'Goes with the territory of being a mum. Don't feel sorry for me. I love it.'

'I can see that.' His gaze dropped to Seamus, and his expression became guarded. What was he thinking? Did he accept Seamus as a son? Or as another problem to be dealt with? When she'd placed the baby in his arms Kieran hadn't known what to do. Even the simple act of holding a child seemed to unsettle him, and when she'd refused to take Seamus back, stepping away from them, he had looked completely lost. Maybe she shouldn't have done that, but she'd sensed he would need some gentle pushing when it came to coping with the children.

She also sensed his vulnerability, and didn't know what to do about it, didn't understand why he felt that way. There was a real possibility of making things worse, not better, unless he opened up and talked about what bothered him. Her stomach clenched. Was this really what she wanted? Kieran becoming involved in the family? Maybe she was setting something in motion that she'd later come to regret, something like having to move to Ireland so they could be closer to each other. A chill slipped over her skin. Leave home and cross to the other side of the world? No way. Not even for the children's sake.

But Olivia and Seamus needed him, needed to know him, and already they were further along that track than she'd expected they'd be on day one. Admittedly when she'd forced Kieran to keep holding Seamus he hadn't been happy, but neither had he protested. Had he thought that would make him appear weak? She hoped not. He wasn't a weak man in any sense. Holding his son for the very first time had to have had an effect on him, one she hoped he'd absorbed and found he enjoyed. She should be feeling thrilled that he'd not given into whatever had bothered him, but instead she felt rattled.

Throughout the long months of her pregnancy and over the fifteen months of being a single parent, she'd never experienced any loneliness, never worried that she mightn't cope. And yet now, with Kieran here in her home, she felt uncertain. She couldn't dispel the sensation of the ground sliding out from under her. Of her life being about to change radically. What if she'd made a mistake bringing Kieran into Olivia and Seamus' lives?

No. She shoved that selfish idea away. She might've done the wrong thing for her but it was right for them.

'Abigail, are you all right?' Kieran interrupted her swarming thoughts. 'You've gone awfully quiet.'

Shaking away her doubts, she tried for a deep breath and the strength to cope. 'Couldn't be better.' *Couldn't I?* These weird, mixed-up feelings would soon pass. They had to if she was to survive the next eight weeks. 'I'm going to put this guy to bed, or he'll be grizzly all day tomorrow.'

So would she if she didn't get a decent night's sleep. She'd lain awake for hours last night, worrying about Kieran's arrival. Tonight she'd just sleep. He was here, and whatever happened would happen, and she could deal with it later. Yeah, right. Who was she kidding?

Kieran watched her with that perceptive gleam in his eyes. If he could read her mind, he'd be as confused as she was. She shrugged. 'I won't be long. Make yourself comfortable.'

But not too comfortable. This is my castle, the one place in the world I usually feel safe from everything and everyone. You could so easily destroy that for me by becoming too involved with us. By making my heart remember how close I came to falling in love with you in Dublin. At the end of your term here you'll go back and leave me with your scent touching my furnishings, my clothes. Your presence will fill the corners, sit at the table, take over my kitchen.

'I'll make us some tea. Or do you prefer coffee?' Kieran still watched her.

'Tea, thanks.' See, they didn't even know the most basic

things about each other. Her face warmed. But they did have an intimate knowledge of each other. As the warmth became hot she fled the room, needing to put space between her and the man who'd made love to her so thoroughly she could still remember every detail two years later.

Singing a lullaby as she tucked Seamus under the cotton covers, the peace that usually stole over her at this moment wasn't forthcoming. Within a few hours Kieran had taken that from her. How much more would he take before he left? Would she survive intact? Would her heart cope? And she'd thought the hardest part of this visit would be the issues surrounding the children. How stupid of her.

'You're singing like an Irish mam.' Kieran spoke softly from the doorway. 'I like that.'

Abby's heart leapt. 'Don't creep up on me like that.' Then she focused on what he'd said. 'Did your mother sing to you?'

'Yeah…' The word whispered across his lips. 'I remember her singing to Morag more than me, but I know I got the same when I was little.'

'What happened to your mother?' No one had ever mentioned her, not even Morag.

'Unbeknown to anyone, she had diabetes. Our father came home one night to find her in a coma on the bathroom floor. She never recovered.'

'Kieran, I'm so sorry.' Her heart squeezed for him. 'How old were you?'

'Four.' There was a lot of pain behind that single word.

'I certainly know how hard losing a mother is, but at least I was an adult.' Not that it had made it any easier, but at least she had been able to understand some of the process.

Kieran stepped into the centre of the room. Of her bedroom. What had happened to making her a cup of tea? Had he been drawn to Seamus instead?

He asked, 'Why does Seamus sleep in here?'

'Because Olivia has the only other bedroom. I don't want Seamus disturbing her when he wakes during the night.'

Tucking the blue cotton blanket around a very sleepy boy, she didn't have to look up to know Kieran was studying the room with its bright red and white curtains and bedspread.

'Hardly ideal. What about some privacy for yourself?'

'There is no such thing as privacy when you have two small children, believe me.' Neither was there a need. It wasn't like she had someone special in her life to share this room with. Her eyes lifted to Kieran. The moisture in her mouth dried. An image of them in bed together filled her head. Trying to shake it away, she swore silently. Kieran would not become that special person. No man would. Hadn't she learned her lesson well?

'Surely you must want to take a break from the children at times?'

'I work so I already get a break.' Did he think the kids were too much for her? She managed very well, thank you. 'Dad helps by taking them over to his house sometimes.' And she began another lullaby.

He didn't say any more, instead wandered over to stand beside her, looking down at Seamus. What did he see? His family likeness? Did he look at Seamus as his son? Her singing dwindled to a halt. It was hard to sing with Kieran standing so close she could feel the heat from his body. She also felt self-conscious. She didn't exactly have a fantastic voice.

Seamus half-heartedly waved a fist at her. Or was it at Kieran? Glancing sideways, she studied Kieran watching Seamus. His hands were jammed into his pockets, and he stood with his legs slightly apart. What she wouldn't give to know what was going on in that head of his.

Reaching into the cot to run the back of her hand over Seamus's warm, soft cheek, her heart squeezed. Her precious, little boy. She loved him so much she could cry. Kieran had missed out on lots already, which was entirely her fault. A fact she readily acknowledged.

Kieran had surprised her by being nervous when he'd first seen Olivia. There'd been something akin to fear in his eyes, and vulnerability. As though he'd felt completely out of his depth. His movements had been stilted, as though he'd never held a child before. And then he'd had to hold *his* child for the first time. She'd thought he'd be very much in control of the situation, of his emotions. From what she knew of him, he usually was.

What about when they'd made love? If that had shown controlled emotions then she was a possum. Her skin tingled at the memory of that night. Never before had she known anything like it. Making love with Kieran had spoiled her for ever. There wouldn't be another man on earth who'd measure up. Which perfectly suited her plan to remain forever single.

Seamus's eyes closed, blinked open. 'The little monkey's fighting going to sleep.' Abby smiled, first at Seamus then at Kieran, who still kept a closed expression on his face. 'He does that every night. It's like he doesn't want to miss out on anything.'

'Does he sleep right through the night?'

'Most of the time.'

From down the hall Olivia called, 'Abby, Teddy's got his foot stuck in a drawer.'

Abby chuckled. 'I'd better go and sort this out as Olivia won't go to sleep without Teddy.'

Kieran watched her leave the bedroom, totally unfazed by the children's demands. Damn, but she was good with them. A natural mother. Warmth stole over him. The kids were extremely lucky. He turned back to the boy, who'd finally succumbed to sleep, one fist pressed against his mouth, the other flung above his head. Kieran leaned forward, reached in and ran the back of his hand over Seamus's cheek, as he'd seen Abby do earlier. The warmth grew as Seamus's soft skin seemed to melt against his harsher skin. Beautiful.

Scary. He tugged his hand away, straightened. His body cooled. He couldn't do this. He didn't have Abby's knack with children. Abby didn't just feed Seamus, she fed him with love. She didn't bath Olivia, she bathed her with devotion. He didn't know how to comfort, to play. It wasn't in him to cherish another human.

Doctoring was about fixing, not nurturing. He didn't know where he'd start if he had to take care of this little man even for an hour or two. Just standing here, he felt responsible for Seamus and that didn't sit comfortably.

The earlier panic began rising again. He could not become involved with Olivia and Seamus, become a part of this family. It would take a wet day in hell before he'd be ready for that. Or capable of doing what was expected of him.

Abby heard the phone ringing in the kitchen and wondered which of her sisters that might be. Stephanie's voice bubbled down the line. 'Hey, Abby, how's things? How's the great man from Ireland? All excited to see Olivia?'

Abby dredged up a laugh. 'Olivia dazzled him.' Which was certainly more than she'd managed.

'I bet she did.'

'She chattered nonstop to him, but wouldn't let him bath her.' Much to Kieran's relief.

'I bet Seamus won him over in an instant.'

'No. That's a work in progress.' Neither of her sisters knew who Seamus's dad was, but they probably had their suspicions. Anyone could do the sum and they'd both known there hadn't been anyone else in her life since Phillip had turned out to be such a rat. Now was probably the time to tell them, but she'd wait until she knew what Kieran would do.

Thankfully Steph changed the subject. 'I bought a new

dress today for a party I'm going to. Can you take the hem up for me?'

What ever happened to 'do you mind?' or 'please'? Abby sighed. What did she expect? She'd always done alterations for her sisters. 'Bring it round on Saturday morning.'

Sometimes she felt Charlie and Steph didn't even consider she might have a life of her own. Certainly neither realised how time-consuming bringing up two very young children could be. What would they say if she left the children with them for a day and went out shopping, visiting the beauty parlour or just lying on a lounger, reading a magazine? She couldn't help the small smile that twisted her mouth. They'd be horrified. As far as Steph was concerned, children definitely didn't go with the image of a lawyer in one of the city's top firms. Neither did Charlie think hotshot real estate salespeople should have kids clinging to their tailored suits. But they loved their niece and nephew, and her. As she loved them.

Six years younger than her, her sisters had always turned to her for help with things since the day she'd come home to nurse their mother. When their mum had died she'd kept right on looking out for them. At twenty-three they didn't really need her to do that now, but she wouldn't have it any other way. Most of the time.

Stephanie was saying, 'I wonder if Kieran would like to go to the party. The girls from the office would love him, especially with that divine accent. His gorgeous looks won't hurt either.'

Abby's stomach plummeted. She knew Kieran loved parties. Her brother had often talked about all the socialising they'd done together. Why shouldn't he go? He was a free agent. Because he'd come here to work, it didn't mean he had to be a saint for the duration of his stay. What he did in his spare time had nothing to do with her. He'd probably be glad of a distraction from the 'children' problem.

'Is Kieran still there? I'd like to talk to him.'

'Sure.' But then she heard a car starting. At her front gate? Kieran? A low, throaty engine roared away. A sports car kind of sound. Definitely Kieran. 'Seems I'm wrong. He's just left.'

Without a word. Whatever happened to saying goodnight? Anger vied with disappointment. Surely she wasn't asking too much? Even if he couldn't handle being a dad, he could've poked his head around the corner and said something before he disappeared. Even if the situation had got too much for him and he'd needed to get away, how hard would that have been? Guess she didn't rate too highly on his list of important people or things. Her shoulders slumped. Was she being impatient? Probably. But she didn't know how to be any different.

Stephanie didn't seem too concerned. 'I'll catch up with him later. I'll bring my dress over on Friday. See you.' Click. She'd gone, too.

Leaving Abby feeling incredibly lonely. At home with two children while their other parent, as such, raced back to town and presumably the safety of his new apartment. So where was the problem? She hadn't expected him to make himself so comfortable that he'd stay to start taking over caring for the children. *Give the guy a chance to get used to all this.*

Two mugs stood on the bench. The kettle was warm to her touch. So he'd got that far with making the drinks. She boiled the water again and took her tea with her to check up on Seamus. Sound asleep, he looked angelic, which he was. Most of the time. A smile tugged at her mouth, despite her gloomy mood. Seamus always did this to her whenever she was out of sorts. One look and she felt better about her world.

Now she studied his face, so like the face that had haunted her over the last two years. Moving away, she sank onto the end of her bed, her thoughts automatically returning to Kieran. Today, when she'd met him at the airport, she'd seen that her memory had been correct. The sharp lines running down the sides of his mouth were still there, as was that lopsided smile that sliced through her every time. Those full lips that had done untold exciting things to her body were exactly as she recalled. Oh, yes, her body remembered him very well.

Too well. Now all she had to do was cope with him being around for two months when just looking at him sent all her hormones into a dance. That was all. *That was all?*

CHAPTER FIVE

DRESSED in non-matching panties and bra, Abby headed down the hall, vigorously towelling her freshly washed hair. How could she have slept in? How had she managed to sleep at all with everything going on in her mind? Mainly things about Kieran. He really had got to her in a very short time. She had to get herself under control, stop thinking Kieran at every turn.

Seamus played with a wooden truck in the bedroom, damp nappies drooping around his knees. She left him to go and start making toast. Olivia was chattering in the kitchen, probably telling Teddy what she wanted for breakfast. Had she dressed herself this morning? Some days she did so, with bizarre results, some days she wanted Abby to do it.

At the kitchen door Abby lowered the towel, looking for Olivia, and gasped. Her heart stopped, then with a thud resumed its regular beat.

'Kieran. What are you doing here? How did you get in?' Hadn't she locked up before going to bed last night?

'Good morning, Abigail.' He looked past her. For Seamus? Surely that had to be a good sign?

'Morning yourself,' she muttered, then realised where his gaze had settled and hurriedly draped the towel around her body. Except the towel was too small and only covered from her breasts to halfway down her backside. Abby started backing out of the kitchen. She'd get dressed properly before asking why he was here.

'I opened the door,' Olivia informed her importantly.

'Haven't I told you not to open the door to strangers?' Abby hesitated in mid-flight and eyed Olivia sternly.

Kieran explained, his gaze now in the vicinity of her face, 'You can blame me. When I knocked and got no answer I came round to the window to see if you were about. Olivia saw me and let me in. There are advantages to being Uncle Kieran.' At last his eyes met hers, twinkling at her. 'Anyway, I'd hope I wasn't a stranger.'

She knew he was referring to his relationship with her, not Olivia. She stuttered, 'W-what b-brings you out here this early?'

'I wanted to apologise for my abrupt departure last night. It was rude of me.' He raised his hands and shrugged disarmingly. 'I admit to being a little overwhelmed. Throw in exhaustion after that damned flight and everything caught up with me in a hurry. But I should've said goodnight.'

'Apology accepted.' He surprised her, admitting he'd been out of his depth. But right now she had to feed and clothe the kids, then get to work on time. No, first she had to get dressed before Kieran began sizing her up again in his toe-curling way.

He said, 'I thought it best to see you before we get to work. It might be a bit awkward explaining in front of other people.'

'Work?' He was joking, right? 'You're not starting today?' She'd been relying on having a few more days before he invaded her work space as well as her home.

'Might as well. There's nothing else on my agenda at the moment, and I understand Michael is already on leave.'

'His son's desperately ill and last week they got word of a liver that might be compatible in Brisbane.'

'Then the sooner I start, the better. Let's hope the operation on his son is successful.'

'Everyone's got their fingers crossed for that,' Abby responded. 'We've seen the pain the family is suffering.'

'I can't imagine being in their shoes.' Kieran turned for the back door. 'I'll see you later on.'

Relieved that he was leaving, she couldn't explain the little gremlin that made her say, 'Since you're here, can you put the kettle on and start making toast? I'm already running late and could do with a hand.'

He slowly turned back into the room, his eyes again roaming over her. The playboy was definitely to the fore this morning, not the overwhelmed man trying to deal with two very small relatives he couldn't quite fathom. 'Of course. Where do you keep everything?'

'Fridge, cupboard and pantry.' Abby beat a hasty retreat to her bedroom.

As she changed Seamus into shorts and T-shirt she could hear Olivia telling Kieran what she wanted on her toast and what Seamus liked, and that she wanted juice. 'No, not in that glass. The other one.'

Then, 'Abby doesn't cut our toast like that. She makes it into squares.' And, 'Not that runny honey. It falls off the toast and messes Seamus's shirt.'

Abby grinned in sympathy for Kieran. He was learning breakfast wasn't as straightforward as he'd previously believed.

Time to rescue the man. Back in the kitchen she placed Seamus in his highchair and put his toast in front of him before grinning at Kieran. 'I heard you getting your instructions from little miss bossy britches.'

Kieran placed a mug of tea on the table in front of her. 'I never knew making toast could be so difficult. I hope your tea is to your satisfaction?' He grinned back before looking over to the highchair.

His eyes fixed on Seamus poking food into his mouth and over his cheeks. A mask of indifference hid whatever he truly felt about his little boy and the situation he found himself in. Were his feelings good ones? Or did he still want nothing to do with the kids? Her heart squeezed for Kieran and Seamus. They needed time together, lots of it.

Seamus dropped a piece of toast on the floor. Wrong way up, of course. And Kieran grimaced. It didn't seem to register with him there was a mess to clean up.

Abby grabbed a dishcloth and wiped the floor. He mightn't have leapt in to do it but looking at Olivia's jam-covered toast now cut into squares, albeit very large ones, he seemed to be getting the hang of breakfast under his niece's tutelage.

Abby asked cheekily, 'Do I get any toast?'

Kieran dragged his eyes around to her. 'Coming up. Squares or oblongs? Jam or honey?'

'Definitely squares and jam. What about you? Have you eaten?'

He ran a hand over his chin. 'I think I've just gone off toast. I'll head away to ED in a moment.'

Abby grinned to hide the flutter in her tummy. He looked totally unlike the perfectly turned-out doctor with a streak of jam now decorating his chin. She reached over with a paper towel and wiped it clean. 'Rule number one with children. Never go out before checking in the mirror. You'll be surprised what you might find.'

Something like horror filled his eyes and he quickly checked his immaculate, crease-free shirt front, flicking a crumb off his tie.

She laughed. 'Relax. You've managed to stay clean despite everything. Now go. I've got to get these two ready.'

'Now who's the bossy britches?' he muttered.

'You're welcome to stay and help some more.'

'I think not. You make it look so easy and I'm learning it's not.'

'I've had more practice,' she quipped without thought to the ramifications.

'To be sure, and whose fault is that?'

Tea splashed over her hand as she jolted from the shock of his suddenly harsh tone. So, Kieran's good mood had been a facade. And the guilt she'd tamped down overnight swamped her again. He would never forgive her.

Abby dashed into ED, pretending to herself she wasn't looking out for Kieran. She wanted to avoid him for a while if at all possible. For the whole day would be better but that would be asking too much. 'Hi, Sally, sorry I'm late but it was a disaster zone at my house this morning.'

That had to be the understatement of the century. For some inexplicable reason Olivia had demanded that she stay home with Grandad instead of going to the crèche workers. Abby had delivered one very grumpy little girl to the crèche. Thank goodness Seamus seemed happy enough to be there with his little friends. At least Kieran had left before all the fuss had started. It might've kept him away permanently. She sighed. She was being unfair again.

All the way to work she'd thought about him, how his usual confidence had been undermined by the children. Would he have coped better if it had only been Olivia he'd had to contend with? Was it because of finding himself a father that he was outside his comfort zone?

Sally tossed a file on the desk in front of Abby. 'I thought you might've given our new boss a lift to work for his first day since he's part of your family.'

Abby dropped onto a chair. She'd given the guy dinner, a son and probably a headache. She didn't need to give him anything else. 'I don't think he'd be happy squashed into my car among car seats and kids.' Or within touching distance of her.

Sally grinned at her. 'Here I was hoping Dr Flynn might not have gone to his new apartment last night.'

Abby snatched the file up and jerked it open. 'I know. You only want to see me happily married.' They'd had this conversation so often Abby knew the lines off by heart. 'Do me a big favour, drop the whole Kieran thing. For ever.'

One thing for sure, Kieran seemed to have way too many hang-ups when it came to family and commitment for her to consider him for the role of husband. But Sally didn't know the score and Abby just couldn't bring herself to explain. The tension in the back of her head wound tighter.

'For now.' Sally looked around the department. 'Can you give Barbara a hand?'

'Sure.' Something other than Kieran to focus on.

'But where is Dr Flynn? I'd have thought he'd be the type to always be early.' Sally flipped through some files, her gaze fixed somewhere out in the department.

Abby shook her head at her friend. This was what Kieran did so well; how he got everyone in a twitter. Then she saw Sally's eyes widen and her mouth slide into a beautiful smile. And she knew without looking around that Kieran had arrived. If he could do this to a sane, married woman, what chance did anyone else have?

What chance did she have?

She turned and faced him, but he was too busy introducing himself to Pete and Rose to see her. The interns were drinking up every word Kieran uttered. 'Making fools of themselves,' she muttered.

Damn but the man knew how to work a scene. She looked to Sally for some sanity and was sadly disappointed. 'Stop drooling, it doesn't suit you.'

'Why not? Everyone else is.' Sally grinned. 'Look at those eyes, that body. Are you sure I'm married?' Then she nudged Abby. 'You've got a patient. And if I didn't know better I'd say you were interested in Dr Charming. Why else are you still hanging around the station?'

She wouldn't lower herself to answer. If only Sally knew the half of it. Kieran hid so much behind those twinkling eyes. He gave away nothing of last night's turmoil at meeting his son for the first time. Laughter carried across the department and caused Abby's stomach to roll over agonisingly. She had to admire his nerve. His world had been rocked right off its axis and no one watching him now would ever guess how he felt about that.

'Hey, Abby, Darren Shore's here again. He's had a wee disagreement with his skateboard.' Barbara took care as she helped a lad onto the bed in a cubicle.

'Hi, Darren, Jim.' Abby nodded at the weary man already slouching in the chair on the other side of the bed. 'Can't trust those skateboards not to want to go their own way.' Abby noted Darren's careful movements. 'Where does it hurt?'

'Here.' Darren tapped his wrist gingerly. 'And here.'

The ulna. Two breaks? Or transferred pain? Abby carefully slid the sleeve of Darren's shirt up and felt the swelling of his wrist. A massive bruise covered most of his arm. 'We'll send you for an X-ray after I get a doctor to look at you and sign a form. First we'll clean you up, see how much skin you've removed. What did you crash into this time?'

'The concrete wall by the school gates.'

'Guess you came off worse than the wall, then.'

'Yeah. Ouch.' The boy sucked in a mouthful of air.

'Let's give you some Entonox to take away the pain and make you feel happy.' Abby handed Darren a mouthpiece attached to tubing leading from a gas tank. 'Take a deep breath of that every time your arm hurts. I think you need a stitch or two in your head to stop the bleeding.' A large bruise had formed there.

Barbara slipped out of the cubicle, saying, 'I'll go find a doctor.'

Darren squinted up at Abby. 'Is my arm really broken? I'll still be able to ride my board, won't I?'

'No, you won't.' Darren's father spoke for the first time. 'That damned board can go in the rubbish. I'm tired of you coming off it and hurting yourself. There's not a day goes by that you're not covered in bruises.'

More bruises? Abby glanced at Darren's legs but he wore jeans.

'Dad, no. You can't throw my board away.' All pain was momentarily forgotten as Darren sat up and glared at his parent. 'Gramps gave it to me for my birthday and he'll go bonkers if you take it off me. It's a really expensive one with the best wheels you can get.'

Jim growled, 'I'll deal with your grandfather. Believe me, that board is trash.'

Abby gently pushed Darren back against the pillow. 'Let's get you patched up, and worry about the board later.'

'I'm going home to hide it.' But Darren's bravado quickly evaporated as pain struck again.

Abby began swabbing the cut on Darren's head, noting an older bruise above his eye. An earlier skating accident? 'Do you wear protective gear? Like a helmet, for starters?'

'Yes. Dad won't let me go out without it.'

'He's right. You don't want to injure your head.' Abby noticed purple swelling on the uninjured arm. 'Darren, I want to remove your jeans and examine your legs.'

His father growled, 'Spends more time falling off than actually riding the damned skateboard.'

Abby could sympathise with both of them. Darren was obviously full of spirits and not put off by his accidents, but what parent would be happy about always taking their child to get stitched up? She'd hate seeing Seamus or Olivia hurt. She might be hiding the skateboard, too, despite knowing life was about getting out there and taking risks.

Taking risks? Like she did? The biggest risk she'd taken since getting engaged to Phillip had been flying to Ireland for the funerals. Then her grief had been so crippling she hadn't thought about dealing with Customs and Immigration and all the things people had warned her about. She'd just clung to her sisters and followed the arrows.

The cubicle curtains swished open, revealing a confident Kieran with a boggle-eyed Barbara in tow. Another victim. Careful, or you'll be dribbling. Abby sighed. As if she could talk. From the moment she'd met Kieran she'd fallen under his spell. Even if he hadn't been so good looking and sexy, he only had to open his mouth and speak in that lyrical accent and her knees weakened.

'I hear some stitches are required.' Kieran spoke into the sudden quiet.

There, just as she'd thought. The Irish lilt. Her knees were ready to dump her on the floor, despite her wariness of him. 'Darren, this is Dr Flynn. Darren's one of our regulars. I'm just going to get his file. I want to check on something. Barbara can assist you, Doctor.'

His brow creased but he didn't try to stop her leaving the cubicle that felt as small as a kennel with five people crammed in there. Especially with Kieran present, all the air seemed to have disappeared. She needed to put space between them before she became a brainless ninny. She'd better get over herself. And especially get over Kieran. At least the accusatory tone Kieran had directed as he'd left her house had gone, no doubt put aside for a more suitable time.

Darren's file lay in the in-tray at the nurses' station. Sinking onto a chair, she read through the notes recording a previous broken arm, and on three separate occasions he'd had cuts requiring stitches. No mention of bruising. So why the excessive bruising today? Her heart slowed. She didn't like to think about what the sudden onset of severe bruising could mean.

Pete sat down beside her to write up notes on his patient. Peering at her file, he asked, 'Why are you interested in that?'

'That Darren's file?' Kieran asked from above her.

'Yes.' How had she missed his approach? She thought she had extra-supersensory feelings whenever Kieran was around. Looking up, she saw him watching her intently. What did he see? Someone suitable to bring up his niece? And his son? Or a woman who he'd once enjoyed a few special hours with? What did he remember of that night in Dublin?

'Are you worried about Darren? You seem a little distracted.'

Of course she was distracted. Who wouldn't be in the circumstances? With a flick of her ponytail she focused on their patient.

'I'm not sure. Darren falls off his skateboard a lot. But I can't find any record here of severe bruising associated with previous injuries. He's got bruises in more places than I'd expect from this morning's accident.'

Pete said, 'He's a boy. Of course he's always falling off and getting bruised. Nothing sinister there.'

But Kieran took her doubts seriously. 'Are you worried that there might be a medical cause?'

'Yes. I think we should be investigating further.' She didn't go as far as to say what tests she'd do if it was up to her. Occasionally even she knew when to keep quiet.

Pete muttered, 'If Dr Flynn has checked him out, why are you concerned?'

'Abigail has a valid point. Darren's bruising is abnormal. It doesn't hurt to take another look. Better to find she's wrong than send the boy away with an illness we overlooked. Always listen to your staff. They see things you might not.'

Abby knew Pete would give her a hard time about this later, but it felt good to have her concerns taken seriously. After all, she did have some knowledge about these things.

'I'm going to take a blood sample from Darren. Clotting factors and a blood count. Is that what you had in mind?' Kieran cocked an eyebrow at her.

'Yes. But I hope I'm wrong about the diagnosis I'm considering.'

Unfortunately she wasn't. The lab rang within an hour.

'Darren has leukaemia.' Kieran's jaw tightened. 'We're sending him to Day Stay for a pathologist to do a bone-marrow aspiration to determine the type.'

Abby's heart squeezed for Darren and his father. Their lives were about to be turned upside down and inside out. Their situation was unimaginable for any parent.

'I'd better go and tell Jim.' Kieran stood as though glued to the floor. His hand dragged down his cheek. 'I hate this part of the job.' Then he muttered something like, 'And today it seems worse.'

'Want me to come with you? Or sit with Darren while you take his father to your office?' Abby didn't know how she'd cope if anyone ever had to tell her something as devastating about Seamus or Olivia.

'How does a parent deal with this?' Kieran croaked.

She shivered. 'Let's hope we never have to find out.'

Telling Jim Shore that his fun-loving son was gravely ill and needed more tests had been one of the hardest things Kieran had ever had to do.

For some inexplicable reason young Darren's plight rocked him on a deep personal level. For the first time during his career as an emergency specialist the sense of regret and pain for his patient felt too close. He couldn't understand his feelings, but they were very real. He'd always found this side of his job hard but today was especially difficult.

Other patients awaiting his attention gave him a much-needed distraction. But later, when the pathologist phoned down as a matter of courtesy to tell him that the bone-marrow results showed acute lymphoblastic leukaemia, Kieran's head spun. Even though he'd been expecting the result, he found it difficult to accept. He'd known what the initial results meant. But Darren was a child, a happy boy full of life.

Just like Seamus. What if something like this happened to his little boy? Would he survive the pain of watching his son becoming extremely ill? How did a man cope as he watched his child being put through intensive and painful treatment?

Abby touched his shoulder lightly. 'Are you all right? I saw you on the phone.'

He shook his head. 'That was the pathologist confirming Darren has ALL.'

Sadness and horror filled Abby's eyes before she quickly turned away, murmuring, 'These are the days I hate my job.'

'I know what you mean.' But today felt worse than ever before. Today he understood on a deeper level what Jim Shore might be feeling. And it was sure to be a lot worse than Kieran could imagine. A band of pain throbbed in the back of his head.

Abby said, 'I feel like rushing to the crèche and hugging the kids tight, to reassure myself they're fine and that nothing can touch them.'

'A natural response, I'd have thought.' He squeezed her hand before moving away. 'Take five to go and see them.'

'Are you sure?' Her eyes widened. Surprised he could be so understanding?

'Absolutely.' Well, he surprised himself at his sense of helplessness right now. The only thing he could think to do was send Abby to see the children.

Her smile was thanks enough. 'Come with me. Seeing the kids might make you feel a bit better.'

He shook his head. 'No, I'm needed here.' As head of the department, how would it look to the staff if he went charging off to see his niece just because of the diagnosis on one of his patients? Damn it, they'd be sending him home in no time at all.

He tried not to watch Abby as she raced away. The ultimate mother with all the right instincts. Could he even come close to that as an uncle or father? Vulnerability squeezed his gut. Sweat pricked his skin. Despite his denials, those two children were already overtaking his determination to remain aloof.

Did that mean he'd begun accepting he had a son? With all the connotations of what that meant? No. It was far too soon for him to be ready. He would never be ready. But the control he had over his life was rapidly becoming a myth.

HOPE. The sign flashed by, and this time Kieran didn't even slow down. He didn't know why the compulsion to see Olivia and Seamus felt so strong, didn't understand the need to reassure himself they were healthy and happy.

To be sure, he knew they were all of those things and more. But he had to *see* for himself. His hands gripped the steering-wheel, stones flicked up as he braked hard outside Abby's cottage. Abby. How did he explain his mad rush from town at nine o'clock at night? She'd think he'd gone crazy.

But it was almost as though she'd expected him if the lack of surprise in those expressive eyes was anything to go by. 'Hey, want a coffee? I've just made a plunger full.'

'That would be lovely. But don't move. I'll get it.'

What was really lovely was Abby. Her legs were curled

under her bottom as she sat in an old rocker on the veranda. A magazine lay open on her lap, her hair spilling around her face, her hands lightly holding her mug. Her soft mouth relaxed into a welcoming smile. The efficient, serious nurse he'd worked beside that day had been put away for the night.

'Thanks. You know where everything is. I'm catching the last of the sun now that the kids are asleep.'

His heart lurched. Disappointment warred with relief. Olivia and Seamus were asleep. He could take a quick peek and get out of here. Forget the coffee. It would keep him awake half the night anyway.

Olivia slept under a light sheet, lying on her back with Teddy clasped to her side in a headlock. Her curls dark against her pale Irish skin. Kieran leaned against the doorframe and watched her. Again he was stunned at the likeness to his sister. Looking at Olivia felt like Morag was still with him. He wanted to talk to his sister, tell her he missed her, explain that Olivia was gorgeous, happy and well cared-for and that she mustn't worry about her.

Kieran shut his eyes, squeezed the bridge of his nose. He could not be tearing up. Not now, not when he'd done his grieving two years earlier. He'd come out here to see the children, not to let the past grip him in a wave of nostalgia. He blinked, sniffed. And stepped up to the bed, bent over and kissed Olivia's forehead. Softly.

'Thank goodness you're safe,' he whispered.

As he straightened up he noticed the collage of photos adorning one of the walls. Morag. David. Olivia. The three of them in different poses—laughing, serious, waving, playing. In the half-light from the doorway Kieran studied every photo thoroughly, his heart feeling as though it was breaking. It was wrong for those two to have died. Abby was doing her best to make up for Olivia's loss but the child would never really know her real parents.

He turned to gaze at his niece again. And fought off the tears once more. 'Goodnight, little one.'

He backed quietly out of the room. He'd just take a quick look in on Seamus and go.

Seamus was a restless sleeper. His feet moved almost continuously, and his hands plucked at the sheet, pulling it in every direction. His stuffed toy, a monkey, lay on the floor. He looked so like the Flynns with his colouring and features that Kieran's heart swelled. With pride? Not likely. How could he be proud of a child he didn't want to acknowledge? He didn't mean the biological ownership. He was definitely this little guy's dad in that respect.

But Abby was a part of Seamus, too. It showed in his easygoing temperament, his enquiring mind and gurgling laugh.

This is a one-year-old. How can you possibly tell so much about his personality at that age? You're looking for things in the kid, making them up as you go along.

Was he? Kieran's hands fisted in his pockets and he rolled on and off the balls of his feet while his gaze never left the infant. Looking for more characteristics to attribute to Abby? Making Seamus more of a Brown than a Flynn? Pushing the kid further away? Trying to justify himself when moments ago he'd thought it a tragedy that Olivia didn't know her parents?

But Seamus had met him, would always know him, albeit distantly. In this case, that was best for Seamus. Far, far better than being hurt by lack of love.

He bit his upper lip. Time to go. The children were as happy and healthy as he'd expect them to be. Abby made sure of that as far as it was humanly possible. As a doctor he understood nothing could be done to prevent a tragedy such as Darren Shore's occurring. As an uncle he felt there had to be something he could do. As a parent? A hollow feeling in the pit of his gut gave him no answers. Except to make him feel worse than ever.

It was impossible to leave. His feet were glued to the floor as he watched Seamus sleeping. When he did finally leave the cramped bedroom Abby had moved inside to watch television and darkness had settled outside.

'Everything okay?' Abby asked as he hesitated in her lounge doorway.

'Exactly as I'd expected.' Except for his own messy emotions, which weren't listening to him when he tried to take control and get on with what he'd come here for. To run an emergency department.

CHAPTER SIX

IT SEEMED Kieran couldn't stay away. Surprising Abby, he turned up at the cottage on Friday after work moments after Steph and her boyfriend, Andrew, arrived.

Olivia charged him down as he stepped onto the small veranda, insisting he pick her up. He hesitated before bending to swing her up into his arms. Olivia giggled nonstop. Her vise-like grip around his neck made him wince. But at least he was playing the game and trying to please his niece.

Abby grinned. 'Guess you'll be wanting a beer, too.'

'Sure thing.' Kieran turned to Steph and gave her an awkward hug with Olivia stuck between them. 'It's great to see you again. Is Charlie here, too?'

'Not yet, but I'm sure she won't be far away.' Steph turned to Andrew and made the introductions.

Abby dragged out the stack of hard plastic deck chairs from the laundry.

'Let me take those,' Kieran said from behind her.

She nearly leapt off the floor. She hadn't heard him following her. 'Thanks.' She could get used to having someone do things for her.

He carefully put Olivia down and picked up the stack with ease, then asked in a nonchalant tone, 'Where's Seamus?'

Yes! He'd asked after his son. Triumph spurted through

Abby. A very small step but, in her book, a step nonetheless. 'With Dad, shifting the irrigation pump.'

'He's quite the little man, isn't he?' Kieran commented, and carried the chairs out to the veranda. 'Where's that beer? A man could die of thirst around here.'

Abby watched Kieran as he separated the chairs and passed them around. He was totally at ease, very different from the serious professional she worked with during the day. A bit like herself, she supposed. As he tipped a bottle to his lips her stomach muscles cramped. He was so darned sexy. To say nothing about his good looks. No wonder she'd never forgotten that night with him. He'd marked her for life.

What did he see when he looked at her? A harried mother and aunt? He wouldn't be impressed with the shapeless clothes she wore to hide what Phillip had often derisively called her fat body.

Those soul-destroying words still hurt. Words that had finished off any desire for marriage or even a long-term relationship. Phillip had dashed her trust completely, making her wise up to the dangers of falling in love. Like Kieran, he'd been charming and fun to be with initially. Then the snide comments about her body shape, her clothes, her hair, her everything had begun. Finding him in bed with her then closest friend had shattered her. Within twenty-four hours she'd returned home, taking nothing with her except a broken heart. And a wedding to cancel.

'Hope there's a cold one for me,' her dad called out as he came through the orchard, swinging Seamus down from his shoulders. 'It's got to be thirty degrees out here.'

Abby watched as Seamus headed straight for Kieran. The surprise on Kieran's face was a nice change from his usual wariness. Then Seamus grabbed at Kieran's knee-length shorts with his grubby hands, and she laughed out loud. 'Hope they're not your best pair.'

His smile was wry, but at least he did smile. 'They are now my "meet Seamus" pair.'

He might be way out of his comfort zone but he was trying, and that pleased her, eased some of the permanent tension making her edgy these days. If he kept this up, soon he'd be a part of the Brown clan, always welcome, always included in the happenings of the family.

But she had to remember not to get any closer to him. He might be the father of her son, but that's as far as it could go. As far as she could afford to let it go. *So there, hormones, behave. Concentrate on helping Kieran learn to love the children. Forget everything else.*

A car pulled up on the roadside and Charlie appeared, carrying a grocery bag. 'Hi, everyone. Hope you're hungry, I've got a ton of steak and sausages here.'

These were the nights Abby loved, when all her family got together for an impromptu meal. Seamus followed her as she headed into the kitchen to make a salad and put potatoes into the oven to bake.

'Don't you ever stop working?' Kieran asked from the doorway, a frown crinkling his forehead.

'I gave the maid the night off,' she quipped, refusing to take his question seriously.

'Anything I can do?'

'You could see if anyone wants another drink.' Just then Seamus tugged the bottle opener from the table. 'That's my boy. Give it to Daddy.'

Kieran gasped. 'What did you say?'

The air whooshed out of her lungs. Where had that come from? She'd intended discussing with Kieran what she should call him when talking to Seamus before she mentioned the D word. She stared at Kieran aghast. He looked as shocked as she felt. 'I'm sorry. I shouldn't have said that. I...'

She spun around to the bench, staring at her shaking hands as she tried to pick up a knife to slice the tomatoes.

He'd never talk to her again. At least not for the rest of the evening even if he stayed now.

'Abby, it's all right.' Kieran's hand touched her shoulder, pressured her to turn to face him. 'I should have a name and I guess I am Seamus's father.'

Seamus bumped between their legs, startling them both into looking down. He held the opener up to Kieran. Shock drained the colour from Kieran's cheeks. 'Did he really understand you? Does he know I'm his father?'

Kieran stared at his son, speechless. Then slowly crouched down and took the opener in one hand. He ran the other hand over Seamus's head, and whispered, 'Thanks, boyo.'

'Morning, Abigail. Late again, I see.' Kieran strode alongside her as she dashed down the corridor towards the department. His tone dampened her pleasure at seeing him.

'Only by five minutes.' At least she had a good excuse. 'Olivia tipped a bowl of porridge over herself and we had to start dressing all over again.' But, of course, he wouldn't know what that was like.

'Olivia must've looked a sight.' Kieran gave her a brief smile. 'But you must allow time for these things. It's not fair on your colleagues if you keep arriving late after the shift handover is under way.'

'Keep arriving late? I don't make a habit of it.'

'Twice last week.'

Who's counting? 'You really don't get it, do you? Kids aren't that easy to organise.' How dared Kieran criticise her? She drew a breath. She hadn't finished. 'While you're at it, tell me where I'm supposed to find any extra time in the mornings. I'm already up by six, running around like a demented chook trying to get the house in order before my children strike.'

Kieran stared at her, amazed. 'Whoa, I only suggested you might try to be more punctual. Careful.' He grabbed her elbow and tugged her to one side as an orderly negotiated a bed past them. 'It's probably only a case of organising everything better.'

She jerked her arm free. The temptation to strangle him was huge. Had he not learned anything about raising children yet? Could he not try to understand how it was for her? 'Organised? Sure, buddy, from now on I'll get up at five, do the vacuuming, make the beds before Olivia and Seamus get out of them, prepare breakfast, hang out the washing in the dark, have my shower and put on make-up and immaculate clothes, and finally drive to work with two beautifully behaved children, beating the rush-hour traffic to arrive in the department all smiles and looking very serene.'

She sank back against the wall. What had got into her? Her tongue was like a runaway roadster. It wasn't Kieran's fault she'd spent the weekend checking the gate to see if he might have turned up. She'd behaved worse than Olivia. Had he stayed away because of her stupid mistake of calling him Daddy on Friday night?

'Buddy?' Kieran stared at her as though she'd gone stark, raving mad. 'Abigail, is something wrong? I've obviously upset you.'

'Upset me?' Totally. Not because of his criticism but because he was never out of her head, keeping her awake hours after she went to bed every night. 'No, not at all. I've got a touch of Monday-itis.'

She spun around and headed for the nurses' station, Kieran keeping pace with her, thankfully staying quiet.

'Abby, don't think you can ease your way in today. It's

crazy around here already.' Sally added to her mounting stress. 'Kieran, cubicle three, please.'

Kieran reached for the file in Sally's hand. 'What have we got?'

'A twenty-five-year-old woman with an aching leg.'

'Abigail, come with me.'

Grrr. Abby wanted to go home and start again. To put on her best smile and pretend she was coping with Kieran reappearing in her life.

Reluctantly she followed him. He paused outside the cubicle, and his wary smile caught at her, undermining her bad mood. 'I apologise if I sound uncaring. I'm not. Guess this shows I don't know anything about parenting.'

She softened her tone. 'There's only one way to learn. It's called the hands-on approach.' A family could be a tie, and it hurt to know Kieran didn't want that.

'I know, and I should've visited over the weekend but I was busy.'

Sure, partying, socialising. Steph had told her he'd accepted her invitation to that party she'd mentioned. 'No rest for the wicked, eh?' Face it, Kieran could be very wicked. In the nicest, sexiest possible way, her brain mocked her.

A burly young man stood by the bed in the cubicle, his arm around the shoulders of a distressed woman. The obvious worry darkening his eyes made Abby take stock and push those distracting images of Kieran away. But she wished she had someone special to care for her as intensely. And she wasn't meaning her father or sisters.

Neither did she mean Kieran.

She was never going to get that close to the man. Or any other man, remember? *Remember?* Yes, she did. So why was she suddenly having all these odd feelings of missing out on something really important?

The young man said, 'It's Jane's right leg. She says it's

agony to stand on. We can't get her jeans off, it's swollen so much.'

'Hello, Jane. I'm Dr Flynn and this is Nurse Brown. I am going to have to remove your jeans to examine your leg. We might have to use scissors.'

'I'll try pulling them off again.' Jane grimaced, but removing the jeans proved too painful.

'I guess there's no choice.' Abby went in search of scissors.

'I've only just bought these jeans,' Jane muttered when she returned.

Abby smiled in sympathy. 'They're gorgeous.' Designer ones, the sort that Abby could never squeeze herself into. 'I bet you didn't get them here.'

'I bought them in Switzerland two weeks ago.'

Kieran's eyebrows rose fractionally. 'What were you doing there?'

'Skiing. Ahh…' The girl sucked a breath as the denim fell away, removing the pressure on the swelling.

'Any accidents or falls? You didn't twist your knee at any time?' Kieran queried as he examined the inflamed leg.

Jane shook her head. 'No, nothing like that.'

'When did you get back to New Zealand? Did you come straight through?' Abby asked, wondering if this could be a case of deep vein thrombosis. She looked up to find Kieran watching her. He nodded imperceptibly, as though to say she was on the right track.

'Two days ago. It's a long haul from Zurich, through Frankfurt, Hong Kong, Auckland. My body clock's only just catching up. I keep wanting to go to bed in the middle of the day.' Jane smiled for the first time. 'Not a good look when I'm supposed to be organising kayaking trips for tourists.'

'I'll bet.' Kieran smiled his big, calming smile.

That smile might not have had much effect on Jane, but it

sent Abby's heart rate soaring. Fickle heart. She wasn't supposed to notice anything about Kieran other than his medical skills.

Next he asked, 'Any history of thrombosis in your family? Have you had a clot in the past?'

Tears welled in Jane's eyes. 'I wondered about that. I don't know of anyone having had clots but I'd have to ask Mum.'

Kieran said, 'Are you on an oral contraceptive?'

'Yes.'

'Did you take any aspirin before or during the flight?'

Jane shook her head. 'Will I be all right? People die of clots.'

'You've done the right thing coming in here.' Abby folded the now useless jeans.

Kieran explained what would happen next. 'I'll arrange an ultrasound scan of your veins. If that doesn't show up a clot, we'll X-ray the knee to see if you did some damage while skiing.'

Jane's lip trembled as she asked, 'Will I be all right? I mean, if it's a clot, what if it moves?'

Kieran reassured her. 'I'll give you blood-thinning drugs to slow any further clots forming, and we'll put that leg in elastic hose. Then we wait.'

Back at the station Kieran filled Sally in on what he required, before turning to Abby. 'You were on to the idea of DVT straight away, weren't you? That's why you asked about those jeans.'

Abby shrugged. 'They're such an unusual style I didn't think they came from around here.'

'You were really good with Jane.' Another of those beguiling smiles lifted the corner of his mouth.

Trying to get back on side with her? Warmth trickled through her, banishing all traces of her earlier mood. If he could try, so could she. 'I do listen to everything a patient says, not just their comments about aches or pains.'

'You have an analytical mind when you're dealing with patients. Ever consider studying medicine? You'd be a brilliant doctor.'

Bam. The warmth evaporated. As quickly as it had come. She reached for the next patient file. 'It crossed my mind once, but nursing suits me better.' Glancing at the notes in her hand, she said, 'Looks like we've got a broken arm in cubicle one.'

Kieran stepped in front of her. 'Why?'

She deliberately squinted at the handwriting on the page. 'Looks like Mrs Webb fell down her back steps.'

'No, why nursing and not doctoring? And don't tell me it's because of the children. Olivia became your ward long after you'd finished your training.'

Abby looked around for Sally, for help. But Sally was on the phone. 'Mrs Webb's waiting.'

'You did look into it, didn't you?' Kieran asked softly. 'What changed your mind?'

'Okay, truth? I started med school but gave it up to come home to look after Mum when she got cancer.'

'You didn't think of going back?' His hand touched her arm briefly.

'I'd enrolled in the local school of nursing while Mum was sick.' She blinked away a tear. 'When she died I had one year left to qualify as a nurse. It didn't make sense not to complete that degree. I always thought I'd go back to med school but first I wanted a couple of years away from studying and to save a bit of money.'

And then Phillip happened. If she hadn't fallen in love with that scumbag she'd have been close to being a qualified doctor now. But he'd been her big mistake, and she'd lived with the consequences ever since. She'd also learned her lesson. Don't trust charming playboys. Ever.

'You'd have made a very good doctor.' Kieran's knuckle brushed her cheek so lightly it was as though she'd imagined it. 'You're also a very good mum.'

Stunned, she stared at him. She'd just spent most of the morning letting him know how angry and frustrated she felt about everything, and here he was building her up to feel better about herself. He was good, no doubt about it. Which only underlined how careful she had to be with him.

Sally hung up and turned to them. 'While I've got you both, most of the staff is going to the pub after work tonight. It's also a welcome for you, Kieran, if you can make it.'

'Sounds good.' Kieran flicked a question at Abby. 'You coming?'

'Count me out.'

'Why? You're a part of the team. You should be there. The evening isn't just about me. It's about colleagues relaxing together.'

She raised an eyebrow at him. 'There's the small matter of two children.'

'Get someone to sit with them for a couple of hours. It won't hurt them.'

'Sure.' She snapped her fingers. 'Just like that, get a baby-sitter in.' Her cheeks reddened. 'I'm a parent, Kieran. That means I go home at the end of my shift and give baths, make dinner, read stories. Children are a full-time job.'

'Believe it or not, I'm beginning to learn that.' He reached across and tapped the back of her hand with his finger. A lot of little touches this morning. What did they mean? Was he trying to get past her bad mood? 'I haven't been the best uncle in the world, but I'm working on it.'

She slowly withdrew her hand and shoved it deep into her pocket, away from the tingling generated by his touch. 'I know you need time.' But he was only talking about being an uncle, no mention of his role as a father. Her heart dropped, the tingling stopped. 'And Seamus? Are you working on what you're going to do about him?'

He met her gaze full on. No winsome smile now. Just a weary shrug. 'I'm getting there. In the meantime I'm trying to help you in ways that you haven't considered. Starting with tonight and drinks at the pub. Look how wound up you are this morning. A little bit of fun would be good for you.'

He was right. She couldn't remember the last time she'd gone out with her colleagues for an hour or two. It wasn't normal for a single girl of twenty-nine to be staying at home all the time. But until now that had never bothered her as much as it seemed to today.

She gave him a tired smile. 'Forget it. I have to go home at the end of my shift. You go and enjoy yourself. Everyone will make sure you have a wonderful time.'

CHAPTER SEVEN

ABBY still couldn't believe that Charlie was ensconced in the cottage, looking after the children. Charlie didn't do kids. Not hands on, getting smudged with mashed vegetables. Abby chuckled.

'What's funny?' Kieran slid another glass of wine in front of her and sat down beside her. Close beside her. Too close, yet not close enough.

'The thought of Charlie in her designer suit down on her knees, washing those two scallywags.'

Kieran's eyes glittered, fine crinkles bunching at their corners. 'Shame on you when she's helping out.'

Now, that was a surprise. 'What did you promise her? It must have been something big and expensive.'

'A little charm goes a long way.'

A knot formed in Abby's stomach. He had truckloads of charm. Look where it had got her. The lilting voice that melted her bones. His warm smile filled with promise. She hadn't been able to resist him. If she wasn't careful, she might find she still couldn't.

'Thank you, whatever it cost.' She could get used to someone taking charge of her life. Someone like Kieran.

'Let's take these next door and have dinner.' Kieran tapped the side of his beer bottle to her glass. He referred to the restaurant attached to the pub.

'Charlie won't be able hold out that long.'

'Actually, she said to stay out as late as we liked. If you'd prefer it, we could drive down to the waterfront and choose a restaurant.'

'Next door is fine.' Sounded like they were on a date. But, of course, they weren't. Abby looked around at her work colleagues. All three of them. When had the others left?

'You want to know something? Charlie was ecstatic when I rang. She told me you never ask for help, that you're always doing things for her and Steph and never letting them do something in return. Why's that?'

Abby sipped her chardonnay, thinking about the question. Was it true? Sometimes she did wish for help but surely the twins could see that for themselves and give her a hand without having to be asked? 'I guess it's a hangover from when Mum was sick and I looked after them. Dad was busy with the orchard so I kind of starting doing more and more around the house for everyone. It was always easier to do a job than argue with the twins about why they should do it.'

'It must've been horrible for you all.' His shoulder rubbed up against hers as they strolled through to the restaurant. 'Then David and Morag's accident happened. Talk about your family taking the hits.'

'I miss them all so much.'

'Yeah.' The word rolled out over a long sigh. 'Me, too.'

Kieran took her hand and wrapped his fingers around it, giving her a sense of togetherness that she'd not known before. It felt good. Neither spoke until they were seated with menus in front of them, each lost in their own thoughts for a few minutes.

Then Abby said, 'It took a while to really grasp the fact that David and Morag were never coming home again.' She swallowed hard. It still hurt. 'Despite the funeral and having Olivia to raise, for a long time it had just felt like David had gone on another sojourn overseas and would one day turn up on the doorstep with a hug and a smile, saying, "How's things, sis?"'

As kids, David had looked out for her at school, then at university. Even when he'd moved to London to specialise, he'd kept in touch regularly, making sure she was okay. The menu shook in her hand. No one did that for her any more.

Kieran reached over and laid his hand over hers for a moment. The gesture made her feel closer to him. They had something in common apart from the children. Some of the hurt dissipated.

When his gaze met hers she saw he felt the same. He said, 'It's the same for me. Morag and I never had a lot of time together, with me being at boarding school.'

'Didn't Morag go away to school?'

'No, she stayed with our father, going to local schools. They were living in the States by the time she reached college level. I didn't see so much of Morag then. Her skiing took up so much of her time.'

'I never knew she skied.'

He withdrew his hand, reached for his beer. 'She was tipped to make the British Winter Olympics slalom team.' He stared out the window, obviously seeing something far removed from Nelson. 'There was an accident. In my flat. At a party my flatmates held. Someone spiked Morag's drink. She didn't usually have more than one, maybe two. But someone got to her. She tripped and fell down the flight of stairs leading to our front door.'

'The injuries meant the end of her skiing?'

'Yes. My fault.'

What? 'Kieran, no. How can you blame yourself?'

But he did. The truth shadowed his eyes. 'As my father said, I couldn't take care of an egg in a carton, let alone look out for my sister.'

'Wait a minute. You said your flatmates had a party. Were you there?'

'No. I'd swapped shifts in ED so one of the guys could go to the party. He'd done most of the organising so it seemed fair, and I really didn't mind. I didn't even know he'd invited Morag.'

'That would've changed your mind about attending?'

He swivelled around to look at her, his expression bleak. 'I doubt it. I thought Morag was capable of looking after herself. How wrong I was.'

Recognition of his pain, of the reason behind his vehemence about being unable to care for Olivia and Seamus crunched in Abby's mind. Finally she was beginning to understand. Finally in a roundabout way Kieran had let her know what drove him to be aloof from what remained of his family. How could a man like Kieran forgive himself? Especially when his father obviously laid the blame squarely at his feet.

'Kieran, you can't go on blaming yourself. There's only one person to blame and that's the horrible individual who spiked Morag's drink.'

'Tell that to my father.'

Their meals arrived then and Abby took time to savour her fish and let Kieran regain his composure. Then as he began eating she changed the subject. 'How are you finding working in Nelson?'

'Great. Everyone's friendly and helpful, and well trained. Their goal is the same as mine, to help people. Yes, I am enjoying it.'

She smiled at him. 'You look surprised.'

'I hadn't really stopped to think about it.' He smiled at her. 'Too many other things going on outside work.'

'The children.' She put her fork down. 'Are you beginning to feel at ease with the concept of being a father?'

His eyes widened, and he took his time answering. Finally, 'I think I'm starting to accept it. I don't deny I got a shock when you called me Daddy on Friday night. And more than a shock when Seamus actually brought me that opener. Though I'm not convinced he understood you.'

'I agree, but with each time I say something like that he's going to learn who you are. And with each little thing you do for him he's going to understand what a daddy is.'

'Steady on. I'm still getting used to the idea.'

'Don't take too long.'

'Don't push me too hard.' Kieran shoved back in his chair, feeling cornered. 'I've only been here a week.'

In front of him he saw hesitancy in Abby's face then she seemed to shrug mentally, as though thinking, What the hell, and said to him, 'Then you've only got seven weeks left.'

He jumped in his seat. What? How dared she? Wasn't he doing his best? Abby obviously didn't think so. Less than two weeks since first learning about Seamus and he was taking too long? *How long did he need?* Which was Abby's point exactly.

'Easy for you to say,' he murmured.

'I wasn't born a mother or an aunt. I had to learn, as does every parent. Unfortunately kids don't come with a manual.'

He stared at this determined woman sitting opposite him. She was only trying to do the right thing for her children. If that meant harassing him, then harass him she would. She was courageous, and honest, and very warm and loving. How many other women did he know who'd give up their dreams to look after, first, her mother, and then someone else's child? Not one. Her revelation about quitting med school had stunned him, but it had also highlighted her decent, selfless nature.

He'd do well to follow her example.

Her knife and fork rattled on her plate. Her hands were

shaking. Because of him? His reaction to her suggestion? Reaching for her hands, he squeezed gently, surprised to feel her trembling. 'You're right, there's not a lot of time. I'll work on speeding things up.'

Caution flicked through her eyes before she drew a breath and said quickly, 'Then you'll be coming to the staff Christmas barbeque next weekend. Everyone takes their partners and kids and we have a ball. Play cricket, swim, run three-legged races on the beach. I'm taking Seamus and Olivia.' She hesitated. 'And you.'

Gobsmacked at her spunk in light of his earlier irritation, he sat looking at her, thinking how marvellous she was. Then a laugh rolled up his throat. 'Oh, no, you're not. *I'll* take you and the kids.'

She grinned back. 'In that tiny sports car?'

'I'll change it for something more suitable.' She deserved that at least. But darn. He did enjoy driving around in that car. 'Now, let's look at the dessert menu. My sweet tooth will not be ignored.'

'I'll settle for coffee.'

'You don't want to share some cheesecake? Or brandy snaps?' Coffee be damned. He could see the longing in her eyes. So why not indulge? It wasn't as though she had to worry about her figure. That was perfect. 'Cheesecake and brandy snaps,' he told the hovering waitress.

And when dessert came he made sure she ate some by holding a brandy snap to her delectable lips. Big mistake. Her lips parted to take the end of the treat. Her teeth bit through the crisp confection. Then, as if that wasn't enough, the tip of her tongue slid past her lips and licked a dollop cream from the snap. He couldn't take his eyes off her. His spoon shook. He might think he had everything in control when he was around Abby but his body was making a liar of him.

Abby reached for the rest of the brandy snap, taking it between her fingers, holding it as though it was a precious jewel. He couldn't take his eyes off her. He certainly couldn't swallow the piece of cheesecake clogging his dry mouth.

Abby's eyes were huge. Her expression startled. He saw her swallow. Waited for her to take another mouthful. Wished she wouldn't. His system couldn't take it. Willed her to. Sighed when she placed the snap on the plate.

The waitress appeared, placed Abby's coffee on the table. And gave Kieran time to gather his senses. What had happened there? Apart from his hormones going on the rampage?

He pushed the dessert aside and asked for the bill. The restaurant had got too hot and stuffy. He needed fresh air, and lots of it. But it was just as uncomfortable outside. Had they heated up the universe? Without thinking, he reached for her hand and felt a zing of current between them. She moved closer, her sweet honey scent teasing his nose, crashing into his senses.

'Abby...'

She turned to face him, her eyes opaque. Desire? She swayed closer. He caught her shoulders, steadied her. And then he kissed her. Her lips were soft. The scent of her teased his nose, racked up the tension that had begun inside the restaurant. And then he tasted her. His senses exploded.

Wrapping his arms around her, he hauled her in against him, trying to make her a part of him. And he kept kissing her. Like a dehydrated man drinking. Everything between them had boiled down to this moment. One heady kiss. A kiss that enmeshed her in his heart. A mind-blowing kiss that sent waves of desire rocketing through his body. A dangerous kiss.

Slowly they pulled apart. Abby stared up at him, swallowed. 'I've never been kissed like that before.'

Only one woman in the whole wide world had ever kissed him back like that. Abigail Brown.

* * *

'You look like you've been knocked down by a tornado,' Sally chirped when Abby arrived at work the next morning. 'A bad night with the kids or a great night with Kieran?'

Abby dropped her bag under the desk and rubbed her aching back. 'I slept on that lumpy old couch of mine. Charlie had snagged my bed and when she sleeps she spreads out like a starfish leaving no room for anyone else. How her previous boyfriend managed I don't know.'

She wouldn't mention that the lumps in the couch hadn't had as much to do with her restless night as images of Kieran feeding her that brandy snap. She got hot all over just thinking about it. If Sally knew, she'd never let it go.

'Here I'd been thinking you and Kieran were having a good time together. He's wearing similar shadows under his eyes.'

'Kieran's here already?' So much for arriving before him.

'Cubicle four. Robyn from the night shift is with him until one of the day shift shows up. That's you.'

'Sally, could you put Barbara with him today?' As well as those food images, shockwaves from last night's kiss were still rolling through her body.

'You know it doesn't work like that.'

'Why do I get to be his right-hand nurse all the time? Give someone else the experience for a change.' She glared at Sally. 'And stop playing matchmaker. It isn't going to work.' Unfortunately. Gulp.

Sally nudged her. 'Cubicle four. A five-year-old boy has been brought in by his neighbours after being found hiding in their laundry. He's badly bruised around the head and has suspected fractures to one arm and a finger.'

Abby shuddered. The poor little guy. 'Where are the parents?'

'Apparently the police were called out last night to a violent argument between them. The boy must've been overlooked or had already hidden, too terrified to come out. When the neighbour found him and took the boy home, no one answered his knocking.'

'How can parents be like that?' Her heart thumped her ribs as she thought of her two children; their trusting eyes, happy faces, soft cuddles. How could anyone want to destroy that?

'Someone from Social Welfare will be here any minute,' Sally told her.

'They should've been there before he got beaten.' Abby stuffed her fists in her pockets. Some people didn't deserve to be parents.

When she slid between the curtains of cubicle four, she had her anger under control. Kieran raised his head as she stepped up to the bed, and the compassion in his eyes for his young patient softened her heart. He'd never do this to his son. Wouldn't that knowledge make him feel more secure as a father?

'This is Joey.' Kieran nodded to the thin child curled up tightly on the bed.

Large brown eyes watched Abby warily as she moved to the bedside. No other part of him moved. Ugly purple bruises stained his arms and forehead. Abby wanted to lift him into her arms and cuddle him for ever.

'Hi, Joey. I'm Abby and I'm going to look after you now.' Those fearful eyes flicked to her face, but he kept quiet. The poor little guy looked exhausted.

'How old are you?' Abby tapped her finger on her lips and screwed up her nose. 'Let me guess. You look too clever to be three, but I could be wrong.'

Nothing.

'Just teasing. You're really four. Although you're quite big for four.'

Joey turned his head slowly to one side and back.

'Okay, I'm really dumb, aren't I? You're six.'

Again the head moved from side to side. Then Joey blinked. His mouth opened enough for him to whisper, 'I'm five.'

'Go on, you're not.'

'Am so.' The whisper was now a little stronger.

'A schoolboy. Wow. Cool bananas.'

'I like school.'

Kieran tapped her on the shoulder. 'We need to get Joey out of his clothes and into a hospital gown. Robyn's getting a warm blanket. I'm surprised he's not hypothermic.'

A middle-aged man spoke from the corner of the cubicle. 'When I found him he was curled up in the washing basket amongst the clean washing so he probably kept warm throughout the night.'

'Thank goodness he went to your place and didn't hide outside, or we could have a whole different scenario on our hands,' Kieran acknowledged, before nodding to Abby to follow him out where he spoke quietly. 'You're doing great with Joey. That's the most we've got from him so far. Can you stay with him while we sort out what's going to happen next?'

'Of course.' Try and keep her away. This child needed her.

'Joey's undersized for his age. Hopefully the paediatrician will admit him for a full assessment.'

'Then what? He'll go home to more of the same.' Abby couldn't help the despair breaking through her resolve to be totally professional with this case. How could she be? That gorgeous little boy was hurting, inside and out. He needed loving, not beating.

'Unfortunately we have to hand him over to the system.' Kieran's finger touched her cheek briefly, his eyes full of the same emotions she felt. 'In the meantime, let's make him as comfortable as possible and show him not everyone's a monster.' Digging into his pocket, he withdrew some money.

'I'm sure there's something in the cafeteria that little boys love to eat.'

'Definitely far more exciting things than what the main kitchen will come up with.'

'You want to go and get something before relieving Robyn?'

'On my way.' Abby snagged the note from his fingers and smiled at Kieran. 'You've got the right instincts when it comes to children. You know that?'

'Not a clue, but with you enlightening me all the time I'm sure I'll catch on eventually.'

Cheeky so-and-so. His smile warmed her to her toes, and she nearly whistled as she hurried to the café, all thoughts of Joey's situation momentarily on hold. Once again her mind returned to Kieran's kiss. A toe-tingling, spine-bending kiss that had blanked her mind and teased her body.

Idiot. She grinned to herself as she bagged a chocolate cake in the café. Idiot, idiot. She was supposed to be keeping Kieran at arm's length. But it was getting harder by the minute to ignore the effect he had on her. She felt more alive than she had in years. Perhaps she should just enjoy Kieran, have some fun, and make the most of whatever happened between them. The problem with that brainwave would be how to get over him when he left again. But her grin stretched further. She couldn't even get over last night's kiss.

Dale Carlisle, Joey's mother, and the social worker arrived simultaneously, the mother causing pandemonium as she ranted and raved at the top of her voice about neighbours poking their noses where they shouldn't. Kieran offered his office to the social worker but Dale refused to accompany her, insisting on staying with her son, then verbally abusing Abby when she tried to take Joey to Radiology.

Kieran intervened, standing between Abby and Joey's

mother. 'Dale, please don't talk to my staff like that. We're only looking after Joey.'

Abby appreciated the protection, although she didn't need it. Having Kieran stand up for her felt good.

Dale sagged into the chair beside Joey's bed and tipped her head back. The hood of her sweatshirt slid off her face, revealing bruises on her forehead and cheek. So Joey hadn't been the only one to take a beating last night.

Abby shivered. It was impossible for her to imagine living with a thug. She knew she wouldn't stand for it but, then, she hadn't been ground down by a lifetime of beatings and bullying.

Kieran tried again. 'Joey needs X-rays. Then he's going to have a cast put on that arm before being admitted to the paediatric ward for a few days.'

'You can't keep him here. His dad'll go ballistic. The kid's coming home with me.' Dale's eyes flicked left and right, left and right, her agitation growing. 'I want to take Joey home *now*. He's not seeing no social worker.'

The little boy curled up tighter than ever on the bed, one small hand clutching at Abby's uniform. Her heart squeezed for him. His gaze seemed fixed on a spot on the wall behind her, as though his mind had gone somewhere that didn't include anyone in this room.

Kieran remained calm in the face of the woman's tirade about hospitals and busybody social workers who didn't have lives of their own so had to interfere in everyone else's. But Abby could see his fingers tightening by his sides. He waited quietly until Dale stopped for air, and then said, 'Listen to me. Nurse Brown is taking Joey to Radiology now.'

Abby swallowed her angst at the young mother. After all, Dale was a victim, too. 'Dale, I'll stay with Joey until the X-rays are taken. He'll be fine with me, I promise.'

Dale muttered something under her breath as an orderly pushed the bed out of the cubicle, but she didn't prevent them going.

When Abby returned from Radiology she looked around for Kieran.

'He's taken a five-minute break,' Sally told her.

'That's not like him.' Abby wondered where he'd gone. He never left his post.

At least the department was quiet so he'd chosen a good time to disappear. Had the Joey incident affected him more than he'd let on? She wasn't going to find out standing here, so she'd make everyone a drink. 'Coffee, anyone?'

Stirring mugs of coffee, she was so absorbed in wondering about Kieran that she didn't hear him approaching until he said, 'Is one of those for me?'

The teaspoon rattled against a mug. 'Gees, you're doing that creeping thing again.' She turned, her breath catching in her throat. He was that close. If she just leaned forward a little, her lips would touch his. Like that. A soft touch. A loving kiss.

A loving kiss? She jerked away, turned back to the coffees. Reached for another mug to make one for Kieran. Anything to concentrate on other than the effect he had on her. Sugar spilled over the bench. She bit her lip. Hard.

Kieran reached for her hand, took the spoon and shovelled sugar into the mug while his other hand rested on her shoulder. If he couldn't feel her trembling then he had to be dead.

'I went down to the crèche,' he murmured. 'I needed to check on the children. Something inside me had to see them, touch them.'

Again she turned, only to find herself within the circle of his arms. 'Because of Joey.'

'I mightn't think I'm any good at parenting but I'd never, ever hit my son. Or my niece. Or anyone's child.'

She touched his lips, this time with her forefinger. 'You're not telling me anything I didn't already know. But I'm glad you felt compelled to go see them. It shows you're thinking like a parent.'

Kieran's pager beeped before he had a chance to answer her. Disappointment warred with common sense. They were at work, and any moment now someone would come to see what had happened to the coffee. Abby sighed and picked up three of the mugs. 'Want to grab the others?'

'Sure. There's a call for me from Radiology. Probably about Joey.'

At the nurses' station, Abby pulled up a chair beside Kieran as he dialled the number on his pager.

'Two fractures in Joey's arm, but nothing else,' Kieran informed her when he'd hung up.

'Well, at least his head's okay.'

Time to change the subject. Abby said to Kieran, 'Did you bring togs with you from Dublin? Or do you have to go shopping before Saturday's barbeque?' She tamped down hard on the image of Kieran naked apart from swimming shorts.

'Togs?' His forehead creased in puzzlement.

'Swimming gear. Shorts.'

'Swimming? Me? I don't think so.'

'You can't go to the beach with children and not get in the water.' She grinned wickedly. 'Plenty of surf shops in town where you'll find something.' *Please don't buy skimpy Speedos.* Her tongue flicked across her bottom lip. There'd be no accounting for her reaction if he did.

Kieran grinned back at her. 'You've got a very expressive face.'

Then he headed toward a cubicle where an elderly lady was being admitted with chest pains, leaving her staring after him in amazement, her cheeks blazing. He couldn't have read her mind. She crossed her fingers.

At the curtain Kieran turned and winked at her. Obviously he had. Picking up their mugs, she went to rinse them, determined her face would have stopped glowing by the time she got back.

CHAPTER EIGHT

'UNCLE KIERAN, why's it called Rabbit Island?' Olivia bounced around his legs, her face and body liberally smothered in sunscreen lotion. Her cute yellow swimsuit accentuated her black hair and blue eyes. So like her mother. His eyes switched to Seamus. Again the dark hair and blue eyes. His heart lurched.

So like his dad.

'Uncle Kieran, are you listening?' She sounded just like her aunt.

He crouched down on his haunches. 'Yes, Princess, I am. Now, about this island that's not really an island. I'm sure it's called that because there are lots of rabbits here.'

Olivia spun around. 'I can't see them.'

'They're hiding in their burrows, away from little girls who'd want to pat them.'

'What's a burrow?'

'A rabbit's house. They dig holes in the ground to race down when there's danger about.'

Olivia's eyes widened. 'Show me.'

A sweet chuckle caught his attention, stirred his blood. Abby knelt on a blanket spread on the sand, plastering sunscreen on Seamus. 'You'll have to find one now.'

Dressed in cut-off denim shorts and a bright red singlet top that barely covered her midriff, her hair swinging in a short ponytail, she looked like a teenager. The compassionate face of the exceptional nurse he knew her for had been replaced by that of a carefree, happy mother. He felt a tug at his heartstrings. The sort of tug any attractive woman caused. Yeah, right. Abby wasn't just any woman. She was beautiful, on the inside and outside.

Abby appeared so confident in everything she did, but he had seen that flicker of discomfort when he'd suggested dessert the other night. Did she believe she had to watch her weight? When her figure was superb? It didn't make sense. Someone had to have made her think like that. Someone who had hurt her. Why would anyone want to hurt Abby? His teeth clenched. He'd like a moment with that person.

'Ah, hello, Kieran?' The woman in his mind waved at him. 'We're looking for a burrow, remember?'

'Shouldn't be too hard to find one close by. I've got reinforcements if I need them.' He waved a hand at the staff members and their families sprawled over this area of the park, resting after an energetic game of cricket followed by an enormous barbeque lunch. He shook his head at how easily Abby distracted him.

Seamus pushed Abby's hand away and struggled to his feet. With arms outstretched, he stumbled towards Kieran. 'Raabb.' His foot tripped over a stick and he plonked down on his bottom. 'Raabb.' He put his hands down to push himself back on his feet.

A piercing shriek filled the air. Kieran jumped. 'Seamus?' He reached for the boy, caught him up just as Abby got there. Immediately Kieran handed Seamus to her, but she shook her head.

'Hold him still while I check him over.'

'Abby.' Panic rose in his throat. What had happened? One moment Seamus was fine, the next screaming his lungs out. Why? 'I'm the doctor. You're his mother. Take him and I'll look him over.' How was he supposed to sooth a screaming little boy? How did he calm his son? 'Abby, take him.'

'You're doing fine. Just hold on.' She gave him a tight smile.

Was that supposed to reassure him? 'Thanks a bunch.'

'I think he's had a bee sting.' Abby took one arm, carefully searched the skin, turned his hand over, checked his palm.

'A bee sting? Has he had one before? Is he allergic?' Anaphylactic shock could kill Seamus, he was so tiny. Kieran stared around at his colleagues and shouted, 'Have we got a first-aid kit with us?'

'I'll get it from my car.' Pete bounded away, a slightly bemused look on his face.

Kieran glared after him. Didn't the idiot understand what could go wrong here? Seamus tensed in his arms. Kieran dropped his gaze to his son. Seamus's face scrunched up as he sucked air for another scream. His eyes registered fury more than anything. His feet pushed hard into Kieran's abdomen, giving him leverage to stretch his body.

Kieran's heart thumped. His boy was hurting, and Abby wouldn't let him do anything about it. 'Abby,' he ground out. 'Hold Seamus. I'll look for the sting. He'll calm down a lot quicker with you holding him.' Seamus was never going to calm down for him.

By now a circle of staff had gathered around them, all offering helpful advice. How much advice did anyone need to find a bee sting? Pete returned with the kit.

'Found it. Hold him still,' Abby muttered.

Damn it, he was trying but who would've known how strong the little guy was?

Abby raised her head. 'There, the sting's out. All better, sweetheart.' And she plonked a kiss on Seamus's cheek. 'Now we'll put some cream on to take away the itch.'

I could do with one of those kisses. I deserve one, too. Kieran held Seamus out to her. 'I'll do that.'

But Abby took the tube of cream Pete handed her and quickly smeared the red spot on Seamus's hand with a good dollop. 'No need. All done.' And after another kiss on her son's cheek, she looked directly at Kieran. 'Just jiggle him up and down, give him a few kisses, and he'll be right in no time.'

'But I can't.' She'd turned away. 'Abby.'

Abby looked over her shoulder. 'Yeah, you can. You've been brilliant so far.' She lowered her voice so that no one else would hear her. 'For the record you just acted like a parent and not a doctor.' She winked at him. Then, damn it, she walked away.

He stared after her. A parent? Him? No, she'd got it wrong. He was a doctor. What was she doing to him? Seamus twisted in his arms and Kieran peered down at him. Soothing a child was definitely not his territory.

Seamus was hiccuping. Taking great gulps of air and building up to another shriek. Kieran felt a weird lurch in the region of his heart again. 'Hey, little man. Take it easy.'

Kieran jiggled his bundle as Abby had suggested, made soothing noises, and began walking around. 'Come on, my boy. We can do this. We'll show your mum we can put smiles back on our faces.'

Doing exactly what she'd intended. Kieran knew that. Knew he was jerking on the end of her string. But, hey, what else could he do? Charge after her and shove Seamus into her arms, crying and distressed? No way. He'd prove he could manage.

Just as she wanted. Cunning woman, he'd give her that. Then he stopped, looked down at his son gurgling and waving his hands around. *Hell. I've done it. Quieted the boy. Made him smile again.* Warm love, pure and simple, spread through

Kieran and he sank to the ground, staring into the young eyes watching him. He glanced around and his eyes clashed with Abby's. Triumph glinted back at him.

Abby clapped and did a jig on the spot. She'd forced Kieran to look out for Seamus as a father, not as the doctor he automatically reverted to. And it had worked out perfectly. Another step towards being a parent achieved. The proud look on his face was worth the uncertainty she'd seen moments earlier, and which had had her wondering if she'd done the right thing. She had. End of story.

A deep laugh had Abby turning her head.

'I saw that, Miss Clever Clogs.' Kieran stood beside her, so close she could smell the soap on his skin, see the flecks of black in his blue eyes. His mouth was mere inches away. She yearned to lean closer to kiss those lips. What was it about Kieran's mouth that made her act out of character? Those lips sent heat flaring along her veins and scorched her heart. Her cheeks flamed. She scrambled backwards.

'Time for a swim.' Anything to cool off. She reached for Seamus and lifted him into her arms, using him as a barrier between her and the man now gazing at her solemnly.

'Let me carry Seamus down to the beach, give you a break.' The Irish lilt washed over her, like a cool, damp cloth on fevered skin.

'Guess I'm used to it.' She clung to Seamus, suddenly unable to let him go, needing a shield from Kieran's magnetism.

'At least let me help while I'm here.' His hands held Seamus's waist, pressing against her bare arms, making her quiver.

She definitely needed total immersion in the cool sea. Relinquishing her grip, she stepped away from Kieran's touch. 'Thanks. If I seem ungrateful it's because I'm not used to people wanting to do things for me. I guess I tend to take over and push people away.'

'No, people come to you because you're so willing to help out. That's how I see it. Others do, too. Who puts her hand up to stay late when a case overruns a shift? Who altered her sister's dress last weekend?'

Warmth slipped in under her ribs. 'But those things are part of my job, of belonging to my family. No big deal.'

Those were the things that mattered, the things that kept her grounded, helped her through the rare days she regretted having to give up her dream years ago. Anyway, what could be better than raising two of the most gorgeous children ever?

Someone to share her life with. Kieran. Shock tripped her. Kieran? As if. She might desire him, but love him? Her skin prickled, her heart slowed. This was the second time that thought had bounded into her brain. She couldn't afford love. Not with any man. She'd paid a huge price last time. Anyway, if she made the mistake of falling in love with Kieran, he'd never reciprocate the emotion. A cold weight of pain lodged in her stomach. She knelt down to place Olivia's water-wings on her arms as Kieran continued down to the water with Seamus.

Sally dropped onto the sand beside her. 'Kieran's spending a lot of time with the children.'

'He's just doing the uncle thing.' Would Sally never give up?

'But he's not Seamus's uncle, is he?' Sally watched, her eyes narrowed, as Kieran coaxed Seamus to step into the shallow water. 'You know, I've never noticed before how alike in colouring Olivia and Seamus are.'

Abby's stomach clenched and nausea soured her mouth. 'That often happens with cousins.'

Sally's eyes turned to her, and her hand found Abby's. 'I agree. But why does Seamus look so much like Kieran?'

Abby twisted away and stared out at the beckoning waters of Tasman Bay stretching for ever, at the smooth sand broken only by footprints.

'It's okay, your secret's safe with me,' Sally whispered. 'I'll stop trying to push you two together now I know about this. Though I still think he's ideal for you if you'd give him a chance.'

'He's a playboy, Sally. Playboys break hearts easier than I can break glass.' But it might already be too late for her. Somehow Kieran had managed to winkle in under her skin in a very short time. So she had to start acting sensibly, stop thinking about those electrifying kisses. Kieran may be her son's father, but he could only be her friend. No matter what.

'He hasn't been behaving like one since he arrived and, believe me, there've been plenty of offers for a good time from the nurses.' Sally sighed. 'I heard talk last Saturday night he turned down two invitations to go clubbing. Hardly the act of a playboy.'

'Saturday night? He went to a party with Steph and her boyfriend.'

'According to Robyn, Kieran worked most of the weekend, including Saturday night.'

Heat pooled in Abby's stomach as relief poured through her. Kieran hadn't gone to the party after all. Her eyes feasted on him now as he shucked out of his outer clothes in preparation for a swim. Again the overwhelming urge to kiss him hit her, rising so quickly it rocked her to the core.

She needed a diversion before she acted on these dangerous impulses. She hauled her top off and popped the stud on her shorts, letting them drop to the sand where she stepped out of them. Across the beach Kieran stood staring at her, his face unreadable. But the flare of interest in his eyes as he took in her bikini-clad body was definitely unmistakable. He wanted her. Plain as day, Kieran wanted her.

And she wanted him just as much. Prefect timing, Abby. Absolutely brilliant. On a family beach with two children and most of her colleagues, and she wanted to make love to this man. Why hadn't she worn knee-length shorts and a baggy T-shirt?

'Race me, Abby,' Olivia yelled, inadvertently creating a much-needed diversion as she tore down the sand towards the water.

Abby raced after her, not to win the dare but to be on hand should Olivia trip and fall into the water. Olivia had had swimming lessons and now knew how to float on her back and dogpaddle in a fashion, and, most importantly, not to panic if her head went underwater. But she was still only three years old and Abby would never let her go into the water alone.

'I'm first.' Olivia giggled. 'Look, Uncle Kieran's undressed Seamus.'

'So he has.' She watched Seamus, as naked as the day he was born, and Kieran, thankfully dressed in beach shorts and not Speedos, make their way in a more dignified manner into the sea.

As Kieran stepped through the water, she watched the level creeping slowly up his firm calves, his muscular thighs, then… She swallowed. Turned away, focused on Olivia until she heard Seamus gurgling gleefully. Turning back, her face spilt into a smile. Seamus, held carefully by a squatting Kieran, was kicking the water into a frenzy while his tiny fists flew in all directions, putting Kieran's head in danger.

But what really grabbed her heart was seeing the look of amazement on Kieran's face. He was enjoying himself as much as his son.

* * *

Late afternoon the next day and the sun still blazed down fiercely. Kieran swallowed a glass of cold water. He enjoyed the heat, but couldn't get his head around the fact that Christmas was less than two weeks away. There should be snow covering the lawn, not roses and lilies flowering in the garden.

In her kitchen Abby had vegetables cooking for the children's dinner. Olivia sat on the floor, reading her doll a story from a picture book. Seamus had opened the pot cupboard and had begun removing everything he could lay his hands on. Kieran leaned against the bench, savouring the scene. Until now he'd believed domesticity to be highly overrated, had thought his married friends had gone gaga.

But what could be better than this? How could his parents not have given him the same sense of security that Abby gave these two? He thought his mother had but his memories of her were murky. Had his father not loved him enough to care how he felt? *Eejit. You know he didn't.* His breathing hitched in his chest. He hadn't been good enough to love. His father had always compared him to Morag, the golden girl. No argument there. Morag had been special, and he'd loved her. But why couldn't his father have loved him, too? Surely he hadn't been as bad as all that? The old bewilderment trudged through his brain, and he still didn't have an answer.

Dragging his hand through his hair, he shunted the unpleasant thoughts aside. No wonder Abby had been the nominated parent for Olivia. Abby knew what family was all about. But could he be a part of Seamus and Olivia's lives? In some capacity?

The thought of Seamus growing up believing his dad didn't love him appalled Kieran. He would do his utmost to make sure both children knew how he felt about them. These days, with emails, Skype and digital cameras, it wasn't difficult to stay in touch and keep a visual presence from afar.

Clattering pots brought him back to the present. He found Abby watching him, a doubtful smile hovering on her soft lips.

'You all right?' she asked.

'Couldn't be better.' His father may have let him down, but this family had begun to make up for his cold childhood. He felt as though he was coming out into the light after a long spell in the dark. Looking around, he drank in the simple things: food cooking, the radio playing in the background, the children. From somewhere deep inside he began to smile; a big, broad smile that he couldn't stop.

He moved to place a kiss on Abby's cheek. 'Thank you.'

Her finger touched her cheek. 'What for?'

'For being you.' For refusing to let him get away with his attempts to remain aloof. For making him face up to learning what he was capable of. Right now, he believed he actually could be a father. Maybe even a good one.

A thump on his shin stopped these thoughts. Looking down at Seamus pushing a pot lid along the floor, oblivious to obstacles, Kieran decided to join his son. Going down on his haunches, he picked up another lid and began 'driving' around the kitchen.

And around Abby's bare toes.

Toes with pink toenails. Toes that curled under when he blew on them. The owner of those toes tapped the side of his head. 'Remind me never to ride with you again. Your sense of direction is appalling.'

He looked up and grinned. 'Just following the leader.' A light air tripped over his skin as those hazel eyes peered down at him, a hint of humour sparkling at their corners.

'Typical. Blame the most inexperienced member of the team,' the focus of his attention quipped.

From his low crouching position her legs seemed to go on for ever. Something inside his chest squeezed. Excitement spun through him. It took all his willpower not to reach out and run his fingers over her smooth skin. Damn. He was supposed to be playing a game with his son, not ogling the kid's mother.

'Brrm, brrm.' Seamus pushed his lid into Kieran's leg. Focusing entirely on Seamus, he pretended to be unaware of Abby. At least, he tried really hard to ignore her. Impossible to do when his groin ached with need for her.

Thankfully the vegetables were soon ready. Kieran didn't know long he could've stayed on the small floor, ignoring Abby's legs.

'Do you want to feed Seamus?' Abby asked.

Absolutely, but he still wasn't overly convinced about the fun of mealtimes. They seemed highly overrated.

He must have shown some hesitancy because Abby laughed as she pushed the highchair forward. 'It's more about directing the spoon than anything else. Seamus loves feeding himself, which is why bathtime is after dinner.'

Olivia scrambled up to the table. 'I can feed myself. And I don't make a mess of my clothes.'

Abby placed plates of food and cutlery in front of the children. 'Don't rush your dinner this time, young lady. Remember what happened last night.'

'I got a sore tummy.'

As Kieran directed Seamus's sticky hand holding a laden spoon he chuckled to himself. Who would've believed a few weeks ago that he'd be feeding a small boy, really more like supervising the feeding of said boy, and enjoying himself. Certainly his mates back in Dublin would be shocked. Face it, *he* was shocked. Who'd have thought staying in for the evening could be more fun than hitting the nightclubs? Certainly not him. Until now.

'Going to share the joke?' Abby queried, one fair eyebrow lifted in his direction.

'I'm amazed at the amount of pleasure I'm getting out of this.'

Her lips curved upward, slightly apart so he saw her front top teeth. 'Yep, it's pretty wonderful all right.' Her hand touched his shoulder, her fingers pressing gently through his shirt.

Don't take your hand away, leave it there. He liked the warmth emanating from her. He liked the whole scenario. The kids playing. He and Abby looking after them. Then later, when the youngsters were tucked up in their respective beds, he and Abby would share a meal. If she invited him to stay on.

Suddenly that's what he really, really wanted. To spend the rest of the evening here, with Abby and the children. But especially with Abby. Did that mean he should be running back to town as quickly as possible? Or should he relax and see how everything panned out?

'Where's the Christmas tree?' Olivia asked, bathtime forgotten.

They'd shopped for a tree earlier in the afternoon. 'Guess what we're doing next?' Abby grinned at Kieran. 'Want to bring the tree in while I find a bucket to stand it in? I also need to get the decorations out of the cupboard, too.'

'Olivia, come and help me.'

Abby watched Kieran take his niece's hand as they headed out to the four-wheel-drive vehicle Kieran had rented the previous week. Far more practical than the sports car but not half as exciting. Never had she seen him so relaxed with the kids.

Kieran seemed to be enjoying himself. No trace of aloofness showed. He hadn't minded sprawling across the not-so-clean floor to play mindless games with Seamus. Neither had he noticed the smear of mashed pumpkin and potato on his arm. Was he getting used to the children at last? Was he beginning to enjoy their company?

'Hey, where's the bucket, daydreamer?' Kieran appeared in front of her.

'Where's the bucket, daydreamer?' Olivia parroted.

'Coming right up.' Abby ducked into the laundry for the bucket then found some large stones to weigh it down and prevent the tree tipping over.

It took nearly an hour to place all the decorations to Olivia's satisfaction. Seamus did his best to pull the crackers open and had to be regularly diverted.

'Great job, team. That's a fantastic-looking tree.' Abby leaned back to survey their efforts. 'You are joining us for Christmas Day, aren't you?' she asked Kieran.

'If that's an invitation, I accept.'

Abby turned to Olivia. 'Bathtime.'

Kieran straightened from picking up pine needles. 'How about I zip into town and pick up a bottle of wine and some food while you're cleaning up these two? I'll prepare dinner.'

'Really?' The question sounded too loud in the tiny lounge, but Kieran had surprised her.

'Yeah, really.' His smile was slow and deliberate, causing a catch in her breathing. She loved that smile. So warm and honest, and sexy. Sexy? Had she said that? Not out loud, thank goodness. But definitely sexy. Kieran Flynn had always been one well put-together package.

Kieran waved a hand in front of her face. 'Hello? Are you going to take me up on my offer? It won't take me long to drive to the nearest supermarket. There's a mall at Richmond, right? I'm more than an able cook. Or would you like me to do something else first?'

So he intended staying here for the evening. Then she'd make the most of having him around. Maybe even get a bit further ahead with integrating him into the children's lives. 'How're your bathing skills?'

'I'm very capable of taking a bath, though I do prefer a shower.' His smile widened into a grin.

Heat flushed her cheeks as an unbidden picture of a naked Kieran in the shower winged through her mind. Of course he'd be naked. How else did anyone have a shower? It had been hard enough, seeing him in his swimming shorts at the beach. That broad expanse of chest, those firm muscles that rippled every time he moved. She swallowed. A flutter of excitement tripped across her skin.

'It sounds perfect.' Then it dawned on her what she'd said. 'I mean, the wine and dinner, not the…' Shower. Getting in deeper here. She drew air into her lungs. Held it, counted to ten, twenty. Felt Kieran standing beside her. Breathed out, and turned to look at him. And immediately wished she hadn't. Similar emotions reflected back at her from his eyes.

His finger lifted her chin up until their gazes caught, held. 'It does, doesn't it?'

His mouth came closer to hers, and closer, until slowly, tenderly his lips brushed over hers, came back and covered her mouth. The kiss was long and slow, and filled with promise, igniting the tiny flame of need that had mostly sat curled in the pit of her stomach since the day Kieran had arrived, so that now it flared through her body, making her tremble and reach her arms up and around him. To hold him, to feel his lean body against hers, to taste his mouth on hers. Bliss. She gave herself up to the moment, to Kieran, knowing full well this was as good as it was ever going to get.

'Abby, are you kissing Uncle Kieran?'

Olivia's high voice screeched across her senses, slamming her back into reality. Jerking away from Kieran, she stared down at her niece as though for the first time ever.

Kieran saved her from having to answer. 'No, Olivia, Uncle

Kieran was kissing Abby.' Then he looked at her, his eyes the colour of the sky on a hot summer's day. 'Guess we'll have to finish this later. Which am I doing first? Bathing?' He grinned. 'Or shopping?'

Shaken by her overwhelming feelings, she shook her head at him. 'I put a bottle of Pinot Gris in the fridge this morning. I hoped you might stay for dinner.'

His eyebrows rose. 'You didn't say anything.'

'Just thought I'd see how the afternoon went.'

'So what am I cooking? I presume you've got that covered, too.' He ran the back of his finger down her cheek. 'You really are a very organised woman.'

Is that a bad thing? 'I have to be, what with balancing my job and the kids, not to mention Dad and the sisters.'

'Take it as a compliment, not a criticism.' Kieran crossed the kitchen to open the fridge. Reaching for the wine, he asked, 'Did you plan on having this chicken? Good. I'll make a Thai dish if you've the ingredients. But first let's have a drink and get these two rascals organised.'

Bathtime was always a hoot, with lots of water finding its way onto the floor as plastic ducks and boats made difficult manoeuvres around legs and bottoms. Getting clean was the least popular part of the whole operation for Seamus and Olivia, but Abby loved this time of the day.

'Looks like you should be back in your bikini,' Kieran quipped from where he leaned against the doorframe, his glass of wine in one hand.

She reached for the drink he'd placed on the window-sill for her, out of danger of being hit by a flying duck. 'Or my raincoat.'

If only this could last for ever. But she had to remember that Kieran would soon leave them to go back to his safe and secure way of life. He hadn't changed that much.

'I'll start cooking shortly. I thought you might like a few moments to sit quietly once these two are in bed.'

'Sounds heavenly.' And it did. She wasn't used to anyone else taking over and giving her a break, but Kieran did it so easily, so naturally, that she found it easy to accept.

Scary stuff. Could it be she was getting too comfortable with him? If so, she'd get a rude awakening when he left Nelson.

The scent of sweet chilli wafted through the cottage when she sat down at the table and Kieran placed the meal on the table. 'A proper grown-up meal.'

'You don't eat the same as you give the children?'

He looked so horrified she laughed. 'Not quite. I'm exaggerating about the adult food because there are the meals I have with Dad and the twins.' She looked up from salivating over her plate. 'But to have something spicy and different, here at home, this is what I miss. I love exotic foods and used to cook them all the time, hence the well-stocked pantry. I suspect some of those spices have lost their taste they're so old.'

'Most seemed fine to me.'

She relaxed, reached for her fork and took a mouthful of chicken. 'Delicious. Thank you for doing this.'

'If we're thanking each other, then thank you for a wonderful weekend.' He caught her gaze. 'I've enjoyed every minute of it. But I'm happy to admit that sitting down to share a quiet meal together without little voices demanding attention all the time has its benefits.'

'You don't mind tempting the gods, then?'

He frowned. 'The ones who keep little children sound asleep at night? Surely we won't hear another peep out of either of them now? They're exhausted.'

'Let's eat and enjoy while we can. Believe me, when it's quiet around here you make the most of it.'

Kieran looked thoughtful throughout dinner and his conversation was desultory. Abby wondered what was going on in his mind. When she looked up from taking her last mouthful his gaze on her was so intent she squirmed.

'What? Have I got sauce on my chin or grown a horn on my head?'

He shook his head, smiling. 'Nothing like that.'

'Then what?' She hated being stared at. When Kieran did it she created all sorts of weird ideas of what he was thinking about her and most of them were bad. 'Are you going to tell me I'm a rubbish mother? Or need a haircut? What?'

'You're beautiful.' His finger and thumb twirled his glass back and forwards, but his eyes never left her face. 'I still remember the time I saw you coming out from Immigration into the arrivals lounge in Dublin. You were so pale and distressed, tired from the travelling and your grief, but my mouth fell open at the sight of you.'

Abby gulped, took a mouthful of wine, the flavour of blackcurrant and something she couldn't identify crossing her tongue. *This* she had not expected. Men didn't usually tell her she was beautiful. 'How much wine have you had?'

'Less than you. I'm not making it up. Plus, why would I tell you to cut your hair? I miss it being as long as it was back then.'

Abby shook her head. Someone tell her she wasn't dreaming, that Kieran really was saying these things to her. 'Unfortunately, having hair down to my waist wasn't very practical with kids.'

'Do you ever think about that night we spent together?'

She blinked. Her stomach squeezed painfully tight. 'Oh, yes,' she whispered. Her fingers trembled. She desperately needed to take another mouthful of wine but doubted her ability to raise the glass to her mouth without spilling the golden liquid.

Kieran reached across the table, caught her free hand between both his. His thumbs rubbed light circles on her wrist. 'So do I.'

'I tried to put it down to the situation we found ourselves in. You know, our grief, the funeral with those two caskets lined up side by side.' Her voice cracked. Were they really having this conversation?

'Go on.'

She swallowed. 'But I couldn't. I don't normally behave like that, jumping into bed with someone without getting to know them.' She rubbed a hand over her forehead. 'That sounds like I make a habit of sleeping with men once I do know them, and I don't.' Kieran had been the first man she'd even wanted to make love with since Phillip. Unfortunately, the night with Kieran had been far more memorable than any night she'd spent with her ex fiancé.

'I never thought you did.'

Kieran's steady gaze burned into her as though looking for something. What? Did he want something from her? Another night in bed? Her toes tingled, her heart tripped lightly. Yes, her body said. Yes, her brain screamed.

Reality said no.

She wanted him, badly, but what would happen afterwards? They'd still have the same issues between them. He'd still go back to Dublin. She knew she'd be foolish to expect anything more than hot, hungry sex. But, boy, oh, boy, what could be so bad about that?

Despite her gut instinct to believe in and trust Kieran, she knew how abysmal her instincts were. They'd failed her big time in the past with the two people she should've been able to trust most. Absolutely nothing could make her believe she'd got it right this time. She had to be the world's lousiest judge of character.

Pushing away from the table, she broke contact, anything

to avoid those eyes, and then she began clearing up the mess on the bench. 'You're not exactly a tidy cook, are you?'

Kieran's hand touched her shoulder. She jumped. She hadn't heard him move. His touch was soft, relaxed and sent her senses into orbit. She wanted him.

Don't go there. You'd be playing with danger.

She spun away, turned and leaned back against the bench. 'I think it's time you went home, Kieran. I'm tired and need to clear up.'

'Don't shut down on me, Abby. We both remember that night for all the right reasons. Is that so bad?'

Absolutely. It undermined her determination to remain uninvolved with him. The memories teased her, tempted her to break her vow never to let anyone near her heart again.

Too late, yelled her heart.

Then she'd just have to undo the damage before it got any worse.

She licked her dry lips. 'I'm being practical. I don't see any point in going over the past. It happened and I've never regretted a moment of it. Not even when I learned I was pregnant.' She faltered, caught a breath and continued. 'But I've moved on. I don't want to repeat that night.'

Liar, screamed her brain.

He took her face in his hands and looked into her eyes. He didn't say a word. When she returned that look the world stopped. No outside sounds invaded their space; even the soft evening breeze paused as though holding its breath.

Slowly, determinedly Kieran leaned forward, brushed his lips against her mouth. Then he kissed her. Gently. Tenderly. And she responded. Her lips parted. Welcomed his tongue, let him explore her mouth. She danced her tongue across his. Slow burning heat unfurled throughout her. Then his arms came up and around her, pulling her in against his muscular body. And the kiss became demanding. She replied in kind.

Meeting heat with heat, tongue with tongue. Desire wound through her, touching her here, there, everywhere.

Kieran tipped his head back and looked down at her. 'Definitely better than the memories.'

'True.' Her heart thumped as though she'd run a marathon. Her lips hated the loss of contact. Memories were colourless, flavourless, in comparison.

All the more dangerous. Her head jerked back. This had to stop. Now. Before they did something she would regret.

How she could ever regret being with Kieran was another issue, not to be dealt with right this moment. Now she had to keep her feet firmly on the ground and act as though she was way more sensible than she really felt. Sliding away from Kieran, she crossed the small kitchen to put space between them.

Kieran's thoughtful eyes watched her carefully. 'So why stop?'

'There are a lot of things we need to clear up between us. Following this through will only make those things even murkier.' Why did she want to leap back into his arms and kiss him senseless? One thing was for sure, she most definitely did not want to be hauling on the brakes.

But someone had to. She had to. Her heart was in jeopardy. So were the futures of her children if she let that heart take over the thinking around here.

'I'd have thought "things", as you put it, were getting hot, not murky.'

The intensity in those piercing eyes slashed through her arguments and floored her defences.

'Kieran, you're not taking me seriously.'

'Oh, I'm very serious.' He followed her across the kitchen, stopping directly behind her, turning her, taking her face between his hands. 'Very.'

His lips brushed hers, a slow burn marking her soul. Her

eyelids fell closed. Air snagged in her lungs. Her hands crept up and around Kieran's neck.

Dimly aware of a cry, she tried to concentrate on its source. Had she made that noise when she'd responded to Kieran's kiss? Must have. There it was again.

'Hell.' Kieran lifted his beautiful head. 'Timing's everything.'

Bewildered, Abby looked around, blinking. Then realisation slammed into her. Embarrassment followed. So much for passion. The cry came from down the hall. Olivia was calling out for her.

Again Olivia had provided a much-needed distraction.

CHAPTER NINE

THE emergency department had been frantic over the week leading up to Christmas Day. Abby stretched back in her chair and didn't even try to stifle the yawn stretching her jaws.

'I love Christmas, but why do people have to go overboard with everything they do?' she grumbled to anyone who'd listen.

'It's the excitement.' Pete elbowed her arm affectionately. They'd got on a lot better since the work barbeque.

'Or the stress.' Kieran glowered at Pete.

'Plenty of that, I agree.' Abby sighed. Sometimes it almost seemed too much hassle for one day. Nah, who was she kidding? 'Christmas is fun. I love it.'

'Have you done all your shopping?' Pete asked.

'Right down to the last stocking filler for Seamus. If I think of anything else, it's too late. By the time we finish here tonight, I won't be going near any shops. It'll be bedlam downtown.'

'And here I was hoping I'd get a dream run when I go to town at lunchtime.' Kieran shrugged ruefully.

'You haven't done your shopping yet?' Pete looked astonished. 'Whoa, man, you'd better take a three-hour break. But, I suppose, you've only got one niece to buy for. Just hit the toy shop and you'll be right.' He grinned. 'They also have great plastic trucks that little boys go crazy over.'

'Thankfully I've already done that. I just need to pick up something on order,' Kieran commented.

Abby scrutinised Pete's face. Had he guessed who Seamus's father was? It wouldn't be that hard. Sally probably wasn't the only one to notice the likeness between her boy and Kieran last Saturday. Not to mention how much time Kieran spent with Seamus.

Pete kept his face blank, but his eyes were twinkling with knowledge. Oh, well, nothing to be done about it. Had Kieran realised? One look at him and she shrugged. If he had, it didn't seem to be bothering him. Now, there was a turn-around. He'd been adamant he didn't want anyone in the department knowing. She sat back in her chair. Did this mean he was accepting Seamus completely? It certainly looked that way. Her feet tapped the floor. Brilliant.

Pete asked, 'We doing any work today?'

Abby grabbed the top set of patient notes in the in-tray. 'Sure. Guess the coffee break's over. Your next patient.' She handed the notes to Kieran.

'The boss has spoken.' He smiled and read the patient details.

'Yep, and here's yours, Pete. Barbara can help you.' Abby stood up and stretched her back before following Kieran to cubicle four. She may be tired but she was enjoying being nurse in charge this week while Sally took leave. It was great experience and she knew she'd done a good job, made easier by working with people she knew well.

Kieran was talking to her. 'I've never been as aware of Christmas as I am this year. While your shops are not as heavily decorated as those back home, and there don't seem to be as many carol singers on the streets and the weather's weird, there's a buzz in the air.'

'Could be something to do with being involved with children.' Let's face it, Christmas must have been lonely, even boring, for him in the past with no little ones around.

'There's something in that.' He tapped her elbow. 'Tomorrow morning with the kids and their stockings from Santa should be fun.'

'You have no idea.' She grinned and slipped into the cubicle where an elderly woman waited.

'Good morning, Mrs Atkins. I'm Nurse Brown and this is Dr Flynn. I hear you've taken a tumble.'

Mrs Atkins had fallen at the shopping mall, sustaining a suspected fractured hip. 'Got knocked down by a boy on his skateboard, more like. I don't know why those people in the mall let skateboarders inside. It's downright dangerous.'

'I have to agree with you.' Abby took Mrs Atkins's wrist and began counting her pulse.

'On a scale of one to ten, Mrs Atkins, can you tell me your pain level?' Kieran asked as he gently shifted the woman's skirt so he could examine her hip area.

'Eleven. Dratted children. Where are their mothers?'

'I'll give you some more painkiller shortly, Mrs Atkins. I see the paramedic gave you a shot of morphine before leaving the mall.'

'Yes, he did. Helped to get me on that stretcher thing. Am I going to be here long? I need to get home. I haven't finished my Christmas baking and the family depend on me for that. My daughter works long hours at the fish factory so I like to do my bit to help her out. She's got five children, you see, had them late, and there's not a lot of money to go round in that house, I can tell you.'

Abby gave her a sympathetic pat. 'I'm sorry but until we know exactly what you've done to your hip you won't be going anywhere except to Radiology. Can I ring your daughter at work and see if she can come in to keep you company for a while?'

'Oh, no, dear. She can't afford to take time off. She needs

the money for Christmas holidays. I don't think the factory owners would pay her while she sat with me, do you?'

Abby thought they might. Most employers gave their staff leave in these circumstances. 'I'll see what I can find out.'

Kieran nodded at Mrs Atkins. 'Let's get your X-ray done. The sooner we know the damage, the sooner you'll be able to make some plans for your family.'

'Thank you, my boy.' Mrs Atkins hesitated, then went on, 'You're thinking I've broken it. I don't suppose I'll be very mobile if you're right. I knew I should've stayed at home to bake the cake instead of racing out to beat the crowds.'

Kieran looked taken aback at being called 'my boy'.

Abby winked at him as they left the cubicle. 'She's got your number.'

'She's one tough cookie. I guess that family is what keeps her so active. Unfortunately that doesn't stop her bones aging and becoming fragile. She's not going to enjoy her Christmas as much as usual this year.'

Abby reached over the top of the nurses' station and lifted the phone to call for a porter to take Mrs Atkins for her X-ray. Before she'd pressed any numbers Kieran leaned close, his aftershave alerting her to his proximity. She sucked in a lungful of man scent, igniting that deep longing she carried all the time now. Why did he have to stand so close? Why didn't she move away?

His arm brushed hers, and she found herself holding her breath. Why? It wasn't as though he would haul her into his arms and kiss her wildly in the middle of ED. Pity. She would give her sisters away for one of Kieran's kisses.

Nothing had happened since the evening they'd decorated the Christmas tree and that interrupted kiss. She should be grateful because it was becoming increasingly difficult to turn off her feelings for Kieran when he only had to touch her and she melted. Grateful be damned.

'Radiology department, Clive speaking.' When had she pressed the numbers for X-Ray?

Swallowing and stepping aside to put space between her and Kieran, Abby quickly arranged Mrs Atkins's visit, then hung up. 'Who's next?'

Looking up, she found Kieran watching her. 'You're flushed. Need to take another coffee break?'

A break from him, more likely. 'I don't think so. What time are you heading downtown?'

'As soon as there's a lull.'

'That could mean never. Go now while you can.'

He laughed. 'Worried I won't pick up your present?'

'Not at all. I just hope you're not taking the sports car because it's way too small for mine.'

'Cheeky woman. Don't you know some of the smallest things are the most expensive?'

'Are you saying size doesn't count?' She grinned. Then really flushed. Bright scarlet. Spinning away, she grabbed another patient file and dashed past the station, Kieran's laughter following her.

'More than cheeky,' he called after her. 'Interesting.'

Of course, it took for ever to drive home with the traffic banked up as far as she could see. It hadn't helped that she'd had to call into the berry gardens to collect the fruit she'd ordered and her father had forgotten to pick up. Christmas pavlova wasn't right without strawberries and raspberries piled on top.

Olivia and Seamus were irritable in the hot car. The air-conditioning didn't work anymore so she'd opened all the windows a crack, with dismal results.

'Finally,' she muttered as she turned into her road. 'We're nearly home, kids.'

'There's a truck at our place.' Olivia pointed across Abby's shoulder.

'The driver must be lost.' What other reason was there for a truck decorated in a local furniture outlet's logo to be parked at her open front gate?

'Can I ask him?' Then Olivia squealed, 'Uncle Kieran's there. And Grandpa.'

'So they are.' What's more, they were both helping some guy carry a large couch towards her front door. 'What's going on?' she wondered aloud as she lifted Seamus out of his car seat in front of her garage.

After putting down his end of the couch, Kieran came to draw Abby inside to her lounge. 'I hope you don't mind but I bought you a new lounge suite.'

Did she mind? No way. The lumps in the old one gave her bruises every time she sat on it. Shaking her head, she stared first at the navy-blue suite that matched her apricot walls perfectly, then at the man who'd bought this furniture. 'It's wonderful, but why? I mean, you didn't have to do that.'

'Oh, yes, I did. If I'm staying the night, I want to get some sleep, which I most certainly wouldn't on your couch. I'd probably never walk upright again. This one folds out into a fairly comfortable bed. I tried it in the shop.'

'If you're staying the night?' Had she misheard him? 'What do you mean?'

'It's Christmas. I thought it'd be fun being here in the morning when the kids open their stockings.' He hesitated, a flicker of doubt shadowing his denim eyes. 'Is that all right with you?'

Her mouth dried. Kieran staying the night? In her house? She'd never get any sleep thinking of him tucked up out here and her just down the hall. 'Sure, of course it is.' Could he see her uncertainty in her face, hear it in the wobble of her voice? Try harder. 'It's a lovely idea. I'm only sorry you had to provide your own bed.'

That heart-melting smile that never failed to tumble her emotions beamed down at her. 'I don't have to use this one.'

'Oh, yes, you do.' Where had her father got to? Had he overheard? A quick glance around. No one else with them. Phew.

Kieran flicked her lightly under the chin. 'I agree. It's not the time for us to be getting too close and personal, what with over-excited children in the house likely to wake up at any hour. More's the pity.'

Pity? Downright shame, her brain screamed. But in her heart she knew it was best. It couldn't happen. Kieran wasn't a stayer, and that was the only kind of man she'd be interested in. Something inside kicked her ribs, and she gasped. What? She was never going to be interested in any kind of man. Remember? But apparently she'd forgotten because it was far too late. She was very, very interested in Kieran Flynn. Somewhere between patients and kids he'd managed to wind a thread around her and draw her in. She was more than hooked. She was a goner.

Abby tripped in her haste to put some space between them, which only brought Kieran closer as he caught her elbow to steady her. She stared up at him, and felt tenderness steal across her tense muscles as she noted the black curls falling over his forehead, giving him a rakish look. Her fingers itched as she fought not to reach up and touch those gorgeous locks.

She pulled away and stumbled out to the car to get the berries and other bits and pieces she'd collected throughout the day. Her heart hammered into her lungs, her ribs. Of all the stupid things to do, she'd gone and fallen for the man now preparing to spend the whole night under her roof.

This particular Christmas Eve would be the longest in the history of Abby Brown.

'I thought you might like to see these.' Abby stood over Kieran as he sprawled across the new couch, watching a lightweight movie. The children were finally asleep. Olivia's excitement about Santa had been a big deterrent to going to bed.

Kieran sat up, aware of the hesitation in Abby's voice, the way her hand wasn't quite letting go of the package she held out to him. His heart sped up. 'Are these the letters and photos you intended sending me and never did?'

She nodded. 'I figure it's time you saw them.' Her shoulders lifted slightly. 'But if you're not interested, that's okay.'

Vulnerability sat over her like a heavy shawl. Had she opened herself up to him that much in these letters? 'Abby, are you sure you want me to read them?' He caught her hand, felt the tremors running through her.

'Yes.' She jerked her hand away, backed to the door. 'Yes, I do.' And she was gone.

Kieran sat back, staring at the manila envelope. Judging by the thickness Abby had written often, or were there mainly photos inside? Suddenly unable to hold off, he tore the envelope open and upended it. Photos and letters, notes even, tumbled out onto his thighs. A photo of Abby holding Seamus as he waved at the camera lay on top. Here was the beginning of Seamus's life. Here was a window into all the things he'd missed out on. Was he ready for this?

Now *his* fingers were shaking as he reached to the pile of photos. Slowly he made his way through them back to the day of Seamus's birth. His breath stopped. His heart expanded. An exhausted but jubilant Abby held a tiny blue-swathed bundle in her arms. She looked gorgeous. If only he'd been there to see that moment. To experience the joy at the arrival of their son.

He'd missed out on that. Whose fault was that? To be sure, he hadn't known about the pregnancy, but even if he had, would he have been there for Seamus's birth? He didn't have the answer.

Tentatively he reached for the first letter, addressed to him at his Dublin apartment. Did he want to know all the details about Seamus's first months? Did he need to know how Abby had felt during those weeks when she'd learned to look after her son? His finger tapped a rhythm on the letter. Reaching for his glass of lukewarm wine, he took a long swallow. Then opened the envelope.

Time passed. The sun set, dropping behind the trees, and Kieran flicked the light on before settling down to read the extraordinary letters all over again. Abby had bared her heart in each of them. He wondered if she realised how much she'd given away of herself as she'd described Seamus to him. Kieran laughed over the boy peeing across the room during a diaper change. He sympathised about the nights when colic had kept everyone awake. And he wiped his eyes when Abby described her panic when Seamus had stubbed his toe the first time and she'd believed he must've caught it on some rusty wire.

'I panicked about tetanus poisoning. A fine ED nurse I turned out to be, but it's so different when it's your child,' she had written.

That Kieran could believe. His own reactions to children in ED had changed since meeting Seamus. He'd changed in other ways, too. He no longer blamed Abby for not telling him she was pregnant. It hurt to acknowledge he'd missed out on so much because of his own stubbornness, but it was the truth. By being so adamant about staying out of Olivia's life, he'd made it an impossible situation for Abby. Whether it had been guilt over Olivia, or a niggling sense of missing out on something indefinable, he thanked his lucky stars he'd chosen Nelson over Adelaide for these two months.

Movement in the doorway caused him to glance up. Abby stood watching him, uncertainty in her eyes. Instantly he was on his feet, going to her, taking her hands.

'Abby, I'm sorry I made it so hard for you to tell me.'

Her eyes widened. 'You are?'

'Absolutely. Under the circumstances I wouldn't have told me either. I can only blame myself for what I've missed out on.'

It was disconcerting, the way she studied him. Then her lips slowly spread into a smile. 'That's the best Christmas present I could have wished for.'

'Here, get that into you.' Abby handed Kieran a mug of coffee. She felt good this morning after a really good sleep. Kieran's apology had wiped away a lot of tension. 'It might make you feel less rough at such an early start.'

'Being tickled awake at five-forty in the morning is certainly a new experience. Why didn't we think of drugging these two last night?' He winked.

Despite his beleaguered expression Kieran looked totally at home. Olivia and Seamus were tucked one each side of him in the pullout bed. Bulging red velvet stockings were strewn over his feet. Abby's heart did a roll. If only this particular Christmas wouldn't be a one-off. If only they were a real family.

Kieran grinned up at her. 'I didn't have a clue what I was in for when I decided to camp here for the night. Is Christmas morning always like this?'

'Yes. Last year Seamus was too young to understand but Olivia and I certainly made up for him. We got excited about what Santa had brought her.'

'Can I open Santa's presents now?' Olivia demanded. 'Uncle Kieran said we had to wait for you.'

'Of course you can.' Abby raised an eyebrow at Kieran. 'Just how did you manage to keep these two in check?'

'You don't want to know. Ouch.' Olivia's elbow connected with Kieran's midriff as she clambered over him to reach her stocking.

A loud knocking on the back door was quickly followed by her father calling out, 'I've come to join in the fun.'

'Do you think we could postpone the party…' Kieran raised two fingers on each hand to indicate brackets '…until I've got up from bed and into my jeans?'

'You'll have to be quick,' Abby laughed. Then her mouth dried.

Kieran had tossed the sheet back and was clambering out, carefully avoiding children and stockings. Dressed in boxers and a T-shirt, he was sight enough to make her temporarily forget all about Christmas. Wow. As his jeans slid up his thighs she knew she should look away but her eyes seemed to have lost the ability to rotate in their sockets.

'Merry Christmas, everyone.' Her father spoke from some distant planet.

'Granpa,' Olivia squealed, and charged him, Seamus toddling right behind her.

Thankful for the interruption, Abby finally managed to drag her recalcitrant eyes away from Kieran and go and hug her father. 'Merry Christmas to you, Dad.'

He squeezed her back before swinging Olivia up into his arms for a big hug.

Then Kieran was at Abby's side, slipping a soft kiss onto her cheek. 'Where's my Christmas hug, huh?' A second silky kiss brushed her now warm cheek. 'Happy Christmas, Abby.'

She turned her head. Big mistake. Her mouth brushed his. Mumbling some silly reply, she jerked away and dashed into the kitchen to make a coffee for her dad.

Fidgeting with the mug and teaspoon as she waited for the water to boil, she stared out into the orchard. The apricots were ripening fast now, their golden colour bright in the early morning light. Or did everything out there look brighter than normal? Yes, even the sky held a depth of blue she'd never noticed this early in the morning before. Had her eyesight changed overnight? It was as though someone had gone around with a paintbrush making everything much more vibrant than usual.

'You going to stir the bottom out of that mug?' her father asked from behind her.

She jumped guiltily. 'Sorry, daydreaming.' And her eyes went in search of Kieran, who was folding away the sheets and turning his bed back into a couch.

'So I see,' her father murmured. 'About our Irishman, I presume.'

'Shh, Dad.' Abby jerked her head up. 'The man's got a good set of ears.'

'Relax, he's busy tidying himself up. Maybe for you.' Her father actually winked at her.

'Don't even begin to think like that,' she growled, and poured the water over the coffee granules.

'Why not? I like the idea.' Max put Olivia down and lifted Seamus up for his hug. 'I bet these two would, too.'

She shook her head at her crazy father. 'It's not going to happen.' And with a deliberate shrug she added softly, 'Let's get on with opening presents. I doubt Olivia can hold out much longer.'

While the adults sipped their hot drinks Seamus and Olivia got busy. Seamus upended his stocking before delving into the treasure trove of treats and small toys, while Olivia removed and opened each present singly, checking it out before dipping in for another.

Abby focused her attention on them, trying not to watch Kieran as he took delight in the children's excitement. But she did chuckle when he said, 'I can't believe how much fun there is in something as ordinary as a colouring book.'

'I should've got you one.'

'You didn't? Damn, there go my plans for the morning.'

Max got down on his knees and reached under the decorated tree. 'It's about time the adults got something to unwrap.' Picking up a brightly wrapped parcel, he passed it to Seamus. 'Want to give that to Mum, little man?'

Apparently not, if the determined look on her son's face was anything to go by. In a very short while he'd got the hang of tearing wrapping paper off his parcels and this one would be no exception. Except Kieran gently helped him hand the present to Abby.

Abby leaned over and placed a kiss on Seamus's soft face. 'Thank you, sweetheart.' And then she tore the paper off a book she'd been hoping to get.

For a while the cottage was filled with happy discoveries and cries of pleasure as everyone unwrapped gifts. Finally Abby handed Kieran a parcel. 'I hope you enjoy your first New Zealand Christmas, Kieran.' And she kissed his chin. First New Zealand Christmas? Did she think there'd be more? She certainly hoped so.

He chuckled at the dictionary of Kiwi slang. Then his face changed, became still when he turned over the photos of Seamus and Olivia in hand-carved wooden frames. She'd had the photos taken in the orchard by a professional photographer who specialised in children.

When he finally raised his head Abby thought she saw tears glinting in the corners of his eyes. 'They're beautiful.' Kieran leaned across and wrapped his arms around her. 'Thank you. I'll treasure these photos for ever.'

Abby slid out of his arms and stood up. 'Time to cook the pancakes.' Time to put a halt to the heat stealing through her.

'After you've opened this.'

She stared at the small package nestled in Kieran's large hand. 'You already bought me a lounge suite.'

'No, that's for the house. This is for you.'

Her fingers shook as she tugged at the tiny gold-coloured silk bow. Why had he bought her something else? Say what he liked, the lounge suite was for her. As she lifted the lid of the jewellery box she felt barely able to contain herself. Just like the kids minutes earlier. Lying on red satin were the most beautiful pair of gold filigree earrings and a matching neck chain.

She gasped. 'They're stunning. So delicate. So intricate.' Too good for her. But already she was lifting one earring out and slipping it in place.

'Perfect.' Kieran sounded smug. 'I knew they'd suit you.'

Her eyebrows rose as she stared at him. He was so sure of himself at times it was hard to believe the same man could feel uncomfortable with the children. What a mix he was. An intriguing mix. Sudden emotion engulfed her, blocked her breathing. Pushing the second earring through her earlobe she muttered, 'I need a mirror,' and dashed to the bathroom before he could see her inexplicable tears.

Of course he followed her. 'Abby? What's wrong?'

Shaking her head, she dredged up a smile. 'Nothing, it's just that I'm not used to anything as beautiful as these.'

'Here, let me help you with the chain.' He lifted it from the box and placed it around her throat, his fingers caressing her skin.

The throat that could no longer swallow for all the emotion stuck there. Why had he done this? Didn't he know how difficult he made it for her to stay uninvolved with him? Because of a piece of jewellery? No, because he'd gone to the trouble to find her something so lovely.

'Th-thank you,' she stuttered, and stepped closer to the mirror to put space between them. 'For these, and for—. Oh, I don't know, just for everything.' A tear slid down her cheek.

'Hey…' His thumb traced the damp track. 'This is supposed to be a joyous occasion.'

'These are happy tears,' she tried to assure him. But she was the one who needed the reassurance. Whatever she needed, first she'd take a shower, put some decent clothes on. Then there were plenty of things that had to be done before everyone started arriving.

Kieran looked unconvinced, but at least he backed out of the tiny room when she flicked the shower tap on. 'I'll start on those pancakes,' he said.

'There's no need. I'll do them.'

One long stride and he was back before her. 'This is your day, too, and I'll help all I can.' Then he placed another of those soft, soul-clenching kisses on her cheek, before closing the door behind him on his way out.

Abby's fingers touched the spot his lips had caressed, and a silly smile lifted her lips. Like a child, she didn't want to wash her cheek. Catching a glimpse of her goofy smile in the mirror, she laughed. She would put on the new dress Steph had given her two days ago for Christmas. She hadn't been going to wear the gorgeous emerald sun frock that made her feel so feminine. It fitted too well, showed all the curves and bumps that she usually tried hard to hide. But right now she felt she could handle it. Today she wanted to look her best. A T-shirt didn't do Kieran's necklace and earrings justice. Her decision had nothing to do with Kieran. Nothing at all.

Yeah, right.

Kieran was whistling as he made his way into the A and E department two mornings later. He felt damned good, so wonderful, in fact, he'd even been for a run around the waterfront earlier. His first run in weeks.

'What are you on?' Barbara quipped as he dropped down onto a chair beside her.

'Not sure but whatever it is, it needs bottling.' He grinned at the nurse. The Brown family and the way they had accepted him as one of them had something to do with his mood. Abby had her role, too. Had her role? *Red alert, boyo. Abby is the cause of this happiness.*

Somehow, despite all his determination to the contrary, he'd let Abby in. Into his lungs. Into his head, his muscles. Into his heart. A soft sigh slid over his lips. Abby. He adored her.

Shouldn't he be panicking? Shouldn't he be leaping up and stomping on the idea that she'd won him over? What if these feelings for her developed further? That would mean breaking his lifelong vow never to get involved with a woman.

Yeah? So? Things change. People change. I've changed. Because of Abby.

Where was she anyway? Running late, as usual? What the heck, they'd manage until she got here. She'd probably slept in, exhausted after Christmas and all the effort she'd put in to making it a wonderful day for everyone.

He reached for the patient notes. 'Who's first?'

As he read the file his heart sank. His fantastic mood wiped out in an instant.

'Sorry I'm late. The car wouldn't start.' Abby sounded breathless as she flew into the department, all smiles. 'How's everyone? Did you all have a great day?'

That car was a problem, Kieran thought fleetingly as he stood up. He'd do something about it soon. But right now there was another problem. 'Abby, come with me.'

'Sure. What have we got?' She fell into step beside him.

'Young Joey's back.' His jaw clenched. 'This time with a suspected dislocated collarbone.'

'What happened?' Kieran asked Joey's mother.

'He got swung around by his arm yesterday.'

'Yesterday? Why didn't you bring him in immediately?'

If they'd been able to treat Joey's shoulder then, it would've been a simple matter of manoeuvring the joint into place. Now surgery was very likely.

'Had to wait until the booze made his dad fall asleep.'

Kieran felt the heat of anger as it gripped him. Anger at the thug who'd done this to his family. The man Joey should be able to trust to protect him. A picture of Seamus smiling as he tore open his Christmas presents blasted into Kieran's head. Never in this lifetime could he understand anyone doing something like this to their child.

Until now he'd always thought his loveless, sterile childhood had been horrible, but it had been a picnic compared to what this little boy suffered. It was time he got over feeling sorry for himself. At least those two little rascals he thought of as his would never suffer physical harm. Not with Abby for their mother. Or him for their father.

A light touch on his shoulder, a gentle nudge at his waist. He glanced around. Abby. Warning him to take it easy. Telling him she was right there with him, that she knew and understood his feelings. Warmth seeped into his muscles, began unravelling the knots. They were on the same side. She was so right. Joey needed his medical skills, not his rage.

CHAPTER TEN

'YOU look gorgeous.' Steph grinned at Abby's reflection in the mirror as she peered over her sister's shoulder. 'I'm really glad you borrowed a dress for tonight.'

'If I couldn't ask you for help with clothes, then who could I ask? You are the clotheshorse of the family.' Abby laughed nervously at her image. This dress wasn't quite what she'd had in mind. The traffic-light-red suited her, but… 'You really think wearing a figure-hugging sheath suits me? What about my bumpy bits?' She touched her stomach, stared at her breasts.

'Suit you? It was made for you. Where're those earrings Kieran gave you? They'll finish the look perfectly.'

There was that word again. Perfect. Kieran had said that on Christmas morning when she'd first worn the amazing jewellery. Perfect didn't usually mix with her. But maybe she had scrubbed up okay tonight. She twisted around, trying to stare at her bottom. 'You're sure I have to wear the G-string?'

'G-string or no knickers at all. Your choice.'

'Call that a choice?' A nervous laugh escaped her lips. Steph and Charlie had dragged her to a lingerie shop and bought her underwear to match the dress. 'Why the push-up bra? I'm starting to look like a woman on the make here.'

'Then mission accomplished.' At Abby's gasp, Steph waved her hands in the air. 'Live a little, sis, and stop being a mum for a night. It's New Year's Eve and you're going to a party with the extraordinarily good-looking Dr Flynn. You'll have his attention firmly on you all night.'

Did she want Kieran's undivided attention? Oh, yes. If he was the playboy, then for one night she'd be the toy. Then hopefully she'd have got him out of her system and could go back to being that mum, happy with her lot.

Abby ignored the knot of excitement that had been threatening to spring apart all afternoon at the thought of going on a real date with Kieran. Instead, she slipped the fine wire hooks through her earlobes and turned to hug her sister. 'Thanks so much. It's lovely to be wearing something that's not stained with kiddy food. I feel like a real person for a change.'

'You're a real person all the time. Don't you think we all appreciate you? Abby, your family loves you. But if a change of clothes makes you feel whole then I'm going to donate my wardrobe to you and start afresh for myself.'

'I don't go out enough to wear that many clothes.'

'I'll have you know I don't have as many as you're intimating.'

Abby merely rolled her eyes.

Steph laughed. 'Hey, don't knock it. I'm the sister with the same shape and size as you.' She tipped her head to one side and walked around Abby. 'Hair up or down?'

Abby tucked one hand under her ponytail and lifted it onto the top of her head. 'Up kind of looks elegant.'

'Down and loose looks sexy.'

Abby's stomach knotted. Sexy. Her? Not really. Did she want to look sexy for Kieran? What sort of question was that? Of course she did. Already Steph was undoing the cord holding her hair in place and splaying it across her shoulders. Seems she didn't have a choice. And it *did* look…um…sexy.

'I'd better wear it up.'

'Coward.' Steph grinned at her then after a moment turned serious. 'Come on, you're keen on the guy. Show him what you've got. Mind you, he'd have to be made of plastic not to already have noticed. You are beautiful, sis.'

Words that Kieran unwittingly repeated when he picked her up half an hour later. His low whistle when she opened her front door to him was involuntary. One look at Abby and his insides turned to mush, warming him through and through. Sensational. Stunning. Desirable. But, then, when hadn't she been?

But he couldn't stop staring. 'Abigail, you are the most beautiful woman I've ever had the pleasure to take out.'

Abby's cheeks suddenly matched the colour of her dress as she turned to lead him inside. Her words tumbled out in a rush. 'Come in. The children have gone across to Dad's but Steph's hanging around to see you.'

Steph gave him a big bear hug and told him, 'Wow, don't you look a knockout, too.' There was a wicked twinkle in her eye. What was she up to?

'Aren't you partying tonight?' He'd bought three shirts that morning because he hadn't been able to decide which matched his jacket best. A jacket he'd no doubt take off within minutes of arriving at Hamish Harrington's home since the outside temperature was in the high twenties. But he'd wanted to look good for tonight. For Abby.

'Of course I've got a party to go to. Two, actually. But I wanted to spend some time with Abby first. Sister bonding, and all that. I'm good for advice on some things.'

Abby took pity on him. 'Do you want a drink before we go? Or shall we get out of here?'

'We should get going,' he replied with relief. These sisters were an act, one he didn't always understand.

Driving back into the city and the Port Hills, where Hamish

lived, Kieran had his hands firmly on the steering-wheel and his mind stuck on Abby. He'd known she was beautiful, even though she seemed to go to extraordinary lengths to hide it, but tonight she was something else. Sophisticated. Breathtaking. The deceptively simple dress highlighted her superb figure, accentuating curves, including the slight swell of her tummy where his son had grown.

His mouth dried. This lovely woman sitting beside him had him hooked. Face it. Inexplicably he'd always been attracted to her. But now she was reeling him in, centimetre by centimetre, stirring his blood, charging his heart, bringing him alive in a way he hadn't known before.

'Stop. You missed the turn.' Abby touched his forearm.

Heat sped through his veins. He braked too quickly. 'Hell,' he muttered, and slammed the vehicle into reverse gear, ignoring the perfectly styled eyebrows raised at him from the other side of the sports car. Thank goodness he'd kept this car when he'd gone back to the dealer to get a more practical vehicle. Tonight Abby deserved nothing less than a swanky car to go out in.

The massive home was easy to find with the numerous cars lining the narrow road and strains of music reaching their ears as they alighted from the car. Taking Abby's elbow, he followed the laughter and voices until he found their hosts, glad to get among other people and put some space between himself and the woman causing his brain to fry.

Introductions over, Kieran turned to Abby. 'Wait here while I get us something to drink.'

But Abby had other ideas and stuck with him as he headed to the bar.

'Are you all right?' she asked, a frown on her brow.

'Couldn't be better,' he told her. 'This should be a wonderful night. Everyone seems geared up to enjoy themselves.'

'No doubt there will be the usual number of headaches tomorrow morning.'

'Then I'm glad I'm not working.' He took the glasses being pushed towards them. 'Let's go party.'

Kieran's prediction was right. Everyone seemed set to have the best night of their lives. The only bad moment was when Hamish informed Abby that Michael's son was extremely ill with everything that could go wrong with a liver transplant.

The evening flew by and Kieran couldn't remember having so much fun in a long time. It rankled when he found he had to wait his turn to dance with Abby. 'You're a popular lady,' he commented when he finally had another turn with her on the floor.

'I don't think anyone recognises me as Nurse Brown.' She grinned. 'It's this dress that fascinates them all.'

He could understand that. 'If the dress means I miss out dancing as often as I want with my date, we might have to tear it off you.'

Her eyes boggled at him. 'Tear it off? I don't think so.' A flicker of doubt crossed those beautiful eyes. 'Not even you would want to dance with me then.'

Want to bet? Putting his fingers under one shoulder strap, he teased, 'Let's find out, shall we?'

She shivered, and he relented. 'Spoilsport. Want a cold drink? Out on the deck? It's stifling in here.'

'Good idea.' She tucked her hand over his arm and strolled outside with him, where they scooped up two flutes of bubbly.

At the edge of the decking Abby leaned over the heavy glass siding to gaze out across the harbour lights. 'Isn't this view amazing? I wonder if Hamish ever gets used to it, takes it for granted.'

Kieran watched Abby, not the view she was referring to. 'I don't think I'd ever take it for granted.'

Abby leaned further over the edge and Kieran slipped his arm around her shoulders. 'Don't want you toppling over.'

It was an excuse to touch her. Dancing together hadn't been enough, especially as most of that so far had been more about shaking and moving and less about holding and touching. He could only hope that before the night was out the band would play some slower tunes and he'd have a reason to hold Abby in his arms.

'As if,' she retorted, but thankfully didn't pull away.

The music stopped.

'Time to fill up your glasses, everyone. Five minutes to midnight.' Hamish spoke above the babble.

'Five minutes to a new year,' Kieran spoke softly. 'What are you hoping for, Abby?' He knew what he wanted. To make love with this woman, to hold her body against his and stroke her skin, to inflame her desire until she begged him for release.

Abby turned and leaned back against the siding. Her eyes were unfathomable. Were her thoughts aligned with his?

She said, 'More of the same, really. The kids to be happy and healthy, maybe a promotion at work, Dad to be okay, and the twins to get what they want.'

So much for being on the same wavelength. 'That's it? What about you? Don't you have a big dream in there?' He tapped her forehead. 'Something just for you?'

'Kieran, I'm a mother. Dreams are on hold. And, truly, I'm happy with that.'

So why did sadness lurk in those hazel orbs? He stared at her, trying to look beyond what she was showing him. 'I'm not buying it.'

'One minute to twelve,' someone called out, and Abby straightened up, looked across to where everyone was gathering.

She took his free hand and tugged him along. 'Come on. Countdown time.'

He went with her, joined in counting down to midnight, and raised his glass in a general toast, before turning to Abby and twining his arm around hers. 'Happy new year to you, the wonderful mother of my son, and a beautiful woman I hold very close to my heart.'

Saying that out loud made it more real. Suddenly a chill settled over him. In four weeks he'd be heading home. Standing on this deck in the summer warmth, surrounded by friendly, caring people, holding Abby's hand, the thought of returning to Dublin felt incredibly bleak.

'Happy new year to you, Kieran. I hope this year brings you everything you want.' She seemed to be looking for something as she watched him over the rim of her glass. She obviously didn't find it because her shoulders rose in a slight shrug before she tipped her head back and drained her glass.

'More bubbles?' He reached for her glass.

'No, thanks. I've probably overdone it already. Let's have our first dance of the year.' And once again she was heading for the dancing, still holding his hand.

Somehow he'd let her down. Damn it, he'd let himself down in some odd way that he couldn't quite put his finger on. But if she wanted to dance with him then he was more than happy to oblige. Hadn't he spent half the evening waiting for his chance to dance with her? Only to have her claimed by some other hot-blooded male before he'd had enough time with her?

And now, as he took her into his arms for a slow dance, he wanted her instantly, all of her. Again. Still. Abby felt right in his gentle hold. He drew her closer. Dropped his chin on top of her head. The familiar, sweet Abby scent teased him, embraced him. Stirred him.

Her feet followed his in time to the music. Her body

moulded into his. Her breath on his shirt warmed him. Her hand fitted perfectly in his, while her thumb caressed the back of his hand. In the pit of his belly a fire burned. The flames licked his soul, scorched his self-control.

Kieran's hand squeezed her fingers so hard she missed a beat, tripped over his shoe. Slowly she lifted her head, tilted back in his arms, and looked up into smoky eyes that appeared ready to devour her. Against her stomach she felt his response to her. Instantly her body reacted in reply. She wanted him. No questions asked. No complicated conversations. Abby wanted Kieran. And the sooner the better.

Something flickered in his eyes. Recognition of her desire. Longing. A question. She nodded once. When he gripped her hand tighter she didn't hesitate but led him away to the sports car. Totally out of character, so wanton, she leaned into him, sought his lips. He kissed her back, hard and fast, and then they were in the cramped car, speeding down the narrow, winding road. Her fingers tapped impatiently on his thigh. Blood pounded in her head. Desire spread out, licking through her body like flames.

Darkened houses blurred past. The night air cooled her fiery skin. Within moments Kieran had parked in his apartment garage. He had her out of the car and into his arms in less time than it took to say 'Happy new year'.

They had to wait for the elevator, precious minutes they filled with hot, hasty kisses. Not those long, bone-melting kisses she'd come to expect from him but kisses that wound her stomach muscles tighter with each quick search by his tongue. Kisses that caught the corners of her mouth, teased at all her senses, drove her so close to the brink that she thought it would all be over before she'd even started.

'Kieran, wait a…' She forgot the rest as his hands spread

down her back, cupped her bottom while his fingers did incredibly sexy things over her skin.

'You were saying?' he teased as his mouth trailed down her neck, making her gasp with need.

'I don't know.' Her hands tugged at the buttons of his shirt. Her tongue tripped over his chest. Under her mouth she felt his shudders, and smiled.

A door crashed against a wall. Abby jerked her head up, stared around. 'Where—?'

'My apartment.'

How had she missed the elevator ride?

Kieran scooped her up hard against his chest and stepped inside, using his hip to close the door behind him, while his mouth claimed hers once more. Pushing her tongue past his lips, she tasted him and imploded at the heat there. Her hands snagged his shirt, hauled it up and over his head, barely breaking their kiss. Pressing her aching breasts against his chest wasn't enough. She needed skin to skin. With one quick movement her dress flew over her head and landed somewhere across the hall. Kieran unhooked her bra and she shucked it off, tossed it away. His hands cupped her breasts, his thumbs circled her nipples, took her breath away.

Then they were kissing again; mind-frying, nerve-jangling, combusting kisses that acted like oxygen to flames. Her stomach ached with longing. Her legs trembled with need. Her shaking hands tracked over Kieran's chest, his belly, circling, stroking, feeling him. Kieran. She wanted him inside her. Nothing else would do.

She wasn't sure which of them fumbled with the buckle of his belt, jerked the zip down. His trousers bundled at his ankles. Quickly stepping out of them, Kieran kicked them aside. Then his hands were on her waist and her legs were wound around his and, yes, at last, she was sliding down, taking him into her, feeling that wonderful moment when her body no longer seemed real. When all reality disappeared in a haze of desire and sensations that tripped her pulse and took her into another world. And Kieran came with her.

Abby stretched out her legs into the sunlight filtering in through the blinds that neither of them had thought to close during the night. She smiled at the gentle aches in her muscles. All her muscles. Every last one of them. What a night. Rolling her head sideways, she focused on the man who'd spent hours giving her enough pleasure to last a lifetime. It still wasn't enough. Her smile stretched. Brazen hussy.

'God, woman, if you purr any louder the neighbours will be calling the noise patrol.'

She laughed out loud and kicked her feet in the air. 'Bit late for that, don't you think?'

Kieran's grin grew. 'You…um…we were a bit loud at times.'

'I bet you get some interesting looks when you leave the apartment today.' Her stomach rumbled, loudly. Her eyes met his, and they burst out laughing.

'There's just no keeping you quiet, is there?'

'Try feeding me. That should work.' She sat up and swung her legs over the side of the football-field-sized bed. 'Food. That's exactly what I need right now. I'm starving.'

'Must be all that exercise during the night.' Kieran followed her off her side of the bed, no doubt thinking it was quicker than moving back across to his side. 'Let's hit the shower then go over the road to a café for a cooked breakfast. I fancy bacon and eggs.'

'And hash browns, tomatoes, mushrooms, sausages.'

'That hungry, eh?'

'Did I mention toast?' She dug through her tiny handbag for her phone. 'I'd better check in with Dad.'

Kieran chuckled. 'You're how old? And you're checking in with Max?'

She slipped his shirt from the night before over her head. 'Think I'd better explain that I'll be a little while yet. He might be expecting me to pick up the kids.'

But her father seemed pleased she'd stayed out overnight.

'Don't go getting any ideas, Dad. We had a great time and neither of us wanted to drive home after the party.' She crossed her fingers at the little white fib.

'Sure thing, love.' Was that an I-know-exactly-what-you've-been-up-to smile in his voice? Couldn't be. This was her father.

He was still talking and she struggled to concentrate. 'Everything's in hand here. I'm going to take the youngsters to the beach later. Steph and Andrew are coming with us. Why don't you two join us after your breakfast?'

'Sounds like a plan.' Steph and Andrew going to the beach with Dad and the kids? Those two seemed to be getting very domestic these days, and spending more time with the family. What was going on? Had she missed something? Could Steph be settling down?

After hanging up, Abby found the bathroom, where Kieran was already under the jets of hot water, soaping that wonderful body of his.

He watched with hungry eyes as she drew her shirt off. When she stepped into the shower, his hands caught her breasts. 'Beautiful.' His fingers kneaded the soft flesh. 'So beautiful.'

Their shower took a lot longer than normal, and mostly had nothing to do with getting clean.

'I can't finish this.' Abby pushed her plate to one side.

Kieran rolled his eyes at the one sausage left. 'A rugby

prop wouldn't have done any better. I'll be surprised if you can get off your chair any time in the next hour.'

'A gentleman wouldn't say things like that.' She grinned, totally at ease with the huge meal she'd just devoured. 'Guess what?'

'Yeah, I know, you're not one.' Not quite true. Mr Playboy was very definitely a gentleman most of the time. She squirmed as memories of the party crept back. Kieran had been very attentive all evening, making sure she always had a drink when she'd wanted one, holding her supper plate for her. Yes, but playboys did that. It was part of their charisma to be so helpful. But he'd turned down all those offers to dance with just about every female at the party. He'd danced with Hamish's wife but it would've been bad manners not to dance with his hostess.

No, for all she'd seen, Kieran had wanted to spend the time with her. If anyone had been out of line, it had been her. She'd accepted every invitation to hit the dance floor that had come her way. How had he felt about that? Had she hurt him by not staying by his side all night? Time for damage control. 'Thank you for such a wonderful time last night, all of it. I can't think when I last partied so hard.'

'You don't go out much, do you?' Kieran watched her through hooded eyes, giving nothing away. 'Tell me why. Is it because of your ex-fiancé?'

Talk about grabbing her attention. 'That's old hat. You don't really want to know.' Why did he have to ask about the man who'd hurt her so badly? Today of all days.

'Yeah, I do. I want to know a whole heap of things about you. I'm really interested. So, why didn't you marry him?'

'Because I found out I wasn't the only female sharing his bed. Even my bridesmaid enjoyed his favours.'

Kieran wrapped her hand in his. 'That must have hurt terribly.'

'It did.' But it wasn't hurting half as much as usual. Had she finally begun to let it go? Because of Kieran? 'I didn't know a thing about his philandering until the day I caught him with my bridesmaid a week before the wedding. After that people at work were quick to tell me about all the other indiscretions.'

'He worked at the hospital?'

'Dr Phillip de Hendez, general surgeon.'

'*The* Dr de Hendez? The one who tarnished his reputation trying to cover up a mistake in the operating theatre by pushing the blame onto his house surgeon?'

'The very same one. I see the hospital gossip mill is still working on that one.' A touch of bitterness coloured her voice. She'd have hoped by now that anything to do with Phillip would've been forgotten.

'From what I hear, it did the hospital a lot of damage. He was the reason I was so rigorously checked out before I got the nod to come.' He still held her hand, and now he squeezed it gently. 'Looks like you're better off without him.'

Oh, yes, heaps better off. Phillip's ego had always needed stroking, bolstering. At the time she hadn't realised she wouldn't be good enough for him. 'You're right.'

He changed the subject again. 'You know something? I had a lot of fun last night, too.' Those all-seeing eyes held her gaze. 'From the moment I picked you up the night became special. I admit to being blinded by the sight of you in that dress. My driving may have been very erratic, for all I know.'

The dress she still wore. Who took extra clothing to a party? 'Yeah, you were a bit fast.' On all accounts. Right down to that morning's shower. And she'd been with him all the way.

Now she wanted more of what they'd shared last night. Not just today, but every day. She wanted Kieran in her life, full time. Like that was ever going to happen. In the end she'd only get hurt. And sooner rather than later as he would be heading home. She should be distancing herself from him, not getting involved. But it had been wonderful.

Glancing at her watch, she sighed. 'I probably should be getting home.'

'That's a shame.' But he stood up and held her chair for her. 'I'll have to talk to Steph and Charlie and make sure they look after the children more so you can have other fun.'

The sizzle under her skin began to fade. 'Kieran, I might have had a wonderful time with you but I don't want anyone else in my life at the moment. Neither do the kids.' Some time between the dancing and the sheets she'd fallen in love with him. Or had that happened long before, two years ago, and only now was she admitting it? Relief settled over her. She would never marry Kieran but at least she could admit to loving him. Sadness replaced her relief. Was she doomed to unrequited love? Yes, without doubt.

'Abby…' He hesitated then went on, 'I'm going back to Ireland soon.' Caution filled his eyes, quickly followed by guilt.

Did he really feel bad about leaving the children? She doubted his guilt had anything to do with her. 'I know that.'

He looked desperate for her to understand. 'Coming here has turned out to be the best decision I've made in a long time. I needed to get to know Olivia. She's my family and I've let her down badly.' He paused, struggling with something deep inside. She could see it in his eyes, in his stance.

'Go on,' she said quietly, knowing she wouldn't like what she heard but needing to get it out in the open.

'Then there's Seamus. He's awesome. I love him. And that's been a revelation. I will help out with him the same way I do with Olivia.'

'Financially.' The word was sour in her mouth.

'I hope you're not expecting me to stay on, to be closer to you and the children. I can't do that.'

Well, she might not understand why he'd want to walk away from his son, but she couldn't say she hadn't been warned. He'd always made it absolutely clear where he stood on the subject of families. His Christmas Eve apology for making it so hard for her hadn't changed his stance.

'Can't? Or won't?' Her stomach clenched uncomfortably. The wonderful morning had fallen off track. Their camaraderie of the last hours was being tested, and failing. She'd always known Kieran had no intention of staying and she shouldn't have expected anything different. But for a few hours she'd forgotten all that and had allowed herself to dream. What a fool she'd turned out to be.

Kieran was good for a one-night fling, maybe even a few more nights over the coming weeks, but there'd never be any more from him. He had warned her. Told her about his commitment phobia, explained why he didn't want or feel capable of being a full-time parent, let alone someone's husband.

The previous evening she'd thought she could do the one-night-stand thing, but she'd been fooling herself. No way could she walk away from what had happened between them and pretend her heart was intact. Not when she loved him.

Kieran said nothing as they walked back across the road to his apartment block garage. He pinged the lock on the four-wheel drive. Back to the practical vehicle. Her date was over. Abby suddenly felt stupid, shabby even. Dressed in last night's party dress, it was obvious for all to see that she hadn't been home. It hadn't mattered until now. Immediately she wanted to be at home, dressed in mother-of-two underwear, comfortable shorts and a baggy T. Cinderella back in the wardrobe.

Why had she fallen in love with Kieran? Another man

who liked to have a good time but did not want to put down any roots? What was wrong with her that she could only love men who couldn't love her back the way she wanted, needed, to be loved?

CHAPTER ELEVEN

INSIDE the vehicle Kieran leaned his head back and sighed. 'I haven't made you any promises that I can't keep.'

'That's true.'

Two very bleak words he was responsible for. He needed to clear the air before the situation got worse. They'd had a wonderful time and he did not want that to be lost because of any misunderstanding.

'Abby, do you trust me to do the right thing by my son?'

Silence hung between them. Her hands fisted in her lap. Her eyes seemed glued to something beyond the vehicle.

Hurt stabbed him hard beneath his ribs. Why couldn't she trust him? He hadn't let her down since he'd come to Nelson. Had he? He couldn't prevent the hurt ringing in his voice. 'You've answered without a word.'

Her words came slowly, as though she was thinking her way through a minefield. 'I do believe you'll try. You'll probably stay in touch regularly, but that's not enough. The way I see it, you're doing to Seamus what your father did to you. Leaving him behind. You mightn't be cruel and undermine his attempts to do things, but he's not going to know you. You're not going to be there when he hurts, when he asks what the moon is made of, when he wants to learn to drive.'

'You don't pull any punches, do you?' he gasped, reeling

from the intensity of her statement. Where had the soft woman who'd spent the night in his arms gone?

'I just want what's best for you all,' she whispered.

So they were on the same playing field. 'So do I.' He took a steadying breath. 'What happens when I hurt Seamus? How do you explain to him that his father had to go away because he failed to be a good daddy?'

She'd seek him out and throttle him, that's what she'd do.

'I haven't got a clue. I can't even get it through to you that you're already a good father. Like me, you have to learn as you go along. Why won't you see that?' She saw everything in black and white.

'Abby, sweetheart, you're a novice when it comes to this. My father worked at it for most of my life to get me to see things his way. Like water dripping on rock, eventually the rock wears away. Take a young child and keep telling him he's useless and he begins to believe that. Take that child as a young man and blame him for everything that goes wrong in their family and it becomes real.'

She turned, and the sympathy he saw in those emerald eyes nearly drowned him. But he didn't want sympathy, he wanted understanding. He needed her to accept he knew what he was doing.

But, of course, she didn't. This was Abby, after all. The woman who believed in families and happy-ever-afters. Although he had to admit those hadn't come her way very often.

She said, 'That's the most terrible thing I've heard, but you're nothing like that. Already your son loves you, because of how you've treated him with care and love.'

A knife turned in his heart.

'Your niece loves you.' A tear rolled down her cheek.

There was more. He just knew it. Except he didn't know what that was.

And Abby wasn't saying.

Kieran stomped hard on the accelerator. If only he had the sports car in his hands. After dropping Abby off, he'd turned in the opposite direction from the city, taking the main highway south, further out into the countryside. He needed speed to shake the shock out of his system that had slammed him between the eyes.

He loved Abby.

He gripped the steering-wheel harder to stop the tremors racking his body.

How the hell had this happened?

He loved her and the despair he'd seen in her eyes rode with him all the way, mocking him. He'd never promised her anything he couldn't give. But now he had to deal with this new development.

New? Get real. He'd probably loved her since that night in Dublin. If he'd ever admit it. How could he have missed it? He jerked the vehicle around a sharp corner. He'd been blind to what had been right before his eyes because all his attention had been focused on the children.

Abby. The woman of his dreams. When he'd allowed himself to dream, that was. Which hadn't been often.

So what was he going to do? Absolutely nothing.

How could he? He was his father's son. Which meant?

He'd be a useless father. That was a given.

He'd be a worse husband.

Because? Commitment scared him senseless. He'd been committed to his dog and Beagles had got run over while he'd been walking him. What about his girlfriend who'd lost their baby? He'd loved her and yet he hadn't been there when she'd miscarried. He'd been committed to Morag, and she'd been drugged and injured while in his flat. It didn't matter that he hadn't been there, he'd trusted the guys he'd shared that flat with. He'd committed to showing his father he could be a success and never once had he heard that his father was proud of him.

So how could he offer himself to Abby?

No. His lifestyle of love them and leave them was safer for everyone involved.

But.

Last night he and Abby had made love. Last night had been about the two of them, about giving and receiving, sharing. He hadn't been able to get enough of her, generous soul that she was. Last night he'd have been happy if they'd flown to the moon to be alone. He had wanted nothing more than Abby. No one else.

Inspiration struck him. What if Abby and the children moved to Dublin? He could set them up in a house near his apartment. He could see them as often as he wanted without making that commitment he was so afraid of. Pleased with the idea, he relaxed as he drove up the Spooners Range for view back to the city.

It would be a win-win situation for them all.

In ED Abby tugged her gloves off and tossed them in the bin, then stripped the bloodstained sheets off the bed and pushed them into the laundry bag.

It had been an uncomfortable few days since the morning after New Year's Eve. She and Kieran had been dancing around one another. He didn't seem any more prepared to break the uneasy truce that had arisen between them than she was. Whenever he'd come out to see the kids she'd made sure to go over to her father's house so there could be no awkward conversations about the future. It bugged her that

Kieran seemed relieved when she did that. She'd hoped he might come round to her way of thinking.

Anyway, she'd come to a decision. It scared her, a lot, every time she thought about it but if, and it was a huge if, it suited Kieran, she and the children would move to Dublin. Then Olivia and Seamus could be as close to Kieran as to her.

The fact she loved Kieran had nothing to do with this. *Yeah, right.* Somehow she would deal with that. Somehow. Some time. In the next million years she'd get over him.

Sally stopped her on the way back to the cubicle with clean linen. 'That young boy Joey is in cubicle one. His neighbour brought him and his mother in while you were with the forestry worker.'

Abby's heart squeezed. 'What's happened this time?'

'Dislocated shoulder again, plus a fractured wrist. We're waiting on the orthopaedic surgeon, but he's in Theatre at the moment.' Sally grimaced. 'That poor kid. When is his mother going to get out of the situation?'

'I guess it's not that easy when you're financially up against the wall and being terrorised by the person you rely on for support. I'll go and sit with them until we get busy.'

Joey was sleeping fitfully when she crept into his cubicle. She spoke softly to his mother. 'Hello, Dale. Is it okay if I check on Joey?'

Dale nodded. Abby took her time counting Joey's pulse, checking his pain medication levels and generally straightening out the blanket. Then she sat on the end of the bed and studied the woman before her. Dale was probably younger than Abby but the defeat in her eyes made her look ten years older. 'Joey's vitals are good. What about you? Have you got any injuries this time?'

'Nothing too bad. Just bruises.'

'I should look at them,' Abby said gently. 'If you'd like me to.'

'Nah, don't worry about me.'

'But I do. It's just as important to look after your health. For Joey's sake,' she nudged.

In the ensuing silence Abby could hear Kieran talking to Sally. As Abby was about to ask Dale if she'd like a coffee, Dale muttered, 'Last time we were here you talked to me.'

'Yes.' She'd mentioned several things, including Dale getting help for herself and Joey.

'Something about a refuge place where we could hide from my old man.'

Abby spoke quietly, afraid of scaring Dale off. 'The women's refuge. They'd protect you and Joey, and provide a room and food for as long as it takes to sort yourself out.'

'It's not about me. But I can't let him hit my boy no more. Don't suppose you know what it's like for us. You got any kids?'

Abby smiled. 'I've got a wee boy, and my niece lives with me, too.'

'Is the father good to his boy? Your boy?'

Kieran put down the radio handpiece. Ambulance Two was bringing in a sixty-one-year-old male, suspected broken femur, abrasions and possible concussion, query other head injuries. He had been unconscious but had come round in the last five minutes.

Nothing overly unusual with those details. But. Concern at what else he'd been told by the paramedic clawed at him. With a heavy tread he headed around the station. Life had a way of throwing up wild cards when you least expected them. Outside cubicle one he hesitated, and overheard Joey's mother ask, 'Is the father good to his boy? Your boy?'

Abby answered, 'He's wonderful. Seems to instinctively know how to look out for Seamus. I couldn't ask for a better father for my son.'

Kieran's heart slowed as his chest took a hit. That was him she was talking about. Saying he was a good father. Better than that even. Warmth slipped under his guard, gave him a sense of belonging, of doing right. Maybe he was parent material after all. Who would know better than Abby? Hadn't she told him the same a week ago? Yeah, and hadn't he thrown it back at her, refusing to believe her? Too busy protecting himself to see how he'd hurt Abby? She'd been hurt enough in her life, he should be looking out for her.

Dale was saying, 'Lucky little boy. Joey's father can't stand him being around.'

Abby's sigh was audible to Kieran. 'Seamus is lucky. His dad loves him very much.'

Talk about a morale boost. Kieran sucked in the praise. Then thought about what he'd been on his way to do when he'd stopped outside the cubicle and the warmth under his skin evaporated. He lifted his chin. Now was his chance to put some things right between them. He'd be there for Abby, would support her over the coming weeks, help her out with anything that needed doing.

He stepped around the curtain. 'Abby, can you come with me?' Kieran took her elbow and led her out of the cubicle, not giving her time to refuse.

'This had better be good.' That aloof tone she'd adopted with him all week hardened. 'I'm finally getting somewhere with Dale. She's talking about the women's refuge.' Abby tried to pull her arm away but he tightened his hold.

'Barbara will see to Joey. I need to talk to you.'

Abby turned to him. He saw apprehension slither through her eyes. 'Kieran? What's going on?'

He led her to a chair before squatting in front of her and wrapping his hands around hers.

Which made her tremble. 'Tell me.'

'Abby, there's been an accident.'

Slam-dunk. Her face paled. 'Seamus? Olivia? I saw them both at lunchtime and they were okay. What's happened?' Her mouth closed over any more questions.

'The children are fine.' Kieran's thumbs rubbed the backs of her hands. 'Abby, Max fell off a ladder in the orchard. The paramedics are bringing him in now.'

'Dad? Fell off a ladder? Why was he up one in the first place? He's got workers to do that.' She leapt up, spun round, fear written all over her face. 'He's going to be all right? Isn't he?'

Kieran quickly outlined the scant details he'd received from the ambulance crew. 'They've put a neck brace on him but they don't believe he has sustained spinal injures. It's a precaution.'

'I know they do that.' Abby blinked at him as though he held a powerful set of headlights directed at her.

Sure, she knew, but this was her father and when she first saw him there was every chance all her training would go out the window.

'How long before Dad gets here?' Another blink.

'Any minute now. Sally will let us know.' Kieran reached for her and held her against him. He could feel her shock in her tense body, in her short, fast breaths against his chest. His hand stroked her back, trying to give her some love.

She pulled back in his arms. 'What else? Have you told me everything?' This was Abby the daughter, not Abby the nurse asking.

'When Max was found him he was slipping in and out of consciousness so we have to assume he hit his head as well.' Kieran kept rubbing her back in circular movements.

Speaking against his chest, 'I need to wait in the ambulance bay.'

'Of course. But you won't be there as a nurse. Sally and the others will do that.'

Sally tapped him on the shoulder. 'They're pulling into the bay now.' Then she reached for Abby's hands, kissed her on the forehead. 'Hang in there, Abby. We'll do everything we can for Max.'

'I know but what if it's not enough?' Her fear made her voice tremble. Kieran had to swallow hard on the lump blocking his throat. Not only was he worried about Max, but this caring, loving woman was hurting badly, and he couldn't prevent that. He *could* look after her father to the absolute best of his ability. Would it be enough? It absolutely had to be.

Abby thought her ribs would break under the thumping they were getting from her heart. Dad. What had he been doing up a ladder? He should know better. He was sixty-one, for goodness' sake. But he'd been up them all his life. Why shouldn't he use ladders now? How else could he check the fruit? God, she wanted to strangle him. Hadn't they had enough horrors in this family?

Family. Her sisters. They needed to be told. Something to do to fill in this fearful hiatus that waiting inflicted. 'I need to call Steph and Charlie. They should be here.'

Sally gave her a quick hug. 'I called Steph a moment ago. She's heading straight in with Charlie.'

Abby felt her shoulders sag. Now what? She couldn't stand still. But as the ambulance backed into the bay Kieran held her back while the paramedics gently rolled out the stretcher. Abby's chest ached. Her eyes stung. Her legs wobbled. And Kieran held her upright.

Get a grip. She was a nurse. She dealt with this all the time. 'Dad,' she choked as the stretcher reached her. She reached for her father's hand.

'Abby, love. I'm sorry.' Max whispered as he tried to lift his arm.

'Take it easy, Dad. You're going to be okay,' she whispered back, and crossed her fingers. At least he was still conscious, but who knew what damage had been done to his head? A severe bruise darkened one side of his face and the eye was swollen shut.

Max's left leg had been put into a splint, and she noted a pressure pad on his thigh. Had the bone pierced the skin? How much blood had he lost before he'd been found?

In the cubicle Sally took baseline obs and compared them with those taken by the paramedics. She quietly showed them to Kieran and the tightening of his mouth made Abby nauseous. Something was going wrong. Panic rose. She gripped the side of the bed with one hand, willing the fear down. She wouldn't help her father by losing control.

'Hey.' Kieran touched her chin.

She met his eyes for a brief moment, saw something almost like love there, but that had to be wishful thinking. She definitely saw real concern for her and her father. He'd do everything he possibly could for her Dad and that's all she could ask. 'Thanks.'

Kieran spoke to Sally in such a quiet voice that Abby didn't hear what he said. But she didn't have to. She knew what was going on, fully understood the procedures. Her father was in the best place possible, receiving the best care available. She wouldn't have wanted anyone else looking after him. Kieran was a superb emergency specialist.

So she needed to get her head together. Be strong. Be strong? Well, if there was one thing she could do, that was it. If things turned out really bad for her father then she'd deal with it. Her throat blocked with unshed tears. *Please give us a break here. Dad doesn't deserve the worst. He's already faced a lot of bad things over the last few years.*

'We're sending Max to Radiology, Abby.' Kieran spoke beside her. 'The orthopaedic surgeon is on his way as well.'

'His head injury?' She stared at her father's forehead.

'X-rays will tell us more, but concussion seems likely.'

The breath she hadn't realised she held whooshed out between her teeth. 'Thank goodness.' If they only had to deal with fractures and blood loss and concussion then things were starting to look up. Very minutely.

How wrong could she be? While the reports about her father's condition continued to improve, it was a different story when she finally got home.

Expecting to find workers busy in the orchard, Abby was shocked to find Fred McCarthy was the only one there. Fred, a semi-retired man who always worked for her father at this time of the year to earn money to pay for his trips overseas, told her he'd been the only worker for weeks now.

The twins joined her soon after Abby learned this devastating news. Steph immediately phoned Andrew to come, and they all crowded around the kitchen table in Max's house to formulate a plan to keep the orchard running. Abby would oversee everything and help with packing the fruit, while the twins and Andrew would pick fruit and see to other jobs as time allowed.

Well after six o'clock Kieran arrived laden with groceries and news of Max.

'The good news is that he hasn't done serious damage to his head. He has a concussion, which will be monitored. The best thing for concussion is to stay in bed and, given his broken leg and three fractured ribs, he isn't going anywhere for a while anyway. The surgery went well. The surgeons had to put a steel pin in his leg.'

The relief around the table was almost palpable. Abby reached for Kieran's hand. 'Thank you for that. We have been trying not to think the worst but it's hard when we didn't know what was going on.'

Kieran dropped a kiss on her cheek and went to cook dinner.

From then on Abby's days were busier than ever. The hours ticked by faster than a speeding train. There was always so much to do. Some varieties of peaches were beginning to come on and needed select picking, packing and getting to the markets. Some trees needed spraying, the grass between the rows needed mowing to make access to the trees easier; boom cannons had to be put in place to scare away the birds. She felt ashamed she hadn't noticed earlier that those things hadn't been done.

Too tied up with Kieran, that had been her problem. Too busy trying to get him to fit into the children's lives to look out for her father. Well, from now on she'd make sure nothing got in the way of doing what was right for all of them. Obviously it was getting too much for her father. From now on she'd stop leaving the children with him so often.

Moving to Dublin would take care of that. But moving to Dublin was no longer an option. She was needed here.

Max saw it differently when she questioned him about the situation on one of her many visits. 'It's time you had a life of your own, my girl. It's not your responsibility to see that I've got everything under control. The fact that orchard workers are in short supply and can demand a lot more money is my problem, not yours.'

'But, Dad, it is my concern. I don't need protecting from anything that's happening with you or the orchard.'

'No, my girl, this is for me to sort out, once I'm out of here. You need to make a life for yourself, one that doesn't involve running around after all of us.'

Abby felt something akin to panic rising in her throat. She loved doing that. It made her feel needed, gave her focus. 'That's me, who I am,' she cried. Never mind that a few days ago she had decided to move to Dublin.

Max reached for her hand. 'No, love. You are a mother first. Then a nurse, my daughter and a sister. But it's time you found your own man to make a home with, to share life with.'

'I'm happy where I am, doing what I do.' Really happy? So happy there was nothing else she wanted in life? Well, she felt safe, at least.

Max studied her. 'Kieran's a good man, love.'

Kieran was a danger to her heart, that's what Kieran was. She might admit to loving him, but that didn't mean she'd risk all to be with him. 'Dad, I suspect you've been hatching plans in your head, but they aren't going to happen. Kieran would be the first to agree with me.'

Now, three days after the accident, Abby stood in her father's office, stretching her back and rolling her head to ease a stiff neck. Where had the day gone? The hours zoomed past when there was so much to do.

The phone rang. 'Hey, how are you doing?' Kieran asked.

'I'm good. Exhausted. But so is everyone, including you.' Kieran had been out at the orchard helping as much as his job allowed. 'I missed you when we came in to see Dad.'

'I was in a meeting with the international interns.' His sigh said it all.

'That bad, huh?' She knew one or two of the interns were hoping to stay on in New Zealand at the end of their contracts with the hospital board.

'Enlightening would be more precise. Hamish also dropped by to tell me that Michael's resigned due to his boy not improving. It's going to be a long time before he's ready to leave Brisbane.'

'How dreadful. We'll miss Michael in the department. He's been an inspirational director. Always takes on the board over financial cuts and staff deployment.' And he'd been good to her when she'd first started in ED, understanding her problems as a single mum.

Kieran was still talking. 'There's some good news. Joey and his mum moved into the women's refuge yesterday.'

'That's great. I am so glad for Joey. Let's hope Dale sticks it out.'

'She sounded pretty determined when I spoke to her. She said to tell you she was sorry about your father's accident.'

'Wow. I wouldn't have thought she'd have noticed anything going on around her.'

Kieran changed the subject. 'Want me to bring Olivia and Seamus out when I'm finished here?'

Charlie had dropped them off in the morning when she'd gone to see Dad. 'That would be great. I know I shouldn't put them in the crèche but how else do I get any work done here?'

'Abby, we all understand. I'll take them up to see Max before we come home.'

Home. If only it was home for Kieran. But that would never happen because he had a damned job in damned Dublin. Blast him. Anyway, her life was here, despite what Dad said. Despite the fact she'd briefly toyed with the idea of following Kieran.

By the time Kieran arrived with the children she'd put all that behind her, if only temporarily. 'Hi, everyone.' She kissed Olivia and hugged Seamus.

Kieran grinned at her. 'Do I get one?'

'Kiss or hug?' The moment the words had left her mouth she wished them back. She could certainly do with one or the other herself. But not the consequences to her heart.

'Both,' Kieran said as he looped his arms around her. Then his lips brushed hers before he withdrew, leaving her shaken and bemused.

And leaving her heart confused. How did he do that to

her? She had no control over her mind or body when Kieran touched her. Well, she'd better find some. The children needed baths.

Kieran was putting groceries away. 'I bought chicken. Thought I'd do a leg of lamb for dinner.'

Abby stared at him, her heart melting. What a man. She loved it that he did this, taking a load off her. 'Sounds wonderful. I know the others will be thrilled, too.' Looking out the window she looked for any sign of the twins. Laughter bubbled up when she spotted Steph.

'Look at this. Steph's driving the tractor with the spray unit, and over the other side Charlie's up a ladder, picking peaches.'

Kieran came to stand by her, too close, but she didn't move away. He said, amusement lightening his voice, 'Whatever happened to your glamorous sisters? They seemed to have traded smart suits for old clothes that a scarecrow would be ashamed to wear.'

Abby chuckled. 'They're really putting their hearts into helping.' A yawn caught her.

'They certainly are.' Kieran cleared his throat. 'How much sleep did you get last night?'

She was glad he'd asked, glad that he spent most of his spare time with her. He'd been there for her from the moment he'd learned about Dad's accident. It felt wonderful to have someone at her side when she had all this to deal with.

Another yawn stretched her mouth wide. 'Not a lot,' she admitted. 'Between Seamus waking up three times, me trying to work out what had to be done on the orchard, and wondering how I could get back to work by next Monday, not to mention worrying about Dad, the hours of darkness were riveting. But certainly not filled with sleep.'

'Forget coming back to work on Monday. Sally's already got your shift covered for the whole week.'

She opened her mouth to protest but Kieran cut in. 'Don't even think it. You're on leave, full stop.'

'Yes, sir. Bossy britches.' She smiled wearily. If only everything else could be fixed so easily.

'Now, how about you see to the kids' baths while I crank up the barbeque? I'll make dinner out on the deck. It's too hot inside.'

'Sounds wonderful. The others will finish in about an hour.' She tapped his shoulder, and when he turned to gaze down at her she almost forgot what she had to say. Almost, but not quite. 'Thanks for everything.' And she kissed him, her lips touching his mouth lightly. She pulled back fast, aware of her need to kiss him thoroughly taking hold. She had to be strong, but as she turned away she saw surprise and warmth in those piercing eyes.

CHAPTER TWELVE

KIERAN leaned back against the railing, observing Abby's family and friends, tiredness dragging at every muscle in his body. Thank goodness for Saturdays. This past week had been exhausting, with the department incredibly busy and his evenings spent out here, in Hope, helping wherever he could.

But happiness overrode his exhaustion. It felt good to have been a part of everything happening in the orchard and in the house. He'd been absorbed into the hustle and bustle as though he belonged. That was the part he liked best. Belonging, however temporarily. No special exceptions were made for him. He'd been treated like all the family.

He smiled, remembering Abby showing him how to use the ride-on mower and then leaving him to the job of mowing the whole orchard.

His eyes had been opened, his brain had finally assimilated what had been so close under his nose it was a wonder he'd been able to breathe these past weeks. This was where Abby belonged. He couldn't ask her to join him in Dublin for his sake. That would be grossly unfair. If she'd even consider the idea.

He'd watched her taking charge, pulling her family together to keep the orchard running. She'd done it in a way that no one minded, although the twins were obviously used to toeing the line with Abby. They gave her a lot of cheek about her bossiness. And to think she'd previously called him bossy.

'Here, looks like you could do with one of these.' Andrew handed him an icy-cold bottle.

'It's thirsty work, being out in the sun all day,' Kieran acknowledged as he lifted the beer to his lips.

'I reckon this is the best part of the day, with family and friends together for a drink and a meal.'

'Is your family as close as the Brown clan?' Kieran asked.

'Not quite. We don't have an Abby to keep us all together.'

'She's certainly been a tower of strength for everyone since Max's accident.' She'd amazed Kieran with her practical approach to the problems facing her once she'd got over her initial shock of finding there were no workers.

He hadn't forgotten her tears for her father either, her fear for his life. And how distressed she'd been on finding out how badly situated financially this place had become. Another problem Max had kept from her. The past days had taken it out of Abby more than any of them. She constantly yawned. Occasionally she'd even been grumpy.

'From what I've seen and heard, Abby's always been a strong one,' Andrew added.

'The twins would've managed without her. People do when there's no choice.' He didn't want to think of Abby having to be strong for everyone again. Not on her own, anyway. He wanted to be there for her, to stand by her, support her, look out for her. From a distance? *How would that work, boyo?*

Abby pushed the accounts aside and stretched out in her father's office chair. Another day nearly done, nothing else needing urgent attention. Everything was working out a lot better than she'd have believed possible on the day of the accident.

Unless he had a setback, her father would be coming home in two days' time. On the orchard front Andrew had been a surprise. He thrived on all the physical work, had even hinted that he'd like to give up his job as an accountant and get into the orchard business. It would certainly solve a lot of problems for her father if he did.

She could hear him out on the deck chatting with Kieran. The twins were in the kitchen, creating dinner. Scary thought. But it gave her the warm fuzzies the way they'd pulled together with her during this crisis.

Through the window she studied the rows of fruit trees. The afternoon offshore breeze had died away. The air was still and hot. Her favourite time of the day. She should join the others. She would. In a minute. First she wanted a moment to herself.

To think about Kieran.

Now, there was another surprise. Not once had he put his hands up and said no to anything asked of him over the last few days. And he'd been outside his comfort zone many times. That hadn't been the surprise, but more the fact that he'd jumped in to do anything he'd seen that had needing to be done. From cooking meals to changing Seamus's diapers to mowing the orchard.

Her fingers curled tightly. Acting like someone who cared what happened to her family. Like a man who cared what happened to her. She gasped. Did he care for her? Maybe even love her? He hadn't said as much, but hadn't he spent the last few weeks showing her? Kieran had been there for her from the moment Dad had had his accident. Easing her through the horror of seeing Dad smashed up, cooking endless meals for her and her family? If that wasn't showing her, then what was? But did Kieran know that? Did he understand his feelings?

He hadn't shown any characteristics of the playboy he was reputed to be. Sure, he'd been friendly to everyone aged from naught to ninety, not just the females.

She'd wanted to believe the playboy image. It saved her from having to face the truth. Phillip had needed the constant gratification of different women to lift his self-confidence. Another part of Phillip's insecurities meant that he continuously put her down, told her she was unattractive, and that she should've been grateful he'd wanted to marry her. He'd shouted at her that no one else would as she'd tossed her bags into her car the day she'd left him.

Kieran had proved him wrong. He'd been loyal to her, helped her out when no one else had even thought to offer a hand. The reputation her brother had warned her about years ago seemed to be a thing of the past. Kieran had probably dated a lot of different women because of his aversion to settling down. And that, she knew, came from his belief that he wouldn't be a good husband or father. He mightn't have had a good role model for either of those roles but somewhere in his life he'd learned anyway. Or was it just an intrinsic part of his make-up to be caring and loving and loyal?

Olivia bounced into the office, Seamus toddling along behind. 'Abby, come and see what I've done for you.'

'You've done something for me?' Abby leaned forward and hugged Olivia to her. The kids. Where would she be without them? She loved them so much.

She loved Kieran so much. And she'd have to learn to live without him being around.

Olivia squirmed in her arms. 'You were sad so I drawed some flowers.'

'Flowers? For me? Sweetheart, that's lovely. Where is this picture?'

'Seamus scribbled on one flower. Bad boy.' Olivia grabbed

her hand and tugged her out to the hall, where she stopped and pointed proudly. 'See? Aren't they pretty?'

Abby gaped. At the wall. The bottom half was covered in vividly coloured shapes. Every colour under the rainbow. Every colour out of Olivia's indelible pen set. 'Oh, my goodness.'

'You like the flowers, Abby?'

Abby sank back against the opposite wall, slid down onto her haunches. 'They're beautiful but…' What was Dad going to say? He'd finished painting the interior of the house only a couple of months ago. There wouldn't be time to repaint before he got home. 'Olivia, darling, why didn't you ask me for some paper to draw on?'

'You were busy.'

She couldn't argue with that.

Seamus toddled up with a marker pen in his hand, ready to add further to the artistic display. Abby grabbed his hand, gently removed the pen. 'No, Seamus.'

She blinked back sudden tears. Another problem. More work to be done. It seemed never-ending.

'Hey, what's going on?' Kieran stopped in the middle of the hall, his mouth dropping open as he took in the newly redecorated wall. 'Oh, blimey.'

'I drawed flowers to make Abby happy.'

'So I see.' Kieran turned to peer down at Abby, his lips twitching.

'Don't you dare laugh.' Two big tears rolled over her cheekbones.

He sank down to sit beside her, his shoulder touching hers. 'Hard not to, to be sure.' His mouth began stretching into a grin, and laughter threatened. 'This is the ultimate in gifts. A permanent drawing to cheer you up whenever you feel down.'

'"Permanent" being the operative word.' She batted his thigh with the back of her hand. 'It's not funny.' But her tears stopped.

'Olivia, go and find Abby a box of tissues, please.' Kieran twisted round to look at Abby, her face so woebegone he wanted to hug her to him and make everything right for her. Instead, he kissed each salty cheek before asking, 'How do we find out what paint Max used in here?'

'There's probably a tin in the shed. He never throws them out.' She was shaking her head. 'I don't believe this.'

'If you're right and there's still paint around, we'll have the problem fixed in no time. Maybe not today, but soon.'

'You're not here for much longer.' Her bottom lip quivered.

'It won't take long to fix this. I'll do it after work one night. Maybe tomorrow before Max comes home. I think that would be best.' Max might not see the funny side of Olivia's home-improvement idea. There again, the man was fairly relaxed about his grandchildren so he might.

'You can paint?' Those delectable lips twitched. 'As in with a roller and wide brush?'

'Can't be too hard. I learned to drive that ride-on mower, didn't I?' He winked.

Now she did an eye-roll. 'Soon you'll be telling people you're a handyman.'

Olivia pressed a tissue box onto Abby's lap. 'A tissue, a tissue, I fall down.' Which she promptly did, giggling as she rolled all over the floor.

'Okay, Olivia, Seamus. Pens, please.' Kieran began to collect the numerous colouring pens.

Olivia began helping. Seamus picked one up and brought it to Abby.

'Give it to Daddy.' Abby blew her nose and wiped her eyes.

'Daddy.' Seamus handed Kieran the pen.

The pen dropped through Kieran's lifeless fingers. 'What?' He stared at Seamus. His throat ached, his ears hurt, his eyes watered. 'What?' he croaked again.

'Daddy.' Seamus picked the pen up and stood looking from Kieran to Abby and back. Almost as though he wasn't sure which one of them was Daddy.

Kieran asked, 'Did I hear right?'

Abby looked as stunned as he felt. Her mouth opened but nothing came out. Was she disappointed? Hurt even? She had every right to be. She'd done the hard yards with Seamus, not him. But he only saw pride in her eyes.

Kieran touched her shoulder, ran his finger down her cheek. His voice sounded scratchy when he spoke. 'That's amazing. I can't believe I heard Seamus speak his first clear word. But it was the wrong word.'

How did she really feel about this? Seamus's first word. It should've been 'Mummy'. He looked closer, saw nothing but joy in her face. She had to the most generous person he had ever been lucky enough to meet. 'Abby?'

Ripping another handful of tissues from the box, she dabbed at her tears. 'That's the most beautiful thing I've heard in for ever.'

'Isn't it?' Now his smile grew, stretching his mouth wide. 'Unbelievable.'

Seamus, unaware of the turmoil he'd caused, tossed the pen on Abby's lap and went in search of another one. Kieran reached for him, lifted him into his arms and held him close. 'Say it again.'

But Seamus had tired of that game. He stared up at Kieran, chuckling and banging his hands on his father's chest. A chest that was about to break wide open with love. Seamus had just done what he'd believed impossible. His son had shown him love was within reach, was simple if he opened up to it.

One little word. A huge word. Daddy. He was a daddy.

His son had told him so. His head banged against the wall behind him and he closed his eyes, shutting the moment in. Then snapped them open again, looking at Abby. This was her moment, too. The first time her son had spoken something comprehensible.

'It should've been "Mummy".' He repeated it quietly but with feeling. He meant it. He'd stolen her moment.

'That doesn't matter. Truly. I'm just thankful I heard it. It's so special.'

'It's magical.' He reached a hand to her and she took it, wrapping her fingers around his.

She nodded. 'The firsts are always the best.'

She never gave up telling him what he might be missing out on when he left. He smiled at her. 'You're wonderful, you know that?'

He saw her swallow before she looked away from him. Didn't she believe him? She had to. He meant it. With all his body. With everything he had. With his heart.

This wasn't about the children. This was about Abby. About the two of them. About the life they could make together. The life he wanted to make with her.

Emotion swamped him as he looked at the woman who'd snagged his heart. Love suffused him. Fear gripped him.

He couldn't leave.

Not Abby or the children.

Not now or ever. This was where he belonged. Not in some large hospital on the other side of the world where his only claim to life was being a very good emergency specialist. No, he was meant to be a father. To Seamus and Olivia.

But more importantly he could never, ever leave Abby. He needed her. He had so much to give her.

Seamus wriggled out of his arms and toddled towards another pen, which he picked up and handed to Abby, triumph lighting up his eyes.

Abby took it, placing a light kiss on her son's forehead. 'Thank you, darling. You clever boy, you.'

Kieran gulped, swallowed, breathed deep. And reached for Abby's hand. 'Abby, I'm not leaving.'

'Of course not. The twins are cooking dinner.'

His fingers took her chin, turned her head so he could look deep into those hazel orbs. 'No, Abby, you don't understand. This isn't about dinner or about tomorrow or the next day. I'm not leaving. I'm staying on in Nelson. I'll apply for Michael's job, and if I don't get that I'll find something else. I can't go away. I—'

She placed her forefinger over his lips. Her mouth spread into a smile, growing wider as he watched. 'You're staying.'

'Yeah, I'm staying.'

Abby was still smiling when, five weeks later, the plane lifted off from Nelson on the first leg of their trip. Beside her Kieran groaned, and his hand gripped hers even harder.

'At this rate every bone in my hand will be broken by the time we get to Dublin.' At least it wasn't her left hand, with the dazzling emerald in its simple gold setting winking at her from her ring finger.

Kieran tried to relax his hold. 'Sorry, sweetheart. But I hate flying. Intensely.'

Sweetheart. The endearment still filled her with warmth every time she heard it, and that was often. 'Maybe we should've stayed at home and you could've organised selling your apartment, packing up the furniture and all those other things by phone and email.'

'You have no idea how tempting that was. But there are some things I have to be present to do. Like saying goodbye to all my staff, and to my boss, the guy who insisted I do some time away from Dublin before I started at Mercy Hospital.'

He chuckled. 'Ethel told me I'd have a beautiful young woman to accompany me on this trip.'

'Ethel?'

'A very intuitive old lady who sat by me for the flight into Nelson. Perhaps I should look her up and invite her to the wedding.'

'Go on. What's one more person?' The wedding numbers were growing by the day. The wedding. Her stomach gave an excited squeeze. She still couldn't quite believe it. She and Kieran getting married had seemed such a remote possibility that there were moments when she thought she must be dreaming.

'I'll call Charlie about it.' She smiled widely.

Charlie had taken over organising the wedding while they were away. Her organisational skills were surprisingly formidable. Had she learned that from her older sister?

Kieran ran a finger down her cheeks, wiping the lines left by tears from when she'd hugged her kids one last time at the airport. 'They'll be fine with Steph.'

'I know.' They'd only be gone for fourteen days but she'd never been apart from them for more than a day at a time. Seamus was too young to understand and seemed more interested in watching the planes taking off and landing. But Olivia had clung to her, crying and wanting to make sure Abby would come back. 'Not like Mummy,' she'd wailed. That's when Abby had very nearly cancelled her flight.

'Olivia will be fine the moment you've gone through the gate,' Steph, who was looking after the children while they were away, had assured her. 'You can phone her every night. Just go and enjoy yourselves. It is your honeymoon.'

Abby leaned over to kiss Kieran. 'Who has a honeymoon before the wedding?'

'People who can't wait for all the red tape regarding a certain Irishman and his wedding being dealt with. People who can't wait to be together. People who love each other so much it hurts.'

'People like us.'

'Yeah, people like us.' And he leaned in to kiss her. Not a peck on the cheek or chin, but a full-blown husband-to-be kiss.

Under his lips Abby grinned. Hopefully he'd forgotten they were thousands of feet up in the air.

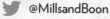

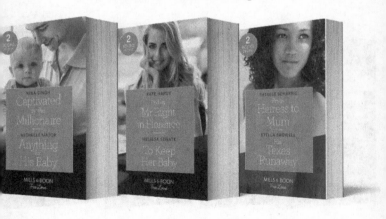